EVERY DAY'S A HOLIDAY

EVERY DAY'S A HOLIDAY

Randy Suits

iUniverse, Inc.
New York Lincoln Shanghai

Every Day's a Holiday

iUniverse books may be ordered through booksellers or by contacting:

iUniverse
2021 Pine Lake Road, Suite 100
Lincoln, NE 68512
www.iuniverse.com
1-800-Authors (1-800-288-4677)

ISBN: 0-595-33435-0 (pbk)
ISBN: 0-595-66928-X (cloth)

Printed in the United States of America

CHAPTER 1

Train up a child in the way he should go, and when he is old he shall not depart from it.

"Please father," begged the little girl as tears washed her blue eyes, "take me with you."

"Child," replied her father softly, "you can't go with your mother and me. We're going to the club tonight."

"But Father," she pleaded, "you never take me with you!"

"Priscilla, Sunday will be the Fourth of July," answered her father apologetically, "I promise you that we'll go somewhere on the holiday."

"But why can't we go somewhere when it isn't a holiday," asked Priscilla in disappointment, "I wish every day was a holiday!"

Though only seven years old, Priscilla had already learned that business and its social ties claimed precedence over her desires. The holidays were the only sure bet that she would spend an entire day with her parents. Harold often said, "You can lose in half a minute all your life's work." Tonight Harold and Elizabeth were to attend a party given by an investment banker who had recently moved to Albany. Mr. Thomas was a very important man in the community and Harold could not afford to fall outside his graces.

Springtime at the Pomp residence was always a splendid sight. The vast expanse of lawn was covered with trimmed hedges and flowers and the birds were making nests. Jonah, the gardener, was planting Zinnia's. The garden was the one area of reality which hadn't been tainted by the ideal-ism of Harold and Elizabeth Pomp. Harold had spent twenty thousand dollars landscaping and preparing the garden for his wife. Elizabeth, how-ever, despised to get dirt under her fingernails. That was the reason Jonah was hired. It was a miracle that the Lord and Jonah had a free hand in this blessed half acre.

Jonah covered the last of the Zinnia seeds and stepped back to gaze over the garden. Peace and tranquility touched the garden this morning and the old man basked in the serenity of the moment. Presently the silence was broken by the warm voice of Priscilla Pomp.

"Good morning Jonah," she said cheerfully.

"Yes my child, that it is. And a very good morning if I do say so myself," replied Jonah as he sat on a bench in the center of the garden.

"Can I sit next to you?" asked Priscilla as she climbed up on the bench beside him.

Jonah reached out to help her onto the bench, but Priscilla pushed his arm aside and chided, "Please Jonah! I can get up here by myself."

Jonah chuckled to himself and replied, "very well my child. You're up early aren't you?"

"Why don't you call me by my first name, Jonah," retorted the little girl, completely ignoring his question.

Jonah was caught off guard by Priscilla's question, but he gathered his wit and answered warmly, "Well, my child…"

"There you go again saying 'my child,'" interrupted Priscilla in chagrin, "my name is Priscilla."

With a great deal of diplomacy, Jonah replied, "I'm sorry Priscilla. I didn't mean to offend you. I'm really supposed to call you 'Miss Pomp'. If your mother heard me call you Priscilla, I could lose my job."

"But I don't like to be called 'Miss Pomp'! Father calls me Priscilla and I don't see him as often as I see you. So why can't you call me Priscilla too? You're my best friend in the whole wide world!" interrupted the little girl as she peered directly into the old man's face.

"Honey," replied the old man tenderly, "this world would be a better place to live in if grown ups would look at things through the eyes of a child. But I must do as your parents tell me or I'll lose my job. This is one of your father's rules."

"I don't like that rule," complained Priscilla, "can't we make up some new ones?"

Jonah thought a moment and ventured a suggestion.

"I can't call you Priscilla in the presence of your parents, but I'll tell you what I can do."

He paused momentarily and studied the anxiety that was teeming in the little girls eyes.

"What Jonah? What can we do?" asked the excited little girl.

"In our little garden, I could call you Priscilla when your mother and father aren't around," ventured Jonah, "but we'll have to keep it a secret."

"Oh goody," exclaimed Priscilla, "I like secrets! Can we start now?"

"Yes Priscilla, we can," he answered as he raised a finger to emphasize the point he was about to make, "but you must remember that our secret world is only within the fences of your mothers' flower garden!"

"Oh yes Jonah," exclaimed Priscilla, "I'll remember."

Priscilla stepped back from the bench and watched the flight of a gold finch flying to its nest. She ran to the tree where the bird was perched, and watched him as he cocked his head to the side to study her.

"Look Jonah," exclaimed Priscilla, "that bird is watching me!"

She anxiously beckoned Jonah to come. The old man lifted his frame from the bench and walked as fast as his arthritis would allow.

"What do you think he's thinking," asked Priscilla.

"Well I suppose he's thinking how good it is to be free and to fly where ever he wishes," answered Jonah with a warm smile.

"I wish I were a bird," replied Priscilla. "I think I would fly to a place where I could find a whole lot of friends like you."

"Thank you honey," replied Jonah with a tear in his eye.

"I think you're a good friend too," he replied softly. Jonah was touched to the heart by the honesty of Priscilla and his voice trembled in emotion.

"If that bird flew away, he couldn't make you and me happy. You see Mr. Goldfinch enriches every day he's around us. If he flew away, he'd leave behind two very sad people. In life we must make the best of each day and do all those things God wants us to do. If we do all we can to make others happy, then we find that we are happy too. Our greatest pleasure is in the joy of friends and family."

"Gee whiz Jonah," replied Priscilla as she watched the bird fly to another tree, "Mr. Goldfinch makes us happy by just being around. Doesn't he!"

"Yes he does Priscilla," answered Jonah as they walked side by side through the garden, "just by being himself and doing what the Lord prepared him to do."

"Who is the Lord, Jonah," asked Priscilla as she took Jonah's hand.

"Well the Lord is the One who made the world and all that's in it," replied Jonah.

"Even Mr. Goldfinch," interrupted Priscilla.

"Yes, even Mr. Goldfinch," answered Jonah as he picked up his spade.

"Where is the Lord," she asked, "I've never seen Him."

"We can't see Him with our eyes," replied Jonah, "we look at Him with out heart. We only see Him when we want to see Him."

"But I want to see Him and I still can't see Him," complained Priscilla.

"Seeing God is like seeing the wind," explained Jonah warmly, "we can't see the wind, but we see the trees sway when Mr. Wind moves through the leaves. We feel Mr. Wind blow in our face and we hear him howl in a storm. So even though we can't see the wind, we know it's there. God is like that. We see Him in the trees, the flowers, the birds, the wind, and the sun and even in each other. God made all things, and every thing that was made was made by Him."

"Can we talk to God," asked the little girl, "I mean if I say 'Hi God. How are you?' Will He talk back to me?"

Jonah started digging a new flowerbed as he thought for a moment about how to answer in a way Priscilla would understand.

"Let me tell you what I do," said Jonah as he continued to dig, "When I go about my business, I talk to the Lord. Like this morning when I saw how lovely the flowers were. I said 'thank you Lord for all these beautiful flowers.'"

"How do you know if He hears you," asked Priscilla, "does He talk back to you?"

"No," replied Jonah, "He doesn't talk back so my ears can hear, if that's what you mean. He answers by giving me more beautiful flowers. You see when we talk to people; maybe they ask how we're doing. They speak words, but nothing happens to change anything if we're feeling bad. Now God is different. If we tell Him we're feeling bad, He touches us with love and makes us feel better."

"What do you ask Him," asked Priscilla.

"I once asked Him for a job, and He gave me this one. I asked Him to bless this garden, and He did that. And I asked Him for a special friend, and He sent you to me," continued the old man with tears in his eyes and a quivering voice.

"Jonah, I think I'm going to talk to God too! I have lots of things I want to ask Him for," retorted Priscilla excitedly.

Priscilla had no way of knowing how her presence thrilled the old man. He was moved with compassion for her partly because he knew the lack of affection she received at home. He was also burdened by memories of his own foolish mistakes when he was rich in worldly possessions. He fought back the tears that swelled in his eyes.

"Yes Priscilla, you go ahead and ask. The Lord will surely hear," he replied in assurance.

Priscilla stayed another hour and talked with Jonah, asking questions, listening to his answer and then asking another question. She enjoyed the opportunity to ask anything she wondered about without upsetting someone. Jonah patiently answered each question with understanding and compassion.

So it was that over the next two years a strong bond of friendship developed between the venerable old man and the little girl. Every opportunity found Priscilla in her mother's flower garden where she could be herself and escape, at least temporarily, the rigid ship of rules her mother ran in the mansion that was her home. In the garden with this peculiar friend were the happiest hours of her childhood. She found happiness, not in material possessions as in her mother's world, but in kindness, appreciation and understanding of Jonah's simple life. Each day when she left the garden, she left behind a world of freedom and returned to a world of tradition, regimented form and pomp. In her father's house, she had anything she wanted yet had nothing.

In Jonah's garden, she had nothing, but yet she had all things worth having.

CHAPTER 2

The fruit of the righteous is a tree of life, and he that wins souls is wise.

Soon after Priscilla's eleventh birthday, she was awakened by a horrible dream. She decided to tell Jonah about it, but the next day was to be one of tumultuous consequences. Harold and Elizabeth had decided to send Priscilla to a boarding school. 'It was time for Priscilla to learn to be a lady' was the way Elizabeth put it. Harold had already delayed the inevitable decision three years for the sake of the tender child, but she must now learn to act like a Pomp and put aside all childish things. "After all," Harold told Priscilla, "you are a young lady of twelve now."

"Father, do I have to stay away all the time like my friends? I'd rather be home with you and mother," Priscilla asked, hoping her father would change his mind.

"Yes Priscilla, you will be required to remain in school until the Thanksgiving break. Then you'll go back to school until Christmas vacation. At that time, you'll have a three week break," said Harold hoping in his clumsy way to encourage his daughter, frightened child that she was.

"Father, I don't want to leave you and mother. And what about Jonah? If I leave him, he won't have any friends at all," exclaimed Priscilla as hot streams of tears bathed her pink cheeks.

"Sweet heart don't cry," begged Harold, "you must do it whether you want to or not. After all, it is for your own good."

Priscilla didn't care that it was for her welfare. She was frightened. Knowing her father as she did, she knew there was no escaping her bitter fate. Never the less, in one desperate attempt to avert the inevitable, she flung herself into the arms of her mother in hope of finding an understanding heart. To her dismay this proved fruitless also. Her refinement had been delayed too long already!

"Your father is right Priscilla," chided Elizabeth, "now stop this crying! You're entirely too old to be carrying on like this."

"You don't love me or you wouldn't make me go away to school," cried Priscilla sobbing in grief and distress, "you're trying to get rid of me."

Harold and Elizabeth were shocked by this outburst of defiance. Her mother grabbed Priscilla by both arms and demanded an apology.

"You apologize to your father and me this minute, "Elizabeth demanded as she shook the little girl in anger.

The unrepentant child screamed, "No! I won't apologize for the truth! You hate me! You hate me! You hate me!"

Priscilla jerked free from her mother's grip and ran out of the house.

"Come back here you little wretch," cried her mother in indignation, "Harold go get her and put her to bed!"

Harold thought a moment and replied. "Elizabeth, she has had quite a trial. I think it best to leave her to herself for a short time. After she has calmed down, she'll apologize, I'm sure."

Elizabeth was not at all satisfied with his answer.

"Harold, that child is unmanageable. If ever a child needed refinement, our Priscilla does! And further more…"

"Elizabeth," interrupted Harold, "all your words are for naught. The child is upset. I suggest we drop the subject and let her cry it out."

Priscilla ran directly to the flower garden, crying as she went. The old gardener turned his gray head in her direction, when he heard her coming. He kneeled down as she ran to him and collapsed in his arms. Jonah felt hot tears dropping on his neck as Priscilla poured out her soul to him.

"Oh Jonah," she caught her breath between sobs, "It's terrible! It's terrible! Mother and father are sending me away. I'll never see you again! I just know it! I just know it!"

"Now Priscilla," consoled Jonah, "It can't possibly be that bad."

"But Jonah! They are going to send me away," she sobbed emphatically, "they don't love me! They're trying to get rid of me!"

"Honey if you'll settle down, we'll get to the bottom of this," said Jonah in assurance.

"It's that dream Jonah! I knew it was bad! It scared me and I knew something horrible would happen," sobbed Priscilla clutching Jonah's neck.

"What dream honey," asked Jonah as he gently pushed his little friend away so that he could look into her eyes.

"That dream! It was horrible," cried Priscilla, "I just hate that dream!"

"Priscilla, please stop crying and tell old Jonah your dream," said the old gardener.

This appeal enabled the little girl to gather her wits.

"Now," Jonah said tenderly, "tell me your dream"

Priscilla drew a deep breath as she and Jonah walked to the bench in the garden. They sat down and she squeezed Jonah's hand as she began to tell him her dream.

"Well," she said gathering courage, "you and I were in this garden laughing and playing games. We were so happy!"

She paused and looked seriously into Jonah's blue eyes.

"Suddenly this bright light appeared and I was afraid, but you told me it was all right. The light came closer and I could see that it was a man whose clothing was as bright as the sun. He reached out and you put your hand in his. Then both of you walked away from me. I yelled at you Jonah! I begged you 'Jonah please come back', but you just kept on going! You didn't even look back!"

At this point, Priscilla could no longer hold back the tears. She buried her head in Jonah's strong shoulder and sobbed uncontrollably. Jonah patted her on the back compassionately.

"It's all right Priscilla. It's only a dream. Is that all?" he asked.

"No," replied Priscilla whimpering, "when you disappeared, I was surrounded by darkness for a little while. And then mother and father took me to a prison and told me to learn how to live. After a while I was happy in prison. Jonah, I just know I couldn't be happy in prison. I just couldn't!"

Priscilla paused a moment for some response, but Jonah remained silent in deep concentration as he pondered her dream. She could tell that he was puzzled.

"All the time I was in prison being happy, that same bright light that came to get you was off in the distance above and behind me. I had to turn to see Him, but He was there!" she said as she clutched his hand and continued. "Then I saw you coming back Jonah and by then I was grown up. But it didn't look like you. Well a little bit he did. He was younger than you, but he had your voice! Oh I know it was your voice!"

Priscilla was becoming engrossed in the story and by now had stopped whimpering. It was clear to Jonah that she was still upset and the old gardener smiled reassuringly.

"But I hated you Jonah! I wouldn't talk to you! Then I started to like you again. Then a dark cloud surrounded you and took you away from me again! The light that was behind and above me came down and stood beside me. I was afraid Jonah, and I cried and begged you to come back! But the Light asked me what I wanted most of all. I said I wanted 'you back again!' He said 'believe and it shall be so.' Then He stood over and behind you, watching all that you did. You finally came back again Jonah and you were sad, and I was sad too, but the bright Light brought us together and we were both happy again!"

Priscilla paused and squirmed on the bench and asked, "Jonah, what does it mean? Do you know?"

Jonah had been drawn near to the Lord God by the past six years of tribulation, and he knew the interpretation of the dream. However, he knew now wasn't the time to tell her. He spoke in his heart "Lord open my lips at the appointed hour, for I know that now isn't the time for the revelation she seeks, though I perceive it will be soon.' At the present time his concern was for the present needs of his troubled little friend. He studied momentarily, and answered her.

"Priscilla, the dream shows your future, and it is from the Lord," Jonah responded, "it says He's going to keep you in His hand, but I want to pray and meditate on the dream, before I tell you the interpretation."

"Jonah, is it bad?" asked Priscilla.

"If the Lord is with you, everything will be all right honey. Always remember that," replied Jonah tenderly.

This was his only response as he sought a way to change the subject before Priscilla could ask another question.

"Priscilla, do you remember that song I taught you about 'one precious moment with you'?" asked Jona.

"Yes, but I don't feel like singing," replied Priscilla sadly.

"Honey, sometimes a song is the best way to defeat your troubles," replied Jonah, "and now is one of those times. Sing with me."

Jonah started the first verse with gusto.

'Sweeter than violets, kissed by the dew,
Stroll through the hedge of roses, thinking of you.
Fairer than spring time, newer than new,
Grander than I can imagine is one precious moment with you.'

Priscilla was caught up in the gay mood and liveliness of the song and picked up the tempo in the vigor of her youth.

'Deep as the ocean, high as the sky,
I've a peculiar notion; you are the reason why,
I love each hour we wander through,
Grander than I can imagine is one precious moment with you.'

They sang the chorus and final verse together with zest. Priscilla grabbed the old man by the arms and they spun around and around as they sang.

'We stroll along, singing a song,
Facing our fate together.
Always we'll be, happy and free,
Laughing and fun forever.

Blessing from heaven, angel divine,
You came to bring me sunshine, I made you mine,
Now and forever, I will be true,
Grander than I can imagine is one precious moment with you.
Grander than I can imagine is one precious moment with you.'

Jonah collapsed on the ground, his energy spent as Priscilla jumped in glee and joy. Both of them laughed in happiness while each caught their breath. It seemed a miracle that Jonah in his uncomplicated and naive manner could bring happiness and vigor from Priscilla's youth. It was only around Jonah that she felt at ease to be herself. She could ask anything, act her age, have fun, and she even felt wanted as well as needed in the presence of the old sage. Heart reached out and touched heart as this uncommon couple chatted, and for a few brief moments Priscilla's soul bathed in a refreshing drink of real communication.

Disaster often strikes as soon as happiness arrives, and it is very likely to stay much longer. Elizabeth had worried when Priscilla didn't return. She searched the house and the entire estate, last of all looking in the garden. By the time she found Priscilla, she was in a fit of frenzy. Finding the old man sitting and resting provided a good target at which to direct her aggression.

"Priscilla Pomp," she scolded, "I have searched this entire estate for you and of all places you're in the flower garden with this second class citizen! And as for you Mr. Wright," she called his name both to belittle and embarrass him, "what are you doing sitting down on the job? We pay you a very good wage for the work you do, and it's very little that you do! Furthermore, you know that this is specifically against the rules. You're always filling this child's' mind with wild ideas and you've been warned before! This child is trouble enough without you confusing her. I'm afraid I'm going to have to dismiss you permanently. You are no longer wanted! Please pick up your final check tomorrow afternoon.

Jonah was shocked and hurt by this unwarranted attack on him, but he carefully concealed his pain for Priscilla's sake. Try as he might, he couldn't hide his bitter anguish and agony of soul from Priscilla. She saw his drooped shoulders as he hung his head in sorrow. Priscilla wreathed in agony with the old man when she recalled the fun they had together. This, coupled with the fact that she'd never see her old friend again, was more than she could bear. She had never seen him broken in defeat, and she ran to him, as she had many times before.

"Jonah take me with you," she begged in tears, "I don't want to stay here without you!"

She threw her arms around his waist and buried her face in his chest, as she wept bitterly.

Elizabeth lunged for her daughter and tore her from Jonah before he had time to console his beloved little friend.

"You little wretch," she screamed, "after all your father and I have done for you, you choose this tramp before us? I'm taking you home! Your father will hear of this," she chided as she dragged Priscilla up the hill to the mansion.

"Jonah take me with you," Priscilla cried out as her mother dragged her up the hill. She cried until Elizabeth pulled her into the house. When the big door closed, Jonah no longer heard her agonizing pleas for help.

CHAPTER 3

That your trust may be in the Lord, I have made known to you this day, even to you.

Jonah lived two miles from the Pomp estate and he usually caught a cab home. Even though his ordeal with Elizabeth had drained his energy, he thought a walk would be good. His mind kept returning to the chaos of the day. He gave no thought to losing his job. The Lord had provided these past three years, and he would provide again.

He was concerned for Priscilla, whose present and future were blue printed by her parents. The child needed love and companionship. How much of either would she receive at the boarding school? Having been enslaved to money, prestige and position in the past, Jonah knew how material wealth could blind even the wisest of men to the ultimate joy and reason for living.

Also, he remembered his grandson, all he had left of a son he had neglected. He had been too busy to watch Roy grow up. He gave him anything he wanted if he could buy it in a few minutes or give him the money to buy it.

But he was young and foolish then and he couldn't see his son slowly withdrawing from him. What a shock when the police found his son dead in a hotel room at the age of 26, leaving behind a one year old son. Then came the shock when Roy's' widow abandoned his grandson and left with a young debonair suitor. When Martha, his wife died one year later, Jonah sought to drown his troubles in alcohol. He shuttered as he recalled how quickly his despondency resulted in one bad business decision after another until he plunged into bankruptcy. The last straw was when the court took his grandson from him because he was deemed incapable of providing a good home for him. He was only seven then. That would make him ten today. He often wondered where little Philip was and if his foster parents provided well for him. This evening his soul was especially troubled as his world was crashing in around him. With his own flesh and blood, he had failed miserably to provide any real happiness or security. All this was before Jonah knew the Lord, before he made his decision to receive the gift of life by receiving the Lord Jesus Christ as his savior. However, knowing the Lord didn't ease the memory of the tragedy of his ungodly past. 'Oh Lord,' he thought, 'Priscilla's parents are sending her down the same primrose pathway of doom.'

Jonah approached a small thicket of trees about halfway home and decided to stop and rest. He saw a tree stump at the edge of the thicket and he sat down and pulled off his straw hat. He tossed it on a large rock close by. With heavy heart and burdened soul, he folded his hands together, looked up to the heavens and spoke to his God.

"Lord, I had quite a day, to say the least, but I give thanks for it. I give thanks because I know that you're going to glorify your name through it," he began in a voice both solemn and sad, "I don't understand why it's happened, but I trust that it's for the best. You've been awful good to me father, better to me than I deserved. The biggest part of my life I spent in blindness to your mercy and grace. I was hopelessly lost in pride and arrogance until you saved me from my sins."

Jonah lifted his head, for it began to droop in heaviness as he prayed.

"When I had great wealth, I put riches before everything. Yet for all my wealth, I was never really happy. Then praise your name," his voice cracked as he felt the touch of the Most High God, "you had compassion on this old stony heart to chastise me and remold my character as I was created by you, and not as I had made myself. I was as filthy rags. The man you have wrought is a perfect work of salvation. Not that I am perfect Lord, but You are perfect who dwells within me. I must admit that I've been a stubborn old cuss at times and I thank you for your patience with me. I even thank you for my suffering, for it has drawn me closer to You. For as the house I built has crumbled, you have rebuilt me as it pleased you. And it has pleased me to know that it pleases you to perfect me. Your servant is grateful for all these things and Holy Father, I thank you for all this."

"It seems that I've lost everything that's been dear to me, except you Lord, and I praise your precious name for that, for how could I have endured without you? How did I endure without you before you saved me? I've lost my wealth, my position, my son, my wife and grandson and now Priscilla. As I look back, I can see why you've taken the others from me. But why you've taken Priscilla, I don't understand. I've been doing the best I can."

Jonah was completely overcome with grief as tears washed his cheeks.

"I'm grateful though for what Priscilla and I had together. Bless those hours to their intended use. I praise your name that I'll never lose you. I'm sorry for letting this situation overcome me Father, but you know how hard I've tried. For three years I've been an outcast of the world, but I've been drawn closer to you. The world thinks I'm alone, yet I'm not alone for you are with me. I count everything I have lost as nothing compared to you. I'm not one to make excuses Lord, but when I've failed it's not because I wanted to. I've found that the only real triumph in life is to do your will and see you face to face. I guess what I'm trying to say is if you'll always abide with me, I'll always be happy."

There was humility in the deep voice of the old man, but what he didn't say in words he more than made up for in spirit. He knew within himself that the Lord understood.

"Lord, I know my time is very near, but there are two things I want to discuss with you. When I neglected my grandson, you took him away from me. I'm not complaining or trying to second-guess your better judgment, for my soul has found relief knowing that he was in your care. Even so Lord, put him under your unfailing grace and deliver him safely from the world. I have found that the only way to subdue the flesh is to overcome it. Godly guidance, teaching and chastisement are purifiers of the soul as fire purges gold of its impurities. You waited until the twilight of my years to chastise me, but I ask you to prepare him, my only grandson Philip, at a very tender age. Purify him with the fire of trial and tribulation in his youth, while he is still a young man that he may overcome and stand firm in your holy word and deliver many from the fires of torment to the glory of your holy name. This I ask for your sake as well as his, for I wasted the best years of my life in quest of riches that passed away," again Jonah was overcome by emotion and he paused momentarily, "if I have found any grace in your sight Lord, remember my grandson Philip."

"My heart also goes out to Priscilla, Lord, for her life is so void of happiness. I know that you have drawn her to me to glorify your name. I ask you to bless her life and forget her not. I know that she shall turn her back on you for a season, but I beg you to be merciful to her. My prayer is that she and Philip, my grandson, might know your love and peace as I know it. Do whatever is necessary to subdue her rebellious spirit to your will, but be merciful, for she did not choose to be what her parents are making of her. You saw her agony and despair. Make her a blessing to all who need a friend. May her parents be blessed through their child. Be a friend to her in hours of need. Lord, I'm so confused and upset. I hope I'm making sense to you."

"All that has been dear to me has passed away or gone on before me. But these two remain. I entrust them to your loving care, asking you to abide with them always. Thank you for hearing your servant. I ask this in Jesus' name. Amen."

In his crude way, Jonah had asked a blessing on the two greatest concerns of his life. He entrusted their care to the benefactor of all mankind, and looked to the Most High God to keep watch over them in his stead. There was no bitterness in his soul or anger toward God for his cruel fate. His attitude was that of a child, trusting and at peace. The Lord had truly prepared Jonah for his reward.

Jonah walked with God on the way home and spent the night in peace. He had left his worries to the One who could solve them and abode in His solace. Tomorrow he must get his things together and pick up his last check. Hopefully he'd see Priscilla one last time.

The sun was peeking over the horizon when Jonah arose the next morning. As he walked to the Pomp estate, he sensed that Elizabeth would forbid Priscilla to see him today. He perceived that this was the day to tell her the interpretation of her dream. However the wise old gardener didn't worry long. He had learned to turn matters over to the Lord when he could no longer handle them. He said in his heart, "Lord, I must see Priscilla today. Please make it possible."

For Priscilla the night had been restless. For the second time she had the same dream which she had revealed to Jonah. How desperately she wanted to see him again. Her mother had left instructions for her to remain in her room. Under no circumstances was she to go to the garden or see Jonah. As she gazed out of her bedroom window, she saw a goldfinch and remembered how Jonah would talk to God. In desperation, she looked up to the sky as she had seen Jonah do many times and spoke.

"Lord, This is Priscilla. You know, Jonah's friend. Do you hear me?" she paused a moment, looking for a physical manifestation, but seeing none, she continued, "Jonah told me that even if you didn't say anything, you would hear me. Maybe you don't know me very well, but Jonah told me all about you."

She stopped again, waiting for she knew not what.

"Lord, It's about Jonah," she continued in remorse, "he's my very best friend. Please don't take him away from me! Mother says that he's dumb, but really he's very smart. And I like him. Any way, if you take him away, I won't have any really good friends."

Having said this, she turned and fell across the bed.

Meanwhile, downstairs, there was a clatter of voices in hysteria. Priscilla heard it and came out of her room. She looked over the banister at the cluster of busy maids below. Two ladies were crying. Confusion was so great that the little girl couldn't quite understand what they were saying, but she heard Jonah's name several times. By the tone of their voices, she sensed that something was desperately wrong. She tried to slip down the stairs unnoticed. Marion, the head maid saw her and quickly grabbed her.

"I'm sorry Priscilla. Back to your room," she commanded.

"But Marion. What's wrong with Jonah," asked Priscilla.

"He'll be all right, so don't worry about it," Marion snapped back, knowing that every word she spoke was a lie. She began leading Priscilla back up the stairs against her will.

"Please Marion! He's my best friend," she cried, "I just have to see him!"

Marion pushed her into her room and locked the door. Priscilla screamed, beat on the door and tugged at the doorknob in vain. The chauffeur heard her screams and ran up the stairs.

"What's wrong with her," he asked in concern.

"She wants out to see Jonah and her mother said she is to stay in her room," Marion replied.

"You are heartless woman," shouted the chauffeur in disgust, "you know that the old man is dying! She's crazy about the old gardener, and you won't let her see him before he dies!"

"I have my orders and she isn't going anywhere," the maid replied defiantly.

"Give me that key," demanded the chauffeur, "She's going to see Jonah!"

"You're not getting this key and she isn't going to see Jonah," Marion retorted angrily.

"Oh yeah! We'll see about that," he replied in determination. He threw his shoulder into the door and jarred it open. Then he took Priscilla's hand and led her down the stairs.

"You fool," screamed Marion angrily, "you'll lose your job for this."

The chauffeur never looked back. Together they ran across the wide expanse of lawn to the garden. Priscilla scanned the garden excitedly for her old friend. There in the center of the garden, lay Jonah with a maid holding his head up. He looked lifeless, but when he saw Priscilla, he seemed to regain some strength.

"Jonah! Jonah!" screamed Priscilla. She kneeled beside him and clasped his waist in a warm embrace, as she dug her face into his chest.

"Good morning Priscilla," replied Jonah weakly, "I've been waiting for you."

"You're going to be all right, aren't you Jonah," said Priscilla in concern.

"Don't you worry any Honey," replied Jonah, "the Lord will take care of us."

"Oh Jonah, I don't want you to go away," begged Priscilla, "please say you won't go away!"

"Priscilla I have to tell you about your dream today," Jonah interrupted, "so please listen carefully because I'm too tired to repeat anything. O.K.?"

"O.K. Jonah," she replied submissively.

He drew a deep breath and began.

"Priscilla that bright light you saw in your dream was the Lord. He's going to watch over you when I leave."

"But Jonah, I don't want you to leave," she pleaded as she looked to him for assurance.

"Honey, I have to go. The Lord's coming to take me to a better home," Jonah replied.

"Well ask Him if I can go too," she begged, "I want to be with you."

"There is much you must do, Priscilla, before we meet again. But we'll meet again," replied Jonah. He was breathing harder and he knew that he must hurry his conversation.

"But Jonah, I…"

"Please Priscilla," Jonah interrupted, "listen carefully for I must hurry. You're going to forget for a time the things you've learned from me. You'll learn to love those things, which you hate now. You'll be just like your mother in a few years."

"Oh Jonah! Say it isn't so," pleaded Priscilla.

"Hush Honey. It's true. Your soul will be in prison, but you'll think that you're happy. The Lord is behind you in your dream because you will turn your back on Him. He's above you because He's above all of us."

"The man you saw is a young man like me. His voice sounded like mine because he will bring you back to God, even as I have lead you to Him. You will despise this man when you meet him, but you will be drawn to him. He will win your heart and he will love you as you will love him."

"The dark cloud means suffering and despair. You will suffer at the hand of the man you love, because you will meddle with the perfect will of God. This is necessary for The Most High God will help you and you will be drawn closer to Him through your suffering. Your husband will be returned to you when you pray for Him and forget yourself. This tribulation will teach you to put God and His work first and yourself last. Then your home will be restored for God, that Great Light, will resurrect your broken home with a miracle."

Jonah's voice had dropped to a whisper and each breath was a gasp.

"Jonah, I love you," sobbed Priscilla, "I couldn't do all those mean things to you."

"Priscilla don't cry," said the old gardener, "where I'm going there will be a new song every day. Every moment will be joy. Every day will be a holiday. We won't be apart very long. Trust the Most High God and look to Him for guidance."

His voice drifted off and his eyes looked to the heavens as peace settled upon him.

"Jonah, please remember me where you go," Priscilla cried rubbing her swollen eyes.

"Yes Priscilla. I will," replied Jonah.

With all his strength, he lifted his arms and squeezed Priscilla for the last time. She clung tightly to him. Tears stained his cheeks and he whispered, "Thank you Lord. Thank you."

Having fulfilled his last wish, his arms slipped lifelessly to the ground and Jonah relaxed in the bosom of the Most High God. Priscilla didn't understand as she sobbed, "Oh Jonah, please talk to me. I love you."

Jonah's work was over and he went to his eternal reward.

CHAPTER 4

There is a way which seems right to a man, but the end thereof are the ways of death.

September brought the beginning of another school year and Priscilla's great fear was realized. She was enrolled in three different schools and each one explicitly refused to allow a future reentrance. Refinement was a ball and chain to the carefree life Jonah lived and taught her. She preferred being herself to acting a role. She clung tenaciously to those principles, which Jonah had taught her in the garden. Jonah was her ideal. He was her standard. The easy, care free life style he had taught her was the epitome of achievement.

She kept a necklace Jonah had given to her a few weeks before he had died. She put it around the neck of her favorite doll Matilda. She had often taken Matilda with her to the garden. She kept it secret, for fear her mother would dispose of the necklace if she knew its' origin. Priscilla treasured the only material gift Jonah had given her. It was half of a heart on a thin gold chain. The letters 'INESS' were engraved upon it. She remembered asking Jonah if it was someone's name. He said that 'it was part of a word.' His wife had an identical half heart with the other half of the word. She had often wondered what it meant.

For nine months, Priscilla had proved more than equal to the challenge of resisting the instruction of a sophisticated world. It was June when Elizabeth began to take the situation in hand. She began by making Priscilla part of her every day activities. She took Priscilla to fashion shows, carnivals and shopping. She even planned events she knew would catch the little girl's fancy. Elizabeth was on the right track. The attention Priscilla received from her mother was a grand new experience. Elizabeth herself became more attached to her daughter. During the summer a new vibrant relationship developed between mother and daughter. Out of this relationship began the evolution of a new and different Priscilla.

Priscilla began enjoying the fashion shows and millinery shops frequented by her mother. There were so many stunning styles and vivid colors to choose from. She would imagine herself with the grace, charm and elegance of the shapely models that displayed the clothing. She would often stand before the mirror in her room and pretend she was modeling a smashing new cocktail dress. This is quite natural for a girl of twelve. Suddenly the world leaps out before her and her eyes are opened to scores of new notions and ideas. Being in the presence of so many rich and high-minded snobs began to make an impression upon her character. She learned the fine art of snobbery. Gradually her thoughts turned inward to herself. All compassion for men diminished to token courtesy, if it suited her fancy at the moment. Priscilla, at sixteen, had indeed become the product of her mother's workmanship. She was every bit as hardened as her mother, seeking only to build her ego at the expense of others.

Priscilla had taken piano lessons since eight years of age and she was a very accomplished pianist. She was sent to the best private tutors in New England where she excelled. Music became her life and her college major. Classical music was her favorite. Beethoven and Straus were her favorite composers. She worked hard at music, but she hardly passed in the general curriculum. This was the new Priscilla. If she liked something, that was great. If her fancy was unmoved, forget it. She graduated at twenty-one with a B. A. in music. A year later she had earned her Masters of music. The following fall she began teaching at Crighton College at Utica New York. She was the youngest instructor in the history of the school.

All visible signs pointed to success and happiness for Priscilla. She was always smiling, but if one observed her closely, her smiles were from the teeth out. Her life was void of happiness.

She felt that the students did not appreciate her talents and musical skills. She could teach them all they needed to know, but the impudent fools took her for granted. Thus her teaching position became a great disappointment. It did not provide the recognition, praise and glory she needed.

These elements were required in colossal quantities to feed her mountainous ego. She used her classroom to tear apart the works of aspiring young students. From her lofty peak of pride, she looked down upon those poorly endowed and untalented students.

Priscilla rarely dated. She had dated Edward Holloway for two years. He took her abuse and yielded to her will. Her brash attitude drove away any young man with an interest in her. She was domineering in every respect and independent to the point that she repulsed many a well-intentioned suitor. She owed nothing to any man. She believed in competing in any way to emerge victorious. Often she would belittle and poke fun at an invitation to get acquainted. Once a hopeful suitor was trying to get acquainted. Priscilla, sensing his intentions, bluntly stated, "Why don't you just ask me out and forget the usual bally hoo."

Needless to say, the young man was startled. He politely excused himself as gracefully as he could, but he never bothered her again. Priscilla laughed at the incident. In her words, "chalk one up for the liberated woman." Priscilla was indeed liberated, as well as proud, arrogant and witty.

Priscilla was blessed with great beauty. She was fair and pleasing to the eye. She stood five feet four inches tall and her figure was very well proportioned. Her blue eyes were set into a full round face, and her naturally curly hair hung to her shoulders. She was pretty and she knew it.

With her beauty and her father's money, she felt she could choose the man she wanted. Thus far Jonah was right. Priscilla forgot all that the old man had taught her concerning the real issues of life and she became just like her mother.

The fall semester at Crighton College began four weeks after her twenty-fourth birthday. With two full years of teaching experience behind her, she was now a seasoned veteran. She had already grown discontent with the dull classroom routine. She decided that this would be her last year of teaching. She wanted to travel for a year. As a child she had traveled the world, but now she felt she would appreciate those sights more.

The only class she enjoyed teaching was Music Theory 314. It consisted of advanced theory and composition. She required two original compositions. One was for a mid-term grade and the other was for the final grade.

Song writing was a talent she never developed, but she appreciated a student with creative aptitudes and talent.

Crighton College had two music instructors, Priscilla and Dr. Stevens. Dr. Stevens was the preferred instructor of the students at large, for he made an effort to understand and work with his students. All music majors, on the other hand, disliked Priscilla. She was unduly strict and her assignments encroached upon infinity. Each year, Priscilla's class consisted of those students not fortunate enough to make the cut for Dr. Stevens's class.

The bell rang for the first session of Music Theory 314. Priscilla stood behind the lectern and studied the students filing past. She stepped to the side of the lectern. She held a list of names in her right hand and with her left hand she flipped her hair over her shoulder.

"I'd like to welcome you to Music Theory 314," she began in a business like tone, "in the next seventeen weeks, we're…."

She was interrupted by two students rushing in late. One was about six feet tall, light brown wavy hair, ruddy complexion and of sturdy stature. He was carefree, happy and light hearted. He was pushing his friend Simeon Worthington in a wheel chair. Simeon had been involved in an automobile accident, which had left him blind and crippled. He was Philip's best friend. The two roomed together. Simeon was the business minded one. They pooled their resources and bought some music equipment to form a band. Philip sang and played rhythm guitar. Simeon played piano and keyboards. Simeon was five feet six inches tall and usually wore sporty clothes. As Priscilla disgustedly watched these two young men parade into her class, her eye paused upon Philip to size him up a second time.

"Just a moment," scolded Priscilla angrily, "The two of you are late! Tardiness is one thing I will not tolerate!"

She shook her finger and drew a bead on the objects of her aggravation.

"Let me make one point clear right now," she continued scanning the remainder of the class, "I allow one absence and one tardy. Each violation thereafter will drop your grade one half point!"

The class was silent as Philip and Simeon remained motionless.

"You gentlemen please find a seat," Priscilla continued, still smoldering from the intrusion, "on second thought, you two men will be seated in the front row seats immediately in front of my lectern. Since you have won my graces, you may honor me with your nearness!" She sought to further embarrass the two tardy students.

"Now," she continued casting a glance and raising an eye brow at Simeon and Philip, "if all the interruptions are over, "I'll Tell you what you can expect to learn, and what I expect of you."

She briefly described the program and handed out the syllabus mapping the topics to be discussed in the coming semester. She told them which books to buy (for quite naturally she chose a different text than Dr. Stevens), and additional materials needed as well. She was specific and concise.

"We will adjourn early today," she said, "but before we leave, I would like each student to introduce themselves, give your reasons for taking this class and tell us a little about yourself. I think we'll begin with this man," she concluded, pointing to Simeon.

Being blind, Simeon was not aware that the ominous finger was pointing at him, so he sat and looked straight ahead. Priscilla waited a moment for his response as all eyes watched her. She thought at once that he was ignoring her.

Indignantly she said, "I'll ask you one more time to…"

She hesitated and noticed Philip gesturing with his hands and eyes that Simeon was blind. She understood immediately and drew her breath. Meanwhile, Simeon perceived Priscilla's anger was directed at him, and he spoke, "I'm sorry ma'am. I'm blind and I didn't realize you were speaking to me."

"Oh! Well I'm sorry," Priscilla replied in embarrassment, "I didn't know."

"That's all right," Simeon answered, "my name is Simeon Worthington. I like music and also discussions with my friends. I hope to better appreciate and understand music from this class."

Priscilla nodded to Philip and he began, "my name is Philip Wright. I'm a senior. I play in a small band with Simeon here. I enjoy music and I do volunteer work at Little Angels Nursing Home. I plan to do administrative work in a children's nursing home when I graduate. I hope this class will help me in composing songs for my friends in the nursing home."

Priscilla couldn't help being attracted to this handsome student. He was peculiarly individual, frank, honest and humble. His voice was mellow. He spoke meekly and words seemed to flow from his mouth. He possessed a depth of character and gentleness that seemed familiar. Her mind flashed back over the past as she tried to remember someone who spoke like that. She was at a loss to recall a face, a time, or a place. As students introduced themselves, Priscilla was strangely entranced. At last introductions were finished.

"That will be all, if there are no questions," she paused and scanned the class momentarily and continued, "we'll meet again Wednesday."

The class hurried out the door, but Philip waited until all had left before helping Simeon into the wheel chair. Priscilla watched him while pretending to write. Philip then pushed Simeon out the door, but looked back at Priscilla before the door closed. She was jarred by the profile of his face. That face. There was something about his face. She felt that she should know his face. Who, in heavens name had she known who resembled this student? She pondered this thought all afternoon and recalled that the old gardener who died in her mothers' flower garden was much like this student. There were many similarities to be sure. She left for home and sat down at her piano to play and relax, relieved that another day at the zoo was complete.

CHAPTER 5

The voice of my beloved! Behold, he comes leaping upon the mountains, skipping upon the hills.

During the next seven weeks, Priscilla continued to be troubled by a burning ember of memory that refused to be extinguished. Each day Philip returned to class, it seemed to gnaw at her mind. Never had any one man been so indelibly stamped in her brain. She knew that voice from her past, and his face resembled one she knew from the past. One evening she pulled out all her high school year books in hope of finding the elusive face that resembled Philip. No one, not even a teacher, resembled him.

At the same time, Philip who found Priscilla attractive the first time he saw her, was growing fonder of her with each class. She became aware of his eyes following her about the class. She knew he liked her and she could see the day when he might not be quite so passive. She pondered the dilemma. On the one hand, it seemed the only way to get acquainted so that she could ask him about his background, which might solve her riddle. Her Victorian respect for rules however, dictated that instructors did not date students. She would have to find an occasion to cool Philip's ideas before they went any further.

Philip was never a man of punctuality, and it was only a short time before he began to be tardy. The next Friday he pushed Simeon into class five minutes late. Priscilla continued to lecture without turning her head, as if she didn't notice. However, she did mark the incident in her grade book.

"Today the first composition is due," she began, "I hope you've spent adequate time on your work, for this is a full eighty per cent of your midterm grade. Please hand them forward."

The class handed their papers forward and Priscilla placed them on the lectern.

"Just out of curiosity, does anyone think they have prepared an 'A' composition," she asked.

Instantly Philip raised his hand.

"May I ask why you think yours is an 'A' composition?" she queried.

"Well Miss Pomp," Philip drawled, "if it isn't an 'A' paper, I figure it's your fault."

"That's interesting," retorted Priscilla, as she blushed, "what do I have to do with your composition?"

"Well," he replied frankly, "you were my inspiration."

The women in the class snickered and Priscilla flushed in embarrassment, and then paled in anger.

"If this is your idea of a joke Philip Wright, I see absolutely no humor in it," scolded Priscilla indignantly.

"I'll remind you that this is a class room and I will not tolerate any cute remarks!" she said angrily.

She stood defiantly and peered angrily into Philips' eyes. To her surprise, he remained calm and smiling.

"I'm not joking Miss Pomp," replied Philip as he leaned back in his chair, "I have an "A" composition. I ain't bragging and I ain't complaining. I'm just bearing the facts."

The coolness of this brash fellow was unnerving Priscilla. Instantly she schemed to belittle him.

"Very well Philip," she retaliated, "you shall know your grade before you leave this class!" She was extremely irate and nervous by this calamity.

"We have five minutes to waste. That should be sufficient time for you to make a fool of yourself," she snapped, flipping her palm in the direction of the piano.

Philip took one step toward the piano, turned and asked, "could Simeon play the piano for me? He can play better and that frees me to sing."

Priscilla angrily nodded her approval, and Philip assisted Simeon into his wheel chair. He pushed him to the piano and lifted him onto the bench. Then he turned on his heal and walked over to the befuddled instructor who had, without realizing it, sat in his seat to listen and critique his composition. He stretched forth the manuscript to her.

"You'll want to follow along," he said softly with a warm smile, "me and Simeon know this tune by heart."

Priscilla gingerly accepted the composition and riveted her eyes on it as Philip returned to the piano. He sat on the corner of the bench with his back to Simeon. He folded his hands together and let them droop in his lap. He was smooth, calm and relaxed. He looked at Priscilla, who pretended to look at his paper, and then addressed the class.

"The title of my song is 'Then You Happened to Me'," he said.

Simeon began playing the introduction and Philip inhaled as all eyes except Priscilla's were fastened upon him. Then he sang in a smooth mellow tone.

'Moon light and music were meaningless things,
Starlight and roses, engagement rings.
I needed someone to call my own,
And then you happened to me.

Romance and love talk were never for me,
Hugging and kissing, that just couldn't be.
I needed someone to call my own,
And then you happened to me.

I never knew what a kiss could be,
Until we kissed at your door.
Now all I know is it's you for me,
Just keep kissing me more.

I never knew there was someone like you,
I never thought I'd be saying I do.
I needed someone to call my own,
And then you happened to me.'

Philip scanned the class and his eyes rested on Priscilla. Try as she might, she could not keep her eyes off him as he sang. He had a magnetic quality about him that drew an audience to him. For a brief moment, she lost herself in the tune. Then her eyes met Philip's. He peered into her very soul and his heart seemed to be calling for her as her sleeping soul was called forth from a tomb of indifference.

As Philip began singing again, the bell rang for the close of the class session, but no one moved from his or her chair. He sang more briskly and robust as he concluded the song.

> 'I never knew what a kiss could be,
> Until we kissed at your door.
> Now all I know is it's you for me,
> Just keep kissing me more.
>
> I never knew there was someone like you,
> I never thought I'd be saying I do.
> I needed someone to call my own,
> And then you happened to me,
> And then you happened to me.'

As the song ended a hush settled over the room and then one clap was followed by a thunder of applause, as all stood except Priscilla. The girls mobbed him excitedly with compliments. All Priscilla could do, was sit and stare in unbelief. Her pride told her to lash out and retaliate again for her embarrassment, but somehow she seemed powerless to act at this disarming moment. In a moment, she knew she could really care for this young man. What a shame that he was two years younger than she, poor and so unrefined.

As the class marched out, she stood up and walked over to the lectern where her grade book lay. She opened the grade book and penned an 'A' beside his name. Philip meanwhile assisted Simeon into the wheel chair and pushed him toward the lectern.

"Is that an 'A'," he asked, looking her full in the face.

"It was quite good Philip," Priscilla replied peering into his eyes. Her face flushed as she looked at him. Her hair seemed to stand on end and goose bumps raised on her arms as a strange tingling sensation swept over her body.

"I must say I was quite surprised," she continued, looking at him again and then down at the floor in nervousness.

"We'll have to be going," said Philip softly, "or we'll be late for our next class."

She stared momentarily at the door as it closed behind Philip, almost in a trance. She laid her grade book back upon the lectern and turned to erase the blackboard. The door opened and Philip poked his head in.

"Miss Pomp, I want you to know that you're a very pretty woman," he said, "and even though you try to act tough, I like you anyway."

She was startled by his statement and retorted, "well Philip I hardly think..."

She didn't finish the statement, for Philip had darted out again and didn't hear her response. She crossed the floor and sat in a chair bewildered. Philip had an uncanny ability to read her heart and see the facade of hardness that covered her soul. With sincerity and rudimentary words, he broke the spell of her self-righteous world and spoke directly to her soul. Against her will he held her attention. In spite of her obstacles, he prevailed. To be so young, he was so mature. What was it about this man that was different from others? Who was it that he reminded her of? Her mind whirled in confusion as she pondered in vain. How could she despise anyone so much and yet be drawn to him?

CHAPTER 6

Turn away your eyes from me, for they have overcome me.

Priscilla's spirit was never subdued for very long. Her competitive drive and strong will were soon to emerge again. When the emotion of that hour wore off, she despised Philip because he had prevailed over her. This singing Casanova might cause the giddy girls of the student body to flock around him, but she wouldn't bow down to any man. Further more, she resented having allowed him to sing the song before the class. The medicine she had intended to ridicule instead blessed him. More than anything else, she despised him because she couldn't fool him. He could see right through her and that troubled her. She recalled that he had already been late for class three times, and she laughed within herself because she could drop his grade one point. Revenge, sweet revenge, she thought. She would announce it in class to humiliate him.

When the bell rang for Friday class, Philip and Simeon were not present. Priscilla smiled in satisfaction and began passing out the graded compositions.

"Look these over and I will be glad to discuss your grade with you after class. If you have questions concerning music structure or related comments with regard to requirements of this assignment, we can discuss those now. I must say I wasn't at all surprised..."

The entrance of Philip and Simeon interrupted her. Both were dripping wet on this rainy day. The floors were freshly waxed and Philip slipped in his hasty entrance. He flopped on his back and Simeon, in his chariot, shot directly toward Priscilla. In fright Priscilla screamed and tried to escape the coming missile. She was swiped just enough to lose her balance and she slipped on the slick floor, breaking the heel of her left shoe and ripping the right knee of her hose. The passing wheel chair tipped the lectern, which fell on her midsection, pinning her to the floor. Simeon sped by and crashed unhurt into the piano at the front of the room. Philip instinctively jumped up and slipped again. He then leaped back up and pulled the lectern off of Priscilla. Her pearl necklace caught the top of the lectern and broke. Pearls rolled in every direction. He set the lectern upright and bent to help Priscilla to her feet. Priscilla straightened her skirt and then looked about the classroom. Philip bent over Priscilla and clutched her left arm and her waist. As he lifted her from the floor, one of her feet slipped on a pearl and she fell backward into Philip, driving him to the floor. She fell on his stomach. This time the room erupted in laughter. Until now the shock and rapid-fire sequence of events had stunned them. The outburst infuriated Priscilla and she leaped to her feet and hobbled on the shoe with the broken heel. She poured forth flames of wrath on the class as Philip righted himself and stood there helplessly embarrassed.

"This class will come to order this instant!" She demanded, "and you Philip…" she couldn't speak the expletive she preferred, so she angrily continued, "sit down before you start an avalanche!"

She was shaking in rage and she hobbled to the lectern. She squatted behind the lectern and gathered in her grade book. Nervously she groped for the compositions that lay at her feet. Many in the class wanted to offer assistance, but all noticed her tears of humiliation and thought better of it. In exasperation, she stood before she had gathered all the papers.

"I am going to dismiss class today. My nerves can't stand another minute of this humiliation. However, Monday we will have a double work load, so don't think for that you're getting off easy!"

Her lower lip trembled and her face again flushed to a deep crimson. It was evident that she was using her last bit of composure to endure a few more minutes.

"Please be careful not to step on any of the pearls," she reminded them, "I can assure you, they can be dangerous."

She hung her head and shook it from side to side as the students filed out. Philip spoke to Eddie Leone for a moment and arranged for Simeon to accompany him the library. Philip would pick him up in a few minutes.

Philip stooped to pick up the scattered pearls. He and Priscilla were alone. As he searched for pearls, Priscilla watched in disgust. What had she done to deserve him? Never had one student so completely destroyed a class hour. And to think that she had nine more weeks with him! Would she endure? She wanted to lash out at him, but she knew if she said even one word, she would explode in tears.

Philip retrieved the last of the pearls and brought them to Priscilla. He stood awkwardly and waited for her response.

"Here's all the beads I could find," he said meekly.

"They're pearls," she replied sullenly.

"I want you to know that I'm very sorry," he said, "I guess I really made a mess of things."

"I'll say you made a mess of things," she retorted sharply, "you've completely disrupted my class, humiliated me before my students, and destroyed a new wardrobe. Just look at me! I'm a shambles from head to toe."

She turned her palms outward in utter despair, as she gave herself the once over. It wasn't until that moment, that Philip took a good look at her. She was indeed a funny sight. Standing with one heel higher than the other, naked right knee, tear stained mascara, and hair in disarray, she was a comical sight. He bit his tongue in an effort not to smile, but the harder he tried to hold back his laughter, the funnier it was. At last, unable to hold it in, he smiled, snickered and burst out laughing. Priscilla was appalled. Her mouth flew open as she raised her eyebrows and pointed a threatening finger in his face.

"How dare you laugh at me Philip Wright," she screamed, "look at me! I'm a shambles! The heel of my shoe is broken and my nylons are ruined!"

She paused a moment to look at herself. How funny she must have looked to the class. Philip was laughing so hard that tears streamed down his cheeks. He was doubled in laughter.

"I'm warning you Philip! Stop this laughter," she shouted. By now the humor of her dilemma was soaking in.

"Please Miss Pomp! Ha ha ha ha ha ha ha," he laughed so hard he could hardly catch his breath, "It's not funny," he sighed breathlessly, "I just can't stop…"

He couldn't finish the sentence.

"Philip, I demand that you stop this laughter at once!" she shouted. She was trying to act angry, but she was very near laughter herself.

"You should have seen yourself when you jumped out of the way of the wheel chair," Philip said laughing. Then Priscilla began laughing.

"Zoom! Simeon streaks toward you! Flop! Down you went," he said.

"You looked quite ridiculous yourself," she laughed, beside herself in hilarity, "rushing in the door and zip, down you go. Zoom! Here comes Simeon! I don't know how I got out of the way," she continued.

"You didn't," retorted Philip, still doubled in laughter.

"Did I scream?" asked Priscilla.

"I'm surprised the windows didn't shatter," replied Philip.

"Look at this shoe," Priscilla said as she stretched forth her left foot, "I must have been a sight walking around up here."

"But when you slipped on those pearls and fell back on me," Philip responded, "I thought my back was broken."

"And that lectern," she continued, "it fell right on me!"

"Yeh! Timber!" replied Philip, "I tried to get up and you slipped back into me and we both fell!"

"Oh! I can't laugh any more," said Priscilla as she held her stomach.

Priscilla wiped tears from her cheeks with a handkerchief. Mean while Philip realized that he still had the pearls and extended them to Priscilla.

"Here. Take these before someone gets hurt," he said.

"Excellent idea," she replied, "I can't remember when I've laughed so hard. Not since I was a child."

"Yeh! It really was funny," Philip replied with a smile, "but I was afraid you might be hurt. You are all right aren't you?"

"Oh yes," she replied with a blush, "I'll probably be sore tomorrow, but I'm all right."

"I am sorry Miss Pomp," said Philip sincerely, "I didn't do it on purpose."

"It wouldn't have been possible to cause that much commotion if you had planned it," she replied with a smile.

Their eyes met and locked momentarily. She felt a pit in her stomach as her pulse quickened. He was a very handsome man. Simple, sincere and in his own way silly. She had to like him in spite of the trouble he had caused her.

"Can I ask you something Philip," she said.

"Yeh!" drawled Philip as he bent over to pick up the scattered papers. She wanted to ask him where his home was. The more she was around him, the more apparent it seemed that he had a tie to her past. She changed her mind though. It was not a rational thought, just intuition.

"Never mind," she replied looking at her watch, "goodness! It's 11:45 and I have a class at one. I must get to my apartment and change! I can't go to class looking like this!"

She scurried to get her things together as Philip collected the last of the papers. He handed them to her and she stuffed them in a leather brief case, and then swiftly exited through the back door. She paused momentarily and looked back.

"Do you have any more classes today," she asked.

"Yeh I do," he drawled.

"Well then do be careful," she teased. She clopped down the hall on a broken heel. She received many a peculiar stare from the faculty and students as well. After these two encounters with Philip what would they do for an encore. 'Heaven help me' she thought.

CHAPTER 7

For he whom the Lord has sent, speaks the Word of God.

The following Monday brought Philip and Simeon to class tardy again. It was just by seconds but nonetheless he was late. Twice before she had intended to bring it Philip's attention, but a calamity prevented it. Her exacting nature demanded a solution. Just before the end of the class she made the announcement.

"At the beginning of this semester, I announced my policy concerning tardiness and absenteeism," she began.

She scanned the room and her eyes settled on Philip, the object of her aggression. He looked directly into her eyes and smiled slightly, perfectly relaxed. Priscilla quickly shifted her glance. His coolness unnerved her.

"Two of my students have been late for class three times now," she continued, "avoiding Philip with her gaze, "Philip will be penalized one and one half grade points of his mid-term grade. I am assuming that Simeon would be here on time if he weren't relying on Philip to get here. I will say that Philips' concern for his friend is commendable. However, his kindness does not exempt him from the rules. Philip I would like to speak with you for a few moments. The rest of you are excused."

As the class filed out, Philip caught Eddie Leone again and asked him to take Simeon to the library. When Eddie and Simeon left the room, Philip and Priscilla were alone. For a moment, no words were spoken. Philip was waiting for Priscilla to begin. She was always excited when she was alone with him. Philip finally broke the silence and said, "Well Miss Pomp, here I am again."

"Philip, it is well known that I am strict. I have found you to be a marvelous student. You're intelligent, creative and sensible. But you must realize that promptness is important," she said regaining her composure, "I don't understand why you can't make it to class on time like the other students."

She looked at him seriously as she leaned on the lectern, but Philip was smiling.

"Philip Wright," she scolded, "what are you smiling about?"

"Miss Pomp," he said frankly, "You're even pretty when you're mad. I guess even a tongue lashing from you is a grand experience."

Priscilla was surprised by his answer and embarrassed to the point of anger.

"Philip, believe me I am serious," she retorted angrily as she shook a finger defiantly and raised her eyebrows.

"And so am I Miss Pomp," he responded sincerely, "I am very fond of you as an instructor and a woman."

"You can keep your opinions to yourself," she retorted as her face blushed, "I want an explanation for your excessive tardiness!"

Unshaken, the smile disappeared from his face as he explained, "I'm a volunteer worker at Little Angels Nursing Home. It's a home for crippled and mentally retarded children. I work with them and encourage them. I guess you might say I love them."

Priscilla shook her head in disbelief. She thought she had heard every excuse but here was a real original.

"Is that your excuse for your tardiness", she asked in disgust.

"Yes," replied Philip.

"Well I find that hard to believe in the first place," Priscilla responded, "and if it is true, I suggest that you think a little less of those misfits and a little more of yourself."

"First of all ma'am, they're not misfits!" Philip snapped angrily, "they're human beings like you and me. They need love, affection and kindness. They ain't got nothing else. It's only right that people should remember them in their suffering."

His face turned white in anger.

"You speak to me with a civil tongue," Priscilla demanded, stepping closer and beaming defiantly in his face, "or I'll…"

"All right Miss Pomp, I'm sorry I lost my temper. You're entitled to your opinion. You don't understand because you haven't seen what I've seen. I've seen little girls cry with no one to console them. I've seen children with scrapes and cuts treated with the latest medicines but without love. Sometimes a hug, a pat on the back or a word of love and encouragement does more good than a world of medicine. Love is the only real balm for a broken heart."

"Don't bother me with someone else's troubles. I have enough of my own," she snapped as she threw her hands up in disgust and turned her back to him. Philip stood and walked to within three feet of her.

He paused as the sentiment of his thoughts tingled in his chest. A tear streamed down his cheek as he continued, "you should see those kids when I go to see them. They come rushing up to me jumping up and down, waving their arms and screaming. We take visitors for granted, but those children don't have any. To them it's like a holiday to have a visitor. You play with them and they laugh and have fun, but pretty soon you have to leave. It's hard to leave those kids knowing that they want to go too. I don't have to consider it a minute, Miss Pomp," he said in determination, "nothing is going to stop me from seeing those kids every day. They need me. If I don't see them, nobody does!"

Priscilla was indifferent and her heart was hardened against him.

"They have a staff and assistants I'm sure. Let them love those children. Don't think for a minute that you're their savior, or that they can't live without you. I advise you to be your own savior, or you'll surely fail this class," Priscilla snapped back.

Philip looked away in disgust. It was useless to talk with her.

Despite her anger with Philip, Priscilla wanted to encourage him.

"Philip, you do splendid work. You're talented and gifted. Don't waste those talents on those barbarians. They don't appreciate your abilities. You can rise to great heights in this world if you'll place important things first. Don't throw your life away by wasting your love on those who can't return it."

"Miss Pomp," replied Philip in disbelief, "to be so well educated you understand so little."

Her eyes opened wide and she started to reply but Philip continued.

"Love is never wasted on God's children, rich or poor. We're all his creation, and He loves us whether we're worthy or not. He promises that 'if we cast our bread upon the waters, it will not return unto us void.' My reward is in their smiles. Though some can't speak, they treasure the warmth of love and concern. Even as you and I, they need to be wanted and loved. And I might add, Miss Pomp, that a little love in your life would soften your stony heart. If you'd come down off your pillar of pride and arrogance, you'd find out what real happiness is. But as I love those innocent children as they are, even so I love you just as you are."

"Philip, I can fail you for that remark," she screamed as she shook her finger in his face, "I demand an apology this instant!"

Philip did not intend to upset her and he regretted his bluntness.

"I'm truly sorry to upset you Miss Pomp. I shouldn't have shot off my mouth. But I'm also sorry that everything I've said is the truth," he replied, "please don't punish me for my honesty."

"Oh you wretch," snapped Priscilla furiously, "get out of here before I completely lose my temper. I hope you're happy. You've completely ruined my day."

As she began to sob covering her face with her hands, Philip awkwardly tried to apologize.

"I'm sorry I hurt you…"

Priscilla interrupted him in rage, "Get out! Get out! I despise you!"

He left with tears in his eyes. His head drooped in sorrow and he walked to the library to get Simeon. Priscilla cried for twenty minutes and left the room before the next class arrived. She called in sick and excused her afternoon classes.

Philip became mute in class and he avoided Priscilla each time he saw her. He was also late for the next five classes. He still cared for Priscilla but he didn't think he would ever have a chance with her. Priscilla despised Philip for he was the one person who could see through her sophisticated front. Several nights she couldn't erase his song from her mind. On another night she saw him eating dinner at a restaurant. Since Philip had come into her life, everything was chaos. Never had anyone been so disrespectful. Never had she been as upset as he had made her. Never had she felt so strange about a person who appeared in her life. Something was wrong and that something was Philip Wright. He was a curse to her happiness.

The last week before Christmas vacation was one of little accomplishment. On Monday Philip wheeled Simeon into class five minutes early then left. Wednesday brought a repeat of the same procedure. Priscilla's heart leaped with joy when the ten o'clock bell rang and Philip was not in his seat. 'Just let him come in now' she thought. What a pleasure it would be to humiliate him. It would be poetic justice. Throughout the lecture she watched the clock.

The bell rang and Eddie Leone assisted Simeon into the wheel chair. Curiosity was gnawing at Priscilla and she couldn't resist inquiring into the mystery.

"Simeon," she called, "may I have a word with you?"

"Sure Miss Pomp," replied Simeon casting a blind glance at her, "If it doesn't take more than two or three minutes. Eddie will wait for me at the library."

"Would you mind if I dropped you off at the library?" she offered, "heaven knows we don't want him to be late."

"It's fine with me," said Simeon.

Eddie left and they were alone.

"I would like to advise you that Philip has now failed this class. Please tell him for me since he can't seem to be here with any regularity, said Priscilla."

"Well Miss Pomp," he answered bluntly, "Philip has already decided to drop this class."

"He couldn't face me himself?" asked Priscilla indignantly," "Oh would I like to tell that boy a thing or two. What a thorn in my side he's been."

"Miss Pomp, Philip didn't mean to upset you or disturb the class. Believe me, he isn't like that!" he assured her.

"I know more than I want to know about him," chided Priscilla.

"May I express an opinion without offending you Miss Pomp?" asked Simeon.

"Sure. Go right ahead," she stated bluntly.

"Philip is the most understanding person I've ever met. He always puts others before himself. Miss Pomp, he's got real musical talent. Why he could be the greatest star this country has ever known," he said enthusiastically.

"You've got to be kidding," laughed Priscilla, "that's ridiculous."

"I know this is right, even though you laugh," exhorted Simeon, "ma'am I wish that you could see him from my eyes and from the hearts of those forgotten souls that Philip remembers every day. He doesn't have to visit those little children, but every morning, there he is, laughing and bringing sunshine into the lives of children who have little else to look forward to. When Philip is around, the whole nursing home comes alive with joy. I've seen him make little boys laugh who had nothing to be happy about. Somehow just being around him is happiness."

Priscilla rolled her eyes in disbelief as she tossed her head and said, "You make him sound like God. If he can do the impossible why can't he come to class on time?"

"He doesn't do the impossible Miss Pomp," pleaded Simeon, "he just takes the time to do what others are too busy to do."

"Well nobody owes those children anything," she replied defensively, "some of us are busy running the world. We're not dreaming with our heads in the clouds. Philip has a hard lesson to learn. There's no doubt about it."

"He is a dreamer Miss Pomp," he explained patiently, "but he brings hope to the lives of many who have no dreams. He likes everyone. I've seen him like people who deliberately gave him reason to hate them. But Philip doesn't carry grudges."

"You're not referring to me I hope," she asked with glaring eyes.

"Please Miss Pomp," pleaded Simeon, "Don't be angry at me. Believe me. You misunderstood everything he did."

Priscilla would have said something but her jaw hung open in disbelief.

"He liked you very much. He did everything he could to make a good impression, but everything went wrong. The more he tried to please you the more upset you became. Nothing seemed to turn out right. At the nursing home, we would have laughed with him, but you took him serious. When he saw you withdrawing from him, he said 'he couldn't stand to hurt the people he cared for.' So rather than cause you more embarrassment, he dropped this class."

"Priscilla couldn't believe her ears.

"This is a fairy tale," she exclaimed, "this can't be happening to me! It's too bazaar! Simeon, you're going to have to stay away from that boy. You're talking just like him."

She backed away and shook her head.

Simeon said nothing more and Priscilla was happy to oblige. She picked up her purse and threw it over her shoulder. She pushed the wheel chair to the library where he was to meet Eddie.

Before she could leave, Simeon leaned toward her and said, "Miss Pomp, I have a problem."

"Oh," she replied curiously, "what is it."

"Eddy's car is broke down and Philip loaned his truck to Dave Milburn, so I have no way to the nursing home. It's Joy's birthday and it's really important that I pick up the birthday cake in time for the party this afternoon. Could you possibly help me out?" asked Simeon hopefully.

"Oh I don't know Simeon," Priscilla sighed, for she really didn't want to be bothered.

"How far is the nursing home from here," she queried reluctantly.

"It's only two miles," he answered.

She was forced by his handicap to comply with his request.

"We'll have to stop at Elburn's Bakery to pick up the cake for Joy," said Simeon excitedly.

"Very well," she reluctantly responded, "I guess I have time but we must hurry!"

CHAPTER 8

He brought me into the banqueting house, and His banner over me was love.

The nursing home was an old two-story frame building. It had been converted from an old apartment into a make shift nursing home. The white paint was flaking and peeling. One of the two bay windows was cracked diagonally, but it was taped on the inside to keep the wind out. The dilapidated gray shingles were hardly adequate to keep the occupants dry.

'So this is the nursing home that takes so much of Philip's time' she thought. It wasn't fit for pigs to live in. She was glad that she wasn't going inside. There was something about children that turned her off. As she slowed to a stop, two boys burst out of the front door into the cold.

"Hey Simeon, did you bring the cake," exclaimed eight year old John, "everybody is all ready!"

"Yeh," shouted ten-year-old Tim, "and Joy doesn't know it either! Boy is she ever going to be surprised."

Wait a minute boys," said Simeon as he opened the door to get out, "one of you boys get my wheel chair out of the back seat for me, please."

The two boys grabbed the door at the same time.

"Hey Tim," complained John, "let go! I got here first!"

"No you didn't," retorted Tim, "I beat you here!"

"Simeon! Simeon!" yelled John, "make him let go of the door!"

"Quit trying to horn in," shouted Tim angrily.

Priscilla was at a loss. This behavior was intolerable. Their attitudes were barbaric and crude.

"Boys! Boys!" she shouted sternly, as both startled boys stopped tussling and stepped back, "What kind of behavior is this?"

She stepped around the rear of the car and opened the rear passenger door. The two boys ran up the stairs. They stopped and looked back from the safety of the porch.

"I must say Simeon," Priscilla said as she pulled the folded wheel chair from the back seat, "Philip has failed to teach these children any etiquette. Honestly, these boys are Neanderthals."

"They're just boys Miss Pomp," said Simeon in defense of the boys.

Priscilla carried the chair up the stairs and turned to Simeon.

"I'll need some help to get you up the stairs Simeon. Is anyone around?" she asked.

"Yes. I'll have the boys get someone," he replied, "boys, get Philip."

They rushed wildly into the house as the door slammed behind them.

The mere mention of Philip's name opened a pit in her stomach. This rude self appointed Savior of the poor was certainly a curse to her. He didn't even have the courage to tell her he was dropping her class.

Philip appeared at the door and paused briefly when he saw Priscilla. He instantly searched her eyes. He was humble but unashamed, nor was his composure shaken. Priscilla pulled her eyes away from him. Philip started down the stairs and spoke.

"Howdy Miss Pomp," he said softly, "This is a pleasant surprise."

"Yes Philip, I'm sure it is," Priscilla snapped, "I'll help you get Simeon up the stairs and I'll be on my way."

"Won't you stay and have birthday cake with us," Philip said, ignoring her indignant attitude, "The kids would be delighted to..."

"No thank you Philip," she interrupted, "I really must go. I wouldn't want to be late for my next class." In spite she alluded to his penchant for tardiness.

"You and I will carry him up the stairs in our arms," he said ignoring her.

He knew another way, but he wanted an opportunity to touch her and have her touch him.

"First," he said," take your left hand and hold firmly to your right arm just above the elbow like this."

She watched and followed his instruction.

"Now," he continued, "just a minute while I help Simeon out of the seat."

He lifted Simeon to his feet and steadied him as he wobbled on weak shaking legs.

"Next we're going to make a seat to carry him in," said Philip, "here, you hold tightly to my left arm and I'll hold yours the same way."

Simeon sat in the seat their arms formed and steadied himself on their shoulders. Though Philip deliberately carried the bulk of the weight, Priscilla found herself in quite a strain. Before she could say a word, Philip started up the stairs. In the firm grasp of his grip, she had no choice but to follow. His strong grip bit into her arm, and she felt as if it would break. Finally, after what seemed an eternity, they reached the top of the stairs and set Simeon in the wheel chair. She was pale, tired and breathless. Priscilla stood in the chilly December wind. Her hair flowed lightly in the wind as sweat beaded upon her forehead.

"You better step inside out of the cold and catch your breath," said Philip. He gently directed her toward the door, as Simeon wheeled inside ahead of them. Even though she had a few reservations, she was too cold and tired to resist.

The nursing home was clean but much in need of maintenance. The feet of the children scuffed the hard wood floors. The rough plaster walls needed painting. The original color looked to have been pastel yellow, but time had paled the luster to gray. Inside the foyer was a bench upon which Priscilla sat, after she dusted it with a handkerchief. She writhed as she observed the filth on her handkerchief, but miraculously, she said nothing.

Philip pushed Simeon into the middle of the playroom next to a long table. It was set with two gigantic punch bowls, and paper plates for fifty people. Three women busied themselves seating the handicapped children who couldn't seat themselves. There was a scramble of chairs as little eyes opened wide in expectation. Busy hands picked up forks and excited lips chattered excitedly.

"Hey kids," shouted Philip, as he tried to get their attention. As they hushed, he continued, "now please be very quiet. I'm going upstairs to get Joy. When we come in we'll all yell 'surprise! Happy birthday!' Ya got that?"

"Yeh!" they responded in unison.

"Remember though," he said, "you must be quiet or it won't be a surprise."

All was quiet as Philip climbed the stairs to get Joy. Priscilla looked at her watch. It was twelve o'clock. She decided to leave. What a relief to leave this God forsaken place. The children were uncouth barbarians. She raised herself and reached for the door. Just then, Philip came down the stairs with a small girl in his arms.

"Priscilla," Philip called to her. When he spoke she felt a tingle in her spine. She paused a moment with her hand on the door.

"Before you leave, I'd like you to meet my little sweetheart," he said as he stopped at the foot of the stairs, "Priscilla this is Joy Palmer. Joy this is Priscilla Pomp."

Joy lifted her face and Priscilla saw a happy smile.

"How do you do," responded Priscilla, not knowing how to respond.

Joy was a tiny girl of seven. Priscilla could see that she had some type of muscular disorder, for her legs were limp and thin. She was pale and her red hair curled. She wore a pink dress with white lace on the sleeves.

"Hi Priscilla," Joy said in a shy but strong voice, "You're a dream come true. You're pretty too! Just like Philip said."

Priscilla was pleased by her statement and asked with a smile, "in what way am I a dream come true."

"Well replied Joy with a smile, "last night I prayed for a special guest today, and here you are!"

Joy was very perceptive and she remembered Philip and looked into his hazel eyes as she continued, "you're a special guest every day Philip, but I wanted a new special visitor. Was it all right to ask for that?"

"Yeh," he replied with a smile, "it was a great idea."

"Philip has something to show me Priscilla," said Joy, "would you like to go with us?"

Priscilla looked at her watch again. It was twelve ten.

"Really Joy, I'd love to stay, but I have to go to work…"

"Oh please Priscilla," pleaded Joy, "it'll only take a few minutes."

"I just can't," Priscilla replied nervously.

"Priscilla," said Philip earnestly, "it will only be a few minutes. If you could just stay ten minutes, Joy would appreciate it."

Even Priscilla's hardened conscience couldn't deny Joy her wish.

"Well…O.K.," she said reluctantly, "but I really have only ten minutes to spare."

Philip lead the way into the play room and opened the door.

"Surprise! Happy Birthday!" the room thundered with the clamor of happy voices.

"Oh Philip!" screamed the delighted little girl, "Oh Philip this is wonderful!"

"Here Joy," said Philip laughing, "let's have a seat and open your gifts!"

"Oh Philip! For me? You've got some gifts for me?" exclaimed Joy with glee.

She was excited beyond words. In her uneventful days, this occasion was the greatest in her life.

"Yes we have several gifts for you," said Philip as he placed Joy in her seat beside himself. Priscilla seated herself beside Simeon, directly across from Philip. Philip gave Joy one of her five presents. Anxious little fingers tore at the ribbons on the box. Priscilla noticed how hard she worked to open the box. Her heart melted as Joy looked to Philip for help. Without saying a word, Philip smiled down on her and helped her tear the ribbons from the package. Joy was to be pitied. Her little fingers wanted to work, but she couldn't use them as she wished. Her mouth flew open as she exclaimed, "Oh! Just what I wanted! A new Doll! Who got it for me?"

"Well," replied Philip as he read the tag, "it's from Melba, Irene and Phyllis the nurses aides."

"Oh! Thank you very much!" she said hugging the doll close to her chest.

Joy opened the next three gifts, which were a new dress from Simeon, a watch from Hilda and Maxine, the two R.N.'s and a large box of grape bubble gum, Joy's favorite, from the kids at the nursing home. Philip had bought that for the children to present to Joy. Last of all came Philip's gift. It was in a small box and Joy shook it beside her ear before opening it.

"This is from you. Isn't it?" she asked, looking up lovingly at him.

"Open it," he replied.

He helped her open the package. Inside was a half heart on a tiny gold chain. On the heart was inscribed the letters 'HAPP'. Joy delicately handled the necklace and held it before her eyes in amazement.

"Oh Philip! It's beautiful! Here," she said, "put it on me."

Priscilla fastened her attention on the necklace. She remembered a necklace she once had that was similar to it. She noticed that inscription on the half heart. What could it mean? Her mind wandered into the past as she tried to tie the loose ends. The necklace troubled her.

"This is your special day Joy," said Philip, "is there anything you would like to do?"

She frowned and thought, and then her eyes sparkled in glee.

"Would you sing that song you wrote for me? You know. 'Every Day's a Holiday'," she said.

"Well…Yes," he said softly as he gave her a hug, "If you and the rest of the kids will sing with me."

"Let's do it like we always do," exclaimed Joy, "I'll sing the 'it's a holiday' part, and you sing the rest of the song. But who's going to sing the Lady's part the first time? Could you Priscilla? Philip has the music! He wrote it! Then we could all sing it the second time. O.K.?"

Before Priscilla could say no, John the eight year old jumped up and ran to the corner of the playroom where Philip kept his sheet music and brought it to Priscilla. He stretched it forth to her and said, "here it is!"

Priscilla caught up in the fun of the moment looked at the music and found it simple. She was an excellent sight-reader and so for Joy's birthday she said, "This will be my birthday present to you Joy. I'll do the best I can."

Simeon slipped into the wheel chair with Priscilla's assistance. She pushed him to the piano and assisted him upon the bench. Philip looked at Joy and smiled cheerfully as Simeon began to play. He kissed Joy on the cheek and began to sing.

'Every day with you is a holiday, honey it's true.
Anything we do it's a holiday, darling with you.
I know that when I'm holding you it's a holiday,
All my dreams come true; it's a holiday,
Every hour is such a shower of blessing with you.
Believe me.
Troubles we go through it's a holiday if I'm with you.
Dreams that don't come true it's a holiday, living with you.
I know that we will always stay; it's a holiday,
So much in love this way, it's a holiday,
I know you'll always say it's a holiday too.'

Philip then sang alone.

'Dear I love you, need you too,
Morning, evening, night time too.
Darling how I would love to make you mine.
Love you know I want you all of the time.'

Priscilla sang her part as if she were singing in a musical production.

'Just picture you and me,
In love and strolling under the stars,
How happy we would be,
T'would be the grandest feeling by far.
Magnificent and sweet,
This love that fills each cell of my heart,
Divine and so complete,
And darling this is only the start.'

Priscilla stood in excitement and called to the girls, "sing along with me!" Girls only!"

All of the girls and female staff at the nursing home joined Priscilla in the song.

'Just picture you and me,
In love and strolling under the stars,
How happy we would be,
T'would be the grandest feeling by far.
Magnificent and sweet,
This love that fills each cell of my heart,
Divine and so complete,
And darling this is only the start.'

Philip called to the boys to sing with him, and they all sang along.

'Dear I love you, need you too,
Morning, evening, night time too.
Darling how I would love to make you mine.
Love you know I want you all of the time.
Sincerely'

Philip, Priscilla the children and the staff joined in the chorus.

'Every day with you is a holiday, honey it's true.
Anything we do it's a holiday, darling with you.
I know that when I'm holding you, it's a holiday.
All my dreams come true; it's a holiday,
Every hour is such a shower of blessing with you.
Believe me.
Troubles we go through, it's a holiday, if I'm with you.
Dreams that don't come true, it's a holiday, living with you.
I know that we will always stay; it's a holiday,
So much in love this way, it's a holiday.
I know you'll always say 'it's a holiday too.'

They joyfully repeated the last chorus.

'I know that we will always stay, it's a holiday,
So much in love this way, it's a holiday.
I know you'll always say 'it's a holiday too.'

When they finished, Philip shouted in glee, as he picked Joy up in his arms, "Let's sing it again."

Simeon started again and the children, the staff and Priscilla joined in. Priscilla was enchanted by the happiness of the moment. For the first time in years, she felt a freedom of expression not bound by form or tradition. She just let herself be free to absorb the joy of the moment. A mode of living long dead, began at this moment to resurrect itself. Priscilla forgot about her one o'clock class.

"Children," interrupted Hilda, "the ice cream and cake are ready!"

Hilda and the three nurses aides busied themselves lighting the candles and serving the cake and ice cream. Philip led the children as they sang happy birthday to Joy. As they sang, Joy looked around the table at her friends and Priscilla. Priscilla experienced a warm glow when Joy smiled at her. The little girl said not a word, but the gleam in her eyes said it all. Priscilla saw the glow in Philip's face as he clutched the tiny girl tenderly in his arms. Philip seemed to be enjoying the gathering more than anyone else.

"Have you made a wish," asked Philip.

Joy put her right hand on her chin and frowned in deep thought.

"Yep," she replied enthusiastically, "I wished you and Priscilla were here every day. Then every day would be a holiday."

Philips' eyes met Priscilla's, but she quickly looked to Joy.

"You're not supposed to tell your wish," said Philip in surprise, "it's a secret."

"But you don't keep secrets from people you love," answered the little girl, looking up at him.

Her words struck Priscilla. What wisdom for such a young girl.

They began to dive into the ice cream and cake when Philip stopped them.

"Wait a minute kids," scolded Philip, "let's say the blessing."

Every head bowed. Philip began and the children followed in unison.

"Dear Lord. We thank you for this food and every blessing of life. Bless us and keep us in your care. We ask in Jesus name. Amen."

The simplicity and brevity of the prayer was new to Priscilla. She always felt a prayer must be long to be heard. The sincerity of the prayer moved her.

As the children dived in to their treats, she glanced at her watch. It was ten minutes until one. She couldn't possibly make it to her one o'clock class on time. How humiliating to walk into her class late! She knew she shouldn't have stayed! No matter what Philip was involved in, it was suicide for her. Without saying a word, she turned to go, but Joy called to her.

"Thank you for coming to my party," she said cheerfully, "you've made it a very special birthday."

"Good bye," Priscilla called over her shoulder.

Priscilla walked briskly to her car. She drove wildly through town in fury. She would be at least five minutes late. Though no one spoke a word, Priscilla knew their thoughts. In her humiliation, embarrassment and anger she forgot how much she had enjoyed herself. She forgot how Philip made a room full of fatherless children happy for a short time. All she knew was that any time Philip was near her, disaster was soon to strike. This was the first time in her life she had ever been late for work. If she never saw Philip Wright again, that would be too soon!"

CHAPTER 9

Cast your bread upon the waters: for you shall find it after many days.

Priscilla laid the book aside and set her hair. Her mind wandered back over the day and she pictured Joy as Philip carried her down the stairs. She wondered what her affliction was. She was such a pretty girl, and yet she possessed an internal beauty beyond words. To be so hopeless, she was so happy.

The locket, which Philip gave to Joy, sprang to her memory. Where did he get it? She definitely remembered having a necklace with half a heart on it. It seemed like it had a name on it too! She knew it was a gift, but she couldn't remember who gave it to her. Her mother bought everything she had ever wanted, but wait a minute. She received that necklace before she and her mother grew close. She remembered hiding it from her mother! The old gardener! That's who it was! What his name? Mother despised the old man. The necklace was mysterious.

The next morning, Priscilla rose early and began packing for Christmas vacation. Suddenly she realized that she was humming the tune of 'Every Day's a Holiday'. It did have a catchy melody. And the words were easy to remember. To be such a bungler, Philip entertained the children. However it was one thing to please those children and quite another to entertain adults. That song could be arranged into a nice piece. But for all she knew, maybe he didn't compose it.

She closed the last suitcase and hurried through breakfast. Then she loaded her car and drove to school. One last day of classes! It was great to be going home.

Eddy Leone pushed Simeon into class five minutes early. Priscilla had only a halfhearted interest in class, as did the students. Time seemed to drag. She dismissed class 15 minutes early, so she could get an early start. The students left quickly. Eddie pushed Simeon towards Priscilla.

"Miss Pomp," said Simeon softly, "I have a couple of letters for you. One is from Joy."

"I will accept the one from Joy," she responded, "but if the other one is from Philip, you can keep it".

Simeon placed the two letters in her hand. She singled out Philip's letter and discarded it in the wastebasket.

"Miss Pomp," Simeon said, "every man deserves a chance to apologize. One owes that much respect, regardless of personal feelings."

She looked into his dark glasses and replied, "I'll do my own thinking Simeon. Philip has been a thorn in my side since the day I met him."

"Well, I'll be going," said Simeon sadly, "merry Christmas."

"Thank you Simeon," she responded warmly.

As Eddie and Simeon left, Priscilla opened Joy's letter.

∾

'Dear Priscilla,

How are you today? Fine I hope. Thank you for coming to my birthday party. You are very pretty and I like you too. I hope you come to see me again soon. Philip is going to give me a ride in Sylvester (his truck) and show me where you live. Well, I'll see you.

Love, your friend,

Joy'

The letter brought a glow to her heart. The print was ragged. It must have been a real effort on her part. If all the children in the home were like her, she might be attracted to the nursing home. Joy worshipped Philip as she once admired Jonah. Jonah! That was the name of the old gardener!

She remembered the lovely hedge of roses in the center of the garden, and how Jonah had once picked a sticker out of her hand. She had tried to pick a rose. Jonah sat down on the bench and wiped the blood off with his handkerchief and soon she was laughing. Joy was much like Priscilla at that age.

She folded the letter and tucked it neatly in her purse. Her eyes fell on Philip's letter and she had a strange desire to read it. It might be interesting to see what he said. What would it hurt? She bent over and retrieved the letter and gingerly opened it.

'Dear Priscilla,

I guess I did it again. I know you were late for your class, and it was not my intention to upset you again. I didn't see any way I could mess you up or I wouldn't have asked you to stay.

Please remember though, that some things are worth paying a price for, like little Joy. You'll never know how much it meant to her for you to be there that day. When you have as few visitors as Joy, you really appreciate a new face. If you'll be honest with yourself, deep down in your heart you enjoyed yourself. For a few short moments, I saw you as you really are beneath all that sophistication. I saw happiness in your heart through the gleam in your eyes. You have pretty eyes anyway, but they're beyond description when the real Priscilla shows herself through them. I saw you laugh the kind of laughter that can only come from a happy heart. It was a joy to my heart to see you enjoy yourself so much, for you have so little happiness in your life.'

Priscilla was touched by the last sentence and tears moistened her cheeks. A tingle moved in her neck as she wiped her eyes.

'I knew the first time I saw you that you weren't really happy. You put forth so much effort to project an image of happiness. Yet though you deny it till the last, I know the sadness of your soul. I liked you the first time I saw you. I still admire you, and I ain't ashamed of my feelings. Please don't laugh to yourself because I can't help the way I feel about you. You don't choose those you happen to love. It just happens.'

Again Priscilla wiped her eyes as the content of the letter plowed deeply into the crust that had hardened around her emotions. She had never received a letter like this, but she remembered that Jonah had the same tact for moving her soul. She bit her lip and continued reading.

∾

'Don't be shocked by my reference to love. We live our lives calling things by false titles. The least of friendships is love. The cooperation of two total strangers is a form of love also. And when I am drawn to you like I am, that's love too. When I'm around you I seem to get nervous. You excite me like no one else I have ever met. I tried to make a good impression, but it seems that everything I did turned out wrong. I prefer to never see you again, than to cause you any more agony. I've never been good at apologies, but please accept mine now. I'm sorry for any and all embarrassment or humiliation, which I've caused you. Every effort will be expended to assure that this never happens again.

You won't believe this but I even allowed myself the liberty to imagine you and I enjoying an evening together. I realize now what a fool I've been and how I've embarrassed you. But then you haven't been the easiest person to understand Priscilla. At times you've tested my patience.'

She wiped her eyes again and finished the letter.

∾

'Well, I guess I'll get out of your life now, before I drive you crazy. I dropped your class because I thought it best for you. I need that class to graduate, but I can take a summer class and graduate.

I just want to ask one thing of you. Let's let things be just like nothing ever happened between us. When we meet, please speak to me, and I'll speak to you just like I always have. You're one person I don't ever want to avoid. If you stay mad at me, I guess I'll never forgive myself. God be with you Priscilla. I thank Him for just having known you. I'll remember you in my prayers.

Your admirer always,

Philip'

Priscilla wept bitterly. She saw a tender side of Philip and felt ashamed that she hadn't understood him nor had she even tried. She cried because his words were true. He had her pegged dead to rights. She sorrowed because she knew a relationship with him would never work. Her family would never accept him. Also, Philip could never provide for her in a way she was accustomed to.

She wiped her face, and patched her mascara. As she left, she walked briskly to her car and drove home. The events of the past few months caused her to do some soul searching, but her pride still burned strong.

CHAPTER 10

Because he has set his love upon me, therefore I will deliver him: I will set him on high, because he has known my name.

Priscilla left her last class and walked directly to her Mercedes. She was off for home. Two grand weeks of rest and relaxation awaited her. Then, thank God, another two weeks, the end of the semester and it would be good-bye to Philip Wright forever.

Snow was blanketing the ground as she pulled out of the parking lot. The weatherman was predicting four inches of snow, but she would be home in an hour. As she approached the light at the end of the block visibility was poor and the roads extremely slippery. The light changed and she drove to the edge of town behind the snowplow. She passed the plow, which was impeding her progress and drove into the driving snow. The wind picked up and blew the snow against her windshield like a white sheet limiting her visibility to five to ten feet in front of her car. She decided to turn around and looked for a side road. She slowed to five miles per hour, looking for any place to turn around. She was desperate now; even a driveway would do. Suddenly she saw a drive way to her right! In haste, she whipped the car into the lane. The road was covered with a thin glaze of ice and she lost control of the car. It slid into the ditch beside the lane. Desperately she tried to back out but the tires only spun. She was alone in the snow. There was no traffic moving. However she had a full tank of gas so she could stay warm until help arrived or the storm passed.

Her engine sputtered and died. Instantly she tried to start it again. The engine only ground. It gave no indication of starting. Though terrified, she looked at the gauges on the dash. The fuel gauge indicated empty. That couldn't be! She had filled the tank this afternoon. Maybe a hole was opened in the gas tank when she slipped off the road!

She was wearing a warm coat, but it soon became apparent that she would need more clothes.

All her clothes were in the trunk. She hated to think about getting out of the car to get them. She sat another twenty minutes shivering in the cold. The wind howled outside and snow had frozen in a sheet over her windshield. She looked around the car. 'Oh Lord!' she thought 'please send somebody, anybody!' The wind howled louder. She simply must get the clothes out of the trunk. As she opened the door, the wind ripped it from her hand. She felt the sharp bite of the angry wind as she wrapped her coat tightly about herself. Her nylons scarcely retained any heat or withheld any cold. Bumps rose on her legs and progressed over her entire body. She stepped into the snow that had swirled into a neat pile beside her car. The chill numbed her feet. Once completely outside the car, she had to hold to it to maintain balance. Each step was a battle with the elements. At last, she reached the trunk of the car. She turned the key in the trunk and it sprang open. Quickly she opened the suitcase with the slacks in it and snatched an armful. She would choose in the security of the car.

Carefully she picked her way back to the door. As she opened the door, the wind caught the door. She slipped into the door and banged her head on the doorpost. Stunned, she dropped the clothes. The storm lashed out at her. She shook her head, fell to her knees and groped wildly for even one pair of pants. She was so hysterical that the stinging cold didn't affect her. After what seemed an eternity, she found a pair of slacks. She turned in the direction she thought her car to be. It had vanished; completely camouflaged by the snow. 'Oh Lord' she thought 'please don't leave me out in the snow to die. Help me! Please, somebody help me.'

Tears burst forth and froze on her cheeks as she clumsily pulled the slacks over her shoes. She was hopelessly lost in the blizzard. In desperation, she began walking and stumbling through the snow in hope of finding her car or any other type of shelter. Aimlessly she pushed through the wind and snow hoping to find help.

It started with a hum, but it was definitely a running engine and a scraping sound like a plow blade on the road. Priscilla knew it was a snowplow. She was down wind of it and she couldn't be sure how far away she was. She wondered if she had enough strength left to reach the plow before it passed her. She couldn't see the lights but she heard the snow plow. With all her strength she pushed her aching body through the deep and drifting snow. She was trudging directly into the wind and her face stung as if it were burned. Several times in her haste, she stumbled and fell face first into the snow. Her whole body was numb and she wondered if she was really walking or merely imagining it. Her fingers and toes had no feeling whatever. The roar of the blade grew louder and she could now see the headlights and flashing warning lights. Her strength was now all but gone. She was walking on determination and courage. She was within one hundred yards of the road. Would she make it in time? 'Oh Lord' she thought 'please don't let that truck pass by without me!' When she was within twenty feet of the roadside, she encountered an old wooden fence. She didn't have enough strength to climb the fence! The truck drew along side of her and with her last bit of energy she cried out, "Help! Help! Somebody please help me!"

The truck passed by but stopped with a crash about fifty feet past her. One of two men in the cab jumped out of the truck to see what they had hit. Priscilla could hardly scream, "Help!" The man couldn't hear her above the howl of the wind and the roar of the big diesel engine. Then the driver jumped out and they discussed the situation.

"It's a small car," said one, "but I don't see anybody in it!"

"I hope they didn't leave the car to find help," replied the other, "they wouldn't last thirty minutes in this blizzard."

"Well, let's get back into the truck and go around it," replied the other one.

"Help! Help! I'm over here!" Priscilla screamed again. She knew it was now or never. She hung over the fence in complete exhaustion.

"Hey wait a minute," said one, "I think I heard someone!"

"You're crazy," shouted the other, "it's the wind howling!"

"Help! Help! I'm over here! Help me!" she screamed.

"There it is again," said one, "it sounds like a woman!"

"You're out of your mind," shouted the driver, "get in it's cold!"

"But I heard someone," the helper shouted, "It sounded like a woman."

"Well I'm getting in the truck," the driver shouted.

The driver climbed back into the truck and the assistant looked over his shoulder and began to climb in also.

"Help! Help! I'm over here," she screamed again. 'Oh Lord' she thought 'please, make him hear me!'

"There it is again! I tell you I hear someone yelling for help," he said emphatically, "give me that flashlight. I'm going to take a look!"

He climbed down from the truck and flashed the beam into the darkness. Priscilla could see the beam cut through the darkness.

"Help! Help! I'm over here," she screamed again.

This time the light fell directly in her face.

"Hey Mike!" the assistant yelled, "It is somebody! I see them down by the fence! Come down and give me a hand!"

Priscilla awoke early Saturday morning wet with perspiration. Her brow was aflame with fever. She felt dizzy and weak. Her mother and father were standing besides her bed peering down at her. She had a sharp biting pain in her chest. A piercing pain interrupted each breath she drew and exhaled. Elizabeth, Priscilla's mother, carried on about how terrible she looked. This left little if any impression on Priscilla. Harold, her father however, spoke very little. The Pomp's were never very affectionate or open with their love.

In about twenty minutes, the doctor entered and informed them that Priscilla was suffering from pneumonia of the left lung. He assured them that it was virtually one hundred per cent curable with rest and medication. The family visited about an hour and since Priscilla was tired and exhausted from her ordeal and illness left for the day, but called again from home that evening for a few minutes.

Priscilla spent a restless day and night. Soon after her parents left, the fever subsided but the pain in her chest continued. Her mind wandered and she looked back over the events of the past few months. Of all people, she remembered Philip the most. She recalled how he fell in class, embarrassed her, and then insulted her and how wroth she was with him. Illness and the weakness that accompanied it strengthened her emotion as she remembered the first time she saw him.

She remembered the song he sang in class, his affection for the children at the nursing home and the song he sang for Joy on her birthday. She was touched in her heart by the memory of a note of apology from a humble and honest man. She realized that in his own awkward way, Philip was a beautiful person. In so many ways he was much like Jonah.

She pondered her childhood and called to mind once more the tenderness of the old man. For a lonely little girl, he was a great companion. He had an understanding of people and desire and ability to console. All these memories coupled with the events of the last few months made her melancholy. She was troubled yet curious about the present and the past. Philip seemed linked to these past events, and yet she couldn't honestly understand why she despised him so much.

She fell asleep thinking of him and tossed all night. She perspired enormously that night. She awoke however with no pain. She was extremely weak. She had a slight headache all day and she was chilled.

When Harold and Elizabeth returned Sunday morning, Priscilla was preoccupied so her mother did most of the talking. She had eaten a poached egg for breakfast and drank a glass of orange juice. Priscilla ate merely out of habit, for she wasn't really hungry. After her parents left, she spent the day watching television and napping.

After the lights were turned out, Priscilla thought about the necklace Philip gave to Joy. The mystery loomed before her again. She would ask her mother if she remembered a necklace like that. As crazy as it seemed, she couldn't forget that necklace.

CHAPTER 11

God is our refuge and strength, a very present help in trouble.

Priscilla awoke at 7:00 in the morning. She felt surprisingly well! Still very weak, she discovered that it was necessary to rest and catch her breath even after a short walk.

Dr. Walton stepped in to see her and checked her medical chart. He was pleased with her recovery, but he advised her that she must stay at least four more days in the hospital. She might have to spend Christmas in the hospital. She was not pleased with his prognosis but she was mending and she would make the best of the situation and be thankful.

At 10:30 Harold and Elizabeth visited. Their visit was very pleasant. Harold teased Priscilla by asking her 'where she planned to spend the holidays.' She laughed and said, "I think I'll stay five more days and leaving will be my Christmas present."

They chatted about Christmas. Elizabeth said that she wanted 'a simple holiday with just the three of them.'

"I never fully appreciated our family Priscilla," her mother said, "but when you were hospitalized, then I realized how very much you mean to me."

"Yes," continued Harold, as he puffed a cigar, "your mother and I did some soul searching and I have to admit that we both neglected the most important part of our marriage. From now on, we're going to do things as a family; one for all and all for one."

Every eye was moist with tears as the Pomp family was being drawn closer together.

"Being here has made me realize some things too," replied Priscilla, "I've been unsympathetic to the feelings of others. I've been a spoiled brat all of my life, but I'll be more understanding from this day forth."

"Hey ma'am," said a soft voice in the hall, "can you tell me where to find Priscilla Pomp?"

"Yes," replied the nurse, "room 333."

"O.K. Thank you," replied the voice.

The sauntering steps drew closer and Philip Wright stood in the doorway. He craned his neck around the door and paused awkwardly before entering. When he saw Priscilla had visitors, his face flushed. When no invitation came, he walked in slowly.

"I believe you have the hardest room in the building to find," he stammered, "first I went up to the seventh floor and that's the utilities room. Nothing up there but ducts and blowers!"

Priscilla began laughing to the discomfort of Philip and soon Elizabeth and Harold laughed too. Philip smiled as the laughter subsided.

"Well, I guess in a way, it is funny," he drawled.

This comment set off another round of laughter as they rolled in hilarity. Finally they had each laughed until they could laugh no more. Philip decided to change the subject.

"The kids at the nursing home and I got you this poinsettia. They all send their best wishes and hope you get better soon," he said handing her the plant.

She took the plant and replied, "Well tell the children I said 'thank you', and Philip I thank you also. They're gorgeous! Just perfect for the holiday season. She set them on the table beside her bed.

"Oh! Before I forget it," Philip said digging in his pocket, "Joy sent this for you. It's her last piece of sour grape bubble gum. She said that she had been saving it for a special occasion, and since you were sick, she thought 'it might cheer you up.'"

"Oh Philip," Priscilla replied gratefully, "Why this must be a real treasure to a girl who has so little."

"This has to be one of the greatest gifts you'll ever receive," nodded Philip in agreement, "It's just a nickel piece of bubble gum, but it's all she has to give. It shows how much she likes you."

"Yes," agreed Priscilla as she remembered her little friend, "she's such a charming little girl.

Tell her I said 'thank you very much!'"

"No-one can say it as well as you," said Philip, "if she could, she would come to see you. When you get back from vacation, drop in and see her. She'd love that. And so would the other children! You were quite a hit that day at Joy's party! Even those two boys you scared said they liked you. It will only take a few minutes, and you'll be so glad that you stopped."

"O.K. Philip," replied Priscilla tenderly, "I'll do that. Tell Joy that I'll see her on my way home from the hospital."

Then she realized that Philip hadn't been introduced.

"Oh," she said with a start, "I'm sorry! Philip you haven't been introduced."

"Well," responded Philip with a sheepish grin, "I guess I just barged in and didn't wait for an introduction."

"Father this is Philip Wright," said Priscilla.

Harold stood and stretched out his right hand while holding his cigar in his left hand. Philip stepped in his direction and they shook hands.

"Philip, this is my father, Harold Pomp," she continued.

"It's a pleasure to meet you young man," said Harold warmly.

"And this is my mother, Elizabeth Pomp," said Priscilla looking at her mother.

Philip nodded his head, as Elizabeth remained seated and smiled.

"It's nice to meet you," said Elizabeth coldly.

"And I'm glad to meet you Mrs. Pomp," said Philip softly.

"Sit down for a while," invited Priscilla sincerely.

"O.K.," replied Philip, "but just for a few minutes. I've got to get back to the nursing home and work with the kids."

Harold had thrown his hat in the chair where Philip was about to sit. He backed up to it with his eyes fastened on Priscilla. He didn't see the expensive Derby hat. Harold, however, remembered the hat and he was reaching for it as Philip sat on it and crushed it.

"For Pete's sake man!" Harold shouted disgustedly, "You've sat on my hat! Get up!"

Philip leaped up as if stuck by a pin, his faced flushed with embarrassment.

"I...I'm sorry Mr. Pomp. I didn't see it," replied Philip in humiliation.

"I guess I did it again Priscilla," he said bewildered.

"I'll say you did," retorted Harold angrily, "I just bought that hat yesterday."

Elizabeth looked at Priscilla and they both began laughing.

"I don't see anything funny about ruining a perfectly good..." Harold could go no further.

He began to laugh boisterously. Philip just smiled in disbelief and dismay. As the laughter died down, Philip glanced at his watch.

"Well I hate to leave, but it's 11:15 and the kids will be wondering where I am. Besides," he said looking at Priscilla, "if I stay any longer, there's no telling what might happen next. So if you'll excuse me, I'll be on my way."

"Philip," said Priscilla as he started to leave, "do come back again."

A note of tenderness was evident in her voice as she continued, "I never knew how much a visit from a friend could mean. I've lived in my own little ivory tower and never needed anything that I couldn't do for myself. You're a good man Philip. Keep up the good work at the nursing home. Tell Joy that I'll stop by to visit her on my way home from the hospital. That should be in six more days. I'm going to buy presents for all the children. Bring a list of names when you come back, or if you don't have the time, call me and I'll write them down."

She said this to guarantee another visit. She had enjoyed his company and she wanted it again.

"Say! That's a good idea! The kids will be excited," said Philip in excitement, "Tell you what! Let's plan a party for the kids!"

Philip was excited as his eyes glowed like a child.

"I do have to go, but I'll see you again. Would tomorrow be all right? I should be able to bring the list with me then," he concluded.

He used the list as an excuse to come back the next day, which also pleased Priscilla.

"Tomorrow will be fine," she replied softly, "come back any time."

As she spoke their eyes met. For a brief moment their gaze seemed glued to each other in enchantment. Then she remembered her parents and dropped her eyes and blushed. Philip turned and left the room without a word.

The conversation between Priscilla and her parents was pleasant. Elizabeth and Harold stayed until noon and left when lunch was served. Priscilla napped in the afternoon and when her parents returned to visit in the evening, the family shared pleasant memories from the past. That evening Priscilla enjoyed an exceptionally restful sleep and she awoke the next morning refreshed.

Philip returned the next day in the morning and again in the evening. They planned the party and she made arrangements for her parents to purchase the gifts for her. Priscilla laughed and enjoyed herself more in those two hours with Philip than she had in a long time. He was funny in his backwardness. His voice seemed to have magnetism. There was sincerity and humility in his manner. A light glowed in his eyes and Priscilla sensed warmness in his presence. There was tranquility in each visit. In the last three days of hospitalization, Philip came to see her twice each day and with each visit this unlikely couple drew closer together. On Sunday, eight days after she was lost in the blizzard, Priscilla was well enough to go home. Still pale and noticeably weak, she was excited and looking forward to the party at the nursing home. Elizabeth tried to no avail to dissuade her daughter from going, for Priscilla was determined to go. She said they could have their family holiday tomorrow. Elizabeth at last agreed under the condition that they stay no more than one or two hours.

Thus at one in the afternoon, the white Continental drove up in front of the nursing home, laden with gifts for forty-one children. As cheerful and shouting children danced for joy, the Pomp family entered the nursing home. Harold and Elizabeth scanned the rough rustic appearance of the outside walls and inside wallpaper. Elizabeth quickly spied the dusty furniture, footprints on the sofa, and cobwebs in the corners of the hall. Chills crawled over her and she would have preferred to wait in the car.

Before Philip could introduce the guests, the children were chattering in expectation. To have been so glib at social gatherings, the two elder Pomp's were uneasy here. Priscilla, however, felt comfortable. She asked the name of each child and then introduced each one to both of her parents. At that time the chauffeur brought in two sacks of toys, and forty anxious children began to chatter and leap for joy. Elizabeth was quite set back by this barbarian behavior, as she rolled her eyes and whispered, "my goodness Harold! These children have absolutely no manners whatsoever!"

Harold nodded his head in agreement but said nothing.

Philip proceeded down the stairs carrying Joy in his arms. She was wearing a red and white gown with puffed sleeves and a broad collar, which Philip had given to her for Christmas. Also she wore white slippers, a gift from the nursing staff. The necklace, which Philip had given her on her birthday, was about her neck. When Priscilla spied it she again tried to remember what could have happened to her necklace, which was similar. About midway down the stairs, Philip began welcoming the guests.

"Well! Welcome to our gala occasion," he said joyfully as he stopped at the foot of the stairs.

"Tim," he directed the chubby boy, "You get our guests' coats and hang them up while I introduce Joy to our friends."

"Mr. and Mrs. Pomp," he continued, "this is Joy Palmer. Joy, this is Mr. and Mrs. Pomp, Priscilla's' parents and today, our special guests!"

"How do you do young lady," said Harold as he puffed on his cigar.

"Hello Joy," said Elizabeth as she handed her coat to Tim.

Joy was careful not to overlook anyone and even Harold was moved with compassion by the sincerity of Joy as she said "it was very nice for you to remember us on Jesus' birthday."

Elizabeth flashed a smile as she was touched by the crippled little girl.

"Why don't we all go to the game room," suggested Philip.

All the children ran to the game room and the nurses and aides assisted the handicapped children in wheel chairs.

"Oh goodie," screamed Joy excitedly as she joyfully squeezed Philip's neck.

Once in the game room, Philip seated the children and said, "Santa Clause is going to pass out the presents. You kids sit still and I'll get him."

Harold and Elizabeth sat beside Priscilla at the table in the center of the room. Philip brought Joy to Priscilla and she held her. Philip stepped into the next room and emerged shortly with a thin Santa Clause in a wheel chair, wearing sunglasses.

"Ho! Ho! Ho! Merry Christmas! Merry Christmas!" shouted Simeon merrily. He threw his right arm up and waved emphatically to the children.

Joy whispered in Priscilla's ear, "That's Simeon! I can tell by his voice and those dark sunglasses. Anyway he was Santa Clause last year!"

Priscilla laughed and squeezed Joy affectionately.

Philip pushed Santa Clause to the tree to distribute the gifts. Each time a name was called a child would scream, jump up and rush to Santa for the present. Upon returning to their seat, the ribbons and paper were ripped off the present. The room was buzzing with chatter when Simeon called Joys' name. Philip took the gift to Joy.

"Oh! Neato! Thank you Priscilla…and Mr. and Mrs. Pomp," she said gratefully, "Philip, sit beside us!"

She tried to unwrap the present by herself. Lacking the finger dexterity to open it by herself, she looked to Philip for assistance.

"Will you help me Philip," she said as she looked up at him.

"Yeh," said Philip with a smile. He broke the ribbon and pealed back the wrapping paper. Her fingers groped at the box and she looked in amazement as she raised her eyebrows.

"Oh! It's beautiful," she exclaimed, "A crown and white dress with sparkles all over it! Hey! It even matches my slippers! Thank you very much Priscilla! Can I try it on now?" she asked excitedly.

"Yes," laughed Priscilla, "mother and I will take you upstairs and help you change. You'll come back as a little princess."

Elizabeth carried Joy upstairs and Priscilla changed her clothes. It was apparent just how seriously Joy was handicapped, and Priscilla's heart melted as she studied her weak legs. She had very little control of any part of her body except her head and neck. Priscilla placed the crown on her head and held her before the mirror.

"Oh goodie," Joy exclaimed with glee, "let's go down stairs and show Philip!"

Elizabeth carried her back down to the game room. Philip walked over to her and said, "Joy you're a doll! Are you always going to be my sweet heart?"

"Come a little closer and I'll show you," replied Joy.

He leaned closer and she reached out shakily with trembling arms and hugged him and then kissed him on the cheek. Elizabeth released Joy and Philip held her again. The children had all opened their gifts and Philip moved toward the Christmas tree and said, "O.K. now kids. We're all going to sing the song we practiced for our guests."

"Let's all be quiet now and Joy's going to announce the song," he said as he looked at her with a smile, "the floor belongs to you, your majesty!"

"Oh Philip! You're a mess," replied Joy as she snickered.

She turned her attention to her guests and said, "We all thank you from the bottom of our hearts for all the nifty presents. Philip wrote a song for us to sing for all of you, but really," she paused and looked at Philip and then toward Priscilla then said, "he wrote it for you Priscilla."

The children laughed and pointed at Priscilla as Philip squirmed in embarrassment.

"He didn't tell me so," continued Joy looking up into his eyes, "but I know it anyway. The name of the song is 'Who Wouldn't Love You.'"

Simeon began a short introduction on the piano and Philip led the children.

'Who wouldn't love you,
Who wouldn't love you,
For there's no one in this whole wide world,
Who wouldn't love you.'

Joy sang the first verse.

'I search for ways each and every day, to prove my love for you,
But though I try, there's no way that I can show my love is true.
And so I say in my usual way, a simple 'I love you',
I must confess that I love you yes, who wouldn't love you.'

All the children sang the chorus in unison.

'Oh who wouldn't love you, who wouldn't love you,
For there's no one in this whole wide world,
Who wouldn't love you.'

Joy and Philip sang the final verse in harmony.

'And so it goes that our love just grows, for no one else will do,
It's you for me and I'll always be so much in love with you.
I know that I'm just a fool at times; I'm crazy over you.
It's love I feel and I know it's real, who wouldn't love you.'

The children sang the chorus, and Priscilla warmed to the music as tears welled in her eyes.

'Oh who wouldn't love you,
Who wouldn't love you?
For there's no one in this whole wide world,
Who wouldn't love you?

Oh who wouldn't love you?
Who wouldn't love you?
For there's no one in this whole wide world,
Who wouldn't love you.'

When the song ended the children shouted and applauded themselves and their guests. Simeon interrupted them to announce, "all you kids climb up to the table and Wanda will start serving the ice cream and cake."

Again a mad dash for the table ensued. The children who needed assistance were brought to their seats. Shouting and laughing the children were enjoying the best Christmas of their lives. As Priscilla watched them run to the table, the emotion of the past few minutes moved her heart with compassion. She quietly slipped out of the room in the confusion and walked out into the hall. Behind the closed door, she poured forth tears of sadness and happiness that filled her soul.

Philip had seen her leave and he waited for her to return. He followed after her when she didn't return. He closed the door behind himself as he stepped into the dark hall. Only the streetlights illuminated the room. As his eyes adjusted to the semi-darkness, he could see Priscilla's small shapely silhouette by the front door. She tried to hide her tears as he spoke.

"Priscilla. Why are you crying," he asked softly, stopping a few feet from her as she kept her back to him.

"Oh, I'm just tired I guess," she replied tenderly, turning to look at him and then looking out the window again.

"You're heart has been moved by these children. Hasn't it," he replied.

"Yes. And also by the words of a simple, yet beautiful song. How do you write such lovely songs?" she asked looking into his eyes.

"Like I told you in class," he replied sincerely, "I have the best inspiration in the world. Do you remember the first day I visited you in the hospital? I came home in the most wonderful mood. I lay in bed and thought about how pretty you looked sitting up in that hospital bed. And I thought to myself 'who wouldn't love you?' The next day when we were planning the party, I got this warm glow all over me as I gazed into your eyes. I thought to myself again 'who wouldn't love you?' When I left you this melody came to me and stayed with me along with the words 'who wouldn't love you'. So I sat down and wrote this song. Then I taught it to the kids to sing for you. It ain't no problem to write if you have a feeling in your heart."

Philip looked out the window at the lights dancing on the snow as Priscilla spoke.

"Philip, this day, these past five days since you started visiting me in the hospital have been the most satisfying days of my life. I feel so vibrant, so excited, and so warm inside. I've never felt this way before. I want to thank you for all you've done. You and these children have been a ray of sunshine to me during these dark days."

"You don't owe me any thanks," replied Philip.

"Yes I do," she replied as tears streamed down her cheeks, "but we'd better go back inside."

She wiped her eyes and collected her composure. Philip nodded his head in agreement and they walked back into the game room together.

CHAPTER 12

It is the glory of God to conceal a thing: but the honor of kings is to search out a matter.

The Pomp family enjoyed the best Christmas in their lives. Harold canceled all business engagements and devoted the next eight days to his family. Elizabeth was especially happy, even giddy at times. She lavished the opportunity to fuss over her daughter. It was as if Priscilla had been gone on a long journey and just returned after many years. Tragedy had brought forth love and concern long dormant in each of their lives.

They spent their days in family activities. Priscilla beat her father at chess, a game in which he prided himself, and he lost his temper for a moment, until Elizabeth shamed him. She could have beaten him the second game, but Priscilla feared adding insult to injury. Harold strutted about the den and launched into a dissertation on the science of the game. Priscilla and Elizabeth then winked at each other. Each evening the family would sit in the den and munch popcorn or some other treat. Priscilla and her mother made candy, cookies and popcorn balls, finding pleasure in merely being together.

Evenings after the family retired were empty and lonely for Priscilla. Memory is a stern reminder to the soul after the body has run down. Philip and Joy haunted her each evening. She tried to read but her concentration would wander back to Utica and Philip. Just the thought of him burned in her heart as an ember. How could this happen to her? Philip was so common.

One evening as she tossed and turned in her bed, the necklace, which Philip gave to Joy, returned to mind. Since she couldn't sleep, she decided to search through her old toys. She eased out of bed and tip toed to the storage room. She found many toys, which brought back many fond memories; her old dollhouse, that ragged old stuffed teddy bear she slept with, a tea set, ice skates, and an old diary. Something was missing! It was one of her favorite toys. Matilda! Where was Matilda? She definitely remembered placing the necklace on Matilda so her mother wouldn't ask questions. She rummaged frantically in search of her favorite doll. She couldn't find it. She turned in disgust to leave and tipped a box of doll clothes. The box broke open and exposed a tiny hand. She quickly fell to her knees and pulled the clothes from the box. There on the bottom of the box lay Matilda! She wore the same red and white checked dress just like she remembered, amazingly similar to Joy's Christmas dress, and about her neck was a necklace, half a heart on a tiny gold chain with the inscription 'INESS'! Joy's necklace had 'HAPP' on it. Together, these two half hearts spelled 'happiness'. Could Philip's half heart be the other half of her necklace? Excitedly she scanned through her memory, trying to piece together the puzzle. Jonah had only one living relative, and that was a grandson. She recalled that Jonah didn't know where he was. The old gardener was very sad when he talked about him. Come to think of it, Jonah's surname was 'Wright'! She gasped! Now it was beginning to make sense. That explained why Philip's face was so familiar. His mannerisms reminded her of Jonah. His gentleness and uncanny ability to see below the surface was just like Jonah. It was almost like Jonah himself was here. What a coincidence this was! She remembered dreaming that Jonah left her and came back. It was almost as if he'd returned! But all this reasoning seemed absurd. It was not at all rational. It was silly to believe that dreams come true or that the imagination of a little girl could forecast the future! She smiled as she recalled that Jonah said that she and the man who returned would be happy. That was a laugh. What else had he said? She couldn't remember the rest. Oh well. What did it matter? Though Philip and she could never be happy together, maybe they could be good friends. She must learn to control her emotions around him. After all, he was only a man. She must talk with him when she returned to work and discuss the matter rationally. She liked the children at the nursing home so maybe she would do some volunteer work.

Priscilla had thought very little about school these past two weeks. She had relished the newfound warmth of her parents home. She had been enthralled in the genuine concern and interest that her parents shared not only for her but also for each other. As she drove back to Albany the pangs of memory bit deep into her conscience. She saw herself as a despot over her students. The fact that Philip and her parents were her only visitors pointed to a less than desirable relationship with her acquaintances. Her illness had not only taught her the value of a friend, but it gave her a new perspective on friendship.

The situation with Philip especially burdened her. She knew that he was too honest and sincere to deliberately hurt anyone. She must apologize to him before the class. She gulped as a lump formed in her throat at that thought.

Priscilla was in an exceptionally good mood as she welcomed the students back to class. She spent thirty minutes talking about her experience in the snowstorm and the Christmas party at the nursing home (leaving out the part about Philip). The students were amazed by this sudden and surprising transformation. When she dismissed class she assigned a light assignment, to the pleasant surprise of her students. Then she walked over to Simeon who was being assisted by Eddie Leone.

"Simeon," she began, "I'd like a brief word with you please."

Simeon replied, "Yes Miss Pomp."

Priscilla continued, "Would you please tell Philip that he is welcome to come to class this Wednesday and every day thereafter until the end of the semester?" She smiled as she spoke.

Simeon was shocked and he sat in the wheel chair dumb founded.

"Please tell him that I realize that I was grossly unjust with him, and that I intend to give him full credit for this course if he will return and continues to do good work," she said.

"After all," she explained, "it seems the only fair thing to do. Don't you agree?"

"Yes ma'am," replied Simeon meekly, "I agree whole heartedly."

He paused a moment and turned his head in concentration.

"But…Miss Pomp…" he hesitated, "Well are you sure that you won't change your mind before Wednesday?"

He was concerned for his friend and still unprepared for this miraculous transformation.

"Oh! Oh," laughed Priscilla, seeing the humor in his concern, "please be assured that I won't change my mind. I have definitely decided upon this course of action. Don't worry Simeon. I have no intention of embarrassing Philip or anyone else ever again."

"Sure Miss Pomp," replied a relieved Simeon, "I'll tell him. It will be good to have him back in class again."

"Yes it will," she answered, "he's a very fine student,"

"Eddie has a class," interjected Simeon, "so if you'll excuse me, we have to go."

"Very well Simeon," she called, "and have a nice evening."

When Simeon told Philip what Priscilla said, he smiled and said, "The Lord has put me back in that class because I did no wrong in his eyes. He's going to deliver Priscilla to me."

"You can't be serious," Simeon scoffed, "there's no place for love, not to mention marriage for two people with such different life styles."

"I don't know how He's going to do it," replied Philip confidently, "but she shall be mine and I shall be hers. I know it, Simeon old pal! I just know it!"

"Philip, as one friend to another, don't get serious about that woman. She's not for you. She'll ruin you," pleaded Simeon seriously.

"It's too late now," Philip replied, "She's the one for me, and I won't settle for anyone else!"

"But I'm afraid for both of you," snapped Simeon, "I'm blind but I can see more than most people with sight. You have an ability to stir people's souls and you have touched Priscilla's heart. I can tell by her conversation. I'm begging you friend. Don't pursue this thing! It can only bring heart ache and sorrow for both of you!"

Philip was unmoved by the rhetoric of his friend. His mind focused on the lovely Priscilla. He loved her. He wanted her and he would have her for his own with the help of the Most High God.

"Some things are worth struggling for," Philip replied, "It's the end product that counts, not the sweat and tears that pay for the reward. Heck, I'd do just about anything to make her happy!"

"That's what scares me," replied Simeon, "you think with your heart. I'm afraid that you'll be so crazy about her that you'll forget those who really need you."

"Don't be silly," replied Philip, "I'd never turn my back on those kids. Let's not even talk about it. I just know that the Lord wants me to have Priscilla and if I have to suffer…Well, love is patient and long suffering. God won't allow us to fail if we trust in Him completely."

The following Wednesday, Philip returned to class. Priscilla shocked the class and Philip with an apology. She promised more leniency if good reasons were furnished. She had made the necessary step to enable Philip and herself to be good friends, just as he had requested in his letter.

CHAPTER 13

Show me your ways, oh Lord; teach me your paths.

The following Friday, Priscilla decided that she would visit the nursing home. She looked forward to the visit all day as she thought of Joy. She also had compassion on the other children and felt that she better understood them. Also she had brought back the necklace that Jonah had given to her. She intended to see if it matched Philip's half. She would give it to Joy and the heart would be complete.

It was nine in the evening when she arrived and to her surprise, all the children were in bed. Their day began at seven each morning and they were ready for bed by eight. The door to the playroom was closed but she heard someone pecking at the keys of the piano. When she opened the door she spied Philip sitting on the bench as he jotted notes on score paper. She drew closer and looked over his shoulder.

"Not bad," she said as Philip looked up in surprise.

"Oh…Uh…Thanks," he replied at a loss for words, "it's a song I've been working on for the benefit. We have to raise fifty thousand bucks."

"If that's a sample of the music, it will be a smash," she replied with a smile, "but on the other hand, it's not always easy to pry people loose of their hard earned cash!"

"Yeh, I know," answered Philip with a shrug of his shoulders, "most of these people are only concerned about their property taxes. They don't give a thought to where these kids go. I'll tell you Priscilla, I've heard these people belly ache for five years now about this place being an eye sore and all that, but I don't see any of them who are willing to turn a hand to change things unless it's to their advantage."

"Where have you raised money in the past," she asked earnestly.

"Oh most of them are too ashamed to donate nothing. They donate a dollar or two and then brag about helping that pitiful nursing home. Then they spend a year worrying about donating another dollar next year. They ought to be thankful that their conscience will let them rest for a dollar," he answered.

Priscilla snickered and replied, "It's because they don't enjoy giving."

"You said it," Philip said, "It's because they don't get enough practice. They're trying to latch on to it all the time. A good giver gives because he wants to, not out of obligation. If the Lord wanted to punish them, He wouldn't shower them with fire and brimstone. He'd make them give all their possessions away and they'd all die of sorrow."

"Philip," answered Priscilla in jest, "you're impossible. Everybody isn't like that. There are some who donate willingly."

"Well," said Philip as he looked back at the keyboard, "not enough. If I had one less volunteer to help me, I wouldn't even have myself. The way it stands, if I die today, I'll just be to busy to attend my own funeral."

Priscilla snickered as he continued to stare at the piano.

"That's a shame too," he said as he paused, "a fellow ought to be around when his friends and family are paying their last respects."

"I don't have time to waste on sympathy," scolded Priscilla, "but I'll tell you what I'll do. I'll help in any way I can."

"Those are welcome words. Believe me," he sighed, "all help is greatly appreciated. Well, what are you doing here tonight?"

"I thought I would stop by and see Joy," she replied, "but I didn't realize that the children were in bed so early."

"Yeh. They get up early and go to bed early, but you can see her if you want to. I've done all I intend to do tonight. I'll go up with you if you don't mind," said Philip.

"O.K.," she replied with a smile, "I'll just be a few minutes."

Together they walked up to Joy's room and turned on the light. Joy was asleep but Philip gently aroused her.

"Oh Priscilla," Joy exclaimed sleepily, "You came to see me again! I was just asking Philip about you yesterday. He said you would be here soon."

Priscilla replied with a warm smile, "I brought something for you."

She dug into her purse and pulled out the necklace, which Jonah had given to her and held it out to Joy.

She continued, "it was given to me when I was about your age."

"Oh Priscilla," exclaimed Joy excitedly, "it's beautiful! Hey! I bet it will go with the one Philip gave me! Philip will you get my other necklace for me?"

He retrieved the necklace for the anxious little girl. She held it beside the one, which Priscilla had just given her. They were perfectly matched! The two hearts formed a complete heart and the combined inscriptions spelled 'HAPPINESS'. Philip stared at the necklaces in disbelief, as Priscilla smiled not the least bit surprised. This was indeed a tie between Philip and Jonah, the old gardener. Philip pondered the situation. He felt that it was a good sign and his heart leaped with joy but he wondered who gave it to her. Priscilla visited another ten minutes and excused herself. Philip bent over to kiss Joy good night, but Priscilla started to leave.

"Hey!" shouted Joy in disappointment, "don't I even get a good night kiss?"

Priscilla snickered and her heart swelled with happiness as she came back to the bed and bent to hug the little girl.

"Good night Joy," said Priscilla as she kissed her softly on the cheek.

"Good night Priscilla. Come back again. O.K.?" replied Joy with a smile.

At the foot of the stairs, Philip asked curiously," Where did you get that necklace?"

"An old gardener gave it to me when I was eight years old," she answered nonchalantly, "isn't it a coincidence that the two matched?"

"If you ask me, it's more than a coincidence," he answered earnestly, "where did the gardener get it?"

"I don't know Philip," she replied, "I suppose he bought it. And what of your necklace? How did you get it?"

"It's all that I have left from my grandmother," he answered seriously, "She and my grandfather had matching hearts made for them by her father who was a jeweler. I'm told that it meant that separated each would bear a broken heart and together they would always have happiness."

"It is a lovely thought. Isn't it?" answered Priscilla, "well, I must be going. It's quite late and I really must grade some papers tonight."

Philips' curiosity was aroused, but for Priscilla, the mystery was solved. Philip was beyond doubt Jonah's grandson. Some peculiar stroke of fate, a mere coincidence, had introduced them.

Just as she promised, Priscilla pulled up in front of the nursing home at six the next evening. She parked behind Philips' old truck. The fenders had rusted out and had several holes in them. He had constructed a make shift tailgate of old used lumber. The windshield was cracked and the right door window had been broken. It was covered with a piece of cardboard. The area of finish not covered with rust was dark red. Sylvester, the name given the truck by Philip, rattled and banged as it rolled along the street. The fenders flopped loosely at each bump.

Priscilla looked over her shoulder at Sylvester as she opened the door to the nursing home. As she closed the door, a short, freckled face girl stopped stacking the blocks she was playing with and ran into the game room.

"Hey everybody!" she screamed, "Priscilla's here!"

There was a clamor of voices and the trampling of little feet as a horde of children stampeded in her direction and swarmed about her.

"Hi Priscilla," said the pig tailed five year old in front of her. This set off a chain reaction of remarks by the excited children.

Not knowing to whom to speak first and being unsure of their names, Priscilla replied, "Good evening children. How are you today?"

No one answered, as they all grew silent with their eyes fastened upon Priscilla. She could see the expectation in their faces, but she was unsure of what they expected.

Tim Rakjovic, the little chubby eight years old, said boldly, "you're too late."

He paused and looked up at Priscilla and continued, "I mean, we already ate. Huh guys."

He looked back over his shoulder for support and nervously poked his hands deep into his pockets before looking back at Priscilla.

"Well, I have already eaten also," replied Priscilla pleasantly, "I'm just here to visit all my little friends."

"Did you bring more presents," asked a voice in the group.

"Yeh!" said another excited voice, as the children began to chatter in excitement, "Did you bring some more presents?"

"No," responded Priscilla, as she clapped her hands together playfully, "not today. I just brought myself. Is that O.K.?"

"Aw, that's all right Priscilla," said chubby Tim, "we like you even if you didn't bring presents. Huh gang!"

The children shouted their approval.

"Is Philip here," asked Priscilla as she slipped out of her coat.

"Yeh," replied Tim in disgust, "he's in the kitchen washing dishes. The cook was sick and he had to do the cooking. That's why I ain't speaking to him."

Tim walked to the front window and looked out into the dark street. Priscilla was set back by his response and asked, "Why on earth would you be angry with Philip?"

Tim turned on his heal and sat on the bench. He propped up his jaw with his hand and disgustedly stared out the window.

"Well, he said cocking his head to the right, "Because he tricked me! That's why."

"What do you mean, he tricked you?" she replied curiously as she folded her arms.

"When he started cooking, I asked him what we were having for dinner. He said quote: 'a good meal with lots of nourishment in it', unquote. Those are his exact words Priscilla."

He earnestly tried to convince her as he continued.

"Right away I think we're having hamburgers, hot dogs and French fries. You know. Something neat like that. But what do we have? Spinach, liver and junk like that. Yuk! That stuff was so bad, I could hardly eat two helpings."

Priscilla snickered but didn't interrupt him. He threw up his arms in disgust and rolled his eyes.

"Any way, Philip keeps telling everybody quote: 'come on kids, eat that spinach and liver. It's good for you. It's nourishing,' unquote. But I watched Philip and he didn't eat any of that nourishment. I went into the kitchen after dinner and there he stood eating a hamburger. Grown ups ain't fair. They make us kids eat nourishment and they eat all the good stuff."

He scratched his head and continued, "but what really made me mad was the black eyed peas.

I like them. I asked for a whole bunch of them and put lots of ketchup on them. But when I took a bite, they weren't black-eyed peas at all! Philip had burned the beans! I told him they were burned and he just said quote:

'when you ask for it, you have to eat it' unquote. So I ate them! Between the nourishment and the burned beans, I might even get food poisoning."

Priscilla very nearly burst into laughter, but she had compassion on him. She walked toward him and placed her reassuring hand on his shoulder.

"You show me where Philip is," she said, "and I'll see if I can't get him to fix some good food the next time he cooks. O.K.?"

"O.K.," replied Tim despondently, "I'll show you where he is, but I ain't talking to him."

He led her through the dining area to a small kitchen. Then he dashed off to find his friends. She walked through the swinging door. Philip was on his knees with his head inside the dishwasher, trying to reach a spoon that had fallen to the bottom. He stood up when he saw Priscilla.

"If you're busy, I could come back later," she teased.

"I was just finishing up the dishes. Boy am I beat!" he said with a sigh.

"Well I received a warm reception," she replied in jest, "The children thought I had brought more gifts."

He laughed as he took off his apron. They walked through the dining area to the playroom and seated themselves. Philip briefly sketched a mental picture of the work to be done and they discussed the best ways Priscilla could assist. They decided that she could best handle the publicity and use her position at the college to help the cause. She would also sell tickets at the door. Philip played the seven songs he had written for the show and briefly outlined the skit. Before she left, Priscilla worked up enough courage to express her feelings.

"Philip I must speak with you concerning matters which have greatly troubled me of late. It concerns our relationship," she began diplomatically, "first of all, I like you very much and I treasure your friendship."

She was careful not to wound his self esteem as she continued, "You and I can never be more than friends for many reasons. I feel that our backgrounds and ideals are much too different to be conducive to a lasting relationship. I enjoy your company and I want to work with these children. I'll look forward to working with you at the nursing home. However, we must remain rational. We can be no more than friends."

"If that's the way you want it," he replied softly as he tried to conceal his great dismay, "that's the way it will be."

He smiled as he quietly and calmly agreed with her. He knew that only the Hand of God would deliver her to him, and he trusted the Most High God to provide the appropriate time, trial or circumstance to open her eyes.

So it was that Philip and Priscilla worked diligently together in an effort to raise $50,000. Each day would find Priscilla giving more time to the project as the big day drew nearer. She gained an insight into Philip and saw the tenderness that poured out over the children. She saw the patience with which he handled the unwanted child or the one in pain. They all loved him. She observed all his strengths and she saw his weaknesses. She perceived loneliness deep in his soul that seemed to be reaching for her. She sensed his need for companionship on a higher plane than was possible with the children. Sometimes she allowed herself the luxury of looking into his eyes. She saw anxiety there, even impatience. She marveled that cool, calm and always collected Philip Wright would ever be impatient. She knew that he was not content with her offer of friendship and that his emotions were roaring deep beneath that calm surface. She could feel it when they were together. She was afraid and she tried not to encourage him. It was hopeless! But in the gleam of his eyes, hope still kindled, ever yearning to burn as a flame.

Though he never touched her, he was growing dear to her. She found tranquility in his presence and understanding in his desire to accommodate. Though he talked as an uneducated man, he was on the contrary very intelligent and his musical ability was superb. He needed someone to watch over him as he did others. His memory was preposterous and his concern for financial matters was nil. Though she wouldn't admit it to herself, she was falling in love with this man who honored her wishes and didn't pursue his affections. Though he sat at home at night and longed to have her close to him, he never tried to kiss her.

When the semester ended, Philip received an 'A' in Priscilla's class. She missed him in class during the next semester and they began to talk in the hall between classes. She was aware of other members of the faculty, nosy Dr. Dickens in particular, observing them. Priscilla trusted reason, not realizing that reason is completely hood winked by love.

On the day of the fund raising benefit for the nursing home, their first concerted effort together culminated. The woman who tried so hard to do what was best was gradually reaching the point of needing Philip as much as he needed her. She began to realize that she actually wanted him. In the midst of her doubts and misgivings, her love for Philip planted the seeds of hope and desire.

Philip arose at six o'clock the next morning to begin preparing for the benefit. He, Simeon and Mr. Quilicy, the nursing home administrator, set up the stage props and made last minute adjustments to the speaker system. Priscilla excused classes for that day to devote time to rehearsal with the children. She made rounds among the faculty and sold $714.00 worth of tickets and called every business she could contact for support that evening. Harold Pomp would have been proud of Priscilla. She even persuaded the local radio station to announce the event and encourage listener participation. At one o'clock, she and Philip had lunch and discussed last minute details of the program. At five o'clock the doors were opened to the auditorium and to the great surprise of Philip the house was packed with standing room only. Philip knew that Priscilla had promoted well for the auditorium had never been even half full prior to this. Priscilla turned ticket sales over to Mr. Quilicy to assist with the children back stage.

The curtain opened upon a frightened but excited group of children. The stage lights brought squints to the eyes of the little performers as each child anxiously awaited Philip's cue to begin. He nodded his approval and Tim Rakjovic stepped forward and sang the first of the seven songs in the play. The words were simple and touching. The songs moved as it were the very core of the heart as the crippled and homeless children acted out the parts. The presence of Joy as the afflicted one in the story moved the audience to the point of tears. In essence, what the words failed to say, the actions and singing of the children more than made up for. Even Priscilla and the staff were drying tears as the curtain closed and the audience stood in ovation. Priscilla quickly hurried the children back on stage for an encore.

By this time, Mr. Quilicy had totaled the receipts and it came to $62,757.00. They had netted $12,757.00 more than their requirement. Philip walked on to the stage to thank the audience for their support. He put his hands in his pockets and humbly spoke into the microphone.

"The children, Mr. Quilicy, Miss Priscilla Pomp, myself and the entire staff of the nursing home would like to thank each of you for your kind support. You've done a good thing, preserving a home for our little friends. In working with them these past five years, I have found untold pleasure in their friendship. Together, here tonight, we have collectively provided for the care of these children and we have all gained an experience that will warm our souls throughout the years to come. I thank God for your concern. It's been an answer to prayer. God is always equal to the task if we will only trust Him, follow His leading and obey His instruction. I thank Him for this night and for giving us all a moment to rejoice together. In an hour like this, I'm sure that the angels themselves are leaping for joy. The theme of our play was that none of us could truly be happy as long as even one of us is left without our needs met. Tonight we have triumphed for the Lord God. We have lifted His banner and He has supplied the victory. Now we're going to bring the kids and all those people who made this endeavor possible, back out on stage. Thank you all so very much. May God bless and prosper you."

As Priscilla, Mr. Quilicy and the staff moved out on stage with Philip and the children, the audience rose in a standing ovation. After applause of four to five minutes the audience filed out of the auditorium. Philip, Priscilla and the staff busied themselves by assisting the children into the busses, which would carry them back to the nursing home.

The program had been a complete success. Priscilla marveled at the unbelievable results. Philip Wright, the dreamer, the great believer, had pulled off a near miracle. As he herded the children into the bus, Priscilla could see that he was very tired. She found herself wanting to comfort him. 'Oh Philip' she thought 'if only there was some way that my parents would accept you. I need you so very much. And tonight I know just how very much you need me.'

She sighed in dismay and walked alone to her car. She spent that night tossing restlessly in sleep. She was now enough in love to want Philip no matter what the cost, believing that their love would overcome any obstacle. Maybe it was the will of God! That's what Philip would say. And yet reason, cold relentless reason, gripped her yearning heart with fear.

CHAPTER 14

My beloved spoke, and said to me, 'Rise up, my love, my fair one, and come away.'

The next day Priscilla drove to the nursing home after work. The children and the staff were exceptionally jovial. Joy was sitting in a chair reading and Priscilla sat beside her until Philip and Mr. Quilicy came out of the office. As they exited, Mr. Quilicy strode toward Priscilla, smiled and said, "well Priscilla, its good to see you today. You look quite well after the very stressful events of the past evening."

"I'm feeling quite well, thank you," she replied graciously, "but I will say that I surely lay in bed until midnight before sleeping a wink. I really didn't expect the marvelous turnout. The results were stupendous!"

"Yes," replied Mr. Quilicy, "the results were staggering to say the least. But I guess I should have been an optimist. Philip said all along we would make our requirement. Right Philip?"

"All things are possible if you believe, work and leave the results to the Lord God," replied Philip meekly.

"I for one am glad that the Lord had a little help," said Mr. Quilicy as he again turned his attention to Priscilla.

"I want to thank you for the effort you put forth these past few weeks. I can assure you that a good portion of those contributions were a direct result of your influence with the business people," he concluded.

"It was very gratifying," replied Priscilla softly, "I found more satisfaction in providing for these children than in anything I can remember. It was a thrill to see their excitement. Don't you agree?"

"Yes, I was pleased with the response of the children," he replied, "Priscilla, we're treating the staff, Philip, and Joy, who by the way was a favorite of the crowd, to dinner at the Palos Park Country Club. A rather wealthy citizen who was impressed by our program yesterday donated this evening. Would you be so kind as to honor us with your presence this evening?"

She was delighted with the invitation.

"That sounds like a delightful idea Mr. Quilicy," she said with a grin.

"Oh goodie," exclaimed Joy exuberantly, "will you ride with me and Philip in Sylvester?"

"Who or what should I say is Sylvester," asked Priscilla.

"Sylvester is Philip's truck. It's lots of fun to hit bumps in Sylvester, because he always gives you a good ride. Huh Philip," Joy replied.

"Yeh," replied Philip with an understanding smile, "but maybe Priscilla prefers driving her car. The ride would be much smoother. You can ride with her if you would rather."

"No Philip. I want to ride with you in Sylvester. Besides," complained Joy, "Priscilla doesn't care. Do you Priscilla!"

Priscilla much preferred her Mercedes. The thought of driving up to a country club in the beat up old truck was revolting, but at the insistence of Joy, she conceded.

Philip had to leave early that afternoon, but Priscilla stayed to play with the children and visit with Joy. She hugged her before leaving. This crippled child warmed her to the heart and she was gradually opening up to the other children. Joy was one person that she and Philip had in common. This little girl had done much to draw them together.

That evening at 6:30 sharp, Philip knocked at Priscilla's door. He carried Joy in his arms to her apartment rather than leave her alone in the truck. Priscilla grabbed her coat and the three of them loaded into Sylvester and started to the country club. Priscilla dreaded driving up and getting out of that old wreck at the exclusive country club. It could be heard half a mile away. Its' fenders rattled and banged at every bump. If she saw anyone she knew, she would surely melt in her tracks. Sure enough, when they arrived, an old acquaintance noticed her, did a double take and snickered. Priscilla cringed and bit her lip in anger. Her dear friend Shirley Stuart could be counted upon to spread the tidings around. She was relieved to find that Shirley wouldn't be in sight during the meal.

Once dinner was served the evening went smoothly. Priscilla enjoyed herself immensely. She sat to the left of Joy and Philip sat to the right of Joy. He seemed preoccupied all evening.

The band began to play and several couples at the table danced. Priscilla wanted to dance but Philip said he didn't know how to dance. She sat and talked to Joy and the other guests. Before she knew it, the evening was well spent. It was 9:00 and Philip said that they must get Joy back to the nursing home. They said good night and left in Sylvester.

All the way to the nursing home Philip was unusually quiet as Joy did most of the talking until she fell asleep. Priscilla was uneasy, being alone in the truck with Joy and Philip. He looked nice tonight. She felt a warm glow in her chest as they bumped alone.

They decided to take Joy home first. Philip carried her to her room and Priscilla helped her into her pajamas. After they each kissed her good night, Priscilla watched as Philip gently tucked her under the covers.

Philip seated Priscilla before climbing into the truck. Neither one had anything to say as they continued toward her apartment. She sensed that he wanted to say something and she wanted to break the silence. As they pulled in front of her apartment, she spoke at last.

"Thank you for a delightful evening," she began softly, "I especially want to thank you for understanding a head strong fool who had all the answers. Those children have become a world of cheer to me. I can honestly say that I feel as though I've really accomplished something that will make life better for children who can't possibly help themselves. I have a satisfaction I can't describe, Philip, and you have been responsible for this newfound joy and insight.

Philip had been listening intently to her words. Now he turned to face her, leaned his arm on the steering wheel and peered into her eyes. There was an air of calm about him, but it was evident that he was nervous.

"The first time I ever saw you, I perceived that you were out of place. The real Priscilla was hiding behind a facade of sophistication and pride. You got awful mad at me when I laid it on the line to you, but you wouldn't have been so mad of it weren't true."

He paused a moment as Priscilla gazed intently at him and smiled warmly. When she didn't offer a remark, he continued, "Well any way, I liked you the first time I saw you."

Priscilla grinned and turned her flushed face toward her apartment. She thrilled to the sincerity of this honest, tender young man who had caught her fancy and was deeply in love with her. She wanted to run, but she felt his soul reaching out to hers.

"That's funny isn't it? I mean that a poor boy like me would flip over a rich girl like you," he said, "but I can't help it if you had a rich father. My heart said that's the woman I want and I chose to let my heart be my guide. In all fairness though, I would have loved you even if you had been poor."

She looked directly into his eyes and then down at her lap considering his tender appeal.

"You believe that don't you?" he asked softly.

Priscilla gazed back at him, nodded her head in agreement and looked down at her watch.

"I know it's getting late, but there's something I just have to say. I don't know how I'm going to say it, but I'm going to say it anyway. Priscilla you're the prettiest woman I've ever seen, and when I'm around you, I feel all nervous and squiggly inside. And when you aren't around, I'm constantly thinking about you. My feelings for you have grown in spite of my efforts to stamp them out. But it ain't no use Priscilla. I know who I want and I want you."

Priscilla would have said something but he continued.

"Before you say anything, let me finish first," he pleaded softly, "I made you a promise that we would be just friends, and I've kept that promise. But I'm telling you right now that after tonight you just better stay away from me, because I'm not going to be able to keep that promise any more. I just can't be around anyone whom I love as much as I love you and not reach out and hold them. I love you so much, that I'm beside myself, but I don't want to put you in an embarrassing situation. Nor would I ever want you if I felt that you didn't feel the same as I do. Tonight we're going to clear the air Priscilla. I know that you care for me, but tonight I have to know just how much."

Priscilla wanted to run and hide but she was moved by his humble and sincere words. As she looked into his eyes again she saw a tear peeking out of the corner of his left eye as anxiety exhibited itself all over his face.

"Philip, I am very fond of you," she began hesitantly, "I think I love you too, but I'm not sure. I mean…Well…I've never felt this way before. I do enjoy your company and you are a lot of fun. But…well, you're a student and I'm a teacher."

Her mind whirled anxiously. She was unsure of herself and reason was abandoning her on the adventurous road of desire. Her self-assurance vanished into uncertainty.

"You know yourself," she continued nervously, "that the college is very strict about student teacher relationships outside of class."

"Priscilla quit throwing me flack and just give me a direct answer," he snapped.

"Well it isn't as easy as saying yes or no," she protested, "you're asking a lot. I'm trying to be rational about this thing but my heart keeps clouding the issues. I think about you too at night. But then I think about how different our backgrounds are and I just know that father and mother would never approve. I'm old enough to make my own decisions, but I would like the blessings of my parents. Beside that, you are two and a half years younger than me. I'd never learn to like that. Philip, everything is against us. I don't want to hurt you and I'm afraid that I'll do just that."

"I believe with all my heart that God intends for us to have one another," he replied earnestly, "just look at all that has already happened between us! We've both tried to be rational and we continue to be drawn closer together. God works in mysterious ways His wonders to perform and only He could have brought us this far against all odds. And as far as being friends, we'll never be just friends again. There will always be a special place in my heart for you."

He reached out tenderly and clutched her hands in his. She felt goose bumps from her legs to the top of her head where her hair seemed to stand on end. She looked into his eyes but held back from him.

"Philip, I can't give you the answer you want most to hear tonight. Only time will tell if what I feel is real. I do agree with you that we are no longer just friends. Please be patient with me. I'm really trying to do what's best for all concerned. If you would like to see me again, I would be delighted to have your company. But until school is out, we'll have to meet away from town. I could lose my job if we get caught," she tenderly replied.

"O.K.," he answered, "that's agreeable with me. I wouldn't want to cause any trouble for you. I'll be thinking about you tonight and I'll call you tomorrow if that's all right with you."

"I'll look forward to it," she said softly. She looked again at her watch and concluded, "I really must get in. I have much to do tomorrow."

"Yeh," he said in relief, as he jumped out of the truck and opened her door. They walked together to her apartment. Both were quiet and uneasy. When they reached the door, Priscilla pushed the door open and turned to face Philip.

"Thank you again Philip," she said in appreciation, "I did enjoy myself tremendously."

"Yeh," he replied softly, "good night Priscilla. I'll be thinking about you."

He stuffed his hands into his coat pockets and sauntered awkwardly down the stairs to his truck as she closed the door behind her.

That night she tossed in bed again and once again found sleep elusive. She really needed someone like Philip. He was a lot of fun and he understood her so well. There was no reason why they couldn't date. She would continue her work at the nursing home and everyone would be happy. There was no doubt about it. Philip was good for her.

For the next six weeks, Priscilla merely went through the motions of teaching. Her mind flashed back to the nursing home throughout each day. She could picture in her imagination Joy's smiling face and the excitement of the other children when she came in. How little these small children needed to make them happy! Philip would be there too. He gave so much of his time to these helpless little ones. But now she could see from her own experiences that just one smile from any one of the children made the whole day worthwhile. Yes, there was something indescribable about cheering another soul. Philip had introduced her to a new way of life that money couldn't buy. She had found a commodity, which even the poor could afford.

Every day Priscilla would drive directly to the nursing home after her last class. Sylvester, Philip's old beat up truck was always parked near the front door and she would park her Mercedes behind it. Once inside, the rowdy rascals would swarm her, one tugging on her arm, another pulling on her coat, little three-year-old Billy clinging to her knees wanting to be picked up and twenty or thirty other shrill voices calling to her excitedly. Today was no exception as Philip entered the room.

"Hey kids," he shouted, "give Priscilla a chance to take her coat off. She will visit with all of you before she leaves if you'll be patient."

As he spoke, some of the children moved back and some left to play. However, three-year-old Billy Lisk still clung to her leg and looked pitifully into her face.

"Hi Pwithilla," he said, inviting her to pick him up. He was especially fond of her for she always held him and played games with him. He had quickly come to expect her attention first and he always slipped through the excited mob to her.

"Well Billy," exclaimed Priscilla compassionately as she bent over to pick him up, "how's my boy today? She rubbed her nose against his and Billy giggled and wrapped his arms about her neck. She squeezed him in a bear hug as he laid his head on her shoulder.

"Let me help you with your coat," offered Philip as he reached for Billy, "I'll hold the little guy while you peel that coat off."

He took the small boy and held him over his head. Billy kicked in excitement and squealed in glee. Meanwhile Priscilla had hung up her coat and she took Billy back from him.

"Are the children all well today," she asked, "I must say, they certainly are filled with energy"

"They always react this way when you come in," Philip replied with a smile, "you have found a place in their hearts. For a cultured lady, I have to hand it to you; you are quite at home with these little uncouth kids. These kids have done a job of reforming you that I could never do."

He was teasing and Priscilla perceived his motive as she laughed and replied, "you know Philip; you do have a point. Once these children begin to grow on you, it seems that you feel compelled to come and visit. Seriously though, I'm almost a slave to these children. But I want to come."

She shifted Billy in her arms and Philip walked with her into the playroom. She sat on the couch beside two girls and talked with them as she held Billy. Philip caught Tim Rakjovic and John Thompson and wrestled with them until he was spent. Both boys complained when he quit for they were still primed for action. But he had to go home and study for an economics class.

Philip told Priscilla that he would call her later and went to Joys' room for a few minutes before leaving. After a short while, he came down stairs and left. At 4:45 p.m. the children began preparing for dinner. Priscilla climbed the stairs to Joys' room to bring her down to the dinner table. Joy was reading when Priscilla entered the room and she promptly laid the book aside.

"Hi Priscilla," she said cheerfully, "You have a pretty dress on today. I have one almost like it. Some day I'll wear it for you. O.K.?"

"You tell me when you'll be wearing it and I'll wear mine again," she promised Joy.

"Hey! Neato!" exclaimed Joy, "then I can be pretty just like you!"

Priscilla laughed and pulled back the covers to pick up the crippled little girl. She noticed that Joy was preoccupied and out of curiosity, she asked, "What is taxing your mind?"

"Well," she said as she sat up, "I began wondering about something."

She folded her arms and rolled her eyes toward Priscilla, as she looked full into her face.

"Are you and Philip getting married?" she asked.

Priscilla was shocked by the bluntness of her question.

"Why on earth would you ask a question like that," asked Priscilla not a little on edge.

"Well Philip acted funny all night when we went to dinner yesterday. He kept looking at you. He likes you a lot because I can tell. When I asked him if he liked you, he just said that you were just a good friend. He can't fool me though. He likes you a lot. A real lot!"

Priscilla raised her eyebrows at the perception of this tender child. She pondered her response but Joy tired of waiting and continued.

"And I can tell that you like Philip a lot too," she said emphatically, "I can tell by the way you watch him when he isn't looking. So if he likes you and you like him, then someday you'll get married! Right?"

"Well Joy," Priscilla stammered, "I do like Philip very much and he likes me very much. But two people don't always marry, even though they are fond of each other. Don't ask me why. The answer is difficult to explain."

Joy looked pitifully into Priscilla's blue eyes and wined, "Philip told me once that if he ever got married, his wife and he would take me to be their very own little girl. He said we would have a nice home and I could have a room of my very own. I haven't ever lived in a real home. That's why I hope that you and Philip get married someday. I want you to be my mommy and Philip to be my daddy!"

Tears clouded the brave little girls' eyes, but she didn't cry. Her pain moved Priscilla with compassion as she squeezed Joy lovingly. Joy lay her head on Priscilla's' shoulder and sniffled.

"Joy, you're a very observant young lady and I love you very much. I can assure you that if, now mind you I said 'if,' Philip and I ever get married," Priscilla held Joy away from herself to peer into her face, "then, yes, you will be our little girl and we will go shopping for some pretty pink curtains and fancy trimmings for your room."

Joys' face lit up again as she laid her head back on Priscilla's shoulder and said, "Philip said that if you want something a whole lot you have to pray for it, and the Lord will hear and answer your prayer. I'm going to pray that you and Philip get married real soon!"

Priscilla smiled and lifted Joys' frail body from the bed and took her to the dinner table. All the way home she pondered Joys' words. 'Oh to be a child' she thought. They believe anything is possible and hope on even a hopeless dream. If she could believe like that, no doubt she and Philip would be married right now. But reality wasn't the pretend world of a child.

Philip called that evening shortly after seven. They talked about fifty minutes and made arrangements to meet a few miles from her apartment to take in a movie.

Philip was shy and extremely inexperienced at dating. He was unable to toss words about flamboyantly as the other men she had dated. On their fourth date, he finally put his arm around her, and even then he lightly draped his arm around her almost apologetically. Then it wasn't until the seventh date that he kissed her when they stopped at her door. What a stark contrast to the guys she had dated in the past. She was accustomed to fighting them off on the first date, and sometimes even on the first date. She appreciated his deep respect for her but until he finally did kiss her, she was wondering if he ever would kiss her! As he gradually felt more at ease with her a deep, warm affectionate bond developed between them. She was more relaxed with him than she had ever been with any other man. He would tell a joke and forget the punch line. Once he left the house without his wallet and Priscilla paid their way that evening much to his chagrin. His memory was formidable and his language atrocious. But he was sincere, honest, tender and understanding. He was always placing her wishes before his own. As she gained a better understanding of him, she began to see just how lonely he really was. Even though he spent so much time with the children at the nursing home, he still needed a companion who could minister to his needs. She began to see the man she once thought of as strong, confident and bold as the man he really was; shy, unsure and reserved. He needed her as much as she needed him. Priscilla was still determined not to marry for circumstances were not conducive to a successful marriage. However, each date brought them closer together. Each night when he kissed her good night, he would softly whisper, "I'll be thinking about you."

Thus they met secretly for six weeks until the Easter break. They successfully kept their secret for only Simeon knew except the two of them. When Priscilla left for Albany to visit her parents, Philip came to see her off.

"Take good care of my girl now," he said tenderly.

She kissed him and promised to call and climbed into her car. As she drove off, Philip stood stooped and dejected as if he would never see her again. She could see him wiping his eyes as he disappeared in the rear view mirror.

CHAPTER 15

By night on my bed I sought him whom my soul loves: I sought him, but I found him not.

Priscilla arrived home to a warm, exhilarating reception. Harold was in a rare mood of gaiety. He strutted about the den puffing on his cigar and talking of old times. Elizabeth had rummaged through some old photo albums and the three of them sat on the floor engrossed in the lighter moments of the past. Each page brought smiles, laughter and even an occasional moist eye. Elizabeth brought out an album filled with baby pictures. The first few pages were of Priscilla as a new born. As she turned the page, Priscilla saw a panorama of her first ten years. They thumbed through the pages until the next to the last page, at which Elizabeth nervously began to close the book. Priscilla noticed the remaining page and prevented her mother closing the book.

"Mother," she said somewhat puzzled, "There's one more page."

She took the album from her mothers' grasp and opened it again to the last page. There was only one picture on the page. It was taken in the flower garden. Priscilla was sitting on the bench in the center of the garden with her feet dangling freely above the ground. She was smiling and looking up as if at someone. It was apparent that she was viewing only half of the original photo. A closer examination revealed that the picture had been folded in half. Elizabeth held her breath as Priscilla lifted the picture from the page and unfolded it. To her amazement, the hidden segment was cast with the person of Jonah Wright. She recognized him immediately. Her eyes opened wide as she studied the rough lines of his gentle face. Even in this old picture, he had that glow in his eyes that she had always remembered. He was delicately holding a baby sparrow in his hands, examining his wing.

She remembered now how Jonah had nursed the small bird back to health. She cried when Jonah set him free. He told her that the bird couldn't be happy unless he was free to go where his will took him. Now she could see even more the distinct resemblance of Philip to Jonah. He had the same round face, an identical square forehead, and a like jutting jaw. Even more striking was the phenomenal expression of face they shared. Priscilla turned to her mother with a glint in her eyes.

"Mother, can you think of anyone who looks like Jonah?" she asked.

"No I can't off hand," her mother answered, "what do you think Harold? Do you know anyone who resembles the old gardener?"

Harold took a couple of draws off his cigar and replied, "I have seen someone quite recently who resembles Jonah, but for the life of me, I can't remember who it is."

"Well I'll tell you," interjected Priscilla as she looked to her mother to observe her response, "it's Philip Wright. I have found from talking to Philip, from gleaning bits of memory and now this picture confirms any doubts, which I may have had, that Philip Wright must certainly be the grandson of Jonah Wright! Isn't that a coincidence?"

Her mother gasped but her father studied the picture more closely and called to mind the image of Philip and said, "By Jove Priscilla, you're right about that resemblance. As I remember Philip, he looks just like the old man returned in the flesh!"

Her mother was more concerned with how Priscilla had learned so much about Philip and she asked, "How do you know so much about Philip? Have you been seeing him?"

"Well mother if you must know," Priscilla replied in disgust, "I have seen him on a few occasions. I count him a very dear friend."

"Are you sure," interrupted Harold, "that Philip is Jonah's grandson? I must admit that he is a dead ringer for the old man, but this is uncanny!"

"Yes father," answered Priscilla, "I'm sure of it. There can be…"

"Priscilla," interrupted Elizabeth, "a word of caution from a concerned mother; don't get involved with anyone you couldn't one day marry."

"Mother," snapped Priscilla indignantly, "I am merely seeing him from time to time. He's a very good friend! He doesn't have any money, influence or position, but he can still be a good friend. In fact…"

"That may be true honey," interjected her mother emphatically, "I'm sure he's pleasant and nice to be with. But…"

Her mother was searching for a diplomatic phrase that wouldn't offend her daughter. Priscilla knew full well what she was so awkwardly trying to say.

"What you're trying to say mother is that he's pleasant and nice to be with and good enough to visit me at the hospital, but not good enough to bring home to dinner. Heaven forbid that Priscilla Pomp should be seen with a commoner," snapped Priscilla.

"Priscilla, please try to understand that I'm trying to encourage what is best for you," explained her mother.

"Are you really mother," retorted Priscilla angrily, "what you're really saying is that I allow protocol dictate with whom I shall spend my time. I am perfectly able to think for myself and I shall choose for myself those with whom I socialize!"

Harold had sat aside to let the conversation move along, but when he saw that it was getting heated, he very wisely played the role of statesman and interrupted the conversation.

"I think we need a change of topic. I would definitely prefer that the conversation switch to a more pleasant vein," he said calmly.

Priscilla realized at once that her father was correct and she felt ashamed that she lost her composure. Nevertheless she wanted to be alone for now. Strangely, she was sad.

"I'm sorry mother. I shouldn't have shouted," she said apologetically, "I guess I'm tired from the trip. I'd like to retire for this evening if you and father would excuse me."

She reached out and embraced first her mother and then her father. She started up toward her room and called back, "Good night all."

Harold, meanwhile, scolded his wife, "Why on earth did you allow such a trivial matter to upset you? What does it matter who she dates? I know Priscilla well enough to see that she will not marry a poor piker like Philip Wright. Let her have some fun and quit interfering!"

"Harold, I don't like this at all," retorted Elizabeth in deep concern, "You know yourself that Jonah Wright came between me and my daughter! I'm concerned at the appearance of his grandson on the scene. It's an ominous sign!"

"Rubbish Elizabeth! Rubbish, I say!" replied Harold angrily, "It's merely a coincidence and nothing will come of it."

"You may say what you want Harold," replied Elizabeth earnestly, "but my intuition tells me that there is more between those two than our daughter is telling us! I saw the way he looked at her in the hospital! And I noticed how he watched her at the Christmas party. I also know our daughter was attracted to him. I know what I saw Harold! I know how a woman thinks, and our Priscilla is infatuated with him!"

"Come now," interjected Harold, "let's go to bed and stop this silly jabbering. I swear Elizabeth, you worry about problems that have no chance whatever to materialize!"

Priscilla, meanwhile, had slipped into bed. Her eyes fell upon the phone beside her bed. She had a desire to call Philip, which was silly since she had just seen him seven hours earlier. Maybe she should surprise him! She lifted the receiver and dialed his number. 'I wonder what he will think about getting a call at one in the morning?' she thought. Then she remembered that he and Simeon played at Leonetti's Lounge on Friday and Saturday nights. She dropped the receiver and decided to call him later.

She crawled into bed and tossed and turned until two forty five. Unable to sleep, she decided to try to call Philip again. She rang again, but he didn't answer. This disturbed her; she wondered what could have happened. Did he have a problem with his old truck, or maybe Joy or one of the other children was sick. At three thirty, she called again with the same result. Puzzled and curious, she lay in bed another thirty minutes before drifting off to sleep at last. It was a restless night, and what she really needed was a peaceful sleep. It was vacation, time to put her worries aside. She promised herself that tomorrow would be a better day.

Priscilla rose early that morning, even though she didn't get to sleep until well past three. She wasn't really sleepy for reasons she didn't understand. Her first thoughts were of Philip and Joy. She decided to call Philip. No answer! A gnawing sensation ate at her stomach as she pondered what this meant. She imagined that perhaps Philip had an accident or maybe Joy was sick. As she finished dressing and went downstairs for breakfast, she remained preoccupied. Her mother mentioned that she appeared lost in thought several times throughout the day, but she shrugged it off and made excuses.

That evening the family spent time together in the den. Harold noticed that Priscilla was preoccupied. She said that she was tired after a long day of shopping with her mother. She used this as an excuse to go to her room, and she immediately called Philip.

"Hello," answered Philip.

She was elated as she sighed in relief. Just the sound of his voice lifted her spirits. She felt like a schoolgirl who had just received a letter from her first boy friend.

"Philip! It's so good to hear your voice! How are you? And how is Joy?" she exclaimed.

Priscilla," replied Philip exuberantly, "gee honey. It's good to hear from you! I'm fine, I guess. But I'm lonesome. It just ain't the same with you not around. I've got so used to seeing you at the nursing home that it doesn't seem the same when you ain't there. Joy misses you too! She's all right though. She said last night that she was going to pray that the days would go by fast so that you would be back real soon."

"Philip, darling, that's wonderful," Priscilla felt a twinge go down her spine, as her excitement burst forth, "you don't know how very much Joy means to me. She's a lovely child. If I could, I would make her my very own!"

"She thinks the world of you too," he replied, "she's come to be as dependent upon you as she has been on me."

He seemed troubled and melancholy.

"Is something troubling you," she asked, "you seem reserved tonight."

"Oh I don't know," he replied, "I hope you don't think I'm a nut, but nothing has been right since you left. I can't keep my mind on anything two seconds until you are right in the middle of my thoughts. Heck, last night I got all the way to Leonetti's before I realized that I didn't have my guitar. I had to come back and get it. We got started an hour late, and had to play until 3:00 this morning. On the way home, I had a flat tire and this morning I bumped my head on that low pipe in the bathroom. I guess I sound juvenile don't I?"

"I've thought about you too Philip," she replied softly, "I called three times last night but you weren't home. It's a relief to know that everything is all right. I was quite concerned that possibly a crisis had developed. You know how you can worry and think the worst."

"Yeh," he drawled, "I got in about four and heard the phone ringing as I approached the door. By the time I got to the phone, it had quit ringing. I figured that it might be you."

"Philip," she began hesitantly.

"Yeh," he replied.

"I'm afraid that we're getting entirely too involved," she said nervously, "I mean we originally started out to be friends. I still think that we should keep it that way."

"Priscilla, I'll tell you. It's already too late for me," he said sincerely, "We both know that we will never be just friends again. We've come too far. We know one another's thoughts, we share common interests, we both love Joy who needs each of us and we're happy when we're together.

No honey, we'll never be just friends again. If our love fades away, there will always be a special place in my heart for you. The mere mention of your name will always bring fond memories.

We've grown to be more than friends and I guess I knew all along that I'd just have to love you if I kept seeing you. I knew it was happening, but I didn't care. I'd rather have you and love you even for a brief moment in time and yearn for you forever, than to never have you at all. Maybe I'm being selfish, but I know that you feel the same way too. I know because I see the want in your eyes. We both have a common emptiness in our lives that is filled when we're together. I can only speak for myself honey. The only woman who can fill the void in my soul is you. It's getting to where that I not only love you more each day, but I need you more too. I'm sorry but I'm beyond the point of no return. There's no use lying about it!"

His voice was breaking with emotion as he finished speaking. Priscilla was stunned and couldn't speak for what seemed an eternity.

"Philip I…" she wanted to burst out and tell him of her deep love for him, but that old fear crept into her mind and instead she changed the subject.

"Why don't we discuss it some other time?" she suggested nervously, "I can't really remain rational and for the time being, I think we should both think about it. How are the children?"

The conversation drifted off to the nursing home, and they talked another thirty minutes.

"Good bye Philip," she said tenderly.

"I'll be thinking about you," he replied as he hung up the phone.

As she lay in bed that night, she pondered his words. She knew that he was right. She loved him and only her fear kept them apart. But there was the problem of her parents. How could she get them to accept Philip? If somehow he could impress her father, then her mother would consent also. The only way to impress her father was with success and money. Philip had precious little of the latter. There must be a way! She fell asleep trying to devise a simple solution to her dilemma.

CHAPTER 16

My beloved is mine and I am his.

When the sun peeped over the horizon, Priscilla was brushing her hair, still scheming to find a way to make Philip acceptable to her family. For almost an hour, she burdened her mind. Why was the solution so evasive? She was at wits end. Every conceivable avenue she could conjure up was inadequate. In utter despair, she decided to discuss her problem with her mother. If either of her parents would understand, it would be mother.

Harold had an appointment with an investment banker that evening. Priscilla and her mother were discussing the new wardrobes they each had purchased for the coming spring season. Since her mother was in a good mood, Priscilla decided that now would be a good time to talk with her mother while her father was out.

"Mother, "she paused searching for the suitable words, "I have made a decision today…a very important decision, I might add,…and I'd like to discuss it with you."

"Well of course darling," she replied cheerfully, "we'll discuss it at length if it will ease your mind."

Elizabeth watched her daughter as she could tell that she was quite concerned if not disturbed.

"I don't really know where to begin. I…well…Oh mother, it's so hard to say it!"

She stared at her mother who was anxiously waiting in suspense.

"Priscilla, what are you trying to say," her mother exclaimed impatiently, "good heavens! You'll make a basket case of me!"

"Well, I guess I might as well say it," sighed Priscilla nervously, "I've fallen deeply in love with Philip Wright."

Elizabeth's jaw fell and her eyes opened wide in surprise. She was spellbound.

"Now mother, I know what you're thinking, and I know that you would prefer that I marry somebody, anybody else. However, I have made my decision! Philip is the man I love and very soon, I know that he will propose."

Priscilla stood and stepped toward her mother, wringing her hands.

"What I'm asking in this round about way is your blessing for our wedding. I'm old enough to choose the man I want, but I do want so very much the whole hearted blessing of you and father."

Elizabeth, still shocked, placed her hand over her mouth, and gazed at the fireplace, before looking back to her daughter.

"Priscilla, are you sure this is what you want," she asked as the sentiment began to soak in and the initial shock wore off.

"Yes mother," replied Priscilla, as she perceived the sadness of her mother. "He's the best reason I know for living! Mother, truly, every day with Philip is a holiday! Not only for how I feel about him, but also for what he has made of me, in the short sweet time I've known him. He loves me, mother, in a way I've never known. It's as if his heart reaches out and wraps me securely in his love and care. He doesn't ever want to say goodbye. He prefers to say 'I'll be thinking about you.' And when I leave him, you'd think that I was never coming back. Mother, there are so many reasons why I love him. I couldn't begin to name them all! He just walked right in, tamed my untamed heart and taught me a free and happy way to live."

"Priscilla, what do you want for," asked her mother, "I'm sure that if you'll wait a few months and reconsider, you will see the foolishness of this decision! When you're married, you're married for a long time; a lifetime to be certain!"

"Mother, a day can be a lifetime when you're not with the one you love," replied Priscilla, "I…"

"But Priscilla," her mother interrupted, "these are the best years of your life. You had best have your fun while you are single. You've more than enough time to marry."

"Mother these past few days away from Philip have been torture. I've enjoyed myself immensely, but my heart has been with Philip. Beside that, I'm tired of living merely to have fun!

I've found that life style to be a sham and a 'never never land' that adults conjure up to keep a childhood that they can never recover! I want to live, like the world has forgotten how to live, to sacrifice for friends, to help the needy, to make others happy, even if it involves suffering with them. There's no real good that comes from pleasing yourself! Philip is right! If we make sure the happiness of others, our own happiness is assured. All my life, I've contented myself with trinkets. I've been too blind to see the real treasures of life. I've laughed without really feeling humor. I've followed all the rules and regulations of society, and yet I have not found a deep-seated satisfaction with life. I've attended church for twenty-five years and not found God. But Philip has found Him in the gutters of society. He has more godly qualities than any man I've ever known! He's simple, yet genuine! There's no sham or pretense about Philip. In this man I can see many qualities, which can only come from a life of service to the Most High God, as Philip would say. I once thought that God was hiding from me, and I prayed that he would reveal His purpose for my life to me. That's when he sent Philip to me. And I do thank Him for that."

"Now surely you don't think that this boy…" snapped her mother.

"He's not a boy mother," interrupted Priscilla defensively.

"I admit that the boy, that is young man, "Elizabeth quickly corrected herself, "is a good man. But he's not God's gift to women. Really…"

"No mother," pleaded Priscilla, "not God's gift to women, but God's gift to me! He's all that I ever wanted. Why he's exactly what I need! And I love him and he loves me! The Lord knows that I've stubbornly turned my head to many of His blessings, but not this one! This one comes gift wrapped in the love of the Heavenly Father!"

"Oh Priscilla," exclaimed Elizabeth in despair, "your father will be so upset! He'll be beside himself in rage if you marry that young man. He can't give you the kind of life to which you're accustomed! The world is full of good men. Can't you find a good man with money?"

"I don't want him for his money. I want him because he loves me. I want him because he needs me. That poor man can't remember his hat," she said lovingly.

"And you want to marry a man like that?" asked her mother," Priscilla, believe me…"

Priscilla interrupted her mother and ignored her remarks.

"He forgets his books and most of all he forgets himself. He's always putting other people first. Well someone has to put him first, and I want to be that someone! Mother, you don't need me like he does! He's so alone with no one to love him and it grieves me to see him like that. I want him to be happy. But most of all I want to make him happy!"

Priscilla searched her mother's eyes for even a hint of understanding. Seeing none, the agony of her soul poured forth in a stream of tears.

"Mother, why can't you understand how I feel? All I ask of you is your consent and approval of the man I love! You wouldn't have settled for any man but father! You loved him as I love Philip! I only know that I can't be happy without the man I love!"

She buried her face in her hands, wheeled and ran to her room weeping. She was disappointed that her mother was more concerned with finding a man with more social standing. Elizabeth slowly walked to her bedroom and sobbed also. She knew that Priscilla would do exactly as she said. She decided not to discuss it with Harold. Priscilla was the best one to discuss it with him. She was the only possible person who could sway her father in this matter.

Priscilla found sleep to be a fleeting greyhound, which sped past her waiting eyelids. She decided to call Philip and tell him of her terrible plight. She must speak with Philip! She must speak with him tonight!

She slipped into her housecoat and donned her slippers, then quietly made her way to the family room. She approached the piano and sat on the bench. She laid her fingers gently on the keyboard and began to play the song that came to her mind. It was another of Philip's songs. He had written it for credit in her music class. As her fingers glided smoothly over the keys, her soul reached out to Philip and she poured her love for him into the song. Tonight, in this hour of pain and loneliness, the words perfectly matched her feelings. She yearned for the comfort of his touch. He was enough for her in any situation. Right now, she needed him. Together they would make a life of their own. Her heart thrilled at the thought of a life with Philip. Yet she struggled with the unyielding view of her parents who seemed to be asking her to choose between them and the man whom she loved. As tears washed her longing lips, she sang with such passion that Philip seemed almost near enough to touch.

'Is it love when I wait for his call,
Is it wrong that he comes first of all?
Is it wicked for me to love him so much?
To feel happy and free by the thrill of his touch,
When he's lonely should I turn away?
If he wants me and needs me each day,
If to love him is wrong, yet I'll love him as long,
As he loves me and needs me I'll stay.
Forever as long as he loves me I'll stay.'

She played through the song once more as tears continued to pour down her cheeks. She did so yearn for the man she loved and needed as never before. All that really mattered was being with Philip. She missed him and her stomach was a bottomless pit. Her heart burned with desire and filled with passion. She stood up and walked as if in a trance to her room. She dialed Philip, but there was no answer. In frenzy she dressed herself, brushed her hair, left a note for her mother and drove back to Utica. At twelve thirty in the morning, she knocked at the door of Philip's apartment.

"Who is it," mumbled Philip half awake.

"It's Priscilla," she exclaimed breathlessly.

Swiftly the door swung open as Philip was straightening his hair with one hand and reaching for her with the other.

"Priscilla! What are you doing here," he asked elated.

She rushed into his strong embrace and laid her cheek against his unshaven jaw.

"Philip! Darling! How I've missed you," she cried. For a few precious moments she wept in his consoling arms with her face buried in his neck.

She pulled her head back and looked into his hazel eyes. He bent his head and she tiptoed up to his waiting lips. She squeezed his neck passionately. They were locked in a warm embrace as two souls fused in passion. When at last his lips released hers, she laid her tear stained face on his shoulder.

"Philip, I love you. I love you so much," she sighed, "I didn't know how much until I was away from you. I'm ready to start thinking about our future."

He eased her slightly away so that he could see her face and looked directly into her eyes as he spoke, "honey, I'm half asleep. Did I really hear what I thought I heard?"

"Yes Philip. You heard correctly," she replied softly, "I can't bear to be away from you and I love you so much. I'm going to stick by you no matter what I may have to face."

He squeezed her firmly into his bosom as tears slipped out of his eyes, "Honey, please be sure you mean that. You know how I feel. If you leave it like this, I won't be satisfied until you are mine and I am yours. Don't build me up for a big let down."

"Philip," she said," I would never joke about a thing like this. I am serious darling."

"Let's go inside," he suggested realizing that they were standing in the hall, "we'll wake the neighbors."

They walked arm in arm and sat on the couch.

"Now," he continued seriously, "Am I really understanding you? You're telling me that you're willing to marry me?"

"She peered tenderly into his eyes and replied softly, "What I'm saying is when you decide the answer is yes."

"Well then," replied Philip earnestly, "I'm asking."

"Philip," retorted Priscilla in surprise, "I had expected you to ask me in a somewhat different manner than just saying 'I'm asking.' I mean, it isn't every day that a man proposes to a woman, and I thought you would be romantic about it. Your songs are perfectly penned and I rather expected you would speak the perfect proposal."

"Well Priscilla," he replied apologetically, "I don't know how I can say what I feel in a song. It's just a gift of God I guess. But being smooth with words is out of my department. I really don't know how to flower up my language. All that really matters is that you love me and I love you. Honey, I'm asking you the best way I know how. Will you marry me?"

"Yes Philip," she replied happily, "absolutely. I will marry you."

Neither one said anything for a few minutes. They merely held each other in a warm embrace and relished the sweet savor of the moment.

Philip broke the silence, "How do your parents feel about this?"

"Well," she replied cautiously as she snuggled in his arms, "mother and I discussed it before I came to see you and…"

"That explains why your eyes are puffy," he interrupted, "right?"

"Mother won't be that hard to convince," she responded, "it's father that concerns me most. Mother knows my mind is set, but father will do anything in his power to prevail when he doesn't approve of a situation."

"It isn't good to displease your parents," Philip cautioned, "I grew up without parents for most of my life. I can hardly remember my grandpa Wright. If there's any way at all we can avoid a family squabble, let's do it! I'd like to have a good relationship with your parents. The only way to do it is to be honest from the beginning."

"Father must be maneuvered in a different way," replied Priscilla, "one has to understand that father thinks that I must marry a very successful man. I know how to convince him, but you must trust me."

"Now wait a minute," he protested, looking suspiciously into her eyes, "let's not do anything rash! You scare me when you start talking like that. When you begin to pull off some wild caper, that leaves me out. He's going to blow his stack when he finds out that way. The sooner we get that storm behind us, the sooner we can start making plans for the wedding."

"Philip, please don't jump to any outlandish conclusions!" begged Priscilla diplomatically, "I have carefully thought this out and believe me, if we have faith, it will work."

"Now that's not what I call faith," replied Philip in disbelief, "we say 'I believe' and pow, just like that your father will come forth and beg me to accept his daughter's hand in holy matrimony. Honey, I believe that God will provide a way, but I honestly think this is more than a little shady."

"Exactly darling," retorted Priscilla, "that is exactly why it will work. This is the only thing father understands. Dealing, with father is like playing chess. One must set up his opponent with his own moves."

"I hate to be a doubter, honey, but before I even hear this miraculous scheme, I'm skeptical," he said.

"Philip, the only thing you have to do is write two songs that an orchestra can play. We're going to a party that my parents are planning."

"Wait a minute now," answered Philip anxiously; "you're taking me into your parents home uninvited? That's no way to improve our relationship with your father!"

"Darling, let me explain," she insisted.

"Yeh," he retorted impatiently, "I wish you would."

"You and I will be part of the entertainment. You write the songs and I'll arrange them. We'll sing them with the orchestra. It can't fail to impress father! It will look like we are meant for each other," she answered.

"And that's all there is to it," he asked still doubtful.

She didn't reply but nodded her head. He hesitated and thought as he searched her eyes for a hint of what she was thinking.

"I still don't believe that you're really serious," he said in shock, "we really should approach your father and tell him of our plans."

Priscilla had more in mind than she was telling him, but she knew that if she revealed her plan to the full extent, Philip would never consent to it. She was in a very precarious situation. She had to sway her father the only way he understood and still convince Philip to be part of the plan. For now she must persuade him to follow her plan to the letter.

"Do you have a better plan," she asked.

"I don't have any plan," he replied uneasily, "I admit that I was thinking about how and when to propose. But the swiftness of these proceedings has just about unnerved me!"

"Philip Wright! Are you beginning to back out," accused Priscilla impatiently, "why only fifteen minutes ago you proposed to me!"

"No. I ain't backing out," he replied defensively, "but honey you are literally scaring the daylights out of me!"

"Philip I have learned to trust you and now I know that you would never do anything to hurt me," she said as she gently rubbed his neck, "why can't you trust me just as completely? Or maybe you don't really want to marry me after all! Are you looking for excuses?"

"Now why would you say a thing like that?" he complained, "if I didn't love you would I ask you in the first place? I just ain't sure that this is the right thing to do, that's all."

"Philip darling," she said softly as she kissed him tenderly, "I love you more than words can express. I also know my father. Do you love me enough to try to persuade my father in a way that he could accept you whole-heartedly into the family? It means so much to me Philip. I don't want to hurt father if there is any way to avoid it. Please Philip. Say that you'll do this for me."

"Aw honey," he said sincerely, "don't misunderstand me. I love you so much that I can't stand to be away from you. But...Well O.K."

"Oh Philip, I knew you wouldn't let me down," she sighed excitedly, "Philip, I do love you so much."

She cuddled in his warm embrace.

"Yeh," he replied in a daze, "I love you too."

CHAPTER 17

I found him whom my soul loves: I held him, and would not let him go, until I had brought him into my mother's house, and into the chamber of her who conceived me.

"Oh Philip! It's you," said Priscilla cheerfully, "you look very nice in that tux!"

"The kids told me I looked like a wet monkey and that's exactly how I feel, "Philip replied, "Heck, even monkeys don't wear suits like this."

"Come on in and help me with my coat," replied Priscilla, pretending not to hear his complaint, "we're going to be pushing it very close as it is."

"Don't worry about it," he answered, "old Sylvester will get us there with time to spare."

"What do you mean," retorted Priscilla in shock, "you don't think for a minute that we're going in that beat up old truck of yours I hope?"

"That's what I'm going to drive," he replied firmly, "so if you're going with me, I suppose that you'll ride in Sylvester too."

They walked to the entrance of the apartment.

"Philip," pleaded Priscilla, "be reasonable. Can you imagine what we'll look like driving up in this old truck? You will embarrass my parents, not to mention me."

"Well the heck with those high minded people," he snapped, "let them see how the poverty stricken of this land live. Why can't they ignore

Sylvester at your folks place? They wouldn't give him a second look any other time!"

"Philip Wright," snapped Priscilla indignantly, "I absolutely refuse to drive up my fathers lane in this…this moving piece of junk!"

"All right then," retorted Philip angrily, "forget the whole thing. I didn't like this idea in the first place! And further more, I don't want you making any more derogatory remarks about my truck. Sylvester's just about part of the family. I ain't ashamed of this truck and I don't want to haul anyone around who is!"

"Philip," exclaimed Priscilla in shock at the thought of calling the evening off, "you can't back out now! I have made the arrangements for an orchestra and many of my friends are expecting to meet you."

"If they don't drive trucks, I don't want to meet them," he snapped.

"Philip," she pleaded, "I'm begging you to drive my Mercedes."

"Priscilla," replied Philip sternly, "I'm going in my truck, or I ain't going at all! I ain't going to argue about it, Priscilla. If you want to go with me, here's the truck."

He turned and walked toward the truck. Priscilla was red with rage, but she stomped toward the truck, stepped into it and angrily slammed the door. He started the engine and they began their journey to Albany. Neither one said a word for fifteen minutes. Priscilla noticed that they were moving at a speed of only fifty-five miles per hour. Her Mercedes cruised at eighty, and at the present speed they would arrive just in time.

"Philip, I suggest that you drive at least sixty-five. It is of the utmost importance that we arrive no less than thirty minutes early," she said diplomatically, "there are a multitude of loose ends which I must tie."

Philip looked straight ahead at the road for a moment before answering.

"If I drive any faster the wheels will shimmy," he said irritably, "If you'll just be patient, we'll arrive in plenty of time. Old Sylvester won't let us down."

"Oh good Lord," exclaimed Priscilla at wits end, "and to think that you would prefer to drive this…this…"

Priscilla withheld her opinion as Philip darted a cold unappreciative glance in her direction. Perceiving his displeasure, she changed her approach.

"Honestly, Philip, your obstinance is juvenile," she insisted, "we could have driven to Albany in comfort and arrived in plenty of time, but you insist on driving this old truck to my great displeasure. And despite all my reasoning, you hold fast to this ridiculous idea. We'll be late! I know it! We'll be late! It isn't enough that I be embarrassed when we drive up that long lane in this piece of antiquity, but we have to be late too! You know how I despise being late!"

"Priscilla, will you stop worrying," complained Philip, "we're not late yet, and if we are late, it ain't no federal case. Just relax."

"Relax, you say! Well of course," she snapped in disgust, "why didn't I think of that simple solution? Philip I can't stress enough the importance of this party! The impression we make on father may well determine if we win his favor! One just can't be late for an occasion of this importance! Philip, I'm not badgering you. Please try to understand what I am saying."

Her worry moved Philip with compassion. He reached for her hand and pulled her close to reassure her.

"I'm sorry honey," he said softly, "I guess I am kind of stubborn. On top of that, I'm about as nervous as a cat about to be thrown in the creek. We're both up tight. Heck, here we are fussing like married folks and we ain't even married."

He took his eyes off the road momentarily to peer into her eyes. He quickly kissed her soft lips and hurriedly looked back to the road. She snuggled closer in his embrace and studied his nervous face.

"It's 'aren't' Philip, not 'ain't'. Please! Do please remember to say 'aren't' this evening. Can you do that for me tonight please? But you are right," she said tenderly, "I really didn't mean all those derogatory statements. Forgive me darling. I am so concerned that this evening produces the desired end. We have so much riding on it. I am well aware that we can get married without the approval of mother and father, but I much prefer that we do so with their best wishes. You can understand that, can't you darling?"

"Yeh," he drawled, "honey, if this works, I'll be the most surprised man you ever saw."

"Philip, it will work. I know it will work," she replied as she looked out the window at the rain, "it simply must work!"

They continued to drive for another half hour. Priscilla was contemplating her plans and Philip was nervously fidgeting behind the steering wheel. Her concentration was broken when Philip slowed to a stop and looked back over his shoulder. He began backing up.

"Where are you going," she asked in surprise.

"I saw a woman walking on the side of the road in the rain," he replied, "and she didn't even have a rain coat."

Priscilla sighed in dismay as she rubbed her forehead. Here they were on the brink of being late and Philip stops to pick up a perfect stranger. She cast a worried look at him. It was such thoughtfulness that had induced her to love him as she did. When the truck stopped, Philip leaned across her lap and rolled the window down.

"Ma'am, where are you going," he shouted in concern.

"Nowhere in particular," she replied, "I'm just walking."

"Well get in and I'll take you to a station or a restaurant where you can get out of this rain," he shouted.

She climbed in and rolled the window up as Philip accelerated. She was young, definitely in her twenties. She had a bandage on her left knee. Her yellow print dress was dirty and it was evident that she had no money. She was fearful like a fugitive and she was shy with nothing to say. She reluctantly said that her name was Bonnie Long. After driving about ten miles, Philip pulled over to a roadside restaurant to let her out. He pulled out his wallet and handed her ten dollars. She looked in disbelief and then almost snatched it from his hand. She thanked him and stepped out, proceeding toward the restaurant. Philip pulled back on to the road to begin the last leg of their journey.

Priscilla snuggled closer to Philip and studied the engagement ring, which Philip had bought for her. It would, without doubt, be the least valuable piece of jewelry at her parent's home tonight. She loved this man of little means and laid her head on his shoulder. Somehow her faith seemed to slip away as the moment of truth drew nearer. Being close to Philip strengthened her for the task, which she very soon must face. In her consternation, she forgot that she was riding up the lane to her father's mansion in Sylvester. It was eight fifty and most of the guests had already arrived. She tugged her engagement ring from her finger and placed it in her purse until she could persuade her father to announce their engagement. It would be best for him to see it after their discussion and not before. She walked into the foyer, disposed of her wraps and quickly introduced Philip to some of her friends for a few minutes. Then she pulled him aside to whisper to him.

"Philip, darling, be sure to review the numbers we will sing with the orchestra," she said as she looked about the room for Juanita the head

maid, "make absolutely sure that they remember to burst forth with a pow-
erful crescendo on the final chorus of 'Oh What a How Do You Do'. I must
see Juanita and then I'll be right back. Instruct the orchestra to play until
ten and we'll sing shortly after ten."

She turned to leave, but stopped and reminded Philip, "Oh yes! Now
remember to say 'eating' in the second song. It sounds horrible when you
say 'eatin'! There's a 'g' on the end of that word. Please speak properly. This
audience is cultured and will notice a thing like that instantly."

"Go on and don't worry about a thing," answered Philip, "we'll come
out O.K."

He smiled reassuringly and Priscilla nodded her head, returned a smile
and nervously walked briskly to the kitchen to talk with the head maid.
Juanita was carrying a platter of hors d'oervre's when Priscilla found her.

"There you are Priscilla," Juanita exclaimed in surprise, "I was beginning to worry about you."

"I was on the brink of panic myself," replied Priscilla in agreement, "but
I made it. We have so little time! Have you taken care of those items we discussed last Friday?"

"Yes I have. I made those special hors d'oervre's you wanted. Now what
did you want me to do," she asked excitedly.

"Listen carefully," said Priscilla in a whisper, "circulate a rumor that
father is going to announce my engagement this evening."

Juanita's eyes popped wide open and her jaw gaped as she covered her
mouth with her hand and said, "Priscilla, are you sure that we can do this
and not get caught?"

"Yes, if you make it appear as a slip of the tongue," Priscilla replied confidently, "Make sure to tell Marlene Benson. We can count on her to circulate that juicy tidbit in no time at all. She'll try to pounce on you once you
let it slip, but act as though you want to get away at once and say no more.
If she doesn't tell Bernard Hayes, tell him also. I believe that she'll get to
him early in her rounds. After he's had a few belts, and he's already had
more than a few I'd wager, if I know him as I think I do, he'll confront
father directly with the matter."

Priscilla's breath was short in excitement and Juanita was trembling in
anticipation.

"Priscilla," replied Juanita excitedly, "only you could get away with something like this. Your father will flip when he hears that rumor, but by then, he will be almost committed to your will".

"Don't rejoice yet Juanita," answered Priscilla with a note of uncertainty in her voice, "I still have that bridge to cross. I think it will work. I pray that it will work!"

"I'm so excited," Juanita exclaimed in glee, "I'd best be going to spread some mischief!"

Juanita walked out of the kitchen snickering. Priscilla drew a deep breath of reassurance and went directly to Philip's side. For the next hour or so, she must be seen by all in the presence of Philip, to add validity to the circulating rumor. Their intimacy would affirm the gossip mill in the minds of their guests and lay the foundation for her father's thoughts when he heard the rumor.

She found Philip standing by himself at the punch bowl. Since he didn't drink, he was not in his element at a gathering like this. He carefully surveyed his surroundings and he was holding a cup of punch in his left hand.

"Are you enjoying yourself," Priscilla asked gaily.

"Not exactly," replied Philip shyly, "this is the worst punch I have ever drank. It tastes like somebody poured vinegar in it. All the punch I ever tasted was sweet."

"I think I'll sample it and see for myself," she said as she chose a cup and lifted it to her mouth, "my heavens Philip! This punch is delectable! You must be tasting the Champaign in the punch. One must develop a taste for Champaign."

"It's hard to understand why anyone would try very hard to like this stuff," he replied shyly.

Priscilla began making her rounds through the crowd while on the arm of Philip, introducing him to everyone she knew, while keeping watch on Juanita as she served hors d'oervre's. She studied intently as she saw Juanita approach Marlene Benson.

"Would you care for hors d'oervres?" she asked pleasantly.

"Yes thank you. I think I will," replied Marlene as she studied Priscilla, who was moving her way with Philip in tandem.

"My goodness," she continued, "this is quite a party Harold has set before his guests. By the way, who is that young man escorting Priscilla tonight?"

"Well, I understand that he's part of the reason for this gathering," replied Juanita teasing her with just enough fact to arouse her curiosity. Marlene didn't catch the inference. As was her habit, she was contemplating her next sentence.

"You know this is the first time I have seen that girl with a man at any gathering! Maybe she's beginning to feel old age slipping up on her. Right?"

Juanita only smiled as Marlene shifted her eyes back to Juanita as the inference struck home.

"Do you know something that you're not telling me?" she asked in expectation, "what did you mean by that statement? Is Priscilla going to marry that young man?"

"Well," answered Juanita coyly, "one never knows for sure just how valid hearsay is. It is possible that an announcement might be made to satisfy your curiosity."

"What are you saying," demanded Marlene," is Harold going to announce the engagement of Priscilla and that handsome young man? Is that what you're saying?"

"You said it," retorted Juanita in a whisper, "I didn't say a thing."

Juanita began to busy herself to escape her questioner and free her to fuel the gossip mill. She had given Marlene enough of a hint to start her tongue wagging.

"Well," responded Marlene in satisfaction, "you certainly never know about these young people do you?"

"Ma'am, what ever you do," whispered Juanita, "don't tell a soul. Especially Bernard Hayes. He's a close friend of Mr. Pomp. He probably knows about it and he might ask who told you. Now you remember. I never told you anything!"

"I'll act as surprised as everybody else when the announcement is made," promised Marlene, with every intention of passing the rumor on to every person she met."

Juanita moved away, set the tray on a table and retired to the kitchen. As she passed Priscilla, she winked and snickered in great delight. Meanwhile, Marlene was making rounds through the crowd. When she approached, she laughed and greeted her acquaintance in the customary fashion, but soon she would be whispering a sentence or two. Then the eyes of that person would focus on Priscilla and Philip. Priscilla took advantage of those frequent occasions to hang on his arm, staying close by his side.

Philip noticed that he and Priscilla were getting a loins' share of attention. This only made him more uneasy. His nervousness was apparent to
Priscilla, but she continued to play the part of an over zealous sweet heart
for the benefit of her curious audience.

"What's the matter with you Priscilla," asked Philip a bit puzzled at her
behavior, "you've never acted like this before."

"Oh I'm just happy darling," she responded in excitement, "this is a big
day for us. Let's enjoy it to the fullest!"

Marlene presently approached Bernard Hayes. Priscilla could see that
she was informing him of the latest. Tonight he was drinking heavily as
usual, and he boisterously responded, "I'm going to ask him myself."

He turned and made a beeline for Harold. Priscilla pretended not to
notice when he slapped her father on the back and threw his arm over his
shoulder to drop the bomb of surprise upon his unsuspecting host. Her
father listened intently and then his face hinted of scarlet as his guest
laughed a deep belly laugh of a drunken man. Priscilla felt her father's eyes
settle upon her and watched out of the corner of her eye as he graciously
weaved his way through the crowded room toward her. He approached
from her right side and firmly tapped her on the shoulder.

"A...Priscilla," he began in a soft voice to camouflage his anger, "I would
like very much to speak with you briefly in my study."

"Oh...Well father," complained Priscilla, "can't it wait? I am enjoying
myself immensely tonight," she continued gaily, "and besides, Philip is not
very well acquainted. Since he is my guest, I believe that I should stay close
at hand."

"Priscilla," retorted her father gruffly but low to avoid drawing attention, "this cannot wait! I assure you that I will be brief! Now come along
please."

He spoke in a polite manner, but he definitely spoke a command.

"Won't you excuse us please," Harold asked Philip.

"Yeh," replied Philip as he nodded his head politely.

Harold said nothing. They walked briskly to his study. His strides got
longer as they neared the study. Her legs seemed to weaken as the music
faded and she became more aware just how alone she would be with her
father. As she began to slow her pace, Harold firmly took her left arm and
pushed her along. He was gentle, but firm. She wished he would say something as they walked to relieve the pressure. A volcano was about to spew

forth! She could only hope that it would be of short endurance. Harold opened the door and closed it behind them. He pulled a cigar from his coat pocket, lit it and puffed vigorously, and peered at Priscilla momentarily.

"Priscilla," he began calmly, "someone has started an outlandish rumor tonight and I think you should know about it before you make a fool of yourself."

He drew on his cigar and exhaled before continuing, "someone has seen you and Philip together, and a few drinks, a comment or two, someone mentions your name and 'bingo'; instant rumor!"

He studied Priscilla's eyes for some type of surprise or disgust. When he saw none, his curiosity was aroused.

"Priscilla, did you hear me," he asked puzzled, "I said someone has circulated an embarrassing rumor. Our family pride is at stake here and you find no cause for alarm?

Priscilla seated herself before answering to spare her weakening knees. She gulped before answering. She had to push the words from her lips.

"Not really father," she replied weakly, "I wouldn't be ashamed for anyone to think that I was engaged to be married to Philip. He's really a wonderful person!"

"But a completely unfounded rumor Priscilla," retorted her father. It was clear that he was losing his self-control, "if I could get my hands on the person who started this slanderous tale, I'd tear them apart!"

"Father," replied Priscilla pointedly, "I don't consider that rumor slanderous. Philip is a worthy person. I wouldn't be ashamed to be his wife…Why…."

The impact of her statement suddenly struck Harold and his arms dropped to his side and he beamed a cold stare into her eyes.

"Young lady, what are you saying," he demanded, "you know very well that you can't marry garbage like Philip Wright! Why I'd be the laughing stock of Wall Street! He isn't in our class and you know it! I don't understand why you would make a statement like that."

"Well father," replied Priscilla meekly, "I think I should tell you that I have accepted Philip's proposal of marriage," she gulped as she rallied all her courage for the last few words and forced them from her lips, "and I had hoped that you would announce our engagement tonight."

Her father realized that he had been duped. He silently receded into shock briefly. As the shock diminished, anger colored his ruddy complexion scarlet as Priscilla drew closer into the refuge of the chair and held her breath for the rage to follow.

"You started that rumor!" he shouted, "You started the rumor thinking that I would have no choice but to announce it after everybody in the house knew it. Well I have a surprise for you little daughter. I will surely make an announcement. After you and that rag a muffin sing, I'll personally escort him to the door and announce that all the talk of marriage between you and Philip was merely rumor. After this party, you and I will talk of this again!"

He turned to leave but as he opened the door, Priscilla rose and called to him.

"Wait! Father please wait," she pleaded nervously.

"Father, I'm sorry for hurting you and embarrassing you this way. I never considered this from your point of view. Regardless of what I've done, please be assured that I love you. But I hope you'll try harder to understand my feelings than I tried to understand you. At times like this, it's so hard to talk to your father. I remember when I was a small girl. I would climb into your lap and smother you with kisses. When I had troubles, you were there to understand. I thought then that no one would ever take the place of my daddy."

She strained to hold back her tears and Harold stood perfectly still with his face away from Priscilla. Tears in his eyes blurred his vision as his anger turned to remorse.

"Father, I wouldn't take anything for those years. I'll cherish them forever. Until a few months ago, I thought you would always be the only man in my life. I have been searching for a man who measured up to you. I wanted a man who was his own man father, like you. I know that you don't see it now, but Philip is that man. I love him father. I want him and I need him."

Her voice broke and quivered but she fought back the tears so her face and eyes wouldn't be puffy when she and Philip did their musical numbers. Harold remained silently fixed at the door.

"But how do you tell your father, upon whom you've always depended that you want to depend on another man? How do you say to the man who has fathered you and loved you throughout your life that you want to love another? Or how do you say to the greatest man in your life to date, that you want to belong to a man that is even greater? Is there an easy way to say 'father I want to make a new life with my husband?' This isn't to say that I don't love you just as much as I ever did. I just had no comprehension how much I would love the man who touched my heart with his soul. Father, I beg you…" she said as she took two steps in his direction, "don't make the announcement you said you would make. I'm not asking for myself. I'm asking for the man I love, the man I intend to marry. Do whatever you choose with me. I deserve whatever comes of this, but I will not stand by and allow you or anyone else to humiliate, persecute or embarrass the man I love! If you cast him out, you cast me out! If my Philip isn't treated with respect and appreciation, we'll never darken your door again! I can't bear to see him hurt! I beg you, father, to reconsider! Please!"

She stood limp and almost lifeless as she drooped her shoulders in shame and agony and studied the back of her father's head. He was hurt and she knew it. The full burden of what she had done lay upon her heart as Harold turned momentarily and gazed through tear stained eyes at his daughter. She felt his gaze pierce her soul and she sensed the tenderness of forgiveness and understanding. Still in those tender eyes stirred a fire of revenge and the backlash of his wounded pride. He stomped out of the room and slammed the door. Priscilla checked the time. It was ten minutes after ten. Philip would be wondering where she was. It was show time! With her last bit of courage, she took her engagement ring from her purse and slipped it back on her finger. For better or worse she was committed to Philip. She didn't care who saw her ring. She was proud of the thin one-quarter carat ring. The fact that Philip gave it to her made it worth more than all the expensive jewelry being brandished tonight! Tonight she would make her stand!

CHAPTER 18

God has made man upright; but they have sought out many inventions.

The lights were dimmed when Philip and Priscilla stepped before the audience to sing. Philip felt more at ease as the lights were dimmed. The maestro stepped up to the microphone and nonchalantly introduced them.

"We have had the distinct honor to entertain many audiences in our travels. In that time we have been permitted the privilege to perform many great works of the most celebrated composers. However, I must say that the next two songs, which you are about to hear, are without question two superb compositions. Listen and decide for yourself if these songs written by Philip Wright and arranged by Priscilla Pomp aren't a masterpiece of art."

The silence was broken by applause as Philip and Priscilla bowed to their audience and walked in opposite directions to the edge of the lights. The conductor raised his baton and the orchestra played through the prelude and then stopped. From the left side of the stage came Priscilla and from the right side came Philip. As they neared each other Philip nodded and said, "How do you do." Priscilla likewise nodded her head and said, "How do you do." Both proceeded away from each other for three paces where they stopped, turned and gazed longingly into each other's eyes as Priscilla began to sing.

'I was strolling one evening with nothing to do,
When I met a young man who said 'how do you do.'
But I quivered and trembled like young lovers do.
Oh what a 'how do you do'.

Oh what a 'how do you do',
The flame in my heart burns anew.
For the ring of his voice took me captive I knew,
Oh what a 'how do you do'.

Philip then took one step forward, stretched forth his right arm toward Priscilla and sang.

'I was passing the day with a stroll in the night,
When an angel from heaven appeared in my sight.
Then my heart skipped a beat and then leaped in delight,
When she said 'how do you do.'

Oh what a 'how do you do'.
The flame in my heart burns anew.
For the ring of her voice took me captive I knew,
Oh what a 'how do you do.'

They moved together and joined hands. Priscilla was careful to grasp Philip's hand in a manner that openly exposed her ring. Their countenances beamed with the radiance of young vibrant love as each slipped an arm around the waist of the other. With eyes locked in a trance, they sang the last verse and chorus as if they were alone in the room.

'Just a mere passing fancy, a chance in the night,
Brought we two here together in wondrous delight.
What was briefly enchanting forever is right,
Oh what a 'how do you do.'

Oh what a 'how do you do',
The flame in my heart burns anew.
For the ring of your voice took me captive I knew,
"Oh what a 'how do you do'.

The orchestra launched into a vibrant crescendo as Philip and Priscilla sang the final chorus.

'Oh what a 'how do you do',
The flame in my heart burns anew.
For the ring of your voice took me captive I knew,
Oh what a 'how do you',
Let me say now to you,
'Oh what a 'how do you do.'

As the song ended, an amazed audience stood almost spellbound and captivated for one of those eternal moments. The orchestra slipped into a musical rendition of the number and the conductor invited them to dance while Philip and Priscilla prepared for the next song. They darted out of the room leaving behind a chattering crowd, which was amazed at the ring they had just seen, and the music they had just heard. They were curious about that which they were yet to hear. Philip waited in the foyer while Priscilla retired to her room to change dresses.

Before the song had ended, a slim mustached gentleman with a silk suit approached Harold and Bernard Hayes. He was middle aged and graying in the temples. He carried a walking cane though he was not troubled with a limp. He stood erect and neat except for his hair, which though thin was laying in the most, convenient position chance had left to it. He walked directly to Harold and addressed him.

"I beg your pardon," he began graciously, "I understand that you are the father of the young lady who is singing with that fine young man."

Before Harold could reply, Bernard retorted boisterously, "You are correct my friend, and I tell you that you are face to face with the luckiest human being on this planet! I tell you everything this man touches turns to gold. Instant fortune! That's what it is. Instant fortune! My friend Harold here has the recipe."

Both Harold and the stranger would have preferred to converse in less adverse circumstances but the drunken banker proceeded before either could speak.

"Even when this guy's daughter falls in love with a poor boy, it turns out to be a golden egg of riches. Imagine it! The optimum investment! A small initial investment, no capital outlay and neglig…neglig…neglig…able expenses. Just advertise and rake in the money. I'm truly happy for you and your wife Harold. I'm truly happy for you."

He dropped his head and then stared with blurred vision at the newcomer. Harold seized the opportunity to speak.

"I am Harold Pomp, thank you," he said politely as he extended his hand, "I'm afraid I haven't had the pleasure of an introduction."

"Yes. Come to think of it," replied the stranger politely, "You are quite right. I am Milt Strohmeier of the Providence Record Company. Your daughter, whom I had the privilege to meet at a concert at Crighton College, invited me. She called me one day last week and insisted that I come here tonight. She said that she had a special surprise which she felt sure would please me. I must say, that she was absolutely right. I have found no greater potential in two people than I have seen demonstrated in this home tonight. The combined talents of Priscilla and Philip could net millions without a doubt. I would appreciate immensely your efforts to enable me to talk with your daughter and fiancé this evening. I am sure that we can agree to terms and begin an extremely lucrative contract."

The mere mention of financial gain never failed to catch Harold's ear. Priscilla had counted on that one factor and this new angle was very much to the liking of her father. He studied the eyes of his guest briefly and emptied his martini before answering.

"Very interesting Mr. Strohmeier," said Harold, "I must admit myself that I was pleasingly surprised at the their performance. I wonder though if the act you mentioned could stand up against the rigid competition in the music industry?"

Harold was never hasty to make any decision where money was involved. He knew that the song just sung was a marketable product, but he queried Mr. Strohmeier to solicit a defense of his argument.

"First of all Harold," replied Mr. Strohmeier, "I may call you Harold I presume."

"Well, of course," Harold answered flashing a broad smile and laying a reassuring hand on his shoulder, "by all means a…a."

Harold stammered a moment until the first name of the gentleman returned to memory, "Milt. I would be offended if you chose to address me any other way."

"Now as I was saying," Milt continued, "any music venture carries with it a degree of risk. I should say by comparison to stocks for example the risk is…oh…with the proper backing and advertising, say, one thousand times as great as blue chip stocks."

"Well then," replied Harold somewhat disappointed with the response, "how could that venture be appealing to my daughter? Priscilla can live happily on a secure income from our interests. I must say, if I may say so without arousing animosities, that I see any venture on her part as foolish."

"At first glance this would appear to be the only logical conclusion," replied Milt lifting his finger ever so slightly and squinting his eyes to emphasize his point, "but consider for the moment any investment on the market which has potential. You know before you sink that first dollar into it, that there is no guarantee that you will get a good or even any return. Right?"

"That's very true my friend," agreed Harold as he raised his eyebrows, "but I do have some very substantial evidence that my gamble has exceptional possibilities."

"Agreed, "nodded Milt, "That is exactly what I am saying. I'm saying that the chance of success for this couple is spectacular. Which is not to say that it will bear me out. However, I am convinced enough that I would like to sign them to a recording contract as soon as possible if all parties can agree."

"Tell me Milt," asked Harold, "what kind of capital investment is necessary for this venture?"

Harold was interrupted by the sound of applause as Priscilla and Philip were introduced.

"I see we're about to have another number," said Milt swishing his glass and then emptying it with one last swallow, "let's listen. Shall we?"

"A very good idea," responded Harold. They continued to talk as Milt raved about the last song. This time Philip stepped up to the microphone and nervously spoke into it. He softly and shyly spoke with the sincerity of a child.

"I'd like to say good evening to you all and welcome you to this occasion. This will be the last song Priscilla and I will do tonight so please let me thank the band for the great job they have done. Also, since I might not get to meet everyone personally tonight, let me say that I have really enjoyed myself tonight. The kind of songs we're singing tonight really isn't my style, but Priscilla wanted me to write some songs for this occasion and she said they were the only type that would fit the occasion."

As he talked, smiles donned the faces of his listeners. He was humble, meek and he possessed the quality to convey in feeling that which he couldn't say in words. His nature and manner won the approval of the crowd despite the fact that he was far from cultured. Even though his language was atrocious, he found favor in the sight of all present. Priscilla winced when he said 'isn't' and her mother silently said a prayer, but to their great surprise, he won the respect and admiration of this upper crust clan.

"Heck," he continued smiling shyly, "to tell the truth, I feel down right silly singing them."

Laughter swept over the room but it was from a people laughing with him and not at him.

"Now I'm not putting this kind of music down," he continued as he poked his hands in his pockets, "don't get me wrong. I'm just saying that I don't feel right singing them."

Again laughter filled the room as a pleased crowd was moved by the unique sincerity of this unpolished young man and tickled by the childish honesty and candor he displayed. He looked at Priscilla who was snickering a few feet to his right and then out over the crowd.

"Well Priscilla wanted me to write these songs and so I did. She has a way of getting her way. I say 'now that ain't the way to do it.' She'll say 'oh but it is.' We discuss it a little while and here I am."

This time the humor of his statement swept over the room like an avalanche. Some doubled in laughter and others wiped tears of laughter from their cheeks. Milt Strohmeier poked an elbow into Harold's ribs and nearly spilled his drink.

"I tell you Harold," he said between laughs, "that kid has got it. He's a natural. Look around. He has this crowd in stitches."

"By Jove Milt, I believe you're right," Harold quipped, "The boy is superb!"

They continued to laugh and talk as Philip concluded his remarks.

"I expected you to laugh at the songs," he said with a grin.

With his left hand he scratched the back of his head while his right hand remained crammed in the pocket of his tux.

"I guess that it was really me that was silly all along," he said, "but I don't mind. Not really. I never felt more natural in my whole life. You might say that folly is my element."

As laughter again filled the room, Philip announced the next song, "This all started out with the intent of announcing the next number and I got side tracked. This song's a waltz and Priscilla and me are going to dance to the melody after we sing. Would you please join us on the floor at that time? It's called 'I Love You for Just Being You.'"

The orchestra began to play and Philip took Priscilla by the hand as he sang the first verse.

> 'There's one sweet little thing that you do,
> That is so unmistakably you.
> I'll reveal how I feel when you're near me,
> It's like walking on air how you cheer me.
> It's like eating a strawberry pie,
> Like the sky on the fourth of July,
> I get carried away and I just have to say,
> That I love you for just being you.'

Priscilla gazed at Philip as she sang.

> 'I've a strange disposition that's new,
> When I'm here in the presence of you.
> And I know that it shows how sincerely,
> My heart wants you and longs for you dearly.
> It's like singing a gay happy tune,
> Like a stroll on a warm night in June,
> I get carried away and I just have to say,
> That I love you for just being you.'

They sang the chorus and final verse together. Each slipped an arm about the other and swayed to the rhythm of the music.

> 'There's a mountain of pleasure together,
> With an ocean of wishes we'll start,
> Making plans, we'll be happy forever,
> The two of us, Sweet Heart,
>
> It is so undeniably clear,
> You're the key to my happiness dear.
> I get carried away and I just have to say,

That I love you for just being you,
Yes, I love you for just being you!'

As the orchestra continued to play, Philip and Priscilla stepped down to the dance floor and began to dance. The delighted guests who swooned to the lively rhythm and light mood of the music joined them at once. The orchestra played for a full five minutes and concluded abruptly. Spontaneously the crowd of guests applauded in a resounding ovation. Philip and Priscilla found themselves surrounded by a troop of well-wishers. In the excitement, no one noticed Harold Pomp slowly approach the microphone.

"Could I have your attention please," said Harold dryly," Throughout the evening a rumor has been circulating that my daughter and the gentleman who accompanied her here tonight and contributed to the entertainment were engaged to be married and that I would announce it."

A hush settled over the room as Priscilla held her breath and prayed a silent prayer 'dear God be with us tonight.' She squeezed Philip's hand and studied her father.

"Let me say," he continued, "that what you heard was indeed a rumor."

He cast a cold stare at his daughter.

"Now let me tell you a fact so that you will no longer remain in darkness," he said as he paused and peered coldly at Priscilla again.

"My wife and I are announcing the engagement of our daughter Priscilla to Philip Wright. I would like to propose a toast!"

A roar of approval went up from the guests and Harold looked into the happy eyes of his daughter as she threw him a kiss. That was just like daddy to keep her in suspense and frighten her before making the announcement. 'Thank you Lord' she thought, squeezing Philip's hand.

"I propose a toast to Priscilla and Philip," shouted Harold exuberantly as he tipped his glass toward them, "may your lives be filled with success and happiness."

As the evening progressed, Philip and Priscilla eventually met with Milt and Harold. Each was brim full of anticipation for the new act. Although Priscilla was very receptive, Philip was unsure and reserved. Having sung for the past seven years at parties and clubs, he knew how demanding success would be. His thoughts were for the children at the nursing home. A music career would take the lion's share of his time from the children. He excused himself and Priscilla and pulled her off to a secluded corner.

"Honey," he said softly, "let's get out of this place for a while," he said as he tugged at the tight collar which was choking him, "I feel like I'm going to suffocate."

"Splendid idea," replied Priscilla, "we'll go to mother's flower garden."

The evening air was especially warm this spring evening as Philip and Priscilla strolled down the walk leading to the garden where Jonah and Priscilla had shared so many good times. Philip was quietly pondering the results of Priscilla's plan. She thought joyfully over the many ways that Jonah had warmed her heart and marveled at the similarity of his grandson, Philip. As they neared the center of the garden, her eyes fell on the spot where the old gardener lay as he died. She remembered vividly for the first time since his death, the horror of that day and the dream as Jonah interpreted it.

They sat on a white washed bench and Philip took her hand and said, "It sure is great to get away from those gold diggers. They swoop down like a hawk after a rabbit when they sense a strike."

He dropped her hand and stood, then walked to the roses bushes about six feet away and turned to face her again.

"I'm beginning to see why you wouldn't tell me all of your plan," he said softly, "you knew that your dad would see illusions of grandeur when he heard the possibilities and that would sell him."

He shoved his hands in his pockets and kicked a stick on the ground.

"Honey, I'm awful afraid that this thing is going to haunt us someday," he continued as he shook his head, "for the moment, your manipulation of the situation has accomplished the desired end, but we can't always control the circumstances where people are concerned. That's what concerns me most."

"Philip," replied Priscilla as she stood and advanced toward him laying her hands on his chest, "I know that you're not pleased with that offer to record. But it has opened the door for our marriage. Remember that we will never have to concern ourselves for an income. All we have to do is record and make personal appearances at our choosing. If you prefer, we can do one show a week. Darling I do want so much for you to be someone of high standing if for no other reason than that everyone thought it impossible. Philip, I'm proud of you and I want the whole world to see the treasure I have found. I'm asking you to consent to the offer Mr. Strohmeier has made. If it doesn't suit you after a few months, we'll stop recording. It's as simple as that."

She gazed into his hazel eyes pleadingly and Philip shook his head and grinned.

"Priscilla, you're going to get us in trouble yet," he said, "you keep asking and I keep saying 'yes'. We'll try it on a trial basis only, but if it takes us away from the kids who need us so much, we'll call the whole thing off. Agreed?"

"Yes darling," she replied in relief, "Oh Philip! I love you so much. I feel as if the whole world must be celebrating with us! My heart is pounding with exhilaration!"

They locked in a tender embrace as their lips met. Priscilla sighed. Philip looked into her eyes and kissed her again. They walked toward the bench but Priscilla stopped and said to Philip, "Darling, what if I told you that the happenings of this night were revealed to me in a dream which your grandfather interpreted in this very garden, fifteen years ago?"

Philip was startled by her statement and questioned her as to how she came to know his grandfather. He also asked how she knew that he was his grandfather. Priscilla told him of the old gardener and how he had been such a good friend in her childhood. She told him of her dream and of the day Jonah interpreted it. She also pieced together the evidence that supported her belief and Philip agreed from the facts that Jonah must surely have been his grandfather. As Philip sat dazed on the bench, Priscilla emphatically said, "Because of these things, I know beyond a doubt, that God Himself has brought you to me and me to you! Don't doubt it darling. Believe and rejoice, for today our lives begin!"

CHAPTER 19

Because you have made the Lord, which is my refuge, even the most High, your habitation; There shall no evil befall you.

"Hey Phil," shouted a young woman as she ran toward him. He didn't hear her and continued walking.

"Phil! Hey Phil!" she called again. This time he heard her and turned to see a woman with brown hair running toward him. He didn't know her and he thought that possibly she was calling someone else. She stood about five feet six and had a shapely figure. Her blue eyes were set in a pretty round face. Her hair covered her neck and flipped at the ends with curls. She was neat in appearance, of light complexion and very pretty. She impressed Philip at first glance.

"Excuse me Phil," she said almost apologetically, "I know you don't know me. I'm Angie Mathews. I'm dating Eddie Leone. We saw you at the coffee house last Friday night. You're very good! I thought you were good enough to be playing in the big time."

"Thank you Angie," replied Philip politely, "It's good to make your acquaintance. Are you going my way?"

It was mid-afternoon and he was on his way to his last class of the day. He looked at his watch and realized that he had but six minutes, so he began to walk briskly. Without complaint she kept pace and the conversation continued.

"I'm not going anywhere in particular," she responded, "I wanted to talk with you about a possible job at the nursing home where you work. I understand that you work with handicapped children. Are there any job openings for a practical nurse at the present?"

"They almost always have an opening of some type," he replied, "you do realize I hope that the job isn't very rewarding if you have no love for children."

He stepped over a puddle and studied her face as she answered.

"I love to work with children," she replied emphatically, "I don't like hospital work because it gets to be such a bore. I would enjoy helping afflicted children. I know I can do the work."

"Tell you what," he answered," talk to Mr. Quilicy at the nursing home this afternoon. I'm sure that they have something either now or in the near future."

"I'll do that," she replied cheerfully, "I really need a job that fits me and I believe that I'm best suited to this type of work. Besides," she concluded blushing, "I'll enjoy working with you."

He turned to climb the stairs to the liberal arts building and called out over his shoulder, "It was nice meeting you."

As he ran up the stairs, he nearly ran over Priscilla. She had been waiting for him and she observed his conversation with the attractive young lady. She playfully punched him in the stomach with a stiff index finger and said, "I've been watching you Don Juan. Need I remind you that you are spoken for?"

"You don't have to tell me about the wedding," chided Philip with a grin, "but maybe you should tell her."

"Listen Mr.! I have a special treatment to take care of you," she threatened playfully, "be nice or I'll unleash my secret weapon on you."

"And what might that be," he replied as he pushed his nose to her nose.

"I'm not at liberty to use it in public. It's much more effective under more intimate circumstances," she retorted as she pinched him on the cheek, "I demand that you drop the playboy role, before you find yourself in an unpleasant situation."

"Listen here, you sassy little shrimp," he snapped in jest, "you aren't too big to be spanked. Maybe your father never tanned your hide, but I believe in the laying on of hands."

She jerked her head back as Philip quickly grabbed her arm in a playful attack.

"And as for your punishment," he sneered in fun, "I'll have some of that any time!"

Several passing students were startled as they passed thinking he was in earnest.

"Let go of my arm you nut," retorted Priscilla being playfully defiant, "these people think you're serious!"

"I am, rrrrrrrrrrrrrraaaaarrr," he growled, "you bring out the animal in me!"

Priscilla blushed and smiled as she replied, "you're a nut."

She leaned toward him and whispered in his ear, "but I love you!"

"Oh heck," exclaimed Philip as he glanced at his watch, "now look what you've done. You distracted me and now I'm late for class."

"What's new? At least this time I'll accept your explanation," she laughed as she pushed him away playfully.

"Listen Honey," Philip replied seriously, "I do have to get to class. You know how Miss Rucker is about tardiness."

He turned to go but Priscilla grabbed his arm and said earnestly, "you and I have a meeting to attend."

He was puzzled as his forehead wrinkled and he spoke, "what kind of meeting could you and I attend on campus?"

"It seems that our dear Miss Rucker, bless her meddling soul, has discussed our engagement with Dean Rogers. You know that there are very definite rules concerning fraternizing with students."

"You mean the big wigs consider an engagement as fraternization," replied Philip with a snicker.

"Philip! This is not a joking matter. Do you realize that I could lose my job? I'm not sorry that we announced the engagement..."

"I'm glad that you said that," interjected Philip in appreciation.

"Philip, be serious! The only thing I know to do is offer my resignation. Oh well," she said as she sighed dejectedly, "The only option that I see is to plead for mercy."

"Well, let's get on with the show," replied Philip as he offered his arm to Priscilla who was caught up in consternation.

They closed the door of the meeting room as they left. Priscilla clung to his right arm and bowed her head dejectedly as they strolled slowly down

the corridor leading to the parking lot. Philip seated Priscilla in her Mercedes and climbed behind the wheel. He drove to her apartment and they
went inside and sat on the couch. Priscilla was the first to speak.

"I simply can't believe that they had no other alternative than to termi-
nate me. You weren't in any of my classes. Further more I never once dated
you while you were a student in my class. It seems so unfair."

"Honey, I'm sorry. I never dreamed that they would make a federal case
of this. I hate it that you lost your job because of me. It's a shame," he said
compassionately.

"Philip, I'm not sorry about our engagement. So don't feel guilty about
it. Darling it just seems that we have one obstacle after another. First it was
my family and now this. Surely everybody doesn't experience the same dif-
ficulty we have endured. I'll be happy when we are married. Then we won't
have to face this dilemma any longer," she said sadly as she snuggled in his
arms and lay her head on his shoulder.

"Yeh," he agreed, "waiting is the worst part of all. Maybe we ought to
elope."

"If we hadn't already made plans, I would be tempted. I can assure you,"
she replied.

"Honey," Philip said softly, "don't worry about it. Something will work
out. It's got to. My grandpa Wright said it would."

"Yes he did. Didn't he," she replied lost in thought.

The following Saturday, Priscilla left her mother's house early to shop
for a wedding gown. She stopped at three exclusive stores that specialized
in wedding garments. That afternoon, she decided that she wanted a dress
from the first store she stopped at that morning. She drove to the outskirts
of town and made arrangements to have the dress prepared for a July seventh wedding.

As she opened the door to her car, a red jaguar squealed to a halt beside
her car and the driver jumped out and ran toward her.

"Priscilla Pomp! How are you doing? You're looking good. You're looking real good," he said. He staggered slightly as he stood before her and his
breath smelled like a brewery.

"Hello Allen," she replied coolly, "you're drunk."

"But I ain't blind baby, and you look nice," Allen repeated, "Hey! How
about taking a ride in my new jaguar? Hey baby let me tell you, it will really
move!"

"No thank you," she retorted sharply, "I don't have the time."

"Well you don't have to be so uppity about it," he snapped angrily, "I've got half a mind to throw you into the car and take you for the ride of your life!"

"Don't be ridiculous! You're too drunk to be driving in the first place. Now I insist that you move your car and let me pass," she snapped.

Priscilla was losing her temper and her attitude only served to infuriate the drunken man.

"Aren't you the proud one?" he snapped. He grabbed her by the arm and yanked her toward his car. Priscilla screamed and resisted but he was too strong. When she braced herself against the car door, he picked her up and threw her in the seat. He held her there with a vice like grip as he jumped into the car, raced the engine and peeled off down the road.

"Hang on baby!" he shouted, "we're going on a joy ride!"

"Allen! Stop this car this minute before you kill both of us! You idiot!" she shouted.

"Watch how it hugs these curves," he exclaimed as he accelerated to ninety miles per hour.

Tires screeched and Priscilla gasped in fear as the car held snugly to the road through the S curve. She held her hat on her head as the wind whipped her hair furiously. She was terrified and her heart pounded in fear. 'Oh Lord! Help me please!' she thought to herself as he accelerated to one hundred.

"We're going to take dead man's curve at seventy baby," he shouted.

In the distance she could see the sign to slow to thirty miles per hour. The road beneath them passed under them like lightning. Her mind whirled in terror as she faced the inevitable.

"Slow down! Slow down!" she screamed.

The Jaguar approached the curve at seventy-five miles per hour. Half way into the curve the tires lost traction and squalled. The car spun crazily off the road and sped headlong into a grove of trees.

"Help me Lord," Priscilla screamed in terror as the car smashed into a tree and folded like an accordion. Priscilla was thrown fifty feet from the car upon impact as the car burst into flames.

CHAPTER 20

And whatsoever you ask in my name, that will I do, that the Father may be glorified in the Son.

Elizabeth was nervous and lost in a trance. Concern for Priscilla consumed her. Harold sat beside her nervously turning his hat by its brim and chewing on his cigar. He tried to comfort his wife. The paleness of his usually ruddy cheeks revealed the pain and fear for his child. Philip was pacing the floor. 'It's been three hours' he thought, 'they have to know something soon!'

Dr. Stone emerged from the emergency room. As he approached the trio, Harold rose and Philip quickly went to his side in anticipation. Elizabeth remained seated as the doctor spoke.

"Folks let me assure you that Priscilla will definitely live," he said as Elizabeth wept in relief, "her vital signs are good. Amazingly she escaped that accident with only a few minor cuts and abrasions on her body and face. I'm going to allow you to visit with her briefly today. She asked to see Philip first. Make your visit short. No more than five minutes each."

He scanned his listeners individually to emphasize his point.

"Two more things before you go in," he cautioned, "first, don't be alarmed by the swelling in her face. This is a normal effect of the impact of the accident. The swelling will dissipate in a few days. Next, don't be shocked when she mentions that she has no feeling in her lower body."

Both Harold and Philip were shook by disbelief as Elizabeth gasped, leaped to her feet and exclaimed, "Is she paralyzed? Will my baby be paralyzed?"

She burst out in tears as she reached out for Harold's hand.

"We don't know yet Mrs. Pomp," was the reply, "that was the reason for the long delay in the emergency room. We can't find any medical reason for the paralysis. The spinal column is intact, there are no broken bones and she suffered only a mild concussion. That would suggest that it is probably only temporary, but at the present time, we can't be sure."

"Dr. Stone," said Harold seriously, "I want the best of everything for our daughter. Money is no object. I want her to have the best of specialists. Fly them in if necessary, but I want our daughter to walk out of here!"

"All those steps will be taken. I can assure you Mr. Pomp," replied the doctor, "we plan to begin tests tomorrow. But first we want Priscilla to rest. Philip you go in for a few minutes. She specifically asked to see you first. Remember now, no longer than five minutes."

Philip nodded his head in agreement and hurried into Priscilla's room. He peeked into the door before entering, but even in her dazed state, she saw him at once.

"Philip," she called weakly. He pushed through the door and walked briskly to her side.

"Oh darling, I've waited an eternity to see you," she whispered weakly.

"Come closer," she said as she weakly lifted her hand to his. When their hands touched she wept.

Philip was cut to the heart by her tears and gulped in an effort to control his emotions.

"Honey, I want to reach out and hug you, but I'm afraid that I'll hurt you." he said tenderly.

"Darling I hurt all over, but I still want you to hold me," she replied weeping uncontrollably.

He delicately leaned over and gently tucked her into his bosom.

"Oh," she winced, "Oh!"

"I'm sorry honey," he said as he relaxed his embrace, but she clung to him as he withdrew.

"Don't let go Philip," she pleaded, "please hold me."

"But Priscilla," he complained in concern, "I don't want to hurt you!"

"Oh darling," she replied in pain, "it hurts much more to be away from you at a time like this. Hold me. It doesn't hurt that much."

For a few moments, she wept and clung to him as Philip was overcome with emotion. Together, they wept bitterly as their hearts locked in compassion and tribulation. They shared this hour of woe and found comfort in being together.

"Priscilla, don't cry," he pleaded, "the doctor said you would be all right."

"He told me the same thing," she replied as she regained her composure and ceased crying.

"It's my legs that I'm concerned about," she continued, "I have no feeling below my waist. The doctor wouldn't give me a direct answer. Philip, I'm so afraid that I'll be permanently paralyzed!"

"Honey, don't trouble yourself needlessly," he replied softly, "trust the Most High God to be with us and strengthen us in this trying hour."

"But I can't help but worry about something like this," she complained, "It's important to me to be a good wife and companion to you."

"Priscilla, honey, listen," said Philip tenderly, "the first thing you have to do is rest. Rest will cure a lot of your ills. I have to leave. The doctor has limited our visit to five minutes for today.

Your mother and father are waiting to see you. I'll be back bright and early in the morning."

He squeezed her gently as she replied, "Philip will you pray with me tonight? Ask God to see our misery and heal me."

Her voice was breaking with emotion as she tightened her grip on his hand.

"Why don't we pray together now," he replied. He took her right hand in his and held her close to him as they prayed in agony.

"Oh Lord! Most High God! We approach you in the mighty name of Jesus Christ, your only begotten son. We thank you for your love and strength in this trying hour. We praise your holy name for miraculously snatching Priscilla from the cold jaws of death. Only you could have spared her. Only you can heal her injuries. We thank you for this day even though tragedy has fallen upon us. We give glory to you Holy Father because your Son has sent the comforter to us.

We do need and cherish your holy spirit. We ask you to stand closer beside each of us and assist us through this trial. Be with Priscilla and strengthen her faith that she might enjoy a closer walk with you. I must leave her for today, but I don't leave her alone precious Father, for you will abide with her through the night until I return again. You can do so much more for her than I and I don't doubt that for an instant. I'm entrusting her to your care to keep her, cheer her, and to heal her. We ask that your perfect will be done. We love you Lord and we need you, for you make the bad times good and the good times better. Be with us and bless us. We ask in this Jesus name. Amen."

A brief silence hung over them as each pondered silently their fears and needs. There is nearness in tragedy that can't be described. When two souls join together and appeal to the highest of all powers, they find themselves graced with the presence of a friend who sticks closer than a brother. The bereaved couple finds peace and tranquility. Thankfully, humbly, they submit to the will and pleasure of the Lord and hope in his promises. Thus while they were locked in a warm embrace, they reached out together to God. Philip had looked to Him many times, but this was only the second time Priscilla ever had to call on a power higher than her earthly father or his money. Her life was in the safe hands of the Most High God. As Philip prayed she had put forth her greatest effort to speak with this being about whom she had heard so much, in whom Philip trusted and loved daily and about whom she knew so little.

"Darling," sniffled Priscilla as she leaned back to see his face, "do you think that God hears me when I speak to him? I have completely turned my back on Him all my life. When we were praying, I felt so unworthy of even His least concern. If He really were all He's said to be, what would my paralysis be to Him? Are there not many like me who call out in despair when tragedy strikes?"

"Honey, that's what makes Him God, the Most High, the lover of the souls of mankind," he replied in reassurance, "He isn't some celestial being way off in some remote land. He's right here in our midst. He's as real as you and me. He has feelings and He's concerned about our problems, because He loves us. We're His children! Right now I feel a warm glow in my chest because He's with us. Sometimes I feel nothing, but I know that He hears and cares. He's always standing in the shadows, keeping watch over His own. Don't you doubt that for an instant! In everything you do, you have to believe. You can't play the piano if you doubt and neither can you recover if you don't believe that you 're going to recover. Look at all that has already happened in your life. The dream you had as a child was inspired by God Almighty the Seer of the eternal future before it occurs. Right before your very eyes it has been fulfilled despite unbelievable odds. Only the Most High God could have prepared the way for us. Now this accident occurs. Why it's a miracle that you're alive! Heck not only are you alive, but you're going to live a long time!"

He peered tenderly into her tear-filled eyes.

"I know that I'll live Philip," she replied in remorse, "but I don't want to be a cripple all my life. Please forgive me, darling, if I worry, but this is more than I can bear. I'm trying to be strong, but I can't"

She laid her head on his shoulder for solace and whimpered like a small child.

"Honey, the doctor is going to run some tests for the next few days," he said, "they should know something soon."

Philip tried to console her as he spoke, "you're tired and worn out now. You need some rest and your parents want to see you. I'll be praying for you and I know Joy and the rest of the kids will pray for you too."

Priscilla smiled and warmed at the mention of Joy's name. Through the ordeal she had only thought of herself.

"I have to go before Dr. Stone comes in after me, but I'll be back tomorrow. Honey I love you. Even though my body walks out the door, my heart will be here with you through this night until I see you again in the morning. Rest well and try to relax because everything will be all right," he said as he kissed her.

"O.K.," she nodded in agreement, "I'll be waiting impatiently."

"Is there any other way my lady would wait," he teased as he rose and walked slowly to the door. He paused momentarily in the door to look back once again. In this moment of parting each one felt agony. They exchanged feelings the way only two people in love can. It was a moment when all eternity seemed to be stuffed into one minute of time. Though neither said a word, each renewed a burning desire and commitment deep within their being.

"I'll be thinking about you," said Priscilla as he turned to leave. That was his line. She had thrilled many times at that simple yet concise truth and somehow the words seemed appropriate for the moment.

"Yeh," replied Philip with a smile.

He disappeared as the door closed behind him. Strangely, she didn't feel alone when he left or even after she visited with her parents. This night brought with it tranquility as she had never before known. For the moment, she chose to believe Philip was right about her injury. He had always been right before. God had never failed him. He would remember her plight also.

CHAPTER 21

My peace I give unto you: not as the world gives, give I to you. Let not your heart be troubled, neither let it be afraid.

Tests filled the next six days. She imagined that she had been given every test known to the medical profession. A special group of surgeons were flown to Mercy Hospital. Each day she would ask if any new clues had developed and each day the answer was indefinite. Philip visited twice each day. He was an eternal optimist, always hoping for the best and never doubting a complete recovery. Her mother tried to hide her concern and her father spoke louder and laughed a little more often, but Priscilla could read their growing concern. She perceived that all the facts weren't being revealed to her. In the solitude of the evening, she prayed and cried. Twice the nurse heard her even though she tried to muffle her sobs by burying her face in a pillow. On the morning of the seventh day, she decided to question her doctor. She would not tolerate a devious response.

Dr. Stone stepped into her room at nine thirty while making his morning rounds. He smiled and greeted her as he looked over her medical chart.

"Good morning Priscilla," he said as he leaned over a vase of flowers, "I see another fan has sent you some moral support today. I guess they had no way of knowing that today you would be released."

"I'm to be released today," she asked in shock.

"That's right," he replied, "there are a few things we need to discuss first however. First of all how are you doing today?"

"I suppose that depends upon what you have to say to me," she replied seriously, "Doctor I have received every conceivable bit of news except the true probabilities it seems. Mother and father have worry written all over their faces and each examining physician has adroitly side stepped my questions, reassuring me and yet informing me of nothing. I want you to be frank with me. I have a right to know my fate. Doctor will I ever walk again?"

"Well Priscilla," replied the doctor cautiously.

"Please don't try to find an easy way to break the news to me," she interjected, "There is no easy way to receive tragic news. I merely want a simple, direct answer."

"At the present time, I can only tell you that we can't be sure," he replied grimly.

Priscilla studied him as he answered.

"We can find no physical reason for your paralysis and loss of feeling. All X-rays are negative and as far as we can diagnose, you are completely recovered. At this time, I would estimate your chances of walking again are about fifty percent."

Even though his answer was better than she expected, the impact of his statement stunned her. "I see," she said in a daze, "it really doesn't come as a shock. Not after all that has happened to Philip and me. Our romance has known travail from the beginning. I might have known from the past experience that fate would deny our desires. How cruel our destinies can be to ourselves and the ones we love."

"Don't be so quick to throw in the towel," said Dr. Stone in encouragement, "with therapy and time complete recovery is a very real possibly."

"What about a music career," she asked as she sat up and fixed her gaze upon the doctor, "will I be able to travel and play the piano on stage?"

"With common sense and proper rest this is conceivable," he replied frankly, "much will depend on you and your willingness to keep your activities within the scope of your physical capabilities."

"I think that my husband and I can be happy in spite of my handicap," she said, "but will I always be numb from my waist down?"

"There is a possibility that feeling will return," he answered, "Should that happen, then in all probability, the paralysis would dissipate also. Even with no feeling in the lower extremities one can live a very fulfilling life."

Priscilla was not hearing the answer to one of her most troubling thoughts and her impatience displayed itself upon her face.

"Dr. Stone, what I'm trying to say or ask," she said as her face colored a faint scarlet, "is…will my condition prevent my being a woman for my husband?"

Her question jolted the doctor and he stood speechless momentarily.

"Doctor, I know a definite answer might be impossible, but I want your professional opinion," she continued nervously, "I simply must have something besides a maybe. The happiness of the man I love is at stake. I can't allow my own selfishness to ruin the life of a wonderful man. As much as it could hurt, I would prefer to see him happy in the arms of another woman than miserable in our marriage."

Her voice began to crack as emotion clouded her eyes and anxiety shook her nervous fingers. She gazed pleadingly into the eyes of the doctor for an answer. Her primary concern was Philip.

"Priscilla," replied Dr. Stone, "be fair with yourself. Don't jump to conclusions."

She broke into tears of desperation and agony as she shouted, "Dr. Stone! Please just answer my question and don't torment me any longer! In my condition, will I be able to make love to my husband?"

The doctor sadly replied, "I wish I could assure you that your condition wouldn't interfere with physical intimacy with your husband. There is some hope that some if not all feeling will return to your lower extremities, but you will probably be unable to bear children"

"What you're saying is that the prospect is dim. Am I correct?" she asked.

Dr. Stone nodded his head sadly but said nothing. Her suspicions were correct. She fell back on the bed and buried her face in her pillow. The doctor stood helplessly for a few minutes and quietly left her with her grief.

Within minutes of his departure, Philip entered her room and swiftly went to her side. He leaned over her and laid his hand tenderly on her shoulder.

"Priscilla. Honey," he said in concern, "what's wrong?"

She turned and sat up but refused to allow him to touch her. She fought back tears and drew a deep breath before speaking.

"Philip, please don't touch me," she said nervously, "it will only make what I must say harder to say. I just ask you to please try to understand that I'm trying to do what is best for both of us."

She wiped her eyes and gazed into the puzzled face of her fiancée. She wanted to run and hide but in her deep sorrow she knew that she must face the situation head on.

"Philip," she began, "I've just spoken to Dr. Stone. He informed me that I am to be released today. After I insisted upon a direct answer, he revealed to me the truth of my condition. I most probably will never walk again and also I will be numb from my waist down."

Philip said nothing as he dropped his head in sadness. Priscilla looked blankly into his mournful face. At this time, Harold and Elizabeth were about to enter the room, but they stopped and remained silent to refrain from interrupting their conversation.

"Darling, I had such great hopes for us. I was determined to be the best companion and wife that a woman could be, but my greatest efforts cannot overcome my physical handicap. I'll never be able to live up to the standards, which I myself have set as a cripple. I'll spend the rest of my life as a parasite, a burden to those whom I love. Before this horrid accident, I had a treasure to offer you, the best years of my life, the beauty of my youth and a desire to share my life with the man I loved. Oh you were going to be a fortunate man, Philip. I fully intended to see to that," she said as she choked in deep sorrow at the thought of all she would lose because of her paralysis.

Philip began to stoop toward her and reached for her, as she demanded, "No Philip. Please don't come any closer! I must finish this while I can yet bear to speak of it."

"We overcame the handicap of different backgrounds, and you taught me a new way to happiness. We endured the social pressures, which worked to keep us apart, and we claimed that victory. We even won my father and mother to our cause and that was a miracle. In short, we have withstood all the obstacles the world can toss at us and won handily. But we're only human Philip. We can't stand when the powers of heaven move against us as they do now.

It appears to me that this marriage was never meant to be. Otherwise how do you explain the fact that a merciful God would allow a tragedy to occur just eight weeks prior to our wedding?"

Philip understood her sorrow and knew it must run its' course and he was content to remain silent as she spoke. He gave his full attention to her words and stood stooped with his hands in his pockets. Just outside the door Elizabeth writhed in sorrow for her daughter then turned to Harold and leaned on his chest and cried quietly so as not to be heard. Harold gently draped an arm around his wife and held her while Priscilla continued.

"But," she said as she looked at her hands, which were nervously entwined in the sheets, "since God knows best, I am convinced that this is a sign that our marriage can never be. I have no intention of being a burden to you. I can never be satisfied knowing that our love is handicapped and God Himself has indicated His displeasure toward our union. Under these circumstances, I see no alternative but to call off our wedding. I'm sorry Philip, but I truly believe it to be best for both of us this way."

She peered directly into his eyes and held back the agony, which was streaming in her soul. Philip scratched his head and walked three steps toward the window. He wiped a solitary tear from his eyes. Outside the room, Elizabeth quietly sobbed on Harold's shoulder. Philip turned and calmly walked to within a step of her bed. Priscilla followed his every move and waited in anticipation for his answer.

"Well," he said with a drawl that suggested contemplation, "I guess you can't be any more specific than that. I ain't as good with words as you are, but I'm going to give you my view. I can understand your sorrow, but as to your logic and intentions, I can sum it all up in one word," he said as he paused and looked deep into her soul, "Hog wash! You're over reacting and............."

"Don't waste your time Philip," she replied sternly, "I know this is best! I'm a cripple!"

She shouted the last sentence and her face turned scarlet as she shook in anxiety.

"And you're going to sit by the wayside and feel sorry for yourself as the world goes by," he said, "Priscilla, I understand your agony, I agonize with you, but I despise this self pity. It's time for you to get hold of yourself and come out of this stupor. Together, we can..."

She was shocked by his response and she retaliated in anger.

"What!" she screamed angrily, "self pity? What would you know of how I feel? It's easy for you to be a judge and toss out encouragement from the safety of your ringside seat! Come out here in the ring where the action is and you'll find out that this is no picnic!"

When Elizabeth heard Philip's response and perceived the anger of her daughter, she was instantly angry with Philip. She turned to push through the door, but was restrained by her husband. She glared at him and said, "Do you hear how he talks to our daughter? He has upset her!"

"Elizabeth!" retorted Harold sternly, "for once in your life, think before you shoot off your mouth. That boy is absolutely right! If he doesn't care enough to dissuade her, she's better off without him."

"Harold Pomp!" snapped Elizabeth, "there's no reason for him to talk to her like that! I'm going to tell that bloke a thing or two!"

"You'll do nothing of the kind," he replied firmly, "we have a very strong willed daughter. She needs a man who can meet her on even terms. You're going to stand here quietly with me. We're going to find out what that boy is made of."

"Harold, that's my daughter and that ruffian is badgering her at a time when she needs understanding," Elizabeth snapped back, "and I won't allow anyone to upset her at a time like this."

"Listen to me Elizabeth," replied Harold sternly, "that boy may be the only hope for the joy and happiness we want her to know. She loves him. He wants her and needs her. In her condition, she'll need something to take her mind off of her handicap. If she's loved and needed, she'll learn to be happy even though she's crippled. You had better think beyond this moment to the dismal future that will be hers without someone to care for her. We have done all we can. We must look to that young man to make her happy."

He relaxed his grip as Elizabeth realized that her husband was right. Philip, mean while, was about to speak.

"We have overcome many obstacles because we dared to love when society said that it just couldn't be. And we're going to win over this nightmare. God has brought us to where we are now. This accident was Satan's last and greatest obstacle in our path. He sought by devious means to take your life to prevent our marriage, but the Most High God forbade him by saving you from certain death. What greater proof do you need? Though He may allow Satan to persecute us, he won't allow him to take our lives to kill our love. I'll agree that the world has given us more than our share of problems and even the heavens have intervened, but we shall be remembered before the angels as the lovers who moved heaven and earth to be together!"

Priscilla was moved by his deep devotion and desire, but she still was troubled by her condition. She loved him and needed him, but she didn't want to be a burden to him.

"Oh Philip," she replied, for the anger and self pity had dissipated, "I'd like to believe you. You just don't know how much I want to believe you." She began to cry as she continued. She could sense that Philip wanted to take her in his arms but she knew if he did that she wouldn't be able to resist any longer.

"Please Philip," she insisted, "don't touch me. It isn't that I don't want you or need you as much as ever. It's because I love you so very much that I can't marry you. I will never be able to have children and that isn't fair to you. I know how much you love children. What kind of wife could I be if I'm unable to bear children for you? Oh Philip! I'm just half a woman. I want to be a whole woman for you."

She burst out sobbing in a torrent of tears. Philip instantly stooped and sat on the side of the bed and folded her into his warm embrace. With his right hand, he delicately lifted her chin so he could see her face.

"Priscilla. Honey don't be foolish. These are just little things," he said tenderly as he peered into her eyes, "Our Lord will take care of all these petty things if we will only trust Him. All I know is that I'm miserable without you. Heck, just being with you makes my whole day better. Why you don't think for a minute that we won't be happy do you? Why we'll be the happiest people God ever created. It's going to be us three. The Lord, you and me. And we can lick any problem old Satan can put before us. We dared to hope when there was no hope, just the love in our hearts. God has enabled our love to grow. Honey, we haven't seen anything yet. 'Eye has not seen nor have ears heard those things that God has in store for them that love Him and are called according to His purpose.' We can't comprehend the blessings we'll share if we trust God completely. Don't be afraid to claim those things that are ours to share. Priscilla, I love you and I don't know what I'll do if you don't change your mind."

Philip cried in the tenderness of his heart and his love for Priscilla. He gently tucked her into his bosom and she limply and willingly cried in his embrace.

"Oh Philip, I need you so much. I love you darling. I love you. You understand me and I need you. I promise you that I'll do all in my power to make you happy," she said.

"I know it honey," he replied softly, "We'll be happy. We'll be happy."

Harold and Elizabeth decided to wait until Philip left to visit their daughter. They walked down the corridor contemplating the events of the past few minutes. They would never reveal to Priscilla or Philip that they had overheard the conversation, but memory would preserve it as a price-less gem. To Philip and Priscilla, the world was only beginning to blossom.

CHAPTER 22

Who is this that comes up from the wilderness, leaning upon her beloved? I raised you up under the apple tree: there your mother brought you forth: there she brought you forth that bare you.

Philip was singing as he played with Joy when Angie walked into the room. She was hired as a nurses aid after her conversation with Philip. She found working at Little Angels Nursing Home a pleasant experience. Philip was good-natured with the children and employees. The children seemed electrified when he was there. He was there every day. Each day he brought the sweet nectar of happiness. The children knew the exact time of his arrival. He took the commonplace and routine day of these forgotten and innocent souls and made it a holiday. It was little wonder that a special fondness for him grew in Angie's heart.

"Say," she said pleasantly as she approached, "you seem to be in a good mood. That's a jumpy melody you're singing. Did you write that?"

"Yes I did," he replied, "I have to cheer up Priscilla. That song seemed like one way to do it."

"Do you write a song for everyone who feels bad," she asked with a smile, "if you do, I'll place myself on the agony list."

"Well I guess if you really needed cheering up and the Lord thought it necessary, He'd give me a song for you too," said Philip.

"You know I don't just dream these songs up," he replied sincerely, "these songs are a gift of God for a special purpose. I seem to get them when I have somebody in my heart. The Lord gives me a song because a song is something you must share. That's why a song never fails. If you convey your message, the happiness is doubled."

Joy smiled and said excitedly, "Jesus always gives you a happy song for sad people. Jesus is wonderful! Isn't he Philip?

She looked expectantly into his face for an answer. Philip chuckled at her response and squeezed her lovingly.

"Just look at this wonderful little girl," he said as he looked back at Joy, "You know the Lord might be better off if we remained children all our lives. Doesn't it make you wonder how adults can be so blind to God's handy work?"

He was caught up in thought momentarily as he gazed out the window. His mind slipped back to Priscilla for it was time for him to assist her with therapy. As he stood with Joy in his arms, he would have left except Angie spoke.

"Haven't you been leaving early these past few days," she asked as she took Joy from him.

"Yes, I have to," he replied in concern. It was apparent that he was preoccupied.

"The doctor has prescribed several types of exercises for Priscilla that should keep her joints limber and muscles firm. Since some of them are a bit strenuous, he advised that someone be near to assist her. She does her therapy right after lunch so I guess I had better be going."

"Why doesn't she have a nurse come in and work with her," Angie asked, "It would seem that a professional would be specially trained."

"Oh she just wants me around I guess. You know how it is when we face trials. It's better to have someone who understands and cares than someone with all the answers and no real concern.

I tell you though," he said as he shook his head in concern, "she's got me worried."

"What are you worried about?" she asked.

"Well," he drawled, "she's got her heart set on walking down the aisle on our wedding day. I'm afraid that her want is bigger than her faith. She's trusting in the wrong things. She expects those exercises to do wonders. They will assist, but that ain't the answer to her problem. When I tell her that God can heal her, she accuses me of preaching to her. So," he continued with a shrug of his shoulders, "what can I do? I just keep praying and trusting God to open her eyes."

"Do you actually believe God heals in this day," asked Angie.

"He still gives life, doesn't He?" Philip replied earnestly, "Which is the greatest miracle? To give life or heal a living being? I say that if God can give life, which is the greatest miracle of all, then it isn't a big deal to heal the worst sickness or injury known to man. Well, I better be on my way. You behave yourself young lady," he said to Joy in jest, "or Angie will report you to me."

"I will," replied Joy as she reached out and hugged him.

"I'll see you tomorrow," said Angie. Angie knew that she could care for Philip very much. She almost hated it that she had arrived on the scene to late to compete for the prize that was soon to be Priscilla's.

Philip went directly to Priscilla's apartment. She had a private nurse on duty at all times but she wanted Philip there during therapy. His presence made the time pass quickly. He was always at ease and confident. She needed his inspiration as each passing day brought July seventh nearer. Her anxiety began to build and her doubts were aroused. In her exhilaration at the hospital, she had vowed to walk down the aisle on their wedding day. Today when Philip entered the room, she was very gloomy.

"Well," said Philip playfully, "how's the best looking woman in the world today?"

She was walking between two horizontal bars. She supported her weight with her arms and dragged her feet partly by the motion of her body and in part with the what little body strength and coordination she still possessed in her legs. Of all her therapy, this task troubled him most. His thoughts flashed back to the lightness of her step and the effortless and graceful manner with which she moved across the floor before the accident. It seemed that she had to summon all her strength to move her legs even a few inches. He could understand how she might become discouraged. He perceived at once that her spirits were low.

"Hello darling," she replied with a sigh as she paused momentarily to catch her breath, "I seem to be so tired today. Goodness, every move I make is such an effort! I guess I'm weary of this seemingly endless exercise and therapy."

"Well you know you can't quit now honey," Philip replied in encouragement, "the wedding is only three weeks away."

"I know Philip. That is my greatest concern," she replied in disgust.

"Philip," she began with a note of despair.

"Yeh," he answered.

She paused, drew another deep breath and said, "Oh Philip! What if I still can't walk on our wedding day? Darling that would be just terrible!"

Her blue eyes mirrored the worry and agony of her soul. She appeared to be pleading for understanding and at the same time begging for a quick sure remedy. Philip shared her trauma and his heart cried out in grief for Priscilla. He sat on the horizontal bar to her left and gazed intently into her fearful eyes.

"Honey, we have lots of time by God's standards," he said, "I keep telling you to believe and work. He will work in His own time. I know that you'll find that it is always just in time."

"Philip, you say that day after day," complained Priscilla wearily, "four weeks now I've dragged myself across this floor, each night I pray and read the Word and I continually yearn for a complete recovery. Where is God? Why doesn't He attend to my needs now? After four weeks of hard work and drudgery, I can hardly move my legs a few inches at a time!"

"Priscilla, now don't get depressed," he replied in an effort to reassure, "rather than start doubting, let's give thanks for your progress. Heck, four weeks ago, you couldn't move your legs at all. Let's be optimistic. You will probably have to wear braces, but if the Lord allows you to walk with braces, then it won't be long until you walk without them."

"I don't want to wear braces in our wedding," she complained, "What kind of bride will I be with my wedding dress and train while my braces clank the sound of cold steel. I don't want to hobble down the aisle. I want to walk straight and gracefully for you."

She was on the brink of tears but she restrained herself and dropped her head in grief. Philip gently laid his hands on her arms and said pleadingly, "Honey lets take what the Lord provides and be happy with that until he provides more. It's senseless to brood over things we can't control. I am convinced that if we make the best of our marriage in spite of your handicap, that God will cause us to prosper to the glory of His holy name. We just can't let this problem beat the best love God ever gave two people."

"I'm sorry darling," she said sadly. She couldn't help being impatient.

"It's just a new experience," she continued, "all my life, I obtained any-thing I wanted at the slightest whim. Now I face a situation that demands patience. I can't alter this to suit myself. I must accept it. I feel so helpless! I'm not accustomed to waiting nor have I experienced a problem that I couldn't decide and change for myself."

She was weary of standing and she shifted her weight to her right arm and peered pleadingly at Philip.

"Darling could you help me over to the chair," she asked with a sigh, "I really must rest."

He assisted her into her wheel chair and seated her. He wheeled her to the piano in her room and when he stopped, she looked back at him puzzled. Before she could inquire of him, he said, "I wrote a new song for us and we're going to sing it together. We have to get these problems off of our minds."

She smiled sheepishly and replied, "Oh Philip! Do you think the answer to all our problems is as easy as singing a song? I only wish that were true. Really darling, I don't feel like singing or playing at the present time. Maybe some other time."

"Nope," he replied with determination," I ain't taking no for an answer."

Before she could resist, he took the liberty to lift her out of the wheel chair and set her on the piano bench. She shook her head in disbelief, but she was too tired to argue.

"I have the sheet music right here. You can use those amazing sight reading skills of yours," he said in delight, "remember that tune I was hum-ming the day before yesterday that you liked? That's the one."

"But Philip, this is the first time I've seen the music." she protested.

"So what," he replied as he shrugged his shoulders, "this isn't a recital. Let's just sing, play and be happy."

She shook her head momentarily and then studied the music. Her agile fingers glided over the introduction and Philip said, "You sing the first verse, then I'll sing the second verse. We'll sing the chorus together."

She cast a quick glance at Philip and sang.

'If you hear my heart go pitter patter,
Hold me tighter for it doesn't matter.
I'm in love with you and love I think it's great.
Further more I think that it's a permanent state.'

Priscilla found herself wrapped in the lighthearted words and lively melody. She picked up the tempo and smiled. Philip draped his arm around her waist and sang the next verse.

'If you meet me and I seem a flutter,
Please bear with me for my mind's a clutter.
I'm in love with you and Love I think it's grand.
Further more I think I'm gonna ask for your hand.'

They both shared the gaiety of the song and sang the chorus and last verse in harmony.

'Cuddle closer there's a future we must plan.
Plan and kiss, and think and kiss and dream and kiss again,'

In jest, Philip extended the verse when Priscilla paused between verses.

'And again, and again, and again, and again and again.'

She playfully elbowed him in the ribs and retorted, "be serious you nut and sing it like it's written."

'When we say I do and bells start ringing,
Throw the rice and let the world start singing.
All the things I want begin and end with you.
Hip hooray we've got some planning we must do.'

Philip shouted and raised his arms in emphasis, "Let's hear it once more for planning."
Priscilla took his cue and dashed through the last line again.

'Hip hooray we've got some planning we must do.'

"Oh you nut," exclaimed Priscilla in laughter, "I might know you would have a song for this occasion. It's silly and so are you."
She looked affectionately into his eyes, kissed him on the cheek and said, "but I love you."
He surrounded her in his strong embrace. Their lips met and they shared a moment of bliss. Priscilla found solace in his arms and his nearness cleared her mind of worry and doubt for the present time. They laughed and talked. Later that afternoon, they decided to change the place

of the wedding from the Episcopal Church to her mothers' flower garden. Much of their plan was sure to meet the disapproval of her parents, but Priscilla decided that she would choose the place and order of her wedding. The first climactic fulfillment of her dream of fifteen years ago was to culminate in the very garden where it's meaning was revealed.

Priscilla liked the idea for it was only fitting that she take her vows in the place where she last saw her old friend. In the spot where he released his faith and met his maker, she was about to begin the new life Jonah had foretold.

In the remaining three weeks, Priscilla worked extensively on her exercises and planned along with her mother in last minute wedding preparations. Her legs strengthened but coordination was the primary problem. The last week before the wedding, she began to walk with the aid of braces and crutches. She prayed desperately that she might at least walk without crutches, and she asked God for restoration of the feeling in her legs if she must bear the affliction yet longer. Two days before the wedding, she did walk with only braces. Though she was quite shaky, she would be able to hold her fathers' arm and walk to her husband. She hugged her mother in joy and together they cried in happiness. The following night, the eve of their wedding, Priscilla began to notice some feeling, like a needle prick in her legs. 'What a heavenly irritation' she thought as she praised and thanked God. On the morning of her wedding, she acquired all the feeling in her lower extremities. She would walk in her wedding and she was no longer dead to feeling below her waist.

CHAPTER 23

Whoso finds a wife finds a good thing, and obtains favor of the Lord.

The carriage lunged forward with a start and Priscilla, Elizabeth, Joy and Harold settled into their seats as seven white horses pulled the coach to the flower garden. The coach like every possession owned by the Pomp family boasted a rich tradition. Built in the eighteenth century, it was originally owned by a Marquis in France. Harold's grandfather had bought it while on a business trip to France and shipped it to New York. It was trimmed in polished brass and the interior was lavishly furnished in leather, satin and velvet. It was enclosed and the driver sat on top in front of the coach. Even in the jet age, the little coach presented a stately air as it approached the garden. The idea, though not unique, was necessitated by Priscilla's condition. She wanted to preserve as much of her strength as possible and she preferred to ride to the garden in the coach rather than her fathers' limousine.

In the garden, the Pomp family and friends were seated to the left of the hedge of roses which were situated in the center of the garden. They were dressed in the finest quality designer fashions. Each lady was adorned with an abundance of jewelry with exquisite diamonds, lavish rings and necklaces. An air of pride and arrogance engulfed the setting.

To the right of the roses sat a small group of Philip's friends and the entire nursing staff and all the children. The children were dressed modestly. They were out of place, but in the excitement, which so becomes the young, each sat entranced by the intrigue of this high society wedding. Many of them studied the rich guests across the aisle to their great chagrin.

On the back row Philip, Simeon, the best man, Eddie Leone and Angie Mathews sat impatiently awaiting the arrival of the coach. It was now one o'clock and the coach drew to a halt at the end of the lane leading to the garden. All eyes focused upon the coach and its' occupants.

The driver climbed off his lofty perch and opened the door for the passengers. First he lifted Joy from the coach and seated her in a motorized wheel chair. She fidgeted nervously. Forty kids chattered and pointed when they recognized Joy. All eyes focused on this shy bashful girl.

She wore a white satin gown trimmed in Allecon and Venies lace. It was formal length and she wore white shoes and hose. This was the first time she had worn hose and that pleased her immensely. Her bouquet was of Stephanotis, variegated Holly, white Roses and red miniature Carnations.

Next, Harold emerged from the carriage in a tuxedo and turned to assist Elizabeth. Last of all, Harold and Lars, the driver, assisted Priscilla from the coach. She stepped out struggling to maintain her balance. The bright afternoon sun danced off of her gown of white satin mist trimmed with Allecon and Venise lace with a satin ribbon inserted. The formal length gown had an empire bodice and bishop sleeves. The veil was of matching Allecon lace Camelot cap with a cathedral length veil of silk illusion. Her bouquet was of Stephanotis, variegated Holly, white roses and miniature Carnations. On her face was the pink blush of a new bride. All sensed the rapture of her heart.

Thus the procession started with Joy motoring slowly along the path which Priscilla and Philip would walk. As she proceeded, Joy spread rose petals along the way in which the semi-crippled legs of Priscilla would tread. When she reached the bench, before which Priscilla and Philip would exchange their vows, she wheeled about, turning her wheel chair toward Priscilla.

At this juncture, Simeon and Philip rose and stepped into the aisle, which ran at a forty-degree angle to the bench and Rose hedges. At the opposite end of the garden stood Priscilla, Elizabeth and Harold. Priscilla clung tightly to the arm of her father to her right and her mother to her left. Slowly they began to walk to meet Philip and Simeon, who slowed their normal pace to coincide with the methodical cumbersome pace of

Priscilla. She was valiant indeed, for each step was a mountain of effort. Even the formal length gown couldn't conceal the jerkiness of her step, but it did conceal the unsightly braces. However each step brought with it the cold clank of steel. Though she tried to conceal the arduous labor of this short jaunt, her face revealed that each step was indeed a monumental struggle. The ladies began digging for a handkerchief to dry tears from misty eyes. Very few of the gentlemen could boast a dry eye as well. Philip's heart ached as he observed the snails pace at which his beautiful bride walked and he bit the inside of his lip to hide his dismay.

Half way to the bench was a marble statue of Christ holding a lamb, and at this point Priscilla and her parents paused. Philip also stopped but Elizabeth and Simeon faced each other, met, and she took his arm and continued toward the bench. (They were fourteen steps apart. Each took seven steps toward one another. Elizabeth turned them in the proper direction and served as guide for the remainder of the walk to the bench.) Upon reaching the bench, each took three steps away from the center, turned and faced Philip and Priscilla.

Harold assisted Priscilla two steps to her right to the statue and she leaned her right arm there to steady herself. Harold seated himself quietly on the front row to the left of the rose hedge. At this point, the pianist began to play the introduction to one of the songs Philip had written for the wedding. At the proper queue, Priscilla breathed deeply and poured her soul into the words of the song.

> 'Darling, today I love you,
> Right now I'm so glad you're mine.
> I'm beaming, I'm gleaming, you love me too,
> Right now, this time.'

Next, Philip sang as he peered directly into her blue eyes.

> 'Proclaim to the world I love you,
> Broadcast it I'm glad you're mine.
> I'm delighted, excited you need me too,
> My love divine.'

Together they sang the remainder of the song, as the tenderness of the moment touched their hearts and tears streamed from the wellsprings of their eyes.

'Close by your side when you need me,
Safe in your arms every day,
Pleasing to live cause you'll love me.
Forever, I pray.

Yours though the world may crumble,
Through thick or thin you'll find,
I'll want you, I'll keep you, I'll love you true,
My love divine.'

As the singing ceased and the music ended, an absolute hush had settled over the guests. Philip gazed in ecstasy at his bride in her radiance. Though maimed, she was the most dazzling sight he had ever beheld. He was proud, happy, thrilled and nervous. But most of all, he was deeply in love with this brown haired beauty in braces. The luster of his complexion seemed to radiate his feelings and permeate the being of each person present that afternoon. Here was a man totally and willingly subjected in love to this woman of his dreams.

Priscilla stood likewise entranced momentarily as she looked into Philip's hazel eyes. She saw the tenderness of his heart and a warm glow swept over her. Beneath the nervousness of her groom, she perceived joy and happiness and her heart burned with passion.

She steadied herself for the most precarious segment of the ceremony. She was determined to walk to Philip under her own power. For eight weeks, she had exercised and worked for this hour and she prayed to God silently and summoned all her strength and determination for this important walk of seven steps. She slowly loosed her grip on the pillar and teetered slightly as she maintained equilibrium. Guests looked on in anxiety. The concern of Philip was evident on his face as he took his first step toward her. He wanted ever so much to walk directly to her, but she had made him promise to allow her to walk to him, against the wishes of everyone. Her head bobbed forward and it seemed her entire right side pushed her hip forward. Her face was set with determination as she stepped next with her left foot. Again the same unsightly bob of the head and graceless, uncoordinated jerky movement of the legs, but now she was two steps closer to him. Each step she took brought a sigh of relief from the crowd and a gleam of excitement on Priscilla's face. Three steps, four steps, five steps and then six. Now she stood but one step away from Philip's strong arms. As she started the final step, she lost her balance and teetered backwards to the dismay of all. However, she regained her balance and composure and pulled herself forward as she fell into Philip's waiting arms. Philip breathed a sigh of relief and Priscilla peered lovingly into his eyes and beamed.

Then they turned and walked slowly down the aisle, a distance of fourteen steps, all of which were consciously counted by the guests. As they walked one step at a time, the braces would clank with each step she took. There was no way Priscilla Pomp wouldn't have made it down the aisle that afternoon. Every viewing eye was helping her each step of the way. Her courage moved the guests with compassion and stirred the heart of all present. In spite of the sadness of her condition, Priscilla radiated happiness as they took their final step together and faced each other. She held firmly to his arms and he held to her waist as the piano once more set the tempo for their final song. Philip began the song as he pulled her closer to him.

> 'When I make these vows today,
> I offer you my love always,
> And ever more your place will be,
> Here in my arms forever.'

Priscilla assumed the lead on the next verse.

> 'Darling when I say I do,
> I promise trust and faith in you,
> And by your side I'll always be,
> Here in your arms forever.'

They joined in harmony and finished the song together.

> 'I will always need your love,
> And I'll always want you.
> God looked down and blessed our love.

I'm yours forever.
I'm yours forever.'

A short pause followed the song and a lull fell upon the scene. Then Elizabeth moved to Priscilla's side and extended the red satin pillow on which was the wedding ring for Philip. Priscilla gingerly took the ring and faced Philip as her mother returned to her place. While continuing to hold fast to Philip's arm, she looked into his excited eyes and spoke softly.

"Within the bounds of my weak earthly vessel, I promise to be an unlimited source of love, affection, understanding and hope. But though I be weak of body, yet I shall be strong in spirit, first of all for your sake my husband and second for my own peace of mind. For I can never be happy or find pleasure knowing that you are burdened. I shall be strength in your moment of weakness, joy in your hour of sorrow and peace in your day of affliction. As the moon shining in the dark of night brings light to a dismal evening, so shall I prevail upon your nights of darkness when life casts a dart of trial, woe or despair. Yet as the moon reflects light from an illuminated source, even so my courage shall come from our love and my belief that as one we will overcome all obstacles no matter how great or small. Our love is greater than the two of us as the sun is greater than the moon. Yet of what profit is it if the sun shines for itself? Shall it boast of great things if it has no avenue of expression? It were better that it had never been or shone or even boasted if there was nothing to illuminate. Therefore the sun shines in the night even as in the day. Through the moon does the sun shine upon its subjects who are prisoners of the darkness. The moon through borrowed sunshine lights the earth. Our love shall be my source of strength and it shall be a never failing spring of satisfaction. I shall not fail you when you need solace for our love will wax greater than any test that can be placed upon it. Though my strength is not of myself, yet it is sure. Of a truth I do borrow my strength and reflect that light of our love, which shines upon me. All that really matters is your pleasure and happiness. I will seek to please you in every way I know and we shall dwell in happiness, content all the days of our lives. Philip, this day I pledge my heart, my soul and my life to you. Let the world know that I choose you to be my husband until death do us part. I place my ring upon your finger as a token of my devotion to show the world that we are locked in endless love."

Philip was visibly more nervous that Priscilla. Simeon hobbled to Philip's side and held forth the pillow on which he carried Priscilla's ring. Philip was moved by Priscilla's vows and he feared that he would cry. However, he maintained his composure and spoke in his unpolished manner with the sincerity and humility that were his essential character.

"Before the Most High God and man. I declare that I willfully and joyfully take you Priscilla Pomp to be my wife for the rest of our natural lives. I thank God today for bringing us together, even though it was under the most impossible of circumstances. He has joined us together, and today we align our finite wills with His infinite all knowing will, knowing of a certainty that he is able to keep us together. It is only right that our Lord, who has favored us, should be first to receive praise and glory. He has given you to me and me to you, and in our wedding we lift our spirits in holy devotion to the one and only Living God. My soul leaps within me for I know that He and all the angels in heaven sing songs of joy and praise on our wedding day. But this is only the beginning of blessings we will share together. As we continue to trust in Him, we will reap blessings beyond all imagination and complete satisfaction in this union, which He has ordained. Our house shall stand for All Mighty God forever and we shall rejoice in his Holy Name. Only separation from Him can pull us apart.

Priscilla, God made you in such a way that I couldn't help but love you. I trusted my heart and God's direction all the way to this alter of matrimony. I promise to do all in my power to make each day brighter and each burden lighter. I trust you with my future and all it holds. I entrust you with all the hopes and aspirations I possess because I know that you will be true through all troubles. With you by my side, we can move mountains. You are my earthly hope, my life and my love. How can I be sad with all of these things wrapped up in the person who will be mine forever? The unbroken circle of our God's love has been about us both now and forever more. It is with an unbroken band of gold that I claim you as my own before God and man."

As he finished speaking, his normally strong voice broke in emotion. He drew Priscilla's hand toward him and lovingly placed the ring on her finger. Then he looked tenderly into Priscilla's weeping eyes and they sealed their vows with a warm affectionate kiss.

CHAPTER 24

And when the woman saw that the tree was good for food, and that it was pleasant to the eyes, and a tree to be desired to make one wise, she took of the fruit, and ate, and gave also to her husband: and he ate also.

Philip and the chauffeur assisted Priscilla into the limousine and then climbed into the car to drive to the Pomp estate. The past two weeks of their honeymoon had been grand for Priscilla.

Philip was amazed at every juncture of the European tour. Priscilla found more enjoyment in his reactions than anything else. She had been to Germany and Switzerland three times previously, but Philip, who grew up poor, enjoyed and revered each old cathedral of ancient landmark. She laughed more at her husband than anything else as he awkwardly maneuvered among traditions and customs, which were unfamiliar to him. Even though she laughed, he was good-natured about it. He was simply happy to see her smiling once more. Despite her handicap, they enjoyed themselves immensely and Priscilla found complete happiness in his presence. With the honeymoon over, they were to dine with her parents. Priscilla pondered the immediate future as the car glided along the highway.

"Philip," she began as she reached out to take his hand, "have you been thinking about what we're going to do now that our life returns to normal?"

He thought momentarily before answering.

"Oh I don't know," he replied with a shrug of his shoulders, "I hadn't given it much thought.

Maybe we could both get teaching jobs close to the nursing home and that way we could work with the kids every day."

"Darling don't you think you would be much happier if you pursued a career that would return more to you than you put into it? I mean," she quickly inserted to avoid offending her husband, "the children are wonderful, but we must also consider our future."

"Honey, there you go again, worrying about things that the Lord will take care of. We're always going to eat and as long as we have each other, well, what else could we want?"

Priscilla carefully chose her words as she continued.

"Darling, I know how you feel about God," she began softly, "the children are your work and you feel He needs you in that capacity. Philip, stop and think for a minute. Do you realize how much you could do for God and other children like these if we made it our goal to raise funds for worthy causes?"

Philip was indeed interested in the idea with which his wife tantalized. Priscilla noted the glint of interest in his eyes as he directed his complete attention to her.

"That sounds like a tremendous idea. How could we do it," he asked, "and besides that, what about the kids at Little Angels?"

"The children would not be neglected," she assured him, "that's the beautiful part of this! We could work two or three days a week and still have plenty of time for the children. Think about the thousands of children just like those at Little Angels who would benefit because of our work! Darling, I get excited, just thinking about it!"

She squeezed his hand in excitement but Philip continued to study her as he concentrated.

"How do you propose to raise all this money," he asked. He was skeptical and suspicious that such a plan would not take massive amounts of time from Joy and the children.

"By performing our songs," she responded excitedly.

"Don't say any more," he retorted pointedly, "I don't like it! It's not the kind of life for two people who are in love with each other."

"Darling! Please Philip," Priscilla pleaded, "listen a moment! I know you have seen all the evils in the lives of other musicians, but does that mean that we couldn't be successful if we tried? Surely you don't think that God gave you this musical ability to sit on! Philip there are so many people in need these days and we can help them! I believe the musicians who find misery in their careers are those with no worthy goal for themselves other than self-satisfaction. We have a purpose! We will know the results of accomplishment! Philip, I know beyond a doubt that we can continue your work and assist thousands of others as well if you'll consent to it. If you want, we can try it on a trial basis for three months."

"Priscilla, you make it sound so easy," replied Philip pessimistically, "it takes time to build a following. It requires a lot of work to put a good show together. Where do we find that kind of time and still have time for the kids? Why are you pushing me into this thing? We have already discussed it on the honeymoon! I told you that I've changed my mind about that recording contract. When a booking agent looks at a performer, all he sees is profits. And if you hit the top, they push you even more. Honestly, honey, I think that this is not the way to please God."

"Does it please God to see millions of his children living in poverty every day of their lives," asked Priscilla pointedly, "would it please Him to know that you could have helped many more children and didn't?"

Philip, who was gazing out the window in concentration, was jolted by her blunt statement as his head snapped back to peer into her face. Sensing his anger, she quickly added, "I'm sorry to be so blunt darling, but I believe that you are not giving this enough thought. I truly believe that God has better things in store for you than being a nobody at 'Little Angels Nursing Home.' If that's wrong, then I'm sorry. I can't help but want you to excel and receive all the credit that is due you. Darling, I'm proud to be Mrs. Philip Wright and I want you to be everything that God Himself wants you to be. Please Philip. I'm begging you. Say you will try it for three months. Then if you don't like it, I promise you that we'll quit."

Philip shook his head in dismay. He was unsure of what to do. Priscilla's argument seemed right in itself, but he felt unsure of the results. Despite the rosy picture and grand possibilities, he sensed something shady in the whole thing. Somehow it was bound to lead to heartache. He knew it. However he thought that if that time came, he and Priscilla could quit the business.

"Well, I tell you what," he replied with misgivings, "we'll try it for three months and if it doesn't work out then the heck with it. I'm going to see those kids everyday if it's the last thing I do. I want you to understand that Priscilla, because I ain't guaranteeing anything!"

"Wonderful," exclaimed Priscilla in glee, "Darling it will work out. I just know it will."

"I wish I could share your optimism," said Philip in reply.

"Philip, Mr. Strohmeier will be at mothers to have dinner with us this evening," she said, "and he will further discuss this matter with us tonight."

Philip said nothing, but he was seething inside. Priscilla had planned this all along. If he tried it then he could fulfill his obligation to Priscilla. For the moment, he would wait and see what developed next.

As the limousine turned into the long lane leading up to the Pomp mansion, Harold Pomp and Milt Strohmeier were discussing the recording contract. They had chatted for the better part of an hour and Harold was convinced to invest a sizable sum into the act for promotion. Milt was to act as their manager. He had connections with many influential people in show business and he could work behind the scenes.

"I am most concerned with the possibility that Philip might throw a monkey wrench into the works by refusing to join us in our venture," said Milt in concern, "he really wasn't all that enthused about a career in show business when we last discussed the matter with him."

"Let that be the furthest thought from your mind my dear Strohmeier," replied Harold boldly.

He puffed his cigar and leaned back in his chair.

"Priscilla has assured me that she will persuade him to try it for at least three months," boasted Harold confidently, "You know what that means now don't you old boy. Once we hook him on the finer life and audiences respond to their performances, he'll come along. I'm convinced that all the boy needs is some polish and our Priscilla comes from a family with plenty of that. He'll learn to be our kind of man. Just leave it to Priscilla."

"I certainly hope you're right, Pomp old boy," replied Milt in uncertainty, "There's a bundle of money in this for all of us if we can swing the deal. Believe me Harold, this is the first time in my life that I couldn't convince a man to try to make millions of dollars."

"They're going to be a smash hit Milt," retorted Harold proudly, "no way those kids can fail. I'll sink so much money into that act that it will have to be a success. It's really all about what Priscilla can do with her handicap. She loves music and she can sit while she plays. It's truly good that she married him. He gave her a reason to live when she wanted to die. That's why it's so important that this thing makes it. You must see to it that they get top billing and.............."

The entrance of Philip and Priscilla interrupted him. Philip held her right arm as she hobbled on crippled legs. Harold rose to greet them and he embraced her. Soon after the greetings Harold brought up the subject of music. Milt took his queue and casually mentioned the recording contract. Philip felt hemmed in for he perceived that all minds were intent upon swaying his prior decision. He was somewhat angry, but his deep devotion to Priscilla and his desire for her happiness brought about his concession. For the time being he would try it and hope for Priscilla's sake that it worked out. He still carried a burden for Joy and the other children at the nursing home. He prayed to God that He would provide for his work with his precious little friends.

Milt wasted no time in his quest to promote Philip and Priscilla in the press. He had many influential contacts from years in the business and thus, he was enabled to book their act in the finest clubs. They began with only Friday and Saturday night performances, at Philip's insistence. He refused to work the proposed four-day week, which Milt suggested. Priscilla very wisely stayed in the wings choosing to influence him slowly and carefully. Harold kept his part of the bargain. He purchased the services of a public relations consultant and invested heavily in advertising for each performance.

The combined actions of Philip's song writing ability, Priscilla's arrangement skills, the music promotional and booking contacts of Milt along with the massive infusion of capital from Harold proved to be a steamroller of success to the great pleasure of Priscilla and the disappointment of Philip. Only a month after they signed the contract, their first album was released. In two weeks 'And Then You Happened to me' was number one on the charts. Six weeks later, "I Love You for Just Being You' was released and in just three weeks it also topped the charts. With Success came increased pressure for more personal appearances. Gradually they were working five nights a week and flying back to Utica to see Joy and the other kids the other two days. Philip would spend twelve hours with the children on those two days and Priscilla would rest for the grueling week that lay ahead of them.

Though busy, Priscilla was in her element. The lime light, prestige and success were necessary in colossal quantities to maintain her ego. She was so happy that she failed to comprehend the sadness that more and more filled Philip's days. Even though Priscilla tried to renege on their agreement to give half of their earnings to charity, Philip stood firm on the issue. His only purpose to push them was for the funds, which they raised.

June brought lucrative contracts from Las Vegas. They performed five nights only. Then they returned to Utica to rest for two days. Though Priscilla pleaded with Philip to rest with her, he visited the children. Joy greeted him with a warm smile and a hug when he picked her up from her wheel chair.

"How's my girl today," he shouted in delight, "you look great! Gee, it's good to see you."

"Fine," responded Joy in glee, "I'm a little tired, but I feel fine."

"Tired," inquired Philip playfully, "why on earth would you be tired?"

"I went to bed early," Joy responded seriously, "but I get so excited when you're coming, that I can't sleep."

Philip was cut to the heart by her statement as he squeezed the tender invalid lovingly.

"Yeh, I know what you mean," he replied earnestly, "last night I was thinking about you too."

"Yeh, me too!" she replied looking lovingly into his eyes, "I miss you and Priscilla when you're gone. I wish we could be together all the time like it used to be. It was like a holiday every day! Remember?"

He remembered those days all too well, and he yearned for them again. His soul ached as he considered the plight of these helpless little ones. He must come to them for they couldn't come to him. Joy didn't understand the agony of his heart but she perceived that something was troubling him. He was lost in thought when she placed her palms on his cheeks and turned his head toward herself.

"Don't worry Philip," she said bravely, "I know that our God will take care of it. Just wait and see. Remember how you said to trust God and He will work it all out?"

He smiled but didn't speak for fear of crying. He didn't want to upset Joy, so he simply pulled her to him again and hugged her tenderly. She wrapped her frail arms around his neck and laid her cheek against his.

Angie entered the room carrying one of the children. When she saw Philip, she smiled pleasantly.

"Hi Phil," she said cheerfully, "you can help me round up these ruffians if you will. It's dinner time and most of them are outside playing."

"Be glad to," he replied softly. He welcomed the opportunity to seat Joy so that he could be to himself a short while. He seated Joy and then chased the other children inside. Then he separated himself to the playground and seated himself in a swing. With shoulders slumped and head bowed, he rubbed his face in an effort to relax and ease his tension. Angie, however, noted that he didn't return and saw him sitting alone on the playground. She walked slowly out to him before he was aware of her presence.

"Why so gloomy?" she asked in concern.

Philip quickly wiped his eyes and turned away from her as he rose from the swing. As he spoke, his voice quivered, "Oh…a…I'm just thinking."

"Phil," exclaimed Angie in concern, "what's wrong?"

"I've just been touched by the love of a child. I'll get over it though," he replied. His voice cracked in emotion as he spoke.

"Yes Phil, you will," she responded, "but you're also not telling all the truth."

"What do you mean," asked Philip as he held back his tears.

"You know what I mean," retorted Angie, "you're not happy and we both know it. You're too good hearted for your own good. You're letting Priscilla make your life miserable."

"Well, I wouldn't exactly say that. I…" he said as he was interrupted.

"Philip, you might convince everyone else in this world about that, but don't try to fool me. I know better," she retorted. She was right and he knew it was useless to try to cover it up. She moved around in front of him and pulled out a Kleenex from her pocket. She wiped the tears from his cheeks. He awkwardly tried to pull away, but she firmly held to his arm and held him as if he were one of the children.

"I'm O.K. Angie," he softly protested. He was embarrassed but appreciative of her concern.

She placed her Kleenex back into her pocket and sat on the swing, which he had just vacated. She was quite pleasing to the eye and he studied her baby blue eyes momentarily as she smiled. At the moment, he needed someone to talk to. She seemed so understanding and sensible. She was able to see through the front he had thrown up these past few weeks.

"You know something," he said meekly. He paused a moment before finishing his statement as she studied his eyes seriously, "I like you. You have a head full of sense."

"Don't change the subject," she replied seriously, "Phil, please don't misunderstand my motive. I don't mean to interfere. I just think that it's time that someone told you that you've changed. I mean look at you! You're miserable! You can't go on this way! It's bound to ruin your life if you don't come to grips with this dilemma and turn this situation around."

He seemed to withdraw as he scratched the back of his head. He sighed and stuck his hands in his pockets. When he looked back at her, he loosened up and felt more at ease.

"I know that you're not meddling. I appreciate your concern," he began humbly. As he spoke the humility and sincerity of the old Philip was manifested.

"You've been right on every count," he continued, "but I don't know how to get out of this mess. Priscilla likes show business. She has this desire to be a step above the common man. She can't help it. That's just the way she is. Well anyway, her parents think we're sitting on top of the world. Heck Angie, we ain't doing anything but making money. Sure we're donation fifty percent to charity, but we're neglecting the more important spiritual needs. There are people in this world who don't know what it is to be loved, and here we go traveling around the country when we should be ministering to more important needs. My problem is Priscilla. Her health ain't real good and there isn't much else she can do in her condition. All she has to do is sit behind that piano and sing with me and that's something she enjoys. The doctor said that it's important for her to be content. Lord knows she's had enough trouble these past few months without her own husband pulling the rug out from under her. When you love someone, it's a hard thing to make them unhappy, even when you know it's for their own good. Now, on top of all that, she's pushing herself beyond her physical limit. We're playing five nights a week and flying back home for two days rest, and it's beginning to take its' toll on her. I'm concerned she's going to collapse on the set one of these days, but she won't listen to me. I tell you, it's either agony or worry."

Just talking about his problem had been a tonic in itself. For a moment, silence enveloped them before Angie spoke again.

"You know what you have to do," she replied seriously, "all I know is that things aren't the same with the kids or even the personnel when the two of you are gone. The few days you have for us are so precious. It's important that you be yourself. Even Joy has noticed that you aren't happy like you used to be. You can't hide your true feelings from those who really care."

"Well Angie," he began dejectedly, "I don't know what I'm going to do, but I want to thank you for your concern. I guess the hour of decision is at hand."

Philip stretched forth his hand to assist Angie from the swing as he said, "I guess I've wasted enough of your time. We'd better get inside and see if we can make those kids smile."

Angie bounced from the swing and strolled along with Philip into the nursing home.

"Angie," said Philip as he watched a swallow circle in the sky," how come you and Eddie aren't married? As serious as the two of you are, you should be tying the knot."

"Eddie is in his first year of medical school and at the present time, we can't afford to get married," she replied, and then changed the subject, "while I think about it, there's a new baby in the nursery. She just came in yesterday. You'll just love her."

Angie was glad to change the subject for her relationship with Eddie was not fulfilling her emotional needs. There was something about Philip that compelled one to like him. A man, who could turn a common day into a holiday for little children, could do the same for her. She wondered 'what would it be like to be with him for an evening'. She dismissed the thought from her mind, but she was aware of Philip observing her out of the corner of his eye.

CHAPTER 25

When I am afraid, I will trust in God. In God I have put my trust.

Philip and Priscilla were relaxing in their dressing room between shows. They were the next act and Priscilla nervously fidgeted while Philip very calmly chewed gum and thumbed through a comic book. His nonchalant behavior aggravated his wife as she ran a brush through her hair.

"Philip," she said sarcastically "how can you sit there and read a comic when the show is only a matter of minutes away? When I try to talk to you, you either make some silly remark or ignore me completely! Really, Philip! You pay so little attention to anything I say. I might as well be here by myself."

He looked up and smiled.

"Honey, you worry too much," he quipped, "heck, you're always anticipating trouble that never comes. Why waste time worrying? If it's going to happen it will happen."

"We're playing Las Vegas and you don't think we should be concerned about our performance?" snapped Priscilla. She was working herself into frenzy. She always did that when Philip didn't respond to her comments like she thought he should. He wasn't concerned about it though. It would pass like it always did. He continued reading the comic and blew a bubble, which popped and covered his face.

"Look at you," she exclaimed disgustedly, "heaven help me Philip. I married what I thought was a man! The only time you apply yourself is at the nursing home with the children. I imagine it doesn't deflate a man's ego to be one of only a few men in the midst of all those young women, especially Angie. She likes you Philip and don't you deny it! A woman can see those things."

He laughed and tossed his comic at her playfully.

"Did I ever tell you that you have a suspicious nature?" he asked as he teased, "Honey, she's just a girl. Sure, maybe she does like me but she and Eddie are planning marriage when he graduates from medical school. Since when is there a law against being friendly and enjoying your work?"

"When you begin enjoying it too much," snapped Priscilla angrily, "that's when!"

"Now you see why I don't talk when you're in one of these moods," he complained, "you're always making something out of what I say. You know how I feel about the kids at the nursing home! They need us and we ain't going to let them down for anybody!"

He was beginning to lose his temper and she knew it was time to drop the subject. She knew just how far to push him and she would take him to that point and quickly retreat. He lay back on the couch and stretched out. He was temporarily lost in a daydream when he broke the silence.

"Honey, you should see that new baby in the nursery. She is a little doll! Poor little thing, she cries all the time. You can tell by the way she reacts that she needs affection. Tell you what though; she seems to sense affection when Angie holds her. She still cries, but not as much. It's beautiful to see an unwanted baby receiving love and attention."

"And I suppose that Angie took time out of her busy schedule to show you the baby," snapped Priscilla sharply. She put her brush aside and angrily gazed at her husband.

"Yes," he snapped back, "she showed her to me. Priscilla, I've begged you to come to the nursing home with me. That's the way it started. You came every day like I did. I haven't changed Priscilla! You have! You belong there right along side of me."

There was a rap on the door and a voice said, "You're on in five minutes."

Priscilla scurried from her bench and hobbled on her braces making last minute adjustments to her face and hair. Soon they were on stage and she was seated. When the curtain was raised, both of them smiled cheerfully as if they had never spoken a cross word. Her crossness was, in part, due to being exceptionally tired. Earlier in the day, Philip had mentioned that she see her doctor before going on stage. She merely brushed the suggestion aside since this was the last show of the week. Just before the curtain rose, she had experienced a brief moment of dizziness.

"Is something wrong?" asked Philip in concern, "you looked like you were dizzy."

"Oh it's nothing," she quickly responded, "I'm just somewhat sleepy."

As the curtains lifted the audience roared approval. Each of their performances brought marvelous press and spectacular crowd response. Philip's songs were perfectly attuned to the times and the mood of joyous living. All could identify with their themes. The show was ninety minutes and the first forty minutes went smoothly.

As Priscilla played the introduction to 'And Then You Happened to Me', Philip noticed that her usually impeccable accompaniment was slightly off-beat. He studied her face and noted that she was playing under a strain. Sweat was visible on her forehead. Her usually rosy complexion was now pale white. Sensing problems, he announced, "This will be our last number folks."

Priscilla played as though she didn't hear his announcement and Philip prayed through the entire song that she would hold up through the song. He wanted to spare her embarrassment. As they began the last verse, her accompaniment became worse. It was still good enough that most of the listeners could not detect it.

Meanwhile, her head was spinning and she played by habit only. She felt as though all her strength was gone and she bobbed backwards on the bench several times during the last verse. As the song ended, Philip could see that she was on the brink of collapse. With microphone in hand, he moved behind her and ostensibly lifted her arm to take a bow. His ulterior motive was to prevent her falling off the bench. The curtain fell just in time. As it did she slumped on the keyboard while the piano sounded the notes of discord. Quickly Philip lifted her from the bench and carried her to their dressing room. One of the stagehands appealed for a doctor to come back stage.

For the third time in eighteen months, Priscilla awoke in a hospital. Philip was by her side looking down over her when she regained consciousness. He was smiling and relieved.

"Good morning beautiful," he said tenderly, "how's my little sleeping beauty?"

He took her hand in his and gently squeezed it. She responded with a smile and reached for him. He bent over and pulled her close to him and then laid her back on the pillow.

"How long have I been unconscious," she asked weakly.

"Oh about eight hours or so," he replied gently pinching her cheek.

"This is getting to be a habit darling," she replied softly. She tried to laugh in spite of her headache. She raised her hand to rub her brow as Philip sat on the side of the bed. Priscilla rubbed her brow as if in pain.

"Here honey. Let me do that," he said softly, "does your head hurt?"

"A little bit," she responded, "I suppose you think I'm a lot of trouble don't you. I'm afraid that if I don't regain my strength that you'll trade me in for a new model."

"Well I wouldn't go that far," he drawled in jest, "I have to admit that you do run me ragged around these hospitals, but this old boy still loves you."

"Oh Philip," Priscilla chided weakly, "You're not old."

"No I'm not," he replied with a smile, "but if you don't start listening to your husband when he's right, I'm going to be."

"I know darling," she replied softly, "I am a bit obstinate, but at times like these I realize just how much I need you. Maybe that's why the Lord has chosen to afflict me again."

She was upset and her spirits ebbed at low tide

"Come on honey. Don't be that way. Let's not worry about why this has happened. We can be happy and thankful for all God's tender mercies. It could be worse you know. As it is, rest will cure all your ills. Dr. Stone flew out here to take care of my girl," he said reassuringly.

She wiped the tears from her eyes and replied, "He's such a wonderful doctor Philip. What did he say?"

"Well, he wasn't aware that you were working five nights a week," Philip replied, "You lead him to believe that we were only playing two nights a week."

Priscilla blushed in embarrassment.

But so much for that," he continued, "he stressed that you absolutely must rest for six months.

Then if you have followed his instructions to the letter, you should be able to return to music. That means no work of any kind for three weeks and then only certain activities for the remainder of the six months."

"Oh Philip that's terrible," whimpered Priscilla, "what about our show? Father and Milt have invested so much into it! We must not let it go for naught!"

"As far as I'm concerned, I don't care if we never see the stage again. We've wasted almost a year that we could have been doing good for people who need us," he replied.

"Please Philip," pleaded his wife, "don't talk that way. You must carry on for the two of us! It will only be six months. Then I'll be able to rejoin you."

"Let's not discuss it honey," said Philip softly, "you rest now. This thing will work itself out if we'll look to the Lord. Pray that He might show us His perfect will and then let's do it. That's the only way we can ever be happy. We began with only God on our side and we overcame. That set the precedent for us. We must be committed to continue in the Lord's will if we are to find rest in this life. If we put Him first, then He'll see to it that we will never be apart."

"Darling, I love you," whispered Priscilla as she again reached for his neck and squeezed him, "you always have the right words to strengthen me in my hour of weakness."

"It's the Most High God who is our strength, honey," he replied tenderly, "let's pray together before I leave."

Philip was at the nursing home at eight o'clock sharp the next morning and the children were waiting excitedly for him. Now that Priscilla was back home, he was lavishing the luxury of spending eight hours daily with these neglected little ones, who so loved his company. Happy screaming voices once again echoed through the rustic old structure. Each day Philip would carry Joy outside and swing with her in his lap. The other children would swarm upon his lap and hang on his neck at every opportunity. Philip was content and the children never seemed so happy. Even the staff was more at ease and an air of optimism engulfed the nursing home. Philip was just the tonic that everyone needed.

CHAPTER 26

Who is this who darkens counsel with words without knowledge?

Now a new dimension moved into Philip's life. It came in the form of little Sabrina. The tiny baby whom Angie had grown to love had now captured the affection of Philip. She needed love and affection, even though she was unable to respond to the attention directed her way. She had suffered brain damage during birth and couldn't suck a nipple. She was tube fed for the first few weeks until Angie discovered that she could drink from a medicine cup. Angie possessed the patience necessary to feed the afflicted girl. At six months, Sabrina was fed baby food and milk. Philip and Angie were the only people with the determination and patience to feed her. She wanted only to drink the milk. Philip would give her a spoon full of meat or vegetable and chase it with milk. Only in this way would she eat. Soon she developed a fondness for peaches and pears. Then they would feed a spoon full of meat and chase it with fruit. Last of all she would be given her milk. During these past two weeks, Philip grew especially fond of Sabrina.

"There," said Philip to Sabrina, "that's a good girl. You ate all your food today. And just look at you! You're all hot and sweaty. Why don't you relax and eat like a big girl?"

He held her before himself and looked into her eyes, as she appeared to be indifferent to his words. He pulled her to him and squeezed her then kissed her on the cheek.

"One of these days, you're going to eat and not fuss and then we'll all be surprised," he teased playfully, "here pumpkin! Sit still while I wipe your face."

He began to wipe the food from her face. This was always an ordeal for she would protest vehemently. As she squirmed and tossed her head from side to side, he awkwardly swiped at her jaws and neck. Her screams could be heard all over the nursing home and soon Angie appeared.

"What are you doing to that baby?" she scolded playfully, "What's the matter Sabrina? Is Philip mistreating the little baby?"

She put forth her hands and took her from Philip, squeezing her warmly. Philip noted the maternal touch in the manner in which Angie handled her. Ever so carefully she supported Sabrina's weak neck and back. Philip and Angie both were deeply moved by the needs of Sabrina. Between the two of them, Sabrina was well cared for.

"Hey look how much this little pumpkin ate," said Philip calling her by his pet name, "she cleaned up the whole dish!"

"She did for me too yesterday," exclaimed Angie, "she's been eating real good these past few days. Haven't you Sabrina," said Angie as she held the baby in the air and talked playfully to her. Philip was moved with compassion by the sight of Angie loving the precious angel who had stolen their hearts.

"She is a precious child," replied Philip as he jostled the right arm of Sabrina playfully.

Philip reached for Sabrina and Angie surrendered the precious package to his strong hands. Together, they walked to the playroom discussing Sabrina and laughing about the way she hated having her face washed. He held her while Angie attracted her attention with an inflated toy fish. Sabrina especially liked the fish for it was never more than half inflated and she could easily hold it. After thirty minutes, Sabrina began to fuss again and Philip decided that it was time for her daily walk. Each day he would walk her through the halls and rooms. She was content to be carried for an hour at a time. She loved to watch the other children at play and peer out the windows at the afternoon sky.

Philip turned her so that her back was to him. She sat on his left arm and he held her firmly with his right arm. Sabrina liked this position for she had a good view of all that was before her.

Angie playfully spoke to Sabrina, "is Philip going to take you for a walk?"

She rubbed Sabrina's neck with the smooth side of a hairbrush and she responded with a smile.

"Hey she likes that," said Philip excitedly, "do that again!"

As Angie reached to tickle the baby again, the clank of cold steel distracted then. Priscilla stood in the door to the playroom and she was not pleased by what she had just observed.

"Well............Hello honey," said Philip nervously, "when did you get here?

Priscilla didn't respond to his question but rather replied with a question of her own.

"Is this the baby you've been raving about?" she said trying to hide her jealousy. She moved closer as she wobbled on her braces.

"Let me hold her Darling," she said, emphasizing darling. Though she didn't look at Angie, the remark was directed at her and Angie knew it instantly.

"Well I have work to do so I'd better begin checking temps," said Angie nervously. She exited quickly.

"I was going to walk her for a while," Philip explained to a very cool Priscilla, "she likes to go for walks. Don't you pumpkin. I take her for a walk every day."

"Philip, I'm ready to go home. I'm really quite tired and I think a short nap will revive me," she said pointedly. She handed the baby back to him and turned to leave the room. Philip followed carrying Sabrina.

"Listen honey," he said softly, "why don't you sit here in this chair for a few minutes and I'll take Sabrina for a short walk and then we'll go."

"Philip," protested Priscilla, "you know that I am under doctors orders to rest and modify my activities. I'm tired and I want to go home!"

"Listen Priscilla," replied Philip quietly but in anger, "I'll just be ten minutes. Now I know that you can wait that long. This baby needs love and affection too so try to understand her needs. I know you don't feel good, but in ten minutes we can go home."

She clamed up and shot daggers in her glance at her husband. She wasn't accustomed to playing second fiddle and it didn't set well with her. Rather than make a spectacle of herself, she sat quietly and pouted until he returned for her.

All the way home, Philip received the silent treatment. He could have shrugged that off, but he knew from past experiences that this was merely the calm before the storm. When she finally did begin to talk the fireworks would start. She was upset about Angie, but Philip knew that shortly the lecture would start and his wife would ultimately come back to the issue of their act and her inability to tour with him. After dinner when he was about to excuse himself, Priscilla broke the ice.

"You and Angie appeared to be quite cozy. I'm not sure whether it was you or the baby she was fussing over. I'm beginning to see why you enjoy your daily visit to the nursing home," snapped Priscilla. She was bitterly jealous and sharp in her criticism.

"Come on Priscilla," retorted Philip angrily, "get off my back!"

"Philip, I didn't like what I saw," she snapped back, "nor do I like what I felt when I saw you two together. She's not a girl like you keep assuring me. She's a woman and a very pretty one at that. If she were only pretty, that wouldn't bother me either. But Philip, I know you. She's the type of woman you could fall for. You would never go for a bar fly or a tramp. It would be a woman like Angie; young, pretty, sweet and most of all possessing those essentials that appeal to you most like purity of heart, intelligence and understanding. I must say that she isn't crippled. It certainly must be nice to watch her sway across the floor gracefully. That's one thing you don't see at home."

Priscilla burst out in tears. She buried her face in her napkin and sobbed. Usually this scene brought Philip to her side but today he was disgusted with her accusations. He felt persecuted and he sat coolly in his chair with nothing to say. His calmness only infuriated her more. In a fit of rage she swiped the table and slapped the dishes off on the floor. She stared furiously at her husband at the other end of the table but he sat motionless looking back at her in disgust.

"Have you nothing to say," she demanded in a scream, "or have I been so accurate in my assessment that you are spellbound? It's rather awkward to find the right words to explain your actions is it not my dear husband?"

Philip moved his chair away from the table. He stood and laid his napkin on his plate.

"If you are through honey," he said softly and coldly, "I think I'll excuse myself."

"Oh no Mr. Wright," shouted Priscilla vehemently, "in no way am I through with you! You are taking advantage of everyone who has put trust in you and I think that it's about time you became responsible. Father and Mr. Strohmeier have expended much time and energy to put us where we are today! Our show, our following and all the good will, which we have built, will quickly dissipate if you don't carry the torch while I'm recovering. I've begged you and pleaded with you but you won't listen to reason. You choose instead to play nurse maid to children who don't even know they're in this world!"

Priscilla was hitting home and his muscles tightened in anger but still he said nothing.

"But dare I speak with the noble Philip Wright about this heavenly commitment? One would think that akin to criticizing God himself! Philip Wright, the self appointed guardian of the little angels. You're not so righteous Philip! Who are you trying to fool? I've been content to allow you to act out this myth, but it's time somebody jarred some sense in your head! You don't want to sing for a living. We haven't worked for twelve weeks now and we are down to our last few dollars. We're not going to father for a hand out! You said that God would provide for us but you're not earning a living by volunteering at the nursing home. You're a fool Philip! A dreamer! A lost little boy who failed to grow up. It's time you acted like a man! You don't want to work Philip. That's your biggest trouble. You putter around that nursing home and waste days on end and think nothing of it. You're lazy! I haven't seen you do a days' work since I've known you!" she concluded.

She had added insult and humiliation to her anger and this added weight on his spirit brought a response to her accusations. He walked slowly toward her and lifted a trembling finger in her face. Priscilla shuddered for she had never seen him so upset. He trembled as he spoke.

"All right Priscilla," he began with voice shivering, "I'll do it! But I'm still going to save time for these children, and you're going to help me and fill in for me while I work on without you. There are some things you can do around the nursing home even if it's only to visit and chat with the kids. I'm going to get Simeon to help me, and we'll put together a group. I hate this! I hate this! I love you Priscilla, but I hate the emptiness of road life!"

He turned on his heel and stomped out of the room. Priscilla sat in deep concentration, considering the events of the past few minutes. At last he would be aggressive. She had been hard on him, but it would be worth it. At last her husband would excel on his own initiative and she could point with pride to his accomplishments. He would be the envy of all who had poked fun at him.

CHAPTER 27

And I looked for a man among them who would make up the hedge and stand in the gap before me for the land, that I should not destroy it: but I found none.

"Simeon it's going to be like old times." said Philip happily, "me singing and playing the guitar and you pecking on the ivories. I've just begun to write some new songs and we'll work on a couple of them tomorrow when we get together for practice."

"Who is going to play base and lead guitar," asked Simeon.

"Well, I've decided to hire Vali Bourbon to play lead. She has always been good with that group she plays with," replied Philip seriously.

"A woman," queried Simeon in disbelief, "we're going to have a woman in the band? How do you expect Priscilla to react to that?"

Philip laughed at his friend and replied, "It might do her some good. Heck, I've humored that woman for two years and it hasn't done a bit of good. Maybe a little aggravation will stimulate her and bring her to her senses. Heck Simeon we're going to hire Rose Nottingham to play base."

Simeon was baffled as he said, "It appears to me that you've thrown caution to the wind. It wouldn't surprise me if Priscilla throws this right back in your lap!"

"You let me take care of Priscilla," responded Philip confidently, "she insisted that I return to show business. I'm hoping that she will do exactly that so I can quit. Now if I can get Angie to sing lead on some of the songs and harmonize with me on a few others that will be good."

"I didn't know that Angie could sing," interjected Simeon, "you know she's Eddies fiancé. You know how jealous Eddie is. Why would you jeopardize a good friendship?"

"Oh Simeon," replied Philip laying his hand on the shoulder of his friend, "don't worry about it. Priscilla will balk when she sees the women in the group and delay it until she can join me and we can continue as before."

"Philip, I've never known you to think this way," replied Simeon in concern, "this isn't like you! I'd advise a more honest approach."

"Simeon, you worry too much," said Philip poking his hands into his pockets.

The phone rang and Philip answered it.

"Angie!" he exclaimed, "I see you got my message. How's Sabrina? Well I'll be there in about three hours. What did you decide about my offer? Will you sing with us?"

His face dropped, his jaw set and concern gripped his countenance.

"You're sure you won't reconsider," he said dejectedly, "well it's a shame, but if you change your mind, let me know."

"Looks like you lose your ace in the hole already," Simeon suggested as Philip hung up the phone.

"Well," mumbled Philip, "I may be stuck that's for sure, but I can still reduce our concerts to a maximum of three each week."

"That evening and four nights of each of the next three weeks, Philip practiced with his new band. They worked through four different songs that he had written. On the eve of his first anniversary, they recorded the songs. Priscilla played keyboards in the recording session. Milt Strohmeier didn't like the songs and was very pessimistic. Philip convinced Harold, that the songs were the latest rage and sure to be accepted by the young record buying public. He launched two records with four of the worst songs ever recorded. Thus phase one of his plan went into operation. Without a doubt this colossal failure would label him as a flop and he would happily submit to a role of obscurity. At last he could work with the children who needed him so desperately. With satisfaction he gave himself a mental pat on the back. A few short days and he would be free forever from this curse of success.

Philip returned from the nursing home to find Priscilla smiling and exuberant. She had set the table with candles and her special china. She wore his favorite dress and placed a green satin ribbon in her hair. Her dress was full length of silk with an orange print carnation pattern. It had an empire bodice and silk sleeves. Priscilla especially preferred long dresses for they covered her braces. Philip was always receptive to her long dresses. He said that she excited him when she wore a long dress.

She welcomed him home with a kiss and sat beside him on the love seat. Despite his sour disposition, she forced the conversation and picked it up again and again when the conversation died. Through their meal she joked with him and pushed aside his suggestion to turn on the lights so that they could see to eat. Then she gave him his present for their anniversary. It was a costume for his newly formed group. This only depressed him more. At last Priscilla could withhold her feelings no longer, and she vented her confusion to her husband.

"Philip," she said in a note of anguish, "what's wrong with you tonight? Don't you know what today is?"

She appealed to her husband with all the anguish in her pining soul. Disappointment and sorrow displayed themselves in her blue eyes.

"Yes honey," he replied dejectedly, "today is our anniversary, but I forgot to get you a gift".

He saw the disbelief and shock in her face and the question in her eyes.

"I mean not something you can see," he added meekly.

"Oh Philip! How could you?" she complained, "our first anniversary and you forget to get a gift. Doesn't this day mean anything to you?"

She dabbed her face with her napkin and sought to control her disappointment.

"You've been an absolute bore all evening," she complained, "this is supposed to be a day of celebration, but you've turned it into a day of mourning."

She burst into tears and turned away from Philip.

"Oh Philip! You've ruined the whole day," she sobbed as she buried her face in her napkin.

"Honey, I'm sorry," pleaded Philip as he rose to console her, "I didn't mean to upset you."

She tried to stand and stumbled but Philip caught her in his arms.

"Honey. Listen to me. Please," he pleaded.

"It's too late Philip," she sobbed, "the whole evening is a total flop."

"Priscilla you have to listen to me," he said softly, "I didn't forget our anniversary. I was just moody that's all. I've been thinking about us all day. That's why I'm so out of sorts. I've been thinking what a lousy husband I've been all year and trying to find the words to express my feelings."

Priscilla calmed herself. She sniffled and wiped her cheeks as he continued.

"This has been a trying year for us," he continued softly, "We've had much success, but we haven't been very happy in the process. Honey, we're pursuing the wrong goals. I'm being forced to do things that are not pleasant for me. I feel that my place is working with handicapped kids. All I ask for is you and a place for us to be at peace with the Most High God."

He turned her so that she faced him and clutched her arms lovingly. He looked down upon her face but she continued to avoid eye contact with him.

"We had all kinds of plans a year ago but they've all been set aside for money and prestige. I wanted so much for you to be walking by now, but our concerts take so much of your energy that when we aren't busy, you're too tired for your therapy. I honestly believe that you would be walking today if not for the strain and tension of the music business. It makes me sad to see you hobbling around because we didn't invest our time wisely."

Priscilla was moved with tenderness by his honesty and concern as she lovingly peered into his eyes. She laid her head on his shoulder and slipped her arms around her his neck.

"Philip, those exercises are so bothersome and boring," she complained, "it seems like I work myself weary for nothing! You don't know how discouraging it is to try and pray with all your heart and soul and never see progress. I've tried to believe like you said, but it's no use. It's hopeless. I'll never walk again," she sobbed.

"Now listen to me Priscilla," Philip snapped with understanding and firmness, "I've heard about all of that kind of talk I want to hear. You are going to walk again honey! You must believe that! Priscilla, one of these days I'm going to come looking for you. You're going to be in your mothers' flower garden, hidden behind the lilac bushes. I'm going to come running down the lane from your mothers' house and I'll call your name. Then you're going to step out from behind the lilac bushes and say 'Philip' and walk without those braces into my waiting arms. And we're both going to praise God for His wondrous mercies to us," whispered Philip, his voice cracking with emotion. He squeezed his precious wife tenderly.

"Oh Philip! I wish I could believe that," she replied wistfully, "but I can be happy my entire lifetime as a cripple as long as I am yours and you are mine."

"Honey, I do have a gift for you," he whispered tenderly, "it's a song I wrote about us. Maybe I can say in song what I feel in my soul."

He carefully picked up his wife and carried her to the piano where he seated her on the bench.

He then sat on the end of the bench.

Priscilla smiled and said, "There isn't as much room on this bench as there once was. I'm sure that I must begin another diet."

"I'm not complaining am I? As a matter of fact, I like the proportion and distribution just like it is," he said in lighthearted jest.

"You're a nut," replied Priscilla in fun, "now am I going to hear a song or must I per chance wait until another day?"

"Well I have to catch my breath you know," he said as he took a deep breath.

"And you say that I haven't gained weight!" prodded Priscilla playfully, "you didn't puff and wheeze when you carried me across the thresh hold."

It's the braces dear," he shot back playfully, "it has to be the braces. Now if you will remain silent for a few moments, I'll sing this song for you."

Priscilla, exercising her marvelous sight-reading ability, played the introduction and he began to sing softly and with affection the song 'Yes I Do'.

> 'Do you feel contented just knowing I'm near,
> Well everything's better just having you here.
> I cherish the privilege of sharing with you,
> A love sent from heaven, yes I do.
>
> Yes I do, I love you, with all of my heart.
> I try to remind you I still feel the spark.
> And darling I tingle when I'm holding you.
> I love you forever yes I do.'

Priscilla played a musical interlude as Philip began a recitation.

'I wake up each morning with you by my side. Each day's sea of misery comes forth as the tide. But you are the sunshine that brightens my day, that breaks up my misery and drives it away. I can't explain dear how you make me a man. Your loves gives me meaning. Your trust helps me stand. I know that God loves me. His wisdom is true. He gave me His love and He gave me you.'

She stopped playing as Philip turned to Priscilla and took her hands in his. He sang the last verse without accompaniment as his wife, moved with passion, listened intently.

'Do you see the wisdom of love in God's plan,
A life in its' fullness intended for man.
Each day you're a blessing, each day I renew,
Our covenant of love, yes I do.

Yes I do, I love you with all of my heart.
I try to remind you I still feel the spark.
And darling I tingle when I'm holding you.
I love you forever, yes I do.
I love you forever, yes I do.'

As the last word of the song resounded in his throat, Priscilla surrendered her lips to him and he kissed her passionately. Locked in a warm embrace, their hearts resounded in love. The hour had blessed them with a perfect anniversary gift. It was the renewal of their marriage.

"Oh Philip," Priscilla sighed tenderly, "you've made me the happiest woman in the world tonight. You've given me the perfect gift that my soul has longed for. Tonight you have given me new hope, a sure prayer and your love. Darling I love you with all of my heart."

CHAPTER 28

Truly God is good to us, even to such as are of a clean heart. But as for me, my feet were almost gone; my steps had well nigh slipped.

It was now two weeks after the release of the first single of the new group, the Keepers of the Flock. Simeon was a dinner guest at the home of Philip and Priscilla. They were discussing the new records, but Priscilla was doing most of the talking. Philip felt very tense throughout the conversation. His conscience was taxed at the remembrance of his underhanded tactics. His wife was enthused about the chances of the release being a hit record. He noticed that even Simeon answered with indirect responses. Simeon knew that the chances of either record being a success were next to nonexistent.

"Philip, darling," began Priscilla gaily, for she was exceptionally light hearted, "you've said very little about the new releases. I should think that you would be full of expectation."

She smiled and studied his countenance as he squirmed in his chair.

"Would you please pass the bread?" he said, forcing a grin?

"There's really no way of telling Priscilla," interjected Simeon seriously, "it remains to be seen if the teen age set will take to the new up tempo music."

"Yes that's what Milt said as well," replied Priscilla, "these songs must make an impression with the youth."

She smiled and looked at her husband with pride and continued, "I'm sure that Philip can sweep those unsuspecting girls off their feet. I should know. He did quite a job on me."

She pinched him playfully on the cheek and said in jest to Simeon, "do you know that he seized my heart before I was really aware it was happening. Actually, he captivated me quite against my will."

She reached out and squeezed his arm affectionately. She was seeking a response but her embarrassed husband was at a loss for words. The phone rang at that moment relieving him at least temporarily of that obligation. The butler answered the phone and entered the room.

"Excuse me," he said politely, "your father wishes to speak with you Priscilla. Would you like to take it at the dinner table?"

"Why that would be a delightful idea Radford," she said joyfully.

She took the phone and said, "Hello father. This is a pleasant surprise. Are you at home?"

She listened for a moment and her eyes began to widen and a gaze of awe and great delight spread over her face. Her mouth gaped wide open as she exploded in excitement.

"Oh father!" she squealed in glee, "that's wonderful! We've just been discussing the new recording. Oh, I can hardly wait to tell Philip! Wait father! Hold on a moment while I tell Philip!"

She leaned excitedly into the face of her husband and squeezed his arm in excitement.

"Oh darling," she gasped in elation, "that goofy song you wrote has sold six hundred thousand copies already and orders are coming in from all over the country. The kids have flipped over that 'Wazzle, Bazzle, Dazzle' or whatever it is. Isn't that wonderful?"

She began to converse with her father in great excitement. Meanwhile Philip was stricken with unbelief. He sat gazing blindly across the table at Simeon.

"Oh darling! Isn't this just divine?" she exclaimed.

"I don't believe it," he said as he pushed his fingers through his wavy hair, "There must be a mistake."

"No Philip," she replied happily, "father and mother are coming over here now and we're going out on the town tonight to celebrate. Oh, isn't this exciting honey?"

Philip raved in disbelief and aggravation, "This can't be real! No way can that song be a hit!

I mean 'Vazzle, Bazzle Wazzle Dazzle', how can that be a hit. Better songs are written on bathroom walls."

He jumped up and stomped back and forth across the floor.

Priscilla was bewildered and said, "Philip! What can possibly be wrong? I have just uttered inspiring words of blessing and you act as though we've been condemned to a cruel punishment. Really Philip! I should think that you would be overjoyed. What does it matter if the song is horrible? It's selling and climbing the charts. Isn't that what it's all about?"

He stammered as he sought for the proper words in confusion and said, "Well…a…honey. It's…a…I just find it hard to believe that song would sell."

"Well then," interjected Priscilla, "if that's all that bothers you, smile. Be happy! God has again favored us with His grace."

Yeh…a…It is a great thing at that," Philip replied still in shock, "Isn't it Simeon. Looks like we get to hit the road again to promote the new music."

His voice contained a bit of question but in her excitement, Priscilla failed to notice. At heart he was numb with agony. Emptiness filled his stomach. However, true to his good nature, he hid his disgust from Priscilla and pretended to be happy. Still the thought of the children at the nursing home haunted him and his face revealed that his mind was not with his company.

"Oh Philip, I'm so glad you're taking this so well," she said happily, "I've been so troubled by your reluctance to accept responsibility. I guess I always knew that you wouldn't fail me. Philip I'm so proud of you! You're uncanny! We're about to become a member of the hit a month club. I just know it. We'll be a dominant force in the music business again! Philip I'm so happy!"

She extended her arms to him, which meant that she wanted him to come to her. He drew near to her, lifted her from her chair and kissed her.

"Well Simeon my friend," he said as he rallied his spirits, "I guess we have much touring to do."

"I suppose that we can do just about anything that we set our minds to," Simeon replied with a smile. He wasn't fooled though. He sensed the reluctance of Philip. He would discuss it later with his friend.

"Which brings me to my eternal concern," Philip said in concern, "what about my little pumpkins at the nursing home? You know my babies have grown accustomed to seeing me on a daily basis for these past few months. It doesn't seem right to go traveling across the country and neglect them."

"Darling you're wonderful," replied his wife cheerfully, "you're always thinking of others. If you'll take care of the music for me, I'll take care of your visitations for you. Fair enough?" she asked as she looked into the eyes of her husband.

"Fair enough," replied Philip with a grin as he affectionately hugged his lovely spouse, "even if you only visit one hour each day, it means a lot those kids. Heck honey, you might even find it to be good therapy."

"There's the door darling," interrupted Priscilla, "that must be father and mother. Simeon would you honor us with your company tonight? We're about to celebrate this gala occasion."

"I'd be delighted Priscilla," Simeon replied sincerely, "it's always nice to share good times" His voice trailed off as he finished his statement. He made it explicitly for Priscilla. It wasn't spoken with real enthusiasm. Today, however, Priscilla didn't notice the pseudo-happiness of her husband and his friend. She was too wrapped up in the excitement of the moment to notice.

Across town, Angie was conversing with her fiancé Eddie Leone. They only saw each other on semester breaks or holidays. Between visits, Angie spent her time waiting for the phone to ring or looking daily for a letter. Consequently she experienced emotional swings of depression and anxiety. After a call, she was exhilarated for two or three days. Then her spirits would sag until the next letter or phone call. Only her great love for him kept their relationship alive. Soon, she told her self repeatedly, this would be over and they could be married. Her spirits leaped this evening when she heard his voice on the phone. Eddie however was tense tonight.

"Eddie, what's wrong," asked Angie in concern.

"Well, it must be this grind. Day after day, I study and prepare for an endless barrage of tests. I'm tired of waiting honey. I want you and my degree now, but that's impossible," he complained.

"Eddie you mustn't be depressed," she replied earnestly, "in one more year, you'll have your degree and you can begin your residency. Then we can get married. I'd like to be with you too, but it just isn't possible."

"I've been tempted to drop out of school and begin playing music again. Remember when Philip and I played together? Those were the good old days," sighed Eddie as he recalled fond memories of carefree days gone by, "Maybe after this semester, I'll drop out of college for a year and join Philip and his band. Now that he married that teacher with all the money, he should be able to help his old friend."

"Eddie! Don't be foolish," scolded Angie, "music isn't the career for you. Philip and his wife have had nothing but trouble and disappointment over music. Philip hates it! Now she's pushed him back into it again and if I see the signs correctly, they will both pay before it's over. That's why I turned down the job offer Philip made to me!"

"Philip offered you a singing job," he asked in astonishment, "why did you turn it down? Angie! That's the solution to our problem! You could make a bundle on that job and we could be married next June."

"But Eddie," stammered Angie.

Eddie interrupted her, "think about it Angie," he said excitedly, "you could make enough in six months to carry us through my last year of school. Angie! Our golden opportunity went down the drain! Hey! Is there any possibility that you could still get that job?"

"Well," she replied reluctantly, "I might be able to get the job, but I don't feel that the easy way is always the best way."

"Angie, you're not making any sense," protested Eddie, "never look a gift horse in the mouth! This is the answer to all our problems."

"But Eddie," she replied anxiously, "I don't feel right about this. There are dangers involved."

She was thinking about her feelings for Philip. The void in Philip's marriage, the constant depression she experienced being away from Eddie and their mutual understanding for each other, might be more temptation than they could endure. It was definitely best to stay away from Philip. At present their relationship was a good friendship and it was best to keep it that way.

"Danger? What are you talking about," demanded Eddie, "what possible danger could be involved in singing with a group?"

"Well," she replied, "you know how night clubs are. There's always a drunk who thinks he's Gods gift to women. It's just too much worry!"

She couldn't possibly tell him the real concern. Nervously she listened as Eddie pleaded.

"Listen honey," he said softly, "we're both being too emotional about this thing. Maybe you're right after all."

She breathed a sigh of relief and sat in a chair beside the phone.

"But listen honey", Eddie continued persuasively, "Why don't you at least give it a try? That would be enough time for you to decide intelligently. Doesn't that make more sense than turning down several thousand dollars, which we desperately need, just because you think it isn't wise."

"Eddie, please," she pleaded, "don't…"

"Wait a minute now," he interrupted, "I'm not through. Angie, I'm begging you to give this a try. Trust me. I know that you'll see that it's right. It's for us that you're doing this. Come on honey. Say you'll do it for us. Will you please?"

"Oh Eddie," replied Angie nervously, "I'm so unsure. I know you believe that you're right, but I still…"

"Listen doll," he pleaded, "would I do anything I thought would hurt you? Give it a try! Eight weeks! Then if you're not convinced it is the right thing to do, quit. O.K.?"

She sighed and succumbed to his will.

"All right Eddie," she said submissively, "I'll do it. I think I can still get the job."

""Great! Good thinking!" Eddie said enthusiastically, "Six short months and we'll be together forever. You won't be sorry honey. Wait and see."

The operator cut into the conversation to charge for more time.

"Honey, I'm out of change," he said quickly "call me this weekend. Bye."

"Good bye," she replied hastily.

As she hung up the phone, she pondered the decision, which Eddie persuaded her to make. She was apprehensive. She had deep feelings for Philip and the only barrier was his marriage. She shuttered to think of the way Philip had of consoling her. He understood her so perfectly. He was more perceptive to her needs than Eddie! He was also fun to be with. She tried to avoid him at work for that reason, yet somehow, in spite of all her efforts, they would meet in the hall and the mere sound of his voice would excite her.

'Oh Eddie' she thought, 'if only you knew the danger involved. If you did, you would never forgive me for these feelings, which I can't control. For our sake, I'll try and pray that it works.'

CHAPTER 29

Lust not after her beauty in your heart; neither let her take you with her eyes.

Philip began a tour across the country that was to take him to thirty-three different cities in the next fourteen weeks. They scheduled two national television appearances also. 'The Keepers of the Flock' had become a household name among the teenage set. The group featured something for everyone. For the men, there were three lavishing blondes, who danced in addition to singing harmony with Philip. Philip was a favorite with the young women. He allowed his hair to grow to just cover his ears. His hair was wavy and it lay perfectly in place. The once drab looking clod was now bold on the stage. His costumes were flashy and brilliant. His trademark was white shoes. He was now a bobbing, weaving light footed dynamo that thrilled and excited the young screaming girls. His strong yet soothing voice and suave manner quickly propelled him to the number one attraction in the country. Milt Strohmeier and Harold Pomp were pleased beyond description, for now the same young man who once complained about excessive bookings was suddenly willing to perform seven days a week. His song writing ability continued to turn out hit after hit. At the time of his return home, he had four hits in the top twenty, one of which was number one; 'Let Me Love You'. Success had come to him in a spectacular way, and it began to show in his everyday life.

Though the world had turned on to Philip, he was greeted in a change of pace upon his next visit to the nursing home. Few of the children paid more than token attention to him. They looked to Priscilla in the same way they once admired him. Even Joy didn't respond to him as she once had. She still loved him dearly, but he was now second to his wife in the little girls' heart. For one who had become so vain, this turn of events was a smashing blow to his ego. As he watched his crippled wife play with the children, he was enraged with jealousy and moped around the playground in despondence.

"This is getting to be a habit," said Angie softly. She had seen him slip out and seized the opportunity to speak with him. She had missed him. The three-month separation from Eddie left her hungry for companionship. Seeing him Phil every day at the nursing home was pleasant and she had come to depend upon his words of encouragement and cheer. Since he understood her, she always felt at ease in his presence. Her emotions were on edge due to the displeasure of Eddie with her failure to discuss the singing job with Philip before the tour began. All he talked about was 'the money she let slip through her hands.' The emptiness and frustration of these past few months had dulled the fear that once prevented her from putting forth her hand.

Philip turned to face her and he unfolded his arms to reach for Sabrina whom Angie carried. A glow returned to his eyes as Sabrina smiled and reached for him.

"Well," he said in response to the warm reception, "at least someone missed me."

As he spoke he searched her eyes for a response to his comment.

"Two somebody's missed you," she replied as she blushed and smiled as she placed the baby in his arms.

"I wish that I could believe that," he replied nervously. He continued to search her eyes for a sign of feeling. He sensed her nervousness and anxiety for she was as uneasy as he. With Priscilla and the staff a few feet away, neither one of then was free to express their complete feelings so they spoke quietly, as if the whole world was listening.

"There are a many things that would be different if you weren't already married," she said in a whisper. As she spoke, the tension of the moment rendered her short of breath.

"Yeh. I feel that way too," he replied softly, "my wife is a good woman, and I love her dearly, but you do move me. It's so easy and comforting to talk with you. Let's be grateful for the friendship we have and make the most of it. It's one of the few things I can be truly happy about.

I really despise the travel. Success has made a slave of me. When I'm here at this little nursing home, I am at peace and content."

"It's hard to imagine that you, the golden boy, who turns melodies and lyrics into riches, could be so low in spirit," Angie said as she shook her head in sympathy.

"It's become a way of life for me," he said sadly, "a few songs and a brief moment of excitement on stage sandwiched between the drudgery of travel and rehearsals. I've gotten so used to it, that I've forgotten how to have fun. But, I have to think of my career," he said in mockery and disgust.

He squeezed Sabrina close to himself as he gently kissed her on the cheek.

"Thank God this little one is too young to understand the sadness that has gripped our lives," he concluded as he patted the baby lovingly on her back.

"Why do you sing if it makes you that unhappy?" asked Angie.

"Are you kidding," he retorted sarcastically, "I'm a star! I have an obligation to my fans, like those girls and young women who scream when I sing. Sometimes I think the world is going mad. The police and security guards hold back screaming crowds and they push and shove like animals to get a glimpse of me. You'd think that I was God or one of the angels come down from heaven to bless them. 'I touched him' one of them will scream. 'Oh! I think I'd die if I touched him' says another. It gets down right sickening. Sometimes, I think that I'll vomit over this whole mess. Then you get on stage, and you smile and dance around a little and they get hysterical. Honestly, I feel like a king out there. Then the show ends and the trip is over. When you get right down to it, none of those people really care about me. They just come to have something to talk about. It's a thankless business. It's all one big farce."

"You're being well paid for this folly," replied Angie with a raised eyebrow.

"Not well enough, actually. When you consider that I'm laying my soul on the line for a few screams, a handful of headlines and all the money that I can spend. Even that's a pittance when you consider that all of if is worthless in the life to come. I guess that makes me the biggest fool of all," he sighed.

"Join the crowd," responded Angie with a shrug of her shoulders, "it seems that we never can have the things we desire most. There's always a barrier of unseen hurdles before us. You're unhappy. Well, join the world."

"The problem with the world is that people sit around and wish for their dreams to seek them out instead of making them happen. Either they do that or they do like you and cling to a hope that may or may not materialize," said Philip frankly.

"What do you mean," she asked.

"You know what I mean," he replied as he sat in a chair, "ever since I've known you, you've been hanging on to he hope that you and Eddie would one day marry. You're often on the top of the mountain of happiness but more likely you're in the valley of despair, trying to hide it from your friends."

Angie was shocked at is bluntness, but before she could deny his statement, he continued.

"Don't deny it Angie," he said, "we both know that I'm correct. Right now, there's something that you want just as much as I, but your fear and this obsession to wait for a tomorrow that may never come is robbing both of us of the happiness that is rightfully ours."

"Phil, I don't deny that what you say is true," she replied nervously and in a whisper, "but it won't work. It just isn't right."

"Angie, you're right. It isn't right," agreed Philip anxiously, "but it's real! I'm not imagining this warmth between us. You don't know how many nights I've laid awake at night and pictured your face. You can't comprehend the satisfaction I feel when you're near. We're such fools! What are we waiting for? Angie, I hunger and thirst for your companionship and love. I'd like to see you tonight."

His heart was pounding and his breathing was heavy.

"Phil," exclaimed Angie quietly, "I know how you feel, but we can't do this. What about Eddie and Priscilla?"

"What about them," retorted Philip anxiously, "they don't have to ever find out!"

"What about us," asked Angie excitedly, "how could we ever hide our feelings for each other?

I find it hard enough to hide them now!"

"Angie, I'm willing to do whatever it takes to be with you," whispered Philip.

"Phil, this is horrible," exclaimed Angie emotionally, "I don't want to talk about this! It is too upsetting."

"Angie, I want you and you want me," he replied seriously, "this thing has already happened in our hearts. It's just a matter of time. All we can do is delay the happening of it."

"Please Phil," she exclaimed, "Stop it! I won't let this happen. Too many people will get hurt!"

"O. K. Angie," he conceded, "we won't discuss it any more. If we ever discuss this again, you will bring it up."

"I'd better get back to work before I'm missed," she said as she turned to leave. She walked quickly back to the nursing home and closed the door. She could feel his piercing gaze upon her back as he watched her every step. She was trembling in nervousness. The authority with which he spoke shook her soul. She prayed that he wasn't right. However the future developed, now was definitely not the time. She didn't dare avoid him completely, for she knew that she would need his understanding again when Eddie failed to call or they had another argument. Then she would turn to Phil like she always did and he would be there as always when she needed him.

Then she remembered that she wanted to discuss the singing job with Phil. She knew that he would be receptive to the idea. She paused momentarily to ponder the situation and decided that now would be as good a time as any to discuss it with him. At least when she called Eddie tonight, he would be pleased. She marched back out to the playground where Phil was carrying Sabrina and talking playfully to her. He stopped and watched her advance toward him.

"Phil, I was intending to discuss something with you, but I was so flustered that I forgot about it," Angie said bashfully.

"I guess I was insistent at that," agreed Philip apologetically, "I'm sorry. I get all worked up when I feel as strongly as I do now."

"Oh it's all right," she replied warmly. She had been extremely upset only moments before, but the sound of his voice had put her at ease instantly. There was no way she could stay upset at him.

"I wanted to tell you that I would be interested in singing with your group if there was still an opening."

She felt uneasy as he peered intently into her flushed face. He was infatuated with her. She moved him and she knew it. She liked that.

"Angie, you excite me," he said softly, "do you know that? I'm not ashamed of it either. I had almost forgotten what it was like to be thrilled over a woman. It's wonderful!"

He noticed that she was nervous again so he bit his lip and smiled as he answered, "I'd be so delighted to have you Angie. I've just written three songs that require a female lead."

"When do you want me to start," she answered excitedly.

"Start tonight," he replied, "We have a band practice at my place at seven. We'll work on a few new numbers that you can sing."

Priscilla had walked up unexpectedly and she overheard his final comments. Angie turned to leave and stopped with a start as Priscilla stood directly before her. Without a word, she stepped around Priscilla and walked directly back into the nursing home. Priscilla stood with arms folded and a definite look of displeasure.

"What, my dear husband was that all about," she asked sarcastically, "this is becoming a habit with you and Angie."

Philip casually smiled at his wife. Priscilla was livid with anger.

"Angie is going to sing with the group. She's going to sing lead on some songs and she'll sing harmony with me on others. Don't look so shocked! She'll be a great addition to the band."

"For you or the public," snapped Priscilla angrily, "she has no experience. She's an added expense and she won't justify that expenditure with her CONTRIBUTION to the group!"

"Oh yes she will! I'll see to it," retorted Philip as he brushed some dirt off of his white shoes, "that she'll be a tremendous asset to the group. I've got some songs that she can sing and she has an excellent voice."

"Vali Bourbon can sing better," interrupted Priscilla, "and you know it!"

He leaped to his feet angrily.

So what," he shouted, "what do I care if she can sing better? I'm running this show and I want Angie to do the singing!"

"You said it Philip," retorted Priscilla fiercely, "YOU want her in the group! I know it, you know it and Angie knows it. That's why I refuse to allow this to happen! Angie WILL NOT be singing in the group and that's not a request; that's a demand!"

Philip walked directly to his wife and stopped three feet in front of her. He lifted his right index finger and launched into a tirade.

"I've listened to your demands for two and a half years now. Since we started dating, you've been such a demanding soul. Well I've had it Priscilla! It's my turn to make a few demands and I demand that Angie stays, and that's final! This is my show, and we've had phenomenal success under my direction. When I need your advice, I'll ask for it!"

"Philip, you can't talk to me like that," she shouted defiantly, "I will not stand for it!"

"I'll talk to you any way I please," he retorted bitterly, "I've been hen pecked ever since we got married, but not any more my sweet. From this day forth, I'm my own man! I'll do as I please!"

"Well," snapped Priscilla vehemently, "then you can find someone else to watch after your beloved nursing home. I've watched over it so that you could sing and travel, but if you don't need my opinions, then certainly you don't need my help!"

"The nursing home! That's a joke," he laughed, "you don't think that's going to stop me do you? I'm through worrying about this place! I've devoted twelve years of my life to this place and the very kids who once worshipped me now treat me like a stranger. Well that's all right. I've got a million screaming fans that pay money to see me and buy my records as well. I now have an obligation to my fans. No way can I let forty-five kids interfere with my duty to millions of the faithful. Is there?"

Priscilla shook her head in disbelief. She couldn't believe that this was her husband.

"Philip! What is the meaning of this crude behavior," she asked bewildered, "You're unlike any semblance of my husband! What's happened to you? This can't be you who raves wildly and feasts on vanity!"

"It's me Priscilla," he replied proudly, "it's the me that's been suppressed all these years. I've made a servant of myself prior to today, but from this day forward, I'll be master of my own destiny. I don't care what anybody thinks. With my new confidence, I've shaken the world and carved my place in the sun. You ain't seen anything yet. I shall be the greatest because that is my goal!"

Priscilla stood spell bound. As she realized the changes, which had swept over her husband, remorse gripped her soul and exhibited itself upon her face.

"Don't look so sad my sweet," he said sarcastically, "You should be the happiest woman alive. You always wanted me to be aggressive. How many times have you complained because I directed my attention to others? You should be glad that I've finally directed attention to myself. As for this group, which so displeases you, just remember that I formed it at your insistence. And I've become a legend in my time. And I've only just begun! Oh yes, and while you're feeling sorry for yourself, just remember that I begged you to forget a musical career. I pleaded to no avail. Yes, my love, you got exactly what you sowed. You wanted me to change, and I have. So feast your eyes on the product of your labors. Rejoice in the harvest for your work is complete. Hence forth I work my own works."

He sneered at his wife and left her presence. She stood weakly, trembling with emotion. The stark realization of the change in Philip left her in a trauma.

"No, Philip, my husband," she said in a trance, "my work has only begun. Oh Lord! What have I done?"

CHAPTER 30

❀

Drink waters out of your own cistern, and running waters out of your own well.

Priscilla faced a dilemma when Philip turned his back on the children at the nursing home. She had threatened to leave if he didn't dismiss Angie. However, his raging did not go unnoticed by the children. He had stomped past a tearful Joy. She had called in vain to him as he bowed his head and charged from the nursing home. When Priscilla came inside, the sight of the tears of the little girl and the realization that the children needed someone to care for them moved her soul with compassion. She began to see them as Philip once had. She sat beside Joy and then carried the child upstairs on her own crippled legs and tucked her tenderly into bed.

"Priscilla," asked Joy meekly, "are you still mad at Philip?"

"I'm disappointed more than angry, "Priscilla replied as she gently stroked Joy's hair.

"Philip said that it's hard to stay mad at people you love," said Joy with raised eyebrows, "he said that one time when you made him mad."

"When did he say that," asked Priscilla.

"Right after you got married and he didn't want to sing. He said that you played a naughty trick on him. Did you Priscilla," Joy asked.

"Yes I did," answered Priscilla, "I took advantage of his goodness. I never really fooled him. He was always too smart for me to manipulate. But I used his good nature to get my own way."

"Do you think that he really meant what he said," asked Joy, "I mean, that he won't come and see us any more."

The eyes of the little girl moistened in anguish. Priscilla moved closer to console her with an embrace.

"I'm sure that he'll return, and soon dear," she replied reassuringly, "unkind words are spoken in moments of anger, but when he collects his wits, he'll remember us."

"You won't leave us, will you Priscilla," begged the little girl.

"No darling," replied Priscilla tenderly, "I won't leave you."

She felt guilty as she recalled her angry words to Philip a few moments ago. She hadn't thought that the children might hear. She wasn't at all sure that, as she had told Joy, Philip would come back, but there was no reason to trouble Joy with that. For the moment, her mind was in limbo. She was unsure whether to press the issue or let it pass. She was positive that Philip and Angie were a deadly threat to her marriage. Even if they had no intention of getting intimately involved, they were a natural combination and too much contact was sure to end in disaster.

She limped on her braces to her car and drove home. Practice was just ending and Philip was about to take Simeon home. The thought of Angie being in her home infuriated her, but she said nothing to avoid another argument. She took notice of when Philip returned home. I took twenty-five minutes. That was just enough time to get there and back. She retired early that evening. Philip sat in the library gazing out the window. He wasn't himself and she didn't know what to do. As she prepared for bed, she kneeled and prayed to the Most High God that He would preserve her marriage. She wept before Him and begged that He would watch over, guide and direct her husband in his rebellious state. She prayed for her healing so that she could be a complete woman for her husband, for she felt that her physical inadequacy might be a source of discontent in her husband. She concluded by saying, "And Lord, Most High God, please forgive me, your servant, for my selfishness and my many sins which contributed to the stress in our marriage. Give me wisdom to know your way and strength to endure that your Name might be glorified. You have given Philip to me and me to Philip, and I praise your holy name for that. In you do we trust, for you can do all things. I claim Philip as our own and my own, remembering what you have said in your Word; 'All Thine are mine and all mine are Thine.' Philip, my husband is caught in the throws of wickedness, but you are the Lord of Hosts and you can do all things. Go forth Lord, both conquering and to conquer and restore our marriage. In Jesus mighty name I pray. Amen."

Philip began a thirty-day tour that was even more successful than his first tour. The addition of Angie to the band was paying dividends. She added class to the group to compliment the savvy and distinction of Philip on stage. She and Philip were an entertaining team. The girls screamed for Philip and the guys yelled for Angie. They released a new single, 'One More Round', on which Angie sang harmony. The song quickly moved to number one in the nation. Reporters were begging for interviews and the smut magazines were running articles about Philip's marriage being on the rocks. Philip's band was being paid top dollar for concerts. Milt Strohmeier, his manager and Harold Pomp, Priscilla's father, were ecstatic. Philip's name would sell any garbage they wanted to promote. Harold liked to boast that he had a corner on the market and it wasn't illegal.

Angie enjoyed the travel. She especially enjoyed being seen and photographed with Philip, but she told Eddie that it was just a necessary part of the job. Just being around Philip was pleasing. He was always suave and calm. No situation would get the best of him. She found herself becoming more entwined with him even though he seemed to be avoiding situations in which they were alone. He was always preoccupied. She sensed that he had deep feelings for her. She felt his piercing gaze as she crossed the room and she perceived more than a casual friendship in his actions on stage. She was puzzled at why he avoided her.

One afternoon after rehearsal, he slipped out of the theater and walked to a nearby zoo. He wore dark sunglasses and donned a hat to hide his identity. He bought a bag of peanuts and tossed them to the monkeys. They would scamper after each nut and look to him to toss more. He stooped down to pick up a small child who had tripped and skinned his knees. He carried him over to the cotton candy stand and treated him. Then he gave the little boy twenty dollars and sent him on his way. That was so like Philip. He could never turn a needy child away. Angies' heart warmed at the sight. As Philip watched the child dance away in excitement, she approached him.

"I've been following you," she said with a warm smile.

"I know," he replied softly with a look of worry on his face.

"How could you know," she asked, "you never even once looked back."

"I always know when you're around," he replied nervously.

"Oh Phil, you're joking," she giggled.

"No I'm not," he replied seriously, "I can feel it when you're around. I'm haunted by your presence at times lately, and I perceive that you are thinking of me as well."

"I have had you on my mind quite a bit lately," she replied tenderly.

"Angie, I know what's been on your mind and it's growing closer to materializing every day. That's what has been troubling me."

For a moment she stood shocked and speechless. He had uncovered her motive and she felt awkward at the unveiling.

"You have a way of seeing right through me, Phil, and quite frankly it scares me. I've never met a man like you," she replied, "You literally unclothe every statement put before you."

Angie helped herself to some of the peanuts, which Philip was tossing to the monkeys.

"Angie, there's no place to hide," he said, "there are rumors and gross stories in the tabloids about us every day. Are you prepared for living in a fish bowl? I despise this life, but I find that I am drawn closer to you every day. What are we going to do?"

"You make it sound so dismal," replied Angie in concern, "The last time we spoke of this, you couldn't wait. We were missing a grand and blessed moment of bliss. Why the change in attitude?"

"I'm really troubled Angie," he continued in deep distress, "I have become a captive of my passions, but it's not too late for you. Get out while you can! Go find Eddie and scratch for a living if you must! Do anything, but get away from me. I'm trouble going somewhere to ruin the life of everyone else. I don't want it to be you."

"Phil, I think you're tired. Maybe we've been traveling too much. You're really not making much sense. I've always known how you feel, but up until now I've been able to keep my distance. I don't intend for anything to come between Eddie and me, even though I might be interested in a few good times. I am very fond of you Phil, but Eddie will always be first," said Angie confidently.

"Do we fools ever listen to good advice," Philip mused shaking his head, "Angie, I've told you the truth and we each stand on our individual decisions. A second love is like a cancer. Two loves cannot abide in the same heart. One will grow and the other will diminish."

"You and your philosophies," she quipped as she picked a flower, "if you don't mind, I feel more confident with my own views."

They stopped before the cage of a playful orangutan and watched his antics.

"That monkey is on the wrong side of the bars," said Philip," We humans should trade sides with them. The most that monkey could do is mangle the body but man has the power to destroy the soul and wreck the happiness of his neighbor."

"Phil," answered Angie, "lately you don't seem like yourself."

"So much has troubled me these past few weeks," he replied, "I can't put my finger on it."

They turned and exited the monkey house and started toward the theater. Phil looked at her with a grin and said, "You're getting braver."

"I'm not sure I know what you mean," she answered.

"You used to run like a scared rabbit when I laid my feelings on the line, but today you stood your ground."

"I'm learning to cope with your peculiar nature," she quipped confidently.

"Just remember," Philip retorted, "that those whom the spirits would manipulate, they first make drunk with boldness."

Priscilla had just finished eating lunch and was about to resume her busy schedule. As she stepped into the playroom, a familiar face loomed before her.

"Oh! Dr. Stone," she said as she caught her breath," you startled me, "and when did you begin making house calls?"

"When my patients miss their third appointment," he replied firmly with a smile.

"Oh! Well I'm sorry," she replied, "my schedule has not allowed for doctor appointments. I've really felt quite well."

"Priscilla you look very tired," he retorted, "come into your office. I'm going to take a look at you."

He led her into her office and sat down as he looked into her eyes and studied her weary face. He shook his head in disgust.

"Priscilla, you know very well that you have strict orders not to over work yourself. I did some research into your activities when you missed your last appointment. You've been averaging twelve hours per day at work. You know that you brought on one physical breakdown because you pushed yourself beyond your ability."

"Dr. Stone," complained Priscilla, "it's all right. I feel fine. The work is good therapy."

"Therapy!" interrupted Dr. Stone as he scolded her, "you're trying to do the work of two people! Priscilla, I must insist that you limit your activities immediately before you ruin your health. Why don't you let your husband assist you more? By the way how is he doing?"

"Oh he's doing fine," she replied, hiding the truth, "now don't excite yourself."

"I don't intend to my stubborn patient," he replied firmly, "I intend to escort you home this very minute. I'm scheduling another appointment for you at nine o'clock in the morning."

"But Dr. Stone," she complained.

"I don't have time to argue with you Priscilla," snapped the Doctor, "Now come along."

The insistence of the doctor and her weariness caused her to comply. On the way out, she left instructions to the head nurse and departed. Her doctor drove her home with instructions to go to bed immediately. She stretched out across the bed and soon was soundly asleep. Priscilla, the crippled matron of Little Angels Nursing Home, was beginning to break under the pressures of her work, but her determination to keep open the haven for unfortunate handicapped children kept her striving against insurmountable odds.

Doctor Stone was not at all pleased with her when she arrived for her appointment the following day. He issued specific instructions to her that she was to limit her strenuous activities to five hours each day. She agreed with his orders, even though she knew that she wouldn't be able to do her work in five hours per day.

When she arrived at the nursing home, she found it a terribly unsightly mess. In aggravation, she plunged into the task of restoring order to the chaos. At about four o'clock as she prepared to leave for home, she received two phone calls from employees who wouldn't report for work. After calling the other staff, she found that no one could cover for the two absentees. They would be understaffed for the evening. They would definitely need help at feeding time. She would nap in her office until six and assist. She asked the head nurse to wake her at six. She slipped off her shoes and dropped to her knees beside the cot in her office. She was extremely tired. Her muscles ached and her injured knees protested in pain. This evening her soul was troubled as never before. Philip had been on tour for three weeks and he hadn't called or written. When she called no one was in. She thought once of going to him, but the nursing home tied her at home. In frustration and fear, she realized how much Philip had done. She recalled having called him lazy. She winced as she remembered how she insulted him. Presently she was keenly aware of just how much burden he had shouldered and how little recognition he received. How the children needed him! How she needed him! Priscilla prayed.

"Oh glorious Father," she sobbed as she reached out to the Most High God in despair, "I'm so weary tonight, but I must speak to you about this terrible mess I've brought upon myself, my husband, these children and your plan. Forgive me Lord, for troubling you. I know that I'm not worthy to call upon your Holy Name, but I simply must talk to someone. I'm so tired; Lord, and I have no one to whom I can turn except You. I drove my husband into the market place of sin and now I fear that I have lost him forever, if You don't undertake. Lord, I beg you to return him to me. I need him so much and the children love him. Be merciful Father, for I have sinned and I confess it all before You. I ask this in Jesus name. Amen"

CHAPTER 31

He that troubles his own house shall inherit the wind:
and the fool shall be servant to the wise of heart.

When Philip returned again for one week, he informed Priscilla that he would begin a world tour for six months. They were to sweep through Europe, North Africa, Asia, Australia and return to Los Angeles before returning home. Priscilla argued against the tour but to no avail. He had made up his mind. Milt had booked all the engagements and he refused to discuss the subject. Each day of the week Philip filled his day with the details of the music profession. He deliberately avoided the nursing home. She needed his help, but her pleas fell upon deaf ears. It was useless to cry for he was insensitive to her feelings.

Priscilla arranged to take Wednesday and Thursday off from the nursing home. She wanted to spend time with Philip, so they planned to drive through the country and have lunch. Then they would return home and enjoy a peaceful evening of solitude alone. On Thursday, she left for the nursing home to sign payroll checks. Shortly after she left, Angie rapped at the door.

"Angie! This is a surprise," Philip said nervously, "what are you up to?"

"I could discuss it better inside," she replied.

"Oh yeh," he answered nervously, "come in."

It was evident by the cast on her face that this was not a casual visit. He could see the far away gleam of determination and the distinct air of uneasiness that accompanies strong desire.

"Phil, I had to talk to you," she whispered. Her breath was short and her tongue thick with anxiety. She gazed wildly into is eyes and trembled as she searched for words which she had just rehearsed a hundred times before knocking at his door. She stood face to face with the man whom she wanted so much.

"Phil,...I...a..." she stammered for the appropriate words which would express her steaming passion, "I hunger and I thirst for your love."

Philip's eyes opened wide in surprise.

"Angie," he gasped in disbelief. He stepped toward her as she rushed into his arms and smothered him with kisses. She trembled in his arms. He was strong and yet gentle. His lips were soft and satisfying. They were drunk in the exhilaration and anxiety of the moment. He thrilled to the touch of her fingers on his neck and her warm body close to his.

"Oh Phil, I'm so excited," she sighed as she lay her head on his shoulder, "I thought I would lose my courage when I saw you. You don't know how my heart has moaned in indecision. I couldn't wait another day. I had to see you today."

"I know how you feel, Angie," whispered Philip tenderly, "I've been torn by desire these past six months just waiting for you to want me as much as I want you."

"I've been so foolish, Phil," she replied softly, "I should have listened to you six months ago. I wanted you then and I knew this would happen, but I was so afraid, sweetheart. I was so afraid, but oh how much we've missed. We have so much catching up to do."

She melted in his arms and their lips met in the hunger of two depraved lovers. After the long wait and the extended tension of their illegitimate relationship, they emptied their passions in each word and kiss as they acted out their unchained emotion.

"Phil, I could stay in your arms forever," she sighed, "Oh Phil. Hold me. I love you so much. I don't ever want to be away from you again."

"Yeh Angie," he replied softly, "we're going to make arrangements to be together Monday when the tour begins. We're going to have lots of time together."

"Phil, darling," she exclaimed, "I can't wait that long. I must see you today!"

"Angie, I can't get away," he protested, "Priscilla expects me here tonight and tomorrow. There's no way I can get out without arousing her curiosity."

"Please Phil," Angie pleaded, "I've waited six months for today. Don't make me wait another minute for your love."

"Priscilla will be back any minute, Angie," he complained, "If she sees us together she'll know what's going on!"

"I don't care about Priscilla or anyone else," retorted Angie, "I just want you!"

"Come on Angie! Be reasonable," begged Philip nervously, "now is not the time for a confrontation. You'll have to leave before Priscilla gets back home!"

"O.K. Phil," she answered softly, "but promise me that you'll see me tonight. Please Phil! I can't wait another day!"

"O.K.," Phil replied in relief, "somehow, I'll get out this evening. I'll see you at about eight. Where shall I pick you up?"

"Come to my apartment, Phil," she answered softly.

"I can't pick you up there! The reporters are flocking around both of us. You took a chance coming here today! Were you followed?" he queried, "some photographer is certain to be lurking around and snap us! The whole world will know it if we aren't careful."

"Phil, you made the rules," she retorted, "it's all or nothing! That's the way it has to be. Don't worry Phil! It will all work out."

She studied his worried countenance and thrilled to the realization that their hour was at hand.

"Oh Phil! I love you," she whispered as she kissed his hesitant lips once more.

"Angie! We have to stop this," he said nervously, "Priscilla will be home any minute now!"

"You're right," she replied breathlessly as she looked directly into his eyes, "Phil, do you love me?"

He gasped as he glanced at his watch and nervously answered, "What a silly question! Would I be worrying myself crazy if I didn't care for you?"

"Phil you've told me you care, you've said that I'm pretty, that you want me. You've said everything except 'I love you," she said passionately.

"Angie, I'm already bound to you by a bond much stronger than words. Why do I have to say it?" he asked, "can't I just show it?"

"Phil, before you show it, you must say it," she replied as she kissed him on the neck.

"I could say it and not mean it, you know," he replied, "how will you know if I really mean it?"

"You just say it. I'll know if you mean it or not," she insisted.

He bowed his head and peered passionately into her eyes and whispered, "Angie, I'm nuts about you. You know that! I love you so much that I can't stand to be away from you anymore."

"Oh Phil. You meant that. I could feel it in my soul! I'll have a perfect day waiting for you to come," she said passionately.

She kissed him and turned to leave. As she placed her hand on the doorknob, she turned again to him and said, "Phil."

"Yeh," he replied affectionately.

"Don't be late darling," she said, "I'm afraid that I'll lose my courage if you're not on time. I'll be waiting impatiently."

She hastily walked to her car and drove off as Philip nervously kept watch for his wife. Just three minutes later, Priscilla pulled into the drive. He hurriedly retreated to the den and picked up a magazine. He acted as if nothing had happened while she was gone. Thus began his personal life of lies. It wasn't easy to hide his guilt, for try as he might, he couldn't shake the nervous tension of the past few minutes.

Priscilla didn't notice his uneasiness, as she was excited about the day, which they were about to share together. She acted like a little girl and laughed and giggled like she once did when they were together. Philip even enjoyed the afternoon. They visited an aquarium and talked, as they hadn't conversed in months. He actually felt tenderness for her. Priscilla seemed so light hearted and gay that the thought of leaving her later that evening repulsed him. It wasn't just. She sat next to him as they drove like she did when they were courting. She was thrilled beyond words just to be together again. He had overlooked this side of his lovely wife in the midst of their marital problems. She was such a tender hearted and delicate woman. She was frail, beautiful, witty and pleasant. He waited for an opportune time to tell her that he must be away this evening. What excuse would he use? How would she react? The opportunity never came. They arrived home at five that evening. Priscilla was worn out and decided to take a short nap. Philip decided that now would be a good time to tell her the bad news.

"Honey, "he began, "I'm going to go to Simeon's tonight and run over a few new songs with him. We're going to be recording Friday and we need to work on the arrangements."

"Well darling," she replied, "I'm rather tired myself. I can take a short nap while you're gone. How long will you be?"

"Oh maybe two or three hours," he replied anxiously, "we'll just cover the basics tonight and work the rest out Friday."

She stepped into their bedroom to slip into her night gown."

"Philip," she called cheerfully, "would you help me with my braces?"

"Yeh," he replied as he opened their bedroom door.

Priscilla had slipped into a pink negligee and a warm glow of tenderness radiated from her face. He knew what that meant. She looked beautiful as she always did. It was months since she had warmed to him this way. In that moment, he knew that it was only Priscilla for him. He loved her and wanted to please her. She needed him and he needed her. They wanted each other and eagerly longed for the tenderness of love. She inspired and moved him like no woman he had ever known. He kneeled and unbuckled her braces. Her legs were soft and warm. They gazed into each other's eyes and then consummated the afternoon. In the peace and fulfillment, which follows true love, they cuddled, played and then napped, with Priscilla securely nestled in the arms of her husband. She thought 'oh the contentment of true love.'

Priscilla awoke at eight fifteen and realized that Philip had scheduled a practice with Simeon at eight o'clock. She shook her husband to wake him.

"Philip! Philip! Wake up!" she said, "You're late for practice!"

He awoke with a start and decided not to go to Angie's apartment as he had promised her. He pulled Priscilla to him and kissed her softly.

"This whole day has been touching and I'm really tired myself," he said tenderly, "This has been a great day. Let's rest and tomorrow I'll help you around the house and the nursing home. It'll be like old times."

He squeezed her tightly, buried his face in her neck and kissed her again.

"Philip," she said, "stop that. You're late again! You made a commitment and now you must go."

"Not tonight honey," he replied tenderly, "I have you to myself for a few days and I'm going to make the most of it. We are more important than the music. I'll call Simeon and cancel."

Tonight Priscilla declined to insist that he keep his appointment. Philip pretended to call Simeon but called Angie instead from the den. She was angry but Philip assured her that it was just a minor delay. He had to appease Angie, and find a peaceful means to defuse the passion Angie had for him. He knew that both his wife and his friend Eddie, who was also the fiancé of Angie, would be hurt. For the next few days he and his wife would renew and restore their marriage. Maybe Priscilla and he could travel together on the next tour. Perhaps someone else could run the nursing home. Maybe Dr. Stone would release her to tour with him again.

The next day, Philip went with Priscilla for her appointment with Dr. Stone. He was adamant in his refusal to release Priscilla and he scolded Philip for not seeing that she had adequate help at the nursing home. They were both disappointed, but Philip encouraged Priscilla and promised that this would be the last music tour he would take until she was able to be part of the act again.

The day passed quickly and Priscilla tired again at midday. She and Philip napped together again. When they awoke, they went to a matinee at the movies and then ate dinner at their favorite restaurant. The stress of her job, the excitement of the past two days and the need of her mending body for extra rest required that she retire to bed early. At seven-thirty, before she went to bed, she reminded Philip about the band practice. Philip had hoped she would forget. He despised living a lie. He had never lied to Priscilla before. Why should he start now? Angie was temptation and he had best avoid her. He wanted to stay home tonight again.

"Honey, I really don't want to practice tonight," he said, "I just want to stay home with you."

"Philip, really" she replied, "If you've made arrangements to practice with Simeon, you should fulfill your obligation. Anyway, I'm so tired and sleepy that I wouldn't be much company. Now go on darling, before you're late."

He heaved a sigh of disgust, kissed her and left. She was so insistent about promptness! As he drove, he determined that he would talk to Angie and break off the relationship tonight! He must not be alone with her. He could never be happy with anyone else but Priscilla. She was the love of his life.

At ten o'clock, Priscilla awoke from her nap, stretched and yawned. She was troubled by Philip's attitude when he left. Now that she was rested, she recalled his reluctance to practice. She could never remember him being quite so insistent. She should have listened to his request for soon he would tour again and they would be apart. He wanted to spend all of his time with her.

She decided to dress and surprise him by dropping by Simeon's place. They could cut the practice short and they could have the rest of the evening together. 'Priscilla' she thought 'you're so blind at times. Your husband wants to show you how much he loves you and you send him off to work.'

She noticed that Philip had taken the Continental. She took the Mercedes. That was odd for he always preferred the smaller car. She drove to Simeon's apartment and knocked on his door. It was strange that she didn't hear music, but possibly they were taking a short break. The door opened and Simeon peeked around the door.

"Who is it," he asked.

"It's Priscilla," she replied, "I've come for Philip."

"He isn't here," he replied politely.

"You mean he hasn't been here all evening," she asked as her suspicions were aroused.

"No he hasn't," he replied sadly, for he too had sensed what had transpired.

"Oh Simeon," she sobbed, "This is terrible. You know where he is too. Don't you?"

He nodded his head but remained mute.

"Priscilla, why don't you come in and get yourself together," he answered.

"No Simeon," she replied bitterly, "I'm going to get my husband from that hussy!"

She turned and crawled into her car, awkwardly lifting each leg into the car. In her wounded pride, she could understand why Philip might want a woman who wasn't crippled. She drove directly to Angie's apartment. She stopped half a block behind Philip's parked car and turned her lights off. There were two people inside, a man and a woman. The man was definitely

Philip. She would know his silhouette anywhere. She cried bitterly as he kissed Angie. Her heart seemed so heavy that it would stop beating and she wished it would. She watched them walk arm in arm to the apartment. As they disappeared behind the closed door, Priscilla bowed her head and in broken spirit sobbed bitterly before the Most High God.

"Oh my dear God," she wailed, "what a wretched soul I am. For that precious and priceless gem which you entrusted to my care is lost to the enemy. I beg you father; don't hold this sin to his charge. Had I been the helpmate I should have been, this would have never happened. Lord, I don't understand why you've allowed this to happen, but I won't question your better judgment. I wish I were blind rather than see the sight my eyes have seen tonight. It were better I had been deaf than hear the rumors and gossip which shall begin after this night. I don't complain for my shame Lord for I deserve all this and more. I am sorry for the shame, which I have brought upon you in the heavenly court. Surely Satan dances with joy at my stupidity and mocks at your righteousness. Lord, I place Philip in your unfailing care. I want him back even though he has grieved my soul. I need him father. I beg you for one more chance to be a woman, a wife and a helpmate to our precious Philip. I ask this in Jesus' Name. Amen."

As she drove home a song Philip had written for the music class she taught whirled through her mind. She wondered at the time how he could write a song so sad. Little did she realize that it could be so true, that it could apply to both her and her husband? She recalled that he said 'that's how the Most High God sees sinful man, as a lost creation which must be restored to its former glory.' That night it played over and over again in her mind until Philip came home. She pretended to be asleep as he slipped into bed as quietly as possible. She prayed for strength to endure the three days until he left for the tour. She must be strong. God would prevail!

When Philip fell into a deep sleep, Priscilla arose and sat at her piano. As the words of Philip's song whirled through her head, she softly sang and quietly played in great pathos.

'Would I were blind than see the sight my eyes behold,
My husband in another's warm embrace,
Would I were deaf than hear the rumors t'will be told,
I'll live each hour in sorrow and disgrace.

I threw away the precious man you gave to me,
I pushed him to another woman's arms.
I cast him into sin and drove him from your sight.
Don't fail me Lord like I failed him tonight.

A fallen angel, that's what he is to you and me.
Lord keep him in your care and bring him back, to what he used to be.
Is there a place in heaven for a wretch like me?
Lord hold my hand and keep me close to Thee.
Lord hold my hand and keep me close to Thee.'

CHAPTER 32

*A virtuous woman is a crown to her husband: but she
that makes ashamed is as rottenness in his bones.*

Priscilla called her mother on Monday morning after Philip left for London on the first leg of the six months World Tour. She insisted that her parents come to her home on Tuesday evening to discuss a matter of great importance. Though her parents had to cancel previous arrangements, they arrived at precisely five-thirty. They chatted and laughed as Harold and Elizabeth waited patiently for the matter to come to light. It wasn't until dinner was served and they sat casually around the table that Priscilla opened the discussion.

"I'm sure that you've both wondered what I could possibly want to see you about," she said.

"Yes we have, my dear," replied Harold with a drag off of his cigar.

"Well, it has to do with Philip and his band," she began seriously.

"Ah, now I could talk about that boy and his fabulous group all day," her father said boisterously, "he's a fountain of blessing to my bank account. Do you know that my business has quadrupled in the first six months of the fiscal year? It's all because I'm his father-in-law, I'll admit, but it all looks the same in the bank balance."

"Father, what I have to discuss is more important than a bank balance. It has to do with my marriage. The success of that group is threatening my home," Priscilla said seriously.

"What do you mean?" said her father in surprise, "I thought Philip was pleased to travel and promote the business. Is he rebelling again?"

"He's more than happy to promote the business," Priscilla retorted, "The trouble is that he doesn't care if he ever comes home. He's perfectly content to travel the globe."

"Well then my dear," interrupted Harold impatiently, "what is it that's troubling you?"

"I want you and Milt to quit pushing him so hard and insist that he slow his pace so that he can be at home at least every other week end," she replied.

"Why in heavens name would we do a crazy thing like that," shouted Harold excitedly, "Priscilla, I'm surprised at you! You know how short a career in popular music can be. You're here today and gone tomorrow. We must continue to milk the cash cow while we can!"

"I'm more interested in preserving my home than providing windfall profits for my father, who already has more money than he can spend," snapped Priscilla disgustedly.

"Priscilla, what's the matter with you," demanded Harold angrily, "who's idea was it to pay off those disk jockeys across the country to promote that horrendous song 'Vazzle, Bazzle, Wazzle, Dazzle'? Your memory is quite short little daughter. I can't invest two hundred thousand dollars into a man and write it off because my daughter suddenly decides it's unhandy for her."

"Father, I'm asking you to slow the pace a bit, not kill the act. My health prohibits me from taking an active part in the act. You are writing me out of my marriage for the sake of more profits," she screamed angrily, "I want my husband and I value him more than any amount of money!"

"I must say that you are more than generous with my money. I only have one thing to say my daughter," he shouted, "I just trained that boy to be a go getter, and I'm not about to slow him down. He's young. He can take the abuse of travel. While he's young is the time to make his fortune. I'm sorry Priscilla but Philip will continue to work at this same torrid pace."

"Well father, I had thought to solicit at least token sympathy," she retorted bitterly, "but now at least there can no longer be any doubt in my mind that I rate a second billing to your checkbook."

"Now see here Priscilla," Harold snapped back as he leaned forward and rapped the table fiercely, "I will not tolerate any disrespect!"

"Is the naked truth not a venomous dart?" retorted Priscilla, "if you won't take action, I will! I know that I can influence Philip to cancel engagements and come back home with me! Then you and Milt can face all those angry promoters who want him at show time!"

"Well, I'll go you one better," replied Harold in fury, "I'm going to foreclose on the mortgage on that run down nursing home. It comes due soon. Now either back off or pay up!"

He laughed as he presented his ultimatum for he knew that she couldn't possibly pay the debt.

"Harold," exclaimed Elizabeth in shock at the harsh threat to her daughter, "don't you…"

"Stay out of this Elizabeth," he snapped, "I'll handle the business!"

"Well it's no deal father," retorted Priscilla, "I want my husband and I intend to stop at nothing until he's spending more time at home with me!"

"Well, that settles it," shouted her father as he leaped from his chair, "Come Elizabeth. We're leaving!"

He pulled his wife from her seat and they hastily slipped into their wraps. Harold pushed his wife out the door ahead of himself. As he was leaving, he stuck is head back inside the door and taunted, "someone from the bank will be out here to see you soon. If you haven't returned to your senses by then, I do hope that you've found a home for the children. Who knows, may be you can find a mansion for them. Ha! Ha! Ha! Ha! Ha! Ha! Ha!"

He laughed as he climbed into the car. Priscilla shuttered as she thought of the dilemma she now faced. It now appeared that she had lost everyone she loved. She didn't want to tell her parents that she and Philip were having marital problems. Now she had to choose between those helpless and innocent children and her husband. Not knowing what to do, she fell to her knees and prayed. It seemed that each day brought a new crisis, but she poured her heart out to the Most High God.

Meanwhile, outside, her mother confronted her husband about his merciless behavior toward their daughter.

"Harold Pomp," she began angrily, "I have stood by you through all manner of questionable business transactions. I have sworn to lies so that you could net thousands. I've allowed you to drag me through the gutters of shame for a dollar, but when you begin to badger our daughter, that's where I draw the line. I refuse to stand back while you steam roll our Priscilla! Did it ever occur to you that maybe she has marital problems as a result of your latest financial boom?

Elizabeth continued angrily, "That girl has problems she isn't telling us and I don't blame her for not wanting to share it with us. I demand that you march in there and apologize to her, or I'm staying with her until you regain your senses!"

"I won't apologize for protecting my best interests," he snapped back, "And her's too, if she could only see it! I'll remind you that I take care of the business in this family!"

"Well good-bye Harold! Take good care of your business," she retorted defiantly as she stepped out of the car, "I'm staying with our daughter. We'll run that nursing home together!"

"Come back here, Elizabeth," he shouted as he poked his head out the window, "Elizabeth! I demand that you come back here!"

She walked as if she didn't hear him. As she drew near the door, he shouted, "I'm leaving for Europe for four weeks tomorrow. It'll really be a blast without you!"

The door slammed and Elizabeth disappeared inside. Harold drove off and raced through town in rage. Inside, mother and daughter faced each other in a happy reunion.

"Mother," said Priscilla in shock, "what are you doing here? Where is father?"

"I left your father outside and I told him that I was staying here to help you. When he comes to his senses, I'll go back home," replied her mother, "but until then I shall reinforce the troops."

"Oh mother," replied Priscilla tearfully, "I didn't intend for you to become entangled in this mess. Go back to father, please. I don't want you to be hurt!"

"What," exclaimed Elizabeth, "am I to stand meekly by as my husband tramples our daughter? I should say not! Priscilla, I've been blind to your needs and troubles in the past, but that won't happen again. I know what type of trouble you must have to risk everything you own and everyone you love. I had no idea that you and Philip were having marital difficulties. I don't intend to pry. You and Philip must work through your problems by yourselves, but I can and will offer my help."

She stepped toward Priscilla and stretched forth her arms and folded her daughter into her bosom. Both of them were overcome with emotion and they burst out in tears.

"Mother, thank you so much for understanding. I have so many worries and no one to turn to. Philip has turned his back on the nursing home and the children who love and need him so. Philip is seeing another woman. Oh mother you can't imagine the pain and humiliation I bear. Now father is going to foreclose on the nursing home. What am I to do, mother," she asked in pain, "What of those innocent children? Why should they pay the price? I have no choice but to go along with father, for I won't make those helpless children pay the price of my husband or my father! As much as I love him, that just isn't right."

"Now don't worry honey," consoled her mother, "your mother hasn't lived thirty years with Harold Pomp without picking up a few of his tricks. We're not about to worry about foreclosure.

We're going to build a new nursing home."

"Mother, how do you plan to do that," asked Priscilla, "Even if you could buy the materials, we have no land on which to build."

"Honey, I have it all figured out," her mother replied with a smile, "Harold Pomp is in for the surprise of his life when he returns from Europe! You sick with your mother. Harold can have this old heap! He doesn't know it yet, but he is going to pay for a new facility."

Early the next morning Elizabeth was on the phone with materials suppliers and building contractors. She also hired an architect, to be paid by, of course, Harold Pomp! She purchased the materials, contracted the labor and designated the spot, which she wouldn't tell to Priscilla.

"It will be a surprise," she said on several different occasions when her daughter tried to coax the location from her. Elizabeth would always smile.

The new building was complete in twenty-eight days from the day Harold left. They loaded the chartered bus with the children and hired a moving van to move the equipment, all authorized by Elizabeth and chargeable to Harold Pomp. As the bus driver proceeded toward Albany, Priscilla was taxing her brain trying to determine their destination. As they reached Albany, the driver took the route which lead directly to the Pomp mansion. Her mouth flew open in shock and she covered her mouth in amazement as the stark realization of her mother's scheme came to light.

"Mother! You didn't build it where I'm thinking," shrieked Priscilla excitedly.

"Oh but yes I did," her mother replied, "we should arrive just about the same time as your father. I'm hoping we're just a few minutes before him. Then we can unload the bus and get the children inside before Harold rages."

"Mother," Priscilla exclaimed, "father will be furious!"

"I don't know why," she said dryly, "it was his idea to put it here. I merely followed his instruction."

"Here we are," she said to the driver as she saw the estate ahead, "that's it just to the left of the lane by the entrance."

She looked back to her daughter and continued, "Do you think he'll miss the nursing home when he drives past. I doubt that he'll need his spectacles to notice."

"Mother, this is nothing to joke about," replied Priscilla in worry.

"Well, Priscilla," replied her mother nonchalantly, "I didn't build it as a joke, and I doubt seriously if your father will take it as such."

The bus slowed to a halt and the children began filing out. The children were ecstatic. Joy glowed with excitement and said, "Oh, Priscilla, a new home for me. I love it! It's beautiful!"

The staff assisted the children who couldn't walk into the nursing home. In less than an hour, all the children were inside and the equipment was unloaded and inside the nursing home.

Before they had time to admire the new facility, Elizabeth spotted Harold's Limousine as it turned into the lane. The chauffeur proceeded up the drive without looking to his left. Harold casually glanced to his left at the structure and puffed on his cigar. All at once his head snapped to the left as he pressed his nose to the window. He shouted to the chauffeur and the car screeched to a halt, then peeled backwards toward the new nursing home.

"Get the kids inside," Elizabeth said calmly, "there's a storm coming."

Priscilla remained inside the front door where she could see and hear the events, which were about to unfold. As the car skidded to a halt, Harold catapulted out of the door and charged angrily toward his wife like a wounded beast. His face was beet red in fury.

"What is the meaning of this? Who is responsible for this?" he demanded as he stood nose to nose to Elizabeth.

She placed her hands on her hips and replied, "The kids needed a place to stay after you closed the nursing home, and you're responsible for this!"

"I'm responsible!" he roared, "How the devil can I be responsible? I didn't order this done!"

"No, but you suggested it, Harold, and don't you deny it," responded Elizabeth.

"Don't be ridiculous! I never suggested this idiotic idea!" he shouted.

"Oh yes you did, Harold," she replied sternly, "do you remember when we were at Priscilla's home and you told her that you would foreclose on the mortgage? Remember what you said as you were leaving? You said, and I quote 'who knows, maybe you can find a mansion for them. Ha Ha Ha Ha', unquote."

She folded her arms and leaned in his face and concluded, "Well, we found a mansion. Ha Ha Ha Ha."

"You can't do this Elizabeth," he shouted as he stomped the ground, "I'll have bull dozers here this afternoon!"

"Oh no you won't," snapped Elizabeth, "you know when you're beaten. The nursing home is here to stay!"

"This just can't be happening," Harold said as he shook his head and mumbled to himself, "I'll be the laughing stock of Wall Street."

He turned to leave then quickly wheeled about in another rage and said, "You think that you have my hands tied! Don't you! Well…I'll be back and this…This…It's going to go!"

He abruptly turned about, threw his cigar down and stomped it. He slammed the car door without waiting for his chauffeur to close it. As the car sped up the lane, he fixed his eyes on the nursing home until the car disappeared over the hilltop.

That was only the beginning of the conflict. Harold did not lose easily. An editorial in the daily newspaper called Harold and Elizabeth benefactors and praised the effort to save the cash strapped nursing home. He still preferred that the nursing home be somewhere else. His pride was torn by the presence of mongrels tearing up the landscape and behaving with all manner of impudence. He was ashamed to invite guests or business associates for fear that he might be questioned as to why he built the nursing home on his estate.

Elizabeth's decision to stand by her daughter was in effect a stand for God. Once she began to work inside the confines of the new facility her eyes were opened to a view of human suffering previously unknown to her. At first, she refused to change diapers or clean up after a child who vomited, but very quickly she developed a fondness and concern for the loving children whom the world forgot. She began to assist with the children in any way she could. She developed a desire to serve others. And as Priscilla had done before her, Elizabeth was hearing and listening to the call of the living God.

A new understanding developed between daughter and mother. Each day they ate breakfast together and prayed for the blessing of the Most High God during the day and for guidance in every situation. They would read a chapter in the Bible and sing an hymn before beginning work. They counseled the employees to treat the children with gentleness and lead them in asking the blessing before each meal. At noon they had lunch together, read the Bible, thanked God for his blessings and asked for strength and guidance for the remainder of the day. At evening, they would sit together in the playroom and discuss the day, sing hymns and pray. Then they would check the children and retire. In this way they each found strength and happiness in serving God, even though their husbands were breaking their hearts and shaming them. Elizabeth even moved into the nursing home with Priscilla, so that she could be near and help in the night.

It was March first and Philip was in Los Angeles on the last leg of his World Tour. Priscilla had not seen him since he left and had only talked with him once by phone. He could never be reached. When he landed in Los Angeles, he was met by a mob of fans estimated at ten thousand. In the past five months, he had written and released seven songs, which sold over one million copies each. Three of those songs were in the top twenty across the nation. The pictures with Philip and Angie together depressed her but then the photographers always snapped suggestive pictures or included provocative phrases around innocent pictures. This one showed Angie and Philip stepping off the plane together.

The next day, Elizabeth was presented with a divorce papers. She wasn't surprised, but her heart was torn and her daughter knew it. One week later, Priscilla opened the paper and saw an article in the Arts section about Philip. The topic heading said 'VALI BOURBON QUITS BAND—TELLS ALL'. The report didn't miss a statement nor did it delete any facts. She stated that Angie and Philip shared rooms and spent the night together.

She hinted that the group was on the verge of breaking up because of internal strife. Even Philip and his friend Simeon were feuding. The article showed a picture of Philip and Angie dancing together in Paris.

Throughout the day this thought discouraged her, though she tried to push it from her mind. She hated Angie, but her heart still very much belonged to Philip. Toward the end of the day, her sorrowful soul began to exhibit itself on her face. When they sat down for devotions Elizabeth decided to ask why Priscilla was depressed.

"Priscilla, I've been reading the paper," she began, "and I saw the article which I believe has drained your soul. Can we discuss that now?"

"Mother, I prefer to discuss another topic if you don't mind, "Priscilla answered.

"I feel it best if we discuss it now, dear," her mother suggested softly, "This can dominate you if you allow it to."

"What is there to discuss," she replied in shame, "another woman has taken my place. Philip definitely prefers her. Why wouldn't he? She's young, pretty, and intelligent and she isn't crippled. How can I compete? Mother, I've never told anyone this, but my handicap has greatly reduced my ability to be a woman to Philip. I must be honest. A man places more importance on those things than a woman. I really feel that my inability to be a lover has done as much as anything to topple our marriage. Under those circumstances, can he be blamed for falling in love with another woman? I hate Angie but I envy her because she can fulfill that role better than I."

Priscilla couldn't cry, but she was in an extreme state of agony.

"I think that I see a good deal of self pity," replied her mother, "I see it as more of a loss for God. Philip was once a Godly man. He's turned his back on all that he once stood for. He hasn't failed you and I. He failed God first. Then all this hardship came upon all those dear to him. You can't allow your personal feelings to blind you to the pertinent facts. Philip is on the road of spiritual destruction and unless The Lord undertakes, he'll be lost forever."

"Mother, please don't preach to me," snapped Priscilla indignantly, "you've never lost father to another woman."

"No, but I've lost him to his business and all those related activities," replied her mother, "Think about all the time your father devotes to business matters. Think about how little time your father and I have together. I have him after he has been drained of his energy and needs someone to complain to. Before God, one case is as ugly as the other. I thank the Most High God that you and I have been delivered from that horrible fate by the Blood of Christ. Priscilla, you and I have a duty to the Lord and our husbands to remain steadfast throughout this trial."

"What can my example do for a husband I never see," asked Priscilla despondently.

"Remember how Philip used to be," asked her mother, "Even though I thought he was crazy, I was impressed by his life style. He was free of all the hang-ups that haunted me. He was good to you and he loved people. I couldn't fathom how anybody could be so selfless. I secretly admired him and wished that I had the courage to be like him. The way we treated him when we first met him was disgraceful. I've come to see that it wasn't Philip that I admired. It was Christ in him. He didn't fit into our ideals. I now appreciate the patience he displayed in submitting to our abuse. He trusted God to work out our salvation. All he did was to let His light shine. It's our turn to be a beacon to our husbands. We can't save their souls, but our husbands need us to be strong for them. If we never see them again, we must pray continually that the Most High God will deliver them from the terrible fate, which is theirs without Christ. It's going to be different on the other side. We both want Harold and Philip there."

Elizabeth began to cry as sorrow and agony crept into her soul and her voice trembled as she concluded her statement on a triumphant note.

"So Priscilla, get your chin up, hold your head high and be a strong warrior for our Lord," she said, "We're going to praise the Lord in song tonight with a song that our dearest Philip penned and the defeat which Satan has presented to us we shall present to God as victory."

Priscilla moved to the piano and played as they sang the song 'I'll Keep Thee and You Keep Me'

'In my weakness Thou art with me,
I have peace and strength within.
Trusting in Thy power completely,
I have victory over sin.
Come to me you heavy laden,
I've prepared a place for Thee.
I recall those words so precious,
I'll keep Thee and you keep me.

When the storms of life beset me,
I find refuge in Thy love.
Love that triumphed over Satan,
From this rock I shall not move.
Come to me you heavy laden,
I've prepared a place for Thee.
I recall those words so precious,
I'll keep Thee and you keep me.

When my burdens over come me,
Jesus share my heavy load.
Precious nail pierced hands assist me,
On that straight and narrow road,
Come to me you heavy laden,
I've prepared a place for Thee.
I recall those words so precious,
I'll keep Thee and you keep me.
I'll keep Thee and you keep me.'

There were tears of joy as they finished the song, but each went to bed with their burdens lifted. Elizabeth was a great help to Priscilla. She was just what her daughter needed, just the help, which Priscilla had prayed for. Together they kept their spirits high and the nursing home operating. In these their darkest hours, they found hope, rest and peace in their faith in the Most High God.

CHAPTER 33

*Every wise woman builds her house, but a foolish woman
plucks it down with her own hands.*

"Phil, when are you planning to get a divorce," asked Angie as they lay in
bed.

"Oh, I don't know Angie," he replied uncertainly, "Divorces are such
nasty proceedings. I hate to get it started."

"Well, someone has to start it," she retorted, "after all, I think I've waited
long enough."

"Yeh, I guess you have," he replied, "I'll see an attorney when we get
back to Albany. It sure will be good to get back home."

"What do you mean by get back home?" complained Angie, "I don't
want you to step one foot inside Priscilla's door! Promise me that you won't
see her again until the divorce is final. We'll see her in court!"

"What are you afraid of," demanded Philip, "I don't intend to go back to
Priscilla."

"I'm just protecting my interests. That's all," she replied, "she handed
you to me but I won't return the favor."

"You really hang on tight, don't you," he said with a smile.

"Now that I have you, I'm not about to let you go. I love you Phil, and I
want to be yours in every way, including your name," she replied.

"When you take possession, you take possession," quipped Philip.

"You got yourself in my arms and you're here to stay," she said as she pulled his jaw toward her. She smiled and peered into his eyes, tenderly kissed him and then laid her head on his shoulder.

"I'm tired Angie," Phil yawned, "let's get some sleep."

"I'm sleepy too," she said as she stretched her arms across his chest and squeezed him tenderly, "would you get the light?"

"Yeh," he replied as he turned off the lamp beside the bed.

Just as he dozed off, the phone rang.

Angie picked up the phone.

"Hello. Yes he's here. Well I don't know. I'll ask him if he wants to speak with you," she snapped hatefully.

She placed her hand over the receiver and said, "It's Priscilla. Do you want to talk to her?"

"Oh heck!" he said in disgust, "I'll talk to her."

He took the receiver from Angie and said, "Hello."

The sound of his voice stirred anguish in Priscilla's soul. Even though she hadn't seen him for six months, her heart still leaped at the sound of his voice. The presence of Angie pushed the knife of sorrow even deeper, but she said a silent prayer and spoke pleasantly and without anger. Philip, however, couldn't see her face for it betrayed her voice.

"Philip, this is Priscilla," she began, "I've been trying to reach you all evening. Joy has been taken to the hospital with internal bleeding. The doctors cannot stop the hemorrhaging, and they advised me to call all friends and family."

"You mean they don't expect her to live?" he asked anxiously.

"They give her a day or two if the bleeding doesn't stop," she replied softly.

"What can I do for her, Priscilla," complained Philip, "if I come back it will just add to the sorrow. Things aren't like they once were and I can't pretend that they are, even for Joy."

"Philip, Joy is asking to see you. You have been a father to her for seven years and she loves you very much. I'm asking you for Joy, Philip. I promise you that I won't interfere in any way. I haven't told her about our problems, so she doesn't know the situation. Philip, you have millions of fans, but the greatest fan you will ever have this side of heaven is dying. She didn't buy your records or come to your concerts, but I've stood beside her each night and listened as she prayed that the Lord would bless you and keep you in his care. Philip, she needs you but she can't come to you. If she could, she would crawl to see you one last time. Philip, I'm begging you for Joy's sake," she burst into tears for a moment but quickly regained her composure and with trembling voice said, "come back and see our precious little Joy before it's too late."

Phil was moved to tears and cut to the heart. Priscilla's tears, Joy's hopeless condition and his own guilt were almost more than his conscience could bear. For what seemed an eternity, he was incapable of speech. Then in a weak and sorrowful voice, he spoke, "O.K. Priscilla. I'll be there as soon as I can get there."

Priscilla didn't say good-bye. She hung up the phone and sobbed. She wiped her eyes and kneeled in the braces, which harnessed her legs and prayed for the healing of Joy and the restoration of Philip.

"Oh heavenly Father, I thank you for sending Philip to our darling Joy in her hour of weakness. Philip is such a ray of hope in her life. He seems the only possibility to lift her spirits enough to want to live. I know that the doctors say she won't recover, but we ask you for a miracle. I try to believe, but I never have had the faith which Philip had before I drove him into the wilderness of sin. Oh Lord, help my unbelief! Grant that Joy might recover and laugh again, that the world may know that there is a God who cares about the suffering of man. Be with Philip that he might again be the inspiring example that he once was to Joy. She believes that he can do anything and she's been praying for his soul as have I. Holy Father, I ask nothing for myself. I pray for Philip, that you might call him again to the work, which you prepared him to do. I beg of you Lord! Hear the pleas of your humble servant. Restore Philip to his commission for the sake of your work on earth, those who need him as he was in your grace and for the sake of my heavy burden of guilt for his soul. I don't ask that you return him to me, even though I'll always love him. I don't deserve to have him again, for I defiled him before your presence, but I do covet his soul for the kingdom of heaven. We ask these things in Jesus mighty name. Amen."

"Phil, you're not going back to Albany by your self," snapped Angie, "it's a trick to get you back so that she can steal you from me! Why do you think that she was so calm on the phone?"

"O.K.! O.K.!" he replied nervously, "you can go with me, but I don't think that Priscilla would lie about something like this."

"Don't kid yourself," Angie said, "a woman will do anything to keep the man she loves."

"I tell you Angie," he said dejectedly, "I'm a rat!"

"Phil! Don't say that," shrieked Angie," are you a rat for loving me?"

She stood motionless on the verge of tears. Philip walked to her and took her in his arms.

"No Angie," he said in tears, "not for loving you but rather for turning my back on those helpless children. Priscilla didn't deserve to be treated like this either. She's an angel and I've walked all over her heart."

"What does that make me?" shouted Angie angrily, "a devil because I love you?"

"No Angie," he said tearfully, "please don't cry. I'm sorry. I didn't mean to upset you. It's just that you don't want to hurt a person, that's all. I've got us into a position where many people are being hurt and I regret it, that's all. I don't in any way regret that I love you. I do love you Angie, and I always will, but try to understand my feelings. Now we have to face the music, and I hate it!"

"As long as you love me, Phil, I can go anywhere and hold my head up high," Angie said, "but don't ever take your love from me. I've come to depend upon it."

She buried her face into his chest and cried. As he held her, he recalled Priscilla and Joy. He bowed his head and wept bitterly.

When Philip entered Joy's room, he just stood there at the entrance and looked at her, unsure of what to do. Priscilla heard him enter, but she said nothing nor did she turn to acknowledge him. Angie stepped into the room and waited by his side. Joy seemed to know when he entered for she opened her eyes and smiled weakly.

"Hi Philip. Hi Angie," she said weakly, "Priscilla said you would be here. I was afraid that I wasn't going to see you again."

She began to cry weakly. She was relieved to see him. Philip swallowed the lump in his throat. He held back his tears for he didn't want to upset his little Joy. He walked over to her bed and hugged her gently to himself. He kissed her cheeks and wiped her tears with his handkerchief.

"Hey," he said tenderly, "my girl isn't going to cry is she. This is home-coming day! We're supposed to be happy!"

"I'm happy," Joy replied with a smile, "but I'm so tired all the time."

"Well now, what can I do to cheer up my girl?" he asked with a smile, "how about starting with a present! Huh? This is going to be like old times!"

He handed her a present wrapped in bright red paper and tied with a green ribbon. Joy's eyes opened wide in excitement for she always liked surprises. Philip laid her back on her pillow and held her hand.

"Priscilla, will you open it," Joy asked weakly, "I never can untie the ribbons."

"Sure darling," replied Priscilla tenderly. Her face was swollen from crying and her eyes were blood shot. Philip felt agony of soul as he sat across from her. She was still beautiful, even with a puffy face. In place of the pride and arrogance of six months ago was humility and tranquility. Priscilla opened the box. It contained a new dress of pink velvet.

"Oh Philip! It's darling! It's beautiful," the little girl exclaimed weakly, "Oh thank you Philip. And thank you too, Angie."

"We picked it out for you to wear home," said Philip.

"Philip, I really knew you'd come, but I worried a little bit," she said in a whisper, "you always said not to worry, but is it all right for me to worry just a little?"

Philip smiled and held back tears, but Angie turned her back momentarily to wipe her eyes.

"Yeh honey," he said as he tenderly laid his hand on her cheek, "because I have to admit that sometimes, I worry a little bit too."

"Philip, could we go to the jungles of the Amazon today?" she asked weakly.

"Well," he replied softly, "maybe we can, but first we have to ask the doctor. But I'll tell you what I'll do. I'll take you on a tour of the everglades right now. How about that?"

"Oh neato!" she exclaimed weakly, "We've never been there have we? I think we've been everywhere else but there."

"Well, first of all we're on a special kind of boat. See that big propeller behind us?" he began exuberantly, "That's what pushes us through the water."

"How big is it, Philip. I can't see it from my seat," replied Joy as she pretended that they were actually in the everglades.

"Oh, it's about…Oh heck! It's taller than me. It must be about seven feet tall," he said as he raised his arms over his head to about seven feet.

"Hey! Look over the side of the boat! There's an alligator ten feet long!" he shouted excitedly.

"Oh Philip, will it hurt us!" shrieked Joy weakly.

"No, he's just a little one," he replied in jest, "man eaters are forty feet long."

Just then the doctor entered to examine Joy. He asked everyone to step outside for a few minutes. When he stepped back out, he spoke with Priscilla and Philip.

"She's still losing blood," he began seriously, "We'll give her another pint of blood, but if the hemorrhaging doesn't stop soon, she won't make it through the night."

Philip dropped his head and sobbed. Angie took his arm to console him. Priscilla bit her lip and held back the tears as she watched Angie standing in her place. She wanted to die, but she knew that she had to be strong for Philip and Joy.

"Incidentally, Joy asked if you could carry her for a short walk," the doctor said, "the walk won't hurt her if you make it short. At present, unless the bleeding stops, all we can do is make her last few hours as pleasant and comfortable as possible."

"Thanks, Dr. Stone," replied Philip sadly, "she always liked to take walks. She always wants me to carry her. We both like that."

His voice trailed off as he remembered how he carried her around the nursing home every day. Without another word, he walked into Joy's room.

"All right doll, are you ready to go for a walk?" he said boldly to conceal his concern.

"Couldn't we sing a song first," she asked softly, "I'd like you to sing a song for me."

"What do you want me to sing," he asked hesitantly.

"Could you sing 'Every day's a Holiday' for me please," she asked as she reached out for his hand and clutched it lovingly in hers.

"Yeh. That's a good song. But we don't have any music," he replied.

"I'll imagine the music. We'll all imagine the music O.K. Priscilla!" she said, ""Oh Philip sing it for me, please Philip. I'll sing the 'it's a holiday' part like I always do."

It was all that he could do to hold back the tears that were straining to empty over his face. It was a happy song, and he did his best to sing it that way. To those who had slipped into the room after he entered, he was clearly not happy. Joy and Philip would sing once more to her great delight. As Priscilla sobbed internally, she witnessed a grand reunion and prayed that it was a fore taste of what was yet to come. 'Bless this hour Lord Jesus' she thought.

> 'Every day with you is a holiday, honey it's true,
> Anything we do it's a holiday, darling with you.
> I know that when I'm holding you it's a holiday,
> All my dreams come true it's a…'

He couldn't continue. His throat tightened and when his eyes met the laughing and suffering eyes of his precious Joy, he cried. He picked her gently out of her bed and squeezed her tenderly as she hugged his neck with all her strength.

"Don't cry Philip," pleaded Joy, with tears in her eyes, "I feel better already."

"Yeh. I guess I look silly don't I? Heck. I should be happy. Right?" he said as he rubbed his moistened eyes.

"Right!" exclaimed Joy weakly in glee, "could we go for that walk now?'

"O.K.," he replied as he picked her up from the bed and situated her in his arms, "here we go."

He carried her through the halls for about ten minutes and brought her back to her room. She was exhausted even though she wanted to walk some more. Phil sat her on the side of the bed beside himself. He supported her with the arm he had draped around her waist.

"Priscilla, will you come and sit with us," Joy asked weakly, "remember how we would sit around the bed and talk at night before I went to bed?"

Priscilla sat on the other side of Joy, much to the chagrin of Angie. Angie perceived the feeling Philip and Priscilla shared when she sat next to Joy. She knew that the sooner she could get him away from Priscilla the better it would be for her relationship.

"Joy, you must lay back down and preserve your energy," said Priscilla in concern.

"But I feel fine," complained Joy weakly, "really I do!"

Despite her protest, Joy didn't have the energy to resist. As Priscilla tucked her under the sheets, Philip turned to Angie and said, "Come over here with us Angie. We're going to have a circle of prayer."

He looked first at Joy and then at Priscilla and Angie and said, "We're all going to pray for Joy before we leave. Priscilla you take Joy's left hand and join hands with Angie. I'll take Joy's right hand and join hands with Angie."

Angie and Priscilla were hesitant about joining hands, but for the sake of Joy, they complied.

"Heavenly Father, we come to you asking you to put forth your healing hand and take away the affliction of our precious Joy. We love her and we trust you to care for her and keep her through the night. We thank you for hearing our request and pray that your will be done. We ask this in Jesus' name. Amen."

When he concluded the prayer, he smiled in reassurance at Joy.

"Joy," he said, "I have to leave tonight, but I'll be back tomorrow morning. I haven't left you alone, for God will send his angels to watch over you. Do you believe that?"

"Yes Philip," she replied with a smile, "everything will be O.K. now."

He turned to go and noticed Priscilla was staying behind. He knew that she would probably stay the night so he stepped back into the room to speak with her. She sat holding Joy's hand, hardly able to keep her eyes open. Priscilla was exhausted. She had no business sitting up through the night. He moved closer and tapped her lightly on the shoulder.

"Why are you staying the night?" he asked in concern, "She'll be all right. Trust God."

"I trust Him, Philip," she replied sleepily, "I just think that he might need some help. I don't want Him to think that we don't care enough to stay by the ones we love when they fight the good fight. Not all of us have faith like yours. For the rest of us, it requires a bit more work."

"Priscilla, if you'll go home and rest, I'll stay with Joy through the night. I agree with you. Someone should be here with her," he said.

"No, Philip. I'll be fine," she replied with a yawn.

"Priscilla, you are not spending the night here," he said firmly, "you are exhausted! You must get some rest. That's the doctor's orders!"

"Philip, I'm not leaving until Joy is safe," she replied.

"Oh yes you are," he said firmly.

He bent over and picked her up from the chair and carried her out into the hall.

"Philip, please," she pleaded, "I'll be all right. Now put me down. Joy needs me."

"We all need you, but you'll be the next one in a hospital bed if you don't get enough rest," he replied sternly, "Angie, stay with Joy until I get back!"

He darted down the hallway before Priscilla could say any more. He drove her to the nursing home and rang the bell. Elizabeth, his mother-in-law, answered the door. He felt ashamed to face her, but she exhibited no animosities, as she looked upon him for the first time in months.

"I'm sorry to wake you at this hour," he said as he set Priscilla's feet on the floor, "but your daughter seemed intent upon occupying the bed next to Joy. Please get her to bed for she's exhausted. I'm going back to the hospital to stay with Joy."

He turned to go, but Elizabeth called to him and he looked back.

"Thank you Philip," she said appreciatively, "she just won't listen to her mother."

He nodded his head in agreement, but said nothing as he made his way to the car. The events of the day had certainly proven that his love for Priscilla was not dead. She was just as obstinate as she ever was, but he remembered her when she was not quite so humble. She was concerned more for others than herself. What a shame to leave a woman like that, but it was a little late to turn around now. Angie loved him. He was grieved as he returned to the hospital. Angie was angry. She finally dropped the subject when he refused to discuss it, but she remained uneasy about her observations.

CHAPTER 34

A new commandment I give to you, That you love one another: as I have loved you, that you also love one another.

When Joy awoke the next morning she was greeted by Philip's smiling face. Angie was asleep with her head on the side of Joy's bed. They had spent the night at her bedside.

"Look Philip," said Joy happily, "I'm all better. I think I'll ask to go home after I eat dinner!"

"Why wait for dinner," teased Philip, "why not leave right now?"

"Because I ordered ice cream for dinner," she replied cheerfully.

"Oh," replied Philip, "so that's the reason."

"Why are you yawning, Philip," asked Joy curiously, "didn't you get any sleep?"

"As a matter of fact," he replied in jest, "we stayed up all night while you slept. Did you know that you snore every other breath?"

"Oh Philip," she replied playfully, "I do not!"

"O yes you do. And every other breath you call the pigs! You call out 'soooooooo eeeeeee, soooooooo eeeeeee'," he laughed as he teased.

"Philip, you're making that up," she snapped back playfully, "Isn't he Priscilla."

Priscilla had just entered, and had no idea what they were discussing, but she remembered how Philip and Joy would tease each other and she played along.

"I'm afraid that I have to agree with Philip," she said without so much as cracking a smile, "and he hasn't told you all of it either."

It pleased Philip that she went along with the game for Joy actually enjoyed the attention.

"Three times last night, you sat straight up in bed and shouted out 'I love Willy Moses'," he chuckled.

"Oh no I didn't! I don't like Willy Moses for a boyfriend," she shouted playfully, "I didn't say that, did I Priscilla."

"Oh yes you did," teased Philip.

Joy looked at Priscilla who shook her head no and smiled.

"See there!" Joy said as she pointed to Priscilla, "Priscilla said I didn't say it."

"Well, whom do you believe," he replied boisterously, "me or Priscilla?"

"Priscilla," she snapped with a smile, "she always tells the truth."

"She always spoils my fun," he remarked in jest.

"I think that the joking has gone far enough," she suggested with a smile.

"Oh well, I had her believing it for a while," he replied.

"No you didn't," said Joy exuberantly, "I knew that you were only teasing."

"Well, I'll tell you what I'm going to do," he said as he bent over closer to Joy, "you give me a big hug and a kiss. We have to get some sleep."

She reached out and hugged him, kissed him and smiled as he laid her back on the bed.

"Will you come back later," she asked.

"You bet we will," he replied emphatically, "we'll be back this evening."

He took Angie by the hand and they left. He noticed Priscilla watching them. He could see the pain in her heart manifested in her eyes. In the fun of the past few minutes, he was swept into the past and acted once more as he did when Joy, Priscilla and he laughed in times gone by. He was saddened that things were different now. He wondered if it were possible to reconcile even if both of them wanted it, given the hurt and mistrust between them now.

As he drove to the hotel, he thought upon the agony, which Priscilla harbored in her heart. This was nothing like the blunt, self-indulgent wife he had left six months ago. He knew that she still loved him and he wished that she would shout at him or be angry. Then, maybe he wouldn't feel so guilty. She looked so tired and he wondered how much she over worked herself, since Mr. Quilicy, the former administrator had retired. She was now the administrator. In her present state of health, she couldn't possibly continue the pace at which she was working. He stopped and looked back at Priscilla.

"Priscilla," he said in concern, "We're going to donate $ 100,000.00 to the nursing home. Please hire enough help so that you can work five eight-hour days and get your required rest. I know that you're over working yourself. I did this work once myself."

"Well thank you Philip," she replied graciously, "we can certainly use the extra revenue."

"Philip," she said in humility, "I once called you lazy and said all manner of cruel insults to you about your work at the nursing home. I am sorry for those grossly unjust and incorrect statements. I know now, that you worked extremely hard and did an outstanding job. Will you forgive me for my insolence?" she asked.

Before he could respond, she continued, "I only wish that I could do half the job which you did. I would also like to encourage you to stop by and visit the children. Angie you come as well. Please don't allow our personal misfortune to interfere with those abilities and gifts, which you execute so well. The children still ask about you, so please do stop by before you leave."

"O.K.," replied Philip sadly, "I'll do that. Well, we'll see you later this evening."

"Good-bye Philip," Priscilla said softly.

"Good-bye Philip," said Joy happily.

Philip and Angie did return that evening and twice the following day. They also visited the new nursing home. They found little Sabrina who had grown five inches longer and now weighted twenty-five pounds. It was sad to see the children after six months away from them. Elizabeth showed Philip and Angie through the new facility as if nothing had happened between them and her daughter. Philip was astounded that both mother and daughter had been transformed. Elizabeth was cordial and in no way did she treat Angie with disdain or spite. She actually went out of her way to make them feel welcome. In the entire visit, there was not even a mention of or insinuation to the marital problems of Philip and Priscilla.

At the insistence of Angie, Philip left Sunday afternoon, after he stopped by to see Joy. Joy was to be released that afternoon to return to the nursing home. He kissed her good bye and left with Angie on a six day chartered cruise. It was relaxing to spend some time away from the stress of travel. But the leisure gave Phil time to ponder his life and the events of the past six months. He yearned for those days at the nursing home when he enjoyed every moment of the day. He missed those snotty nosed kids and stringy hared children with whom he played and teased, like Joy and Sabrina. He also missed Priscilla. Yes, Priscilla most of all. They were all a part of him that would never die. Angie noticed his preoccupation and she also knew that he was being haunted by memories from Albany, with Priscilla and the nursing home.

Once again, they began to tour all the major cities of the US. The Keepers of the Flock packed each performance and received accolades in the news media. Philip was writing songs and each release was a hit. He had booked the group seven days a week, but they finally had a day off after working fourteen consecutive days. The only way to escape his memories was to stay excessively busy. Angie encouraged him, for she wanted to keep him away from Priscilla as much and as long as possible.

However, with the increased activity, came more strain on the band, which had many conflicts before the tour began. Phil was becoming impatient and independent. The finesse with which he once managed the group disappeared. He gave orders that were to be followed without question. He never associated with anyone but Angie. Even his friend Simeon was spurned. She deliberately manipulated him away from his close associates. Angie was now giving orders and Phil backed her up. Thus an impasse developed and the other three members of the band decided to voice their views and objections during practice one day. They chose Simeon as their spokes person.

"Phil, we would like a word with you before we end the practice," began Simeon humbly.

"Wow, people," Philip joked, "are you all going to gang up on me at once or one at a time?"

"We have been talking among ourselves and we have a few grievances we would like to express," said Simeon respectfully.

Philip perceived that they wanted to air their complaints and he instantly took the offense.

"All right cry babies. What is it now? Do you want more money? Do I have to give you all of my wealth," he shouted angrily.

"Philip, we don't want to cause turmoil," replied Simeon calmly, "but we don't want to be scheduled for any more seven day weeks. Five or six days we can go along with, but this is ridiculous. Nor do we want to take any more six-month tours. We like to see our friends and family on a regular basis. And we refuse to take orders from Angie. We expect everyone in the band to be treated the same."

"Philip remained silent, but each demand enraged him more. He ignited and spewed forth his anger upon his three assailants.

"You guys make me sick. You're a bunch of crybabies. I pay you more than other musicians make who are better than you. I have to pamper you and bow down to your whims. Well, let's get one thing straight. I run this show! I made this show! Without me, this group couldn't draw flies. The mob of fans screams for me. You people are just along for the ride! You're leaches, a bunch of free loaders! Now if any of you don't like the way I run the show, they can quit. I don't want to hear these petty complaints again! I've made my decision. Now, you make yours!" he shouted.

"Phil," replied Simeon in shock and grief, "I'll stay with you until the end of the tour, but when we get back to Albany, you can find another piano player. You're running from a past that haunts you daily. You're running scared. You're not the same person any more. Gone is the light-hearted' good-natured Philip we all knew. There's just a shell and a trace of the memory of the friend I used to know. The real Philip Wright is dead! An impostor has taken over his body and he's destroying all that Philip Wright stood for. These tears in my eyes aren't for me. They're tears of mourning for an old friend who has passed on. He has died to greed, pride and arrogance. You, whoever you are walking around in my good friends' body, I wish you would get out and defile that which remains of him no more!"

Philip was hurt and angry with himself, but he lashed out at his friends in rage.

"Get out! Get out I said!" he shouted as they retreated toward the exit, "you're all fired! I don't need you any more. Since you're so miserable, I'll spare you the agony of performing on stage with me. They'll scream just as loud for me and Angie, and we won't have to split the pie in so many pieces."

Angie and Milt, the producer, stood spellbound by the rapid-fire events of the past few minutes. Philip grabbed Angie by the arm and marched toward the exit. He shouted back over his shoulder to the producer, "Get a band for me! Get the best! Money is no object!"

"But where will I get one on such short notice!" he asked nervously.

"Pay whatever it costs," he snapped back angrily, "Just make sure you get the best!

They left the club and drove to their room. Angie said nothing and Philip brooded. As they entered the hotel, a small boy stood in the door selling candy. He asked Philip to buy some candy but he shoved the boy aside and he fell crying to the floor. Philip stopped and threw twenty dollars at him and stomped off.

"Take that and get out of here!" he shouted.

"Phil!" screamed Angie, "what is happening to you? Get hold of yourself!"

She grabbed him by the arm and led him quickly from an angry parent and a flock of reporters. He followed her like a scared little boy to their room. She seated him on the bed and sat beside him. Then she took his hand and kissed it and wrapped her arm about his shoulders. With his head bowed and shoulders slumped, he looked himself in the face for the first time in nine months.

"Simeon was right about everything," he mumbled sadly, "Angie, nothing is right and everything is wrong! Every time I turn around, I'm slapping my friends and loved ones around. I can't understand it!"

"Phil, maybe we're working too hard," she said sympathetically, "when this tour is over, we can take three weeks and go into recluse. It will be good to get away from the mobs of people. It'll be just you and me. Then we'll tour together. There won't be any more arguments with a band. You don't need one. You can ask for what you want. Don't be discouraged. Together we'll build a new world, a new hope and a new dream. Oh Phil, our day has just begun!"

She laid her head on his shoulder and kissed him tenderly on the neck. Philip wrapped his arm around her and folded her securely in his strong embrace. His mind was numb from the chaotic and discouraging occurrences of the day. He wanted to lock their door and stay safe from the screaming, fainting, arm waving mob of girls and women.

"Angie, I just don't know any more. It seems like the brighter the lights shine on me, the farther into darkness my soul plunges. You're all that I have left that I can count on, and you are stolen from another. You are forbidden fruit. What if I drive you away too," he said despondently, "I'm afraid Angie. I can't be trusted with love or friendship. I' bound to bring despair to you too."

"Phil," Angie pleaded, "you must not talk that way! It will be all right. Believe me, it will be O.K."

"That little boy that I shoved aside," he said sadly, "I don't know why I pushed him. I was mad at myself and I shoved an innocent little boy. Someone else's son, that's who I push around. The son I always wanted and never could have. But then what kind of father would I make for a child. I don't deserve a son. I can't even treat someone else's son with tenderness."

"I didn't know that you wanted children," whispered Angie, "wouldn't that be wonderful to someday have a son to run around the house? He would be so much enjoyment on tours. By the time he started school, we would probably be ready to settle down. Oh Phil, cheer up. Every thing's going to be all right."

"Angie, I don't know what I'd do without you," he replied softly, "it's times like this that make me know how much I need you."

"Phil, I love you. I'm going to take care of everything," she promised in a whisper, "Phil, you're tired and upset. Let's lay down for a while. I'll make it all better, Phil. I'll make it all better."

CHAPTER 35

Judge not that you be not judged.

And Priscilla dreamed a dream. She saw herself in a courtroom in heaven. On her side of the court were a multitude of angels. To her surprise, these angels were not happy, as she had always assumed angels would be. She heard them speaking behind her. 'This is she who wants to be relieved of her burden, which is to grievous to be borne.' On the other side of the court, sat Philip in the defendant's chair. He was sad and meek. Behind him, were a band of happy angels. These beings were sinister in appearance, not at all godly, but evil. Though they sat on his side of the courtroom, they were very much against him, and laughing because they knew that he would be found guilty.

"Your honor, in summation, this Philip Wright, one of God's wayward servants and errant children, is guilty of neglect of his responsibilities. He has turned his back on his beloved wife, spurned the affection of a precious group of orphans who need his care and who he, himself, has caused to expect his attention and affections. This man is not worthy of a greater mission. He is filled with iniquity. We have proved and substantiated his erotic behavior with Angie Mathews and his deliberate transgression of the law of the Most High God. The prosecution submits that this man is an impostor! He is not what he pretends to be! He is in fact a demon-possessed fool, filled with blasphemy. Let him hurt his loved ones no longer. Let them no longer bear his burdens. Let him pay the price of death!"

"Oh no!" screamed Priscilla as she stood to protest the suggestion of her attorney, "You can't take his life! There's still hope that he might change!"

"Out of order," retorted the stern judge as he rapped his gavel to restore order, "you will sit and remain silent while this trial resumes!"

She sobbed as the attorney for the defense stood and sadly spoke, "Your honor, I'm afraid that I can only appeal for mercy for my client. You see there is no-one on earth who will speak on his behalf."

"I'll speak on his behalf," sobbed Priscilla as she stood in uncontrollable anxiety, "Your honor, I will testify on his behalf!"

"Objection, your honor. She cannot be both accuser and friendly witness in the same proceeding. She has put forth her petition and it is too late for her to change now!" shouted her attorney.

"Your honor, he doesn't deserve to die," pleaded Priscilla, "I never intended that he should die. I merely wanted to be relieved of the terrible burden, which he brought upon me. I don't hate him your honor. I still love him, but I'm no longer able to bear this grievous burden."

"Order in the court!" demanded the judge again, "Order in the court!"

The judge studied Priscilla momentarily, then said, "this is without precedent, but since a man's life hangs in the balance, and since no other witness has come forward, you may answer a few questions that have come to my mind as the trial has proceeded. First of all, if he was and still is such a scoundrel, how did you fall in love with him?"

"Well, your honor, he used to be tender and meek. In fact," she said lovingly as she gazed upon Philip, "he still is. But this past year he hasn't been himself."

"When did he change?" asked the judge.

"Shortly after we married," she replied.

"Why did he change?" he asked.

"I don't know," answered Priscilla uncomfortably.

"Did you do anything to encourage or aggravate the negative changes?" he asked pointedly. "Your honor, I'm not on trial," she protested, "am I?"

His piercing gaze unnerved her. His questions seemed aimed more at her than Philip.

"Why did he turn away from the nursing home and spurn the children," he continued.

"To pursue a singing career," answered Priscilla anxiously.

"I have done a bit of research in the archives concerning Philip Wright, and the records indicate that he disliked professional singing and was pushed and encouraged into it by another person. What is your response to that?" he asked pointedly.

"Well," stammered Priscilla nervously, "it's true your honor."

"Who is that person?" the judge asked.

"It was I," answered Priscilla in shame.

"The accuser has stated that Philip was a glory hound and only pretended to serve Jehovah. What is your response to that charge," he asked.

"Not true, your honor," she answered softly, "Philip loved his God and his work. He never ceased praising God the Father or talking of the nursing home. That is, until I humiliated him and taunted him against the Father's will."

"Why do you say 'against the Father's will'," he asked.

"Because that's all he talked about when we traveled," she replied.

"Why didn't he pursue his goal?" asked the judge.

"Your honor, must I answer these questions?" she again protested.

"No, but remember that the life of your husband is on the line. So far, his sin seems to be that he listened to the voice of his wife instead of the voice of the Lord. That was the primary factor in his separation from the Most High God, which is the real root of this problem," the judge explained, "now will you answer my questions or shall we proceed with the sentence on this very limited evidence in his defense?"

Reluctantly, Priscilla answered, "the truth is that I persuaded him quite against his will, to pursue a career in entertainment. I confess that it was I who caused him to turn away from his chosen profession, indeed the profession to which God called him. I thought that the two of us could travel and continue the partnership of his song writing and my arrangements, which coupled with our combined musical talents, would provide a good income. I insisted that he continue even when my health rendered me physically incapable of the rigorous stress of travel. Because he loved me, he agreed to promote the music business, on the condition that I assist with the nursing home. But, your honor, I wanted him to be someone outstanding. Why should he waste those musical gifts? He was quite content to be unheard of, your honor, and he has such marvelous talents as a songwriter and singer. I merely wanted what I felt was best for him."

"You were in effect, doing God's thinking for Him," he said sternly, "I understand your thinking, but the problem is that you don't understand the thinking of the Most High God. You were Philip's helpmate, but you actually contributed greatly to his demise."

"But sir, I didn't know," she complained.

"Yes indeed," he replied, "that is your salvation. Nonetheless, you have never really made an effort to understand him. Have you?"

"No, your honor," she answered with head bowed down, "I'm sorry to say that I haven't"

"Why have you stood in his defense," asked the stern judge, "You've done nothing but complain about him to date. Is this not strange?"

"Yes, your honor, I suppose that it is," she answered, "but I feel responsible for this whole thing. Even your questions, point to me as the culprit."

"On the contrary," answered the judge, "you can't be blamed any more than your husband. You were both at fault in that neither one of you has done the will of the Father. However, your constant complaint about the consequences of your sin has brought this matter before the throne of judgment. Can grace abound at the throne of judgment? Prayer, supplication, and fasting; these things can change your present and alter the future. But all your railing accusations can only serve to destroy him. Don't you know that your husband has trials also? He has already succeeded far more than you! The fact that he is presently bogged down in the mire of sin, does not undo all the good works and loving service he performed before he slid back into transgression. Was he not a pillar of strength when you needed him? Did he not faithfully witness to you? If his message had seeded in your heart, this catastrophe could have been different. Do you think that the tempter could not have been prevented from enslaving your husband in the bondage of adultery? If God has allowed it, who can prevent it? God, who can do no wrong, has allowed this to culminate. But if you turn earnestly to Him in prayer, will He not hear and act on your behalf, according to his will? I say to you that your actions affect all that is dear to you. Be not deceived. You heard Lucifer that devil; ask for your husband's life. He will also ask for yours, when it suits his convenience. He sought to separate you and Philip, in the infancy of your love, by attempting to take your life. That failing, when the Most High God intervened at Philip's pleadings, he now seeks to destroy Philip. The possibilities for the two of you are grander than you can imagine! God has been, and is even now appealing to you, to place your fate in His never failing care."

"What will become of Philip? "asked Priscilla in tears, "is there any hope for him?"

"Only The Most High God can save him," replied the judge, "Lucifer has bound him and will not surrender without a battle. That deceiver has boasted that he used the woman God gave to Philip and destroyed him with her."

"Is there anything that I can do to help my husband?" asked Priscilla in tears.

"Pray and carry on his work in hopes that the Lord of Hosts will be merciful to your household. Satan has deceived you into being the greatest accuser of your husband on earth. By trusting in the Lord Jesus Christ, God's only begotten son, you can find courage to defeat that serpent and assist your husband from the pit of sin. Finally, be a believer, even as Philip was and still is! Yes, he is still a believer, even though the enemy has him in his sway. If you can believe as strongly as Philip, you can overcome Satan, that liar and murderer. It will be a fierce battle, but the victory will be worth it all!"

"Your honor, I beg you to have mercy on Philip and forgive me for accusing him. I am not worthy to accuse anyone!" she pleaded.

"I can not change the verdict of death," the judge replied sternly, "only God can do that, for with Him all things are possible. I can, however, delay the penalty in hopes that he can restore himself in the grace of the Most High God."

"Objection your honor!" shouted the attorney defiantly, "he is guilty and worthy of death! Let be now! It must be now!"

Priscilla leaped to her feet and charged the attorney.

"Why you're the devil himself," she shouted, "you can't be human! You're a murderer!"

She grabbed the attorney by the arm and turned him around to see his face. She was shocked to see that the face of the prosecuting attorney was her own!

She sat up in bed as terror filled her soul. Oh how she wanted and needed Philip!

"Oh Heavenly Father! Help us!" she prayed, "Please don't take my Philip from me!"

CHAPTER 36

Hope deferred makes the heart sick, but when the desire comes, it is a tree of life.

"Yes Philip," Priscilla said softly, "the children are fine. Yes, I did hire extra help. We have three extra nurses aides and another full time registered nurse."

"What about you," Philip asked in concern, "are you taking those two days off the doctor told you to take? You know that you're still under a doctor's care. Don't try to work like you used to. You'll never be able to bear the strain. You just aren't able."

"I'm doing fine. The extra personnel definitely enabled me to better schedule my time. I do take more time away from the job," she said appreciatively.

"Tell Joy that I'll be seeing her in a couple of weeks. I'll bring a bag of toys for the kids. Don't tell them though," he said cheerfully, "I want it to be a surprise."

"Phil, how are you," asked Priscilla, "you've talked about everyone except yourself."

"Oh heck, you know me," he stuttered awkwardly, "doing quite well, I guess. We're still selling out our concerts"

"Yes, I know" she replied pleasantly, "I read about your appearances and we listen to your songs on the radio. Philip, I've been concerned. The songs you've written and recorded lately have been so depressing. I see in them sadness and burden. I'm not suggesting anything," she quickly interjected, "but I know that you've strayed from God. Philip make things right with the Lord and your world will be filled with laughter once more. This is the third time in two weeks that you've called. You're reaching for hope. I'm not that hope. Only the Most High God can fill the void, which presently fills your heart and soul. Trust Him again and go to Him in prayer like you used to do. I'll continue praying for you and you know that Joy mentions you every day in her prayers."

"Priscilla," he replied and then paused.

"Yes," she answered expectantly.

"Never mind," he responded hesitantly, "take care of yourself and kiss Joy for me. I have to get to rehearsal."

"Good-bye Philip," she said tenderly.

"Good-bye," he sighed as he hung up the phone.

When Elizabeth went to the playroom that evening for devotions, she found Priscilla playing the piano. Her face was set as if she were being transported on a scenic cruise. Elizabeth seated herself on the end of the bench and listened until Priscilla ended the song.

"That's a pretty song," she said as she hugged her daughter, "it's rather sad. I seriously doubt if the Lord would approve of our mourning. We're to be happy in our work."

"I know mother, "Priscilla replied sadly, "but I was remembering the happy days with Philip and the nursing home and thanking the Lord for the twenty one months of happiness we had together."

"Isn't that another of the songs Philip wrote?" asked her mother.

"Yes it is. It's titled 'I Won't Be Happy til I Have You Here with Me'. He wrote it when I was spending the Easter break with you and father. He said that he missed me terribly, sat down and wrote this song," she said dreamily, "It's quite ironic that I would be playing it now."

"You must be careful that you don't get carried away in your hopes and dreams," warned her mother, "Philip called again today didn't he."

"Yes, he did," replied Priscilla sadly, "he's miserable. He's reaching out to anyone who can console his weary spirit. Mother, it hurts to see him this way. He has fallen down to the gutters of hell. Philip was always happy, perpetually optimistic and always ready to lend a hand to others. Mother, I know that he still loves me. I can feel it when he talks to me. But he doesn't know how to come back and be free of his entanglements. I feel as if the

Lord will bring him back to me and restore our marriage. I know that's what he wants. But Angie will do all she can to keep us apart. At the hospital and the nursing she hung on to him and made sure that we were never alone. Then she rushed him out of town as soon as possible."

"Priscilla, remember that you must be concerned for the soul of Angie, too," said Elizabeth.

"Why should I be concerned for her," retorted Priscilla indignantly, "she stole him from me. She deserves to lose him. She didn't care how my heart ached when she broke up my home. She didn't lie awake nights and worry about me while she made love to my husband. Mother, whose side are you on?"

"I'm on the Lord's side," she answered tenderly, "that is the only way I can really be on your side. God demands that which is best for all his creation. Priscilla you must also include Angie in your prayers. God will not restore your home until you conduct yourself in a Godly manner. He's just as concerned for Angie as He is for you and me. Your father is beginning to see the light. He spoke with me about calling off the divorce if I would forget about this nursing home. I could turn my back on these children and you and return to a life of splendor and luxury, but what would I have? I'd have the same problems we've had for thirty years. No, Priscilla, when your father comes back it will be on God's terms."

"Mother you're right again," Priscilla apologized, "but tonight I can't help but be sad. Let's have our devotions. Maybe that will lift this burden off my heart and I can rejoice again."

They read scripture, studied and discussed the Word, and sang 'The Old Rugged Cross' and 'Victory in Jesus'. Her mother was tired and she said good night, kissed Priscilla and retired to bed. Priscilla still ached in her heart for her husband and sought an avenue to release her emptiness. She turned to the music of Philip's song and sang.

'I've tried a thousand ways to escape your memory,
I strive in vain each night to sleep; you're haunting me,
I can't go on like this for my heart just won't be free,
I won't be happy till I have you here with me.

Time after time I've tried to pretend I didn't care,
That I don't need your love or keep you in my prayers.

Each day is heartache and it will be eternally,
I won't be happy till I have you here with me.

Why do I always cry, why can't I be gay and free,
Who else is there but you, who can put my heart at ease? (Tell me)
When will we meet again, when will you come back to me,
Then will my smiles begin, I will live again.

Angels in heaven can surely see, my misery,
They hear this heart of mine my sweet, calling to Thee,
I wait and long for you for my heart, just won't be free,
I won't be happy till I have you here with me.
I won't be happy till I have you here with me.'

Priscilla cried through the song as she sang it, but it was a relief to express her pain. She not only thought of herself and Philip but also her mother and father. Both Priscilla and her mother were enduring the hardship of a broken home and each yearned for the restoration of her home.

Angie stepped out of the rain and seated herself in the front seat of the car. Philip laid his writing pad with a newly penned song on the dash and kissed her as she shook the rain from her rain cap.

"Hey, be careful," he exclaimed as he turned his face from the scattered drops, "you're getting me all wet."

"Why didn't you come to the door and get me," she teased, "I'm supposed to get special attention from now on. Doctors orders."

"Oh yeh! What did he tell you? It's all in your head?" he laughed.

"No. He told me it's all in my tummy," she answered with a smile.

"What are you doing, getting an ulcer or something?" he teased.

"Or something," she replied.

"Hey! Come on now," he demanded in jest, "what did he say?"

"He said that I am pregnant," she answered bluntly as she watched for his reaction.

"Come on Angie! Seriously, what did he say," he retorted in aggravation.

"His exact words were 'young lady, you are pregnant.' He told me that at this early stage, both mother and baby are well. And he gave me our approximate due date," she replied, looking to Philip for support and excitement.

"Oh no!" he complained as he slapped the steering wheel, "how could it happen to you? You're a nurse!"

"That doesn't make me immune from the laws of nature," she retorted defensively, "I wish I could say that this isn't true, but it is! We're going to have a baby!"

"This is going to kill Priscilla," he moaned.

"What? I'm pregnant with your baby and you're worried about Priscilla!" screamed Angie, "don't ever mention her name around me again! Ever!"

"You did this on purpose," he accused as he pointed his finger in her face.

"You think that I trapped you!" she screamed, "is that what you think? Well, good-bye Philip Wright! I hate you! I hate you!"

She opened the door to step into the rain. Philip reached out and clutched her by the arm, pulling her back inside the car. She was sobbing uncontrollably and attempting to pull away from his grasp.

"Angie!" he shouted as he tried to calm and reassure her, "you can't go out there. It's pouring rain. Angie, please settle down. I'm sorry. I'm sorry. I didn't mean it that way."

"Well how did you mean it," she demanded angrily, "Philip, I did not get pregnant deliberately to trap you! Do you understand that?"

She screamed in his face and trembled in anger, as she repeated, "Do you understand that?"

"O.K., honey. O.K.," he replied nervously, "I believe you."

"Well don't act like you're the only one who suffers," she cried bitterly, as she allowed him to nestle her in his strong and comforting embrace.

"Didn't I tell you that I was trouble going somewhere to ruin someone else's life," he said sadly, "but you wouldn't listen."

"Phil, I'm sorry," she cried bitterly, "I had hoped you would be happy about it!"

"Angie! Honey! Please calm down!" he pleaded tenderly, "I'm not sorry that we're having a baby. I just hate the circumstances. Angie, I love you and I'll love our baby. Why did it have to happen like this?"

She laid her head on his shoulder and looked into his eyes. She wrapped her arms around his neck and squeezed tightly.

"You're not ashamed of me?" she asked.

"No Angie. How could I be ashamed of the mother of my baby?" he said softly, "I just hope we have time to get the divorce and get married before the baby is born,"

"If you had listened to me, you would have started the proceedings five months ago when we were in Albany," she whimpered, "but you didn't want to hurt Priscilla's feelings."

"Well, one thing about it," he replied, "she won't contest the divorce now."

"Wait until the papers get word of this," Angie said dejectedly, "We'll get a full page article. Oh Philip, this is the worst part of this business. Those vultures swoop down on you in your most humiliating moments."

"Yeh, but I'm getting used to it," he replied.

They sat silently for a few moments before Philip broke the silence.

"What a mess," he mumbled, "What a fool I am! May God forgive me my pride and stupidity."

Philip was right. Priscilla made no effort to stop the divorce when she learned that Angie was pregnant. She remembered how Philip would conquer defeat and disappointment and said to the Lord in her heart 'I give thanks for this, for I know that the Most High God will glorify His Name through this development.' Afterward, she wept bitterly for the entire evening but she regained her composure and experienced an inner peace she had never known before. The matter was settled at last. She could put it out of her mind.

However, she still continued to pray for his soul. She asked the Lord, daily, to restore him as he was. The divorce weighed upon her mind. She worked even harder to escape the heartache that accompanied leisure. The divorce wouldn't be final until two weeks after the expected due date of the baby. She wished that the baby could be born with Philip's surname. Secretly she wished that the baby had been born to Philip and her.

During the next seven months, Philip drastically reduced his number of personal appearances. During the last four months of the pregnancy, Angie didn't join him on stage, but she traveled with him. All the controversy only served as free publicity. Philip continued to release a hit every month. He received accolades from across the world. He contracted to an hour long special in which he was to sing many of his greatest hits. At the end of the show, he would be awarded for his contribution to rock music. At

Philip's insistence, it was scheduled three weeks after Angie's due date so that she could be with him as his wife.

Priscilla made the best of her lot, but Philip and Angie enjoyed the last seven months before Angie's delivery. They looked forward to the baby with great expectation. He wanted a son. Angie had no preference. He showered her with attention and affection and he began to revert back to himself. He was happy and soon to be the father of a son. He hoped.

Eddie Leone, Angie's former fiancé, had now graduated from college and was serving his internship as St. Joseph's Hospital. He had also offered to stop by the nursing home to examine the children on a monthly basis. As he closed his medical bag, Priscilla entered the room.

"Eddie, I can't tell you how much your contribution is appreciated," she said appreciatively, "it seems strange though, after all that has happened that you would offer a hand."

Eddie knew what she referred to but he didn't want to discuss it.

"If you're referring to Angie and what's his name," Eddie replied dryly, "I prefer to discuss another topic."

"I merely mention them because they're living here in Albany and I wouldn't be surprised if Angie delivers in St. Joseph's Hospital," she replied, "They're just a few miles from the hospital."

"Well Angie did me dirt and Philip double crossed me," said Eddie angrily, "he was a real friend. He took my girl while I was away educating myself so that Angie and I could get married."

"Eddie, let me say something," she replied earnestly, "we both played big roles in that affair. I pushed Philip to make it big in show business and drove him from my arms. I was too blind to see that he was hungry for affection. You had a good girl waiting for you while you were going to college. You should have known better than to encourage her to sing with Philip. It was at your insistence that she took the job. You handed her to Philip. She led a lonely life waiting for you. Philip needed someone to boost his ego after I humiliated him. Please, Eddie, for your own conscience as well as the welfare of every one involved, forgive them and get this barrier from between you and the Lord."

"Priscilla, It's hard to forgive when you've been hurt in love," he retorted bitterly.

"But It's easy to love when you've forgiven," replied Priscilla warmly.

CHAPTER 37

How often shall my brother sin against me, and I shall forgive him? Until seven times? 'I say to you, until seventy times seven.'

Angie's travail was a long and arduous labor. Philip brought her to St. Joseph's Hospital at five in the evening on Saturday. The severe labor began at about midnight. At about three a.m. the pain became extremely intense. Philip was in the labor room and she called to him for relief.

"Phil," she moaned, "rub my back. Harder! Rub harder! Oh Phil! It hurts! It hurts!"

"I am rubbing, Angie," he said nervously, "Where does it hurt?"

At the base of my back," she winced, "Oh no! Not again!"

She stiffened and rolled on her side digging her fingers into Philip's wrist. She wondered how much longer the hard labor would last.

"Phil, I'm sorry for crying out," she said in pain, "I said that I would be brave, but it hurts! It hurts so much!"

He watched helplessly and nervously stood by through each contraction, until it ended and she would relax again. All his money and fame were of no value to him now. His child and the mother of his child were in the hands of God. She was now in her thirteenth hour of labor and he cried out in his soul 'Lord please get these pains over with soon! Don't make her suffer any longer than necessary. Deliver Angie and the baby safely through this ordeal. Please Lord! I beg you! Hear my prayer. In Jesus name I pray. Amen'.

"Oh!" she groaned again, "Go! Get a nurse quick!"

"He darted into the hall and returned with a nurse. He waited outside the labor room until the nurse came out.

"What's wrong?" he asked anxiously.

"Everything is all right now," she replied, "it won't be much longer now."

In thirty minutes, she was wheeled into the delivery room. Before she left, she reached up and hugged him with tears in her eyes.

"It will all be over soon," she said confidently, "we'll soon have our baby."

Philip walked into the delivery room to wait. He found that a minute of waiting was like an hour of activity. There were three other men waiting with him and each time a doctor entered the room his heart leaped in expectation. One of the fathers knew that his baby would be born dead. 'Oh Lord! Don't let anything happen to our baby' he thought. Then he realized for the first time that Angie's life could very possibly be in danger. What if it came to a choice between Angie and the baby? He would rather save Angie than the baby. He prayed silently in his heart 'Please Holy Father, be with Angie and the baby. Bring both of them safely through the delivery.' He walked the floor and then sat down for a few minutes. Then he repeated this pattern about every ten minutes. He was tired and nervous. At last the doctor entered and Phil studied his face for any sign of an announcement.

"Congratulations, Mr. Wright," he said as he extended his hand, "you are the father of a seven pound boy!"

"How are they?" he asked anxiously.

"The baby is fine," he replied soberly, "but Angie had a very hard delivery and her condition is serious. She had complications which have left her in an extremely weakened state."

"She'll live won't she?" he exclaimed grabbing the arm of the doctor.

"We'll keep her under observation for twenty four hours," he replied seriously, "we'll have a nurse with her around the clock. Don't panic Mr. Wright. We won't know her exact condition for a few hours. The first twenty four hours will tell the story."

Can I see her?" he asked nervously.

"Yes, but only for few minutes," the doctor replied," she may be a bit incoherent, but don't be alarmed. It's the effects of the anesthesia."

He led Philip to the recovery room and instructed him to wait until the nurses left the room. As they left, he entered and found Angie holding their son. He moved closer and began to look at their son. He beamed as he looked for the first time at their healthy baby boy. He cried as he thrilled at the sight of his first-born and he wanted to shout his joy to the world. He watched intently as the nurse took his son from Angie and left for the nursery. With teary eyes, he walked to her side and beamed at the mother of his son. She was weary from the long labor, but she was thrilled to see him. She reached out for him and he bent over her and held her close. She sobbed softly and wrapped her arms weakly around his neck.

"Oh Phil, I'm so happy," she sobbed, "He's so strong and pretty."

"I never thought new babies were pretty, but he's the best looking baby I've ever seen," said Philip proudly.

"I was afraid that all the hard labor would hurt him," she replied as she looked at Philip in concern, "did you notice anything wrong with him? He has all his fingers and toes. Oh Phil, you must examine him closely."

"Angie, he's fine. Don't worry, "he replied in consolation, "he's tough as a pine knot. You just rest now. He'll be fine."

"You should have heard him when he was born," Angie replied softly, "he was born crying. He was so loud that I thought the whole hospital heard it."

"How do you feel," asked Philip in concern, "you look worn out."

"I am tired," she replied wearily, "I didn't want to fall asleep before you got here."

"I would have had to wake you up if you had been asleep," Philip replied with a smile, "how could I leave here without seeing you first?"

"I love you Philip. We did good, didn't we?" she said sleepily, "Phil, something is bothering me."

"What is it honey?" he asked anxiously, "What could trouble you at a time like this?"

"I never told you, but I dreamed the same dream twice before today," she said as she laid her head back on her pillow and held his hand tenderly.

"We were walking through the nursing home together. I was carrying our son and we were laughing and talking. An old man was showing some visitors through the nursing home. He called the children by name as he pointed each one out. Then he pointed to our baby and said 'this one is Priscilla's baby.' The visitors all gathered around our son. But they all kept saying 'isn't Priscilla's baby beautiful!'"

"Now honey, don't get all upset over a dream," he said in encouragement, "It's only a dream."

"Oh Phil, I love you," she said, "We won't let them take our baby away, will we!"

"No Angie. He's our son and that's how it is," he replied tenderly, "why don't you get some rest and I'll get some rest too. I'll come back in a few hours to see you again."

"Oh, yes Phil," she replied wearily, "I'm so tired."

"I love you Angie," whispered Phil as he kissed her tenderly, "rest honey. I'll be back soon."

She seemed to be sleeping as he walked out of the room. He paused momentarily at the door and looked back. She was beautiful even in her weary state. As he left, he proceeded toward the nursery to see his son again, but he was halted by a piercing scream.

"Phil! Oh Phil," screamed Angie.

He wheeled about and ran to her room and soon emerged from her room shouting, "Get a doctor! Anybody! Get a doctor!"

Two hours later, Philip was at the nursing home pleading with Priscilla. She was angry, but Philip was persistent with his plea. Priscilla, however, had hardened her heart to his request.

"Priscilla, please go and see her," he begged.

"For the last time Philip, the answer is no," she firmly replied, "I have no feeling for that woman!"

"Priscilla," he said with trembling lips, "Angie is just clinging to life. She wants to be reassured that her baby will be cared for if she dies! You could encourage her to recover, and you would, if you were really a child of God! I've been in the grace of the Lord and I know that he demands some hard things at times. All I can say is that if she dies and you haven't helped her, then you've failed to witness at a time when Angie might need it most!"

"I have no intention of seeing her no matter what you say," she retorted stubbornly, "you'd best get back to her for I'm sure that she needs you."

He rushed out the door and jumped into his car. He returned to the hospital to Angie's side. Priscilla angrily hobbled to her office and sat behind her desk. She began to read a report as her mother entered and sat in a chair opposite her.

"I couldn't help hearing," she said in concern, "you were quite loud! Do you think that your response was the best decision for the glory of God?"

"Mother!" exclaimed Priscilla disgustedly, "Don't you start too! Do you actually think that I should go to the bedside of the woman who destroyed my home and stole my husband from under my nose?"

"Should God have come to us after we failed our husbands and had no-one else to whom to turn," asked her mother softly.

"Do you know what she wants me to do?" asked Priscilla angrily, "she wants me to take care of her son! I'd say that takes guts! She asks me to care for her son, the son I always wanted and never could have for my husband! I won't do it mother! I wouldn't do it for anyone!"

"Priscilla, you have been a mother to forty-five children for over a year now," her mother replied earnestly, "their parents could be murderers or thieves for all we know. And yet, I haven't seen you mistreat any of the children for what their parents may have done. Nor have I seen any indication that it has even crossed your mind. You have just been paid the highest compliment that can be paid by one woman to another woman. When a mother thinks that her time is near, she worries first about her children. Angie may have sinned against God and in the process stole your husband, but she will do all in her power to protect her child. In her opinion, the most reliable and dependable person she knows and would trust her baby to is you, Priscilla. God will hold you accountable for this if you don't do that which you know in your heart is His will. It is written, 'all Thine are mine and all mine are Thine.' That goes for the baby and it includes Angie. Did not her spirit spring forth from the same creator as yours? We're all part of the same master plan. The only barrier is the one you have built in your heart. Priscilla, I implore you honey, 'don't harden your heart.' Priscilla, let's pray about it."

"Oh, mother," Priscilla sobbed, "it won't do any good! I can't do it! I just can't do it!"

Elizabeth clasped her daughter's hands in tears and they prayed together. When they finished praying, Priscilla and her mother slipped on their coats and drove to the hospital.

At the hospital, Priscilla wrestled with herself. She despised Angie. She was jealous of the happiness which she and Philip shared at the birth of their son. She very nearly balked at the parking lot but the Holy Spirit encouraged her to go to Angie. They walked past the nursery and she stopped to view Philip's son. She saw the name and her heart was pierced with agony. At the same time, she was warmed as she watched the tiny infant kicking angrily. She had compassion on him and wondered if he was hungry. He was strong and lovely. She followed her mother to Angie's room. She hesitated momentarily, and then entered as her heart pounded. Philip was slumped over Angie as he held her right hand. When he saw Priscilla, he burst into tears of thanksgiving and relief as he sobbed to Angie, "Priscilla's here."

She stirred weakly and tried to raise her head. As Priscilla drew nearer so that she could see her face, Angie wept.

"Priscilla," she said softly, "God has sent you to me today. I've prayed that you could come. There's so much to say."

"Wouldn't it be best to save your strength," Priscilla suggested.

"I have to speak to you," she insisted weakly, "I've wronged you and taken that which God did not give to me. Now I am paying the price. I'm sorry Priscilla. I'm truly sorry. But, I don't want my baby to pay for my sins. Would you please care for him as your own and love him as I would if I were here. I may not recover, but my baby still needs a mother."

"Yes, I will Angie," replied Priscilla. She was choking with emotion, but she held her peace while Angie resumed.

"I just want to say," she whispered softly, "that I love you as a sister. I always have. I never intended to hurt you. I thought that only Philip and I would know. I wanted him so much that I was blinded to the sorrow that I caused to you. We committed the sin of wanting each other against the will of the Most High God. At our own insistence, we took one another and brought about this great shame. I am truly, truly sorry for what I've done Priscilla. I've asked the forgiveness of God and now I ask you. Will you forgive me?"

Priscilla was overwhelmed by the confession of Angie and the simultaneous moving of the Holy Spirit in her heart as her soul wept for Angie. The hatred, which only minutes before stood as a great chasm between them, was removed in forgiveness as Priscilla fell upon Angie and embraced her in love. She and Angie wept together. Philip, Elizabeth, Priscilla and Angie were immersed in the healing power of forgiveness and the love of God.

"I forgive you Angie," Priscilla sobbed, as she looked into her eyes, "I too have been at fault and I beg your forgiveness. I have despised you just as bitterly as you despised me. Angie, you must get well for the sake of your baby. I'll care for him until you recover, but he will need his mother. God wants you to live! He intends for you to see your son grow to manhood, but you must look to him for strength. Trust Him Angie, and God will heal you!"

"Would God heal me after all the horrible things which I have done?" asked Angie in tears.

"All have fallen short of the glory of God," replied Priscilla softly, "but He is quick to forgive those who seek Him out and trust Him."

"Priscilla, I want to live. I do want to live. I want to raise my baby," she sobbed as she held tightly to the hand of Priscilla.

Priscilla remembered what Philip did in Joy's hospital room and decided to lead prayer.

"Mother," she said as she looked over her shoulder, "you come and join hands with Philip and I. Philip and I will hold Angle's hand and we'll form a circle of prayer."

After joining hands, Priscilla prayed.

"Our precious Heavenly Father, We come to you to speak of our needs. We thank you for the love of your son who made our salvation possible with his death and resurrection. We praise your Holy Name that you have restored the love of your son among us and destroyed the barriers, which Satan placed between us. We leave the destroyer to your sure hands and come to you for guidance and deliverance. Deliver Angie from the hand of the one who threatens her life. Holy Father heal Angie. Deliver her for the glory of your name, that others may know the power of the true and living god. We believe that you are with us and we expect you to move with mighty power to the glory of your eternal kingdom both now and ever more. We ask this in Jesus' mighty name. Amen."

CHAPTER 38

They that wait upon the Lord shall renew their strength;
they shall mount up with wings as eagles; they shall run
and not be weary; and they shall walk and not faint.

Angie did recover. All who knew the circumstances said that a great miracle was performed. God took a hand in it to be sure. However, the greatest miracle was not apparent to the human eye. The most marvelous miracle of that dark hour was the destruction of the hatred, which had separated these three young people. God had bridged the gap with the tonic of confession and testimony. The healing of Angie was merely a sign of that relationship miracle which had been wrought by a wonderful and loving God.

Priscilla forgave completely. She took little Kevin to the nursing home with her and she placed the crib beside her bed. Angie spent three weeks in the hospital. While she was confined, Kevin couldn't have had a better keeper. He brightened Priscilla's day and added excitement and pleasure to the nursing home. Priscilla visited Angie each day to give a progress report on the baby. Angie also called two or three times each day.

Philip, however found himself in a peculiar situation. With his son in the care of Priscilla, he spent more time at the nursing home. He was becoming ever more attracted to her. Being in her presence daily stirred his emotions and drew them closer. However, he had committed to Angie, and also there was the matter of their son, Kevin. For the first time in months, he began to pray daily. After all his worry and prayer, he still had no answer. There was nothing he could do to remedy the situation. At last, he remembered what he once did we he had exhausted his own means. He brought the problem to the alter of God and laid it before Him. He put the problem from his mind and left it with the Most High God to solve it in his own divine way and perfect time.

In the third week of her hospital stay, Angie spoke with Philip about a burden, which had been troubling her. Now she was well on the way to complete recovery and they were walking the halls together.

"Phil, your divorce will be final in a few days," she began solemnly, "I feel, that under the circumstances, you should stop the proceedings."

"Angie, are you serious?" asked Philip bewildered, "I can't stop it now! I can't adopt our son until we're married."

"Phil, I've been thinking," she responded earnestly, "would our marriage be founded on principles as unshakable as those that enabled Priscilla to cling to the hope of her marriage being restored?

Her marriage was built upon the firm foundation of love and the blessing of God. She didn't steal you from another or break the law of God to have you. She hoped and trusted in faith that you and she would one day be wed. When trouble came to her marriage, she was able to lean upon the Lord in her trials and hope for a brighter tomorrow. She did much to bring on her problems, but the Lord was with her when she acknowledged her sin. Phil, as long as Priscilla is alive, I could never take you, as my husband and feel that we were fulfilling Gods will for us. Knowing that she still loves you as much as ever, I would be taking advantage of her love and friendship to marry you."

"Are you saying that you don't want to marry me?" he retorted in disbelief, "you couldn't wait until I began divorce proceedings! You don't want to get married now?"

He was shocked and angered by her argument. He hadn't thought of calling off the divorce. That was her suggestion. He had been praying for God to show the way, but he thought that the Lord would prepare Priscilla for the decision, which he had to make for his son. Marrying Angie was the only logical choice with the baby in the picture. What of Kevin, their son?

"Yes, that's what I'm saying," she replied sadly, "Phil, as much as I love you, it isn't God's will. I know it in my heart. I want you as much as ever, but we must control our passions and seek out truth, if we are to see and do the perfect will of the Most High God. Look what all our self indulgence has brought to us and our families and friends."

"Angie, what of our son," he exclaimed, "we now have a baby. What about his family. We, you and I, are his family."

"He was God's child when I conceived him in sin," she replied softly, "he is ours for a season. But he is God's for all time. The Lord will show the way very soon if we trust Him. We must take this stand on faith. The Lord will solve it to the glory of His holy name and in the best way for all concerned. If we must bear a portion of sorrow to correct the wrong which we've done, then I am prepared to bear it for the Lord's sake."

"Angie this makes no sense at all," replied Philip in tears, "I love you and we have a son who needs for us to be together as a family. Are you out of your mind? You said you love me! What are you trying to do to me?"

"Philip, this is the hardest thing I've ever done in my life," she sobbed, "please don't make it any more difficult than it is. I've learned that it isn't enough to take because I want. To be happy and at peace with God, I must accept you as His gift to me. He hasn't offered you to me like that. If I please myself, I cause the very ones I love to suffer. No, Philip! I have loved you because I wanted you and see how I've hurt you. It's finished Philip! You're confused and hurt now, but very soon you will understand that this is right. God will provide for you, Priscilla and our son. As for me, I don't know what is in store for me, but I wait for His direction. I throw myself at His feet and seek mercy and forgiveness."

Philip left the hospital without further argument. Angie returned to her room. He drove directly to the nursing home to see his son. As he stood beside the bed of his sleeping son, he hung his head in sorrow and wept as he gazed tearfully upon his innocent son.

"My son. My son," he sobbed, "what is to become of you? May God spare you this great pain."

Priscilla stood in the aisle and overheard and sorrowed for her husband. She still loved Philip but she sadly laid him on the altar of the Most High God and assumed that he and Angie would now soon be married.

Angie prayed and read the scriptures, trusting in faith that the Lord would remember her. Later that afternoon, Eddie stopped in to visit her. He said that it was at the instruction of the attending physician. He was very professional, but Angie felt the stirring of their emotions. She knew from that one visit that she still loved him. Her heart broke as she realized that she could no longer offer the chastity that every groom wanted. After that day, Eddie would make a routine daily visit both in the morning and in the afternoon. His act had Angie convinced, but the hand of God is always present when His trusting servants need support and He intervened on Angie's behalf.

"Everything appears to be in order," he said seriously, "I'm looking forward to Friday. Then I can check you out with a good bill of health."

"Yes, I'm looking forward to that myself," she replied appreciatively.

"Very well," he commented dryly, "I'll be by to see you tomorrow morning."

He turned to leave as one of the nurses walked into the room. She was surprised to see Dr. Loene and she smiled at him and asked, "Do you love this place so much that you spend your time here on your day off?"

CHAPTER 39

*The steps of a good man are ordered by the Lord: and he
delights in his way.
Though he fall, he shall not utterly be cast down: for the
Lord upholds him with his hand.*

Philip did delay the divorce proceedings. So much had happened in the
past four weeks that he found it hard to collect his thoughts. After the initial shock of Angie's decision not to marry, he accepted her decision. He
accepted that as God's will and waited upon the Lord for direction. The
matter with Priscilla was far from settled, but a truce was in place. Philip
tried to speak with her each day, but the activities of her job always inter-
fered as they were about to get down to personal matters. He needed to discuss his feelings with her. Now he had to begin rehearsals for the one-hour
live special in his honor. He flew to Hollywood and spent four days there.

He hadn't performed in five weeks and he wasn't anxious to begin the
rigorous routine again. He was sluggish through the rehearsals for the live
one hour show. He knew that he would have to get up for the show. The
more he thought about show business, the more discouraged he became.
He tried to call Priscilla four times one day but she was either out of the
building or unavailable. Was she avoiding him? It was understandable if
she was. His heart was with his son and the children at the nursing home.
Tonight, he would be alone on stage. Angie was unable to perform and he
had fired his entire band eight months ago. How he wished that he had

Simeon with him again. He had made such a mess of every relationship in his life. As he waited for the show to begin, a massive burden of guilt and dismay weighed heavily upon his heart. A knock at the door meant that he was to take his position on stage. The show would begin in five minutes. He'd just fake it for one hour and he'd be home free. He could do it once more. He had done it before.

As he was introduced, the young girls in the audience screamed and waved their arms frantically. He walked out on stage and raised his hands for silence. After a minute, he could be heard above the noise. He wore his white shoes and a white suit with a red shirt and emerald tie. However, he was humble that evening. The cockiness and boldness was gone. As he spoke, his words were deliberate and sincere. He spoke from the heart.

"I'm going to start the show with a new song which I've just released. It's called 'The Great Stone Castle."

'I built me a great stone castle, in the middle of a desert land,
I said I'll put forth my hand, do my will, take a stand and I'll do anything that I can.
All the people of the world will look upon me, and they'll bow to my least command,
As they gaze in amazement at my great stone castle in the middle of a desert land.

There was weeping and wailing in the dungeon and there was laughter in the party room,
There were statues and idols in the garden and the joy slipped away in gloom.
All the friends in my house shouted please let me out, cause I can't get away too soon,
And I stood all alone in my great stone castle in the middle of a desert land.

I deserted my great stone castle, built a cabin in a grove of trees,
I said I don't want nothing but the joy of God's peace and I'll keep it through eternity.
He restored all my friends and he saved me, when I met Him on my bended knees,
And I'll never more miss my great stone castle in the middle of a desert land.

Now there's laughter and shouting in the cabin, we have good times and brotherly love,
And the light of God's favor shines down on the cabin bringing peace from the Father above.
No more weeping and wailing, all we got is smooth sailing, as we journey in the Lord's right hand,
And I'll never more miss my great stone castle in the middle of a desert land.

The crowd roared their approval and the girls screamed when he took his bow. Several tried to climb on the stage and were restrained by ushers. Pandemonium broke loose as he smiled at his worshippers. Tonight the screaming girls only saddened him. As visions of Priscilla, his son Kevin, Joy, Sabrina, Angie, Simeon, Eddie and a host of other lost friends whirled through his mind, he was present on stage in body only. His great moment of triumph, the unsurpassed hour of glory that was his, meant nothing to him. One scripture was indelibly stamped in his mind and it replayed over and over in his thoughts, 'vanity of vanities, all is vanity saith the preacher'. He raised his hand again to silence the crowd. Then he humbly introduced the next song, "I'm honored to be here tonight and I hope you enjoy this next song. Its sold more copies than any song that I've recorded. It's called 'Rockin with the Good Times'.

'Rockin with the good times, groovin cause a you're mine,
Got me goin, goin, goin, goin gone.
Singin cause I feel fine, laughin in the sunshine,
You're too much, how you turn me on.
Swingin through the bad news…'

The band continued to play but Philip couldn't sing. His throat tightened in sadness and he choked up. The musicians continued to play even though they sensed that something was amiss. Phil turned and stopped them with raised arms.

"Thanks guys," he said to the musicians, "you did your best to cover for me, but let's try it again from the top. All right! Let's rock it!"

The musicians launched into the music again and Philip tried to sing with his usual enthusiasm. His heart wasn't in the song. He was so disturbed that he couldn't continue the masquerade. Nonetheless, he began the song.

   'Rockin with the good times, groovin cause a you're mine,
   Got me goin, goin, goin, goin gone.
   Singin…'

He choked again and now tears seeped from his eyes. He wondered how ridiculous he must look to Priscilla and the children who said they would be watching. He had never experienced such low spirits. Always before, he could smile long enough to make it through a show. He stopped the band again and looked out over the puzzled mob of fans. All eyes were fastened upon him and the crowd was silent. They sensed his despair. He put his hands in his pockets and the once bold, dynamic performer walked slowly, with shoulders slumped to the front of the stage, looked out over the audience and spoke in a broken voice.

"I'm sorry friends, but I just can't sing tonight," he said sadly. He tried to swallow the lump that threatened to choke off his voice.

"I feared when I started in this business two and a half years ago, that this day would come. I've been the most successful singing artist in pop music during that time because I made it my business to be the best. I have made every sacrifice necessary to make it to where I am today. Tonight, the world honors me for that work. By the world's standards, I deserve to be honored, for I have sold more recordings than anyone else in the business before me and through the present day. I have traveled more miles, performed more shows, and entertained more people in that short span than anyone before me. I have made money for every company I endorsed and I have amassed more wealth than I could spend in seven lifetimes. By worldly standards, I have done great things. I'm honored to be so privileged.

"And yet I cannot be happy, for before The Most High God, my life story to date is one of great tragedy. My God given talents I have used to discredit my Lord, the giver of those talents. I was trusted with great heavenly treasure, but to my great dismay, few have ever done a more complete job of forsaking that trust. The greater I have become in the eyes of the world, the lower I have fallen into this spiritual and emotional chasm of hell. Thus has God made my great day of honor into a moment of shame. Though I have acted out my part letter perfect, I am a mockery of the success that I portray. I've been a fool!"

At this point, he could no longer hold his emotion within and he reached into his pocket, pulled out his handkerchief and wiped his tear filled eyes. At the nursing home, Priscilla and the children were watching. Tears streamed down her cheeks. She couldn't bear to see him so distraught. Her heart reached out in sympathy to her sorrowful husband. In the audience every eye was moistened and handkerchiefs dried tear stained cheeks. When he regained his composure, he continued with a voice that trembled in sadness and grief.

"I turned my back on the Lord and that was the beginning of my sorrows. Since then, I've stepped on friends and bullied business associates. I have tarnished the life of everyone I have known whether it was family, friend or business associate. The Midas touch, which I've acquired, has been a curse to me and all I hold dear. Of a truth, my loved ones and friends have paid for my success. Worst of all, I have walked all over the heart of a faithful wife who has endured all manner of shame and humiliation because she loved me. I repaid her love and trust with pain and shame. Yet she continued to pray for me, day and night. I thank God for this angel whose name I am not worthy to speak. The Most High God has rightfully separated me from her. I am not worthy of her.

And now I stand alone before God in my sin and it is indeed a very lonely feeling. What good work can I present to Him? When I speak of all the records which I have sold, He shall surely remind me of all the hearts which I've broken. If I tell Him of all the miles which I've traveled to entertain His creation, He will surely ask how many steps I've taken to feed the hungry or care for the afflicted in that same time. How shall I answer Him? He will have none of my filthy gifts! All I can do is fall down before Him and plead for mercy and forgiveness. But before I face him, I must first make amends with my friends, whom I've treated unjustly. To those whom I've treated unjustly, I make public apology for those injustices. To those whom I've cheated, I will pay back double. Then I must find my wife and beg her forgiveness. I feel that when I find her, I will find the Lord right there with her. I can't expect her to take me back, nor will I ask that of her. I must, however, clear my conscience of these horrid deeds if I am ever to be happy again. And to you friends, I humbly say 'I'm Sorry'. You came to see an extravaganza and you've been presented with a sad tale of woe. I don't know what tomorrow holds, but for today, I must find the Most High God again before my life has any real meaning."

He slumped and broke down in emotion. For a moment, that seemed an eternity, a hush fell over the sobbing, tear stained crowd. At the nursing home, Priscilla wept tears of joy as little Joy leaned on her side and cried. The nursing staff and the children were touched at the sight of the broken man whom they once knew as a friend.

Then scattered applause rang out through the crowd. Soon more joined the applause and then more. At last the crowd rose to applaud Philip Wright because he confessed openly his sin before God and man. At the nursing home, Priscilla stopped wiping her eyes and clapped for joy. She said 'the Lord has turned his defeat into victory!' Soon the staff, Joy and all the children applauded with her. Philip received more acclaim for one broken testimony of defeat than he had for all of his much-publicized deeds.

CHAPTER 40

Trust in the Lord with all your heart; and lean not to your own understanding.
In all your ways acknowledge Him and He shall direct your paths.

Philip rose early the next morning to call Priscilla. He knew that the sooner he set things straight, the sooner he could be at rest and peace again.

"Priscilla, I want to apologize for all the heart ache that I put you through," he said sadly, "I know that doesn't change what I've done, but I am sorry."

"You were forgiven long ago," she replied tenderly, "I saw your show last night. Joy, the nursing staff and all the kids watched it too. It was your best, in my opinion."

"Well, I really messed that up, but I got my misery off my chest," he said sadly, "one of the producers is going to sue me for ruining the program."

"Father said that would probably happen," replied Priscilla pleasantly, "but mother said that if they sue, they would pay the damages!"

"Are your father and mother back together?" he asked.

"Yes they are," she replied softly, "they have been happier than I can ever remember, like two people on honey moon. It's been two weeks now."

"Praise the Lord! That's great news," he replied enthusiastically.

"The Lord has been at work in a marvelous way. Angie and Eddie are back together," she said excitedly, "they're to be married in a few weeks and she's going to work part time in the nursing home until they get married. I told her to bring little Kevin to work with her and I would take care of him. Oh, and Eddie is going to be our physician."

"You know that's a relief," he replied, "Angie needs someone to share her life with. She's a lot like you. She needs to be needed and loved."

"How do you know that about me," she asked tenderly.

"Oh…Well," he stuttered nervously, "I haven't forgotten everything."

"Neither have I Philip," she replied tenderly.

"Priscilla…" he said hesitantly, "How are you?"

"I could be better," she said.

"Would it be all right if I stopped by the nursing home tomorrow to see the kids," he continued, "I'd like to see them one last time."

"Of course you can. The children were hoping that you would come back to work," she said nervously, "I would be glad if you considered being the administrator of the nursing home. It's really too much responsibility for me in my condition. Would you consider that?"

"Priscilla, I have been trouble to everyone I've known these past two years," he said sadly, "I want to visit the kids because I don't see any way that I could do any harm. But I have to get off to myself and try to put all the pieces together. I just don't want to be a heart ache to anybody again."

"Very well Philip," replied Priscilla disappointed, "what time shall we expect you tomorrow?"

"I'll be there about nine in the morning," he replied sincerely, "tell all the kids that I'll bring gifts."

"Very well Philip," she said softy, "Good-bye."

The next morning Angie was bathing baby Kevin in the therapy room at the nursing home. Priscilla was exercising on a therapy table. Angie laid him on a changing table and began to dress him. She put a fresh diaper on him and positioned him on the towel with which she had dried him. The end of the towel draped over the side and touched the floor. As she was dressing him, a nurse's aide called her to the phone.

"Oh goodness," Angie exclaimed as she patted her son lovingly, "you lay still. Mommy will be right back."

Priscilla was stretching her legs on the therapy table. She had continued with her daily exercises and therapy even though she never expected to walk without braces again. As she finished the exercises, little Wally Peterson crawled into her room, spied the orange towel and proceeded toward it. In alarm, Priscilla instantly called to Angie.

"Angie, come quickly," she shouted excitedly.

She reached for her braces, but before she could put them on, Wally was tugging at the towel and pulling the baby toward the edge of the changing table. Priscilla moved to the closest edge of the therapy table. It was still twelve feet to the baby! Wally pulled the blanket again and Priscilla saw that Kevin would surely fall upon the floor. She leaped from the table and ran across the room. She caught the baby in mid air and folded him securely in her bosom. Kevin wailed in terror as Priscilla consoled him.

"Oh Angie!" she exclaimed in relief as Angie entered the room and stopped with a halt, "Wally almost pulled Kevin off the table! I caught him in mid air!"

"Priscilla!" exclaimed Angie as she looked in amazement at Priscilla's legs, "how did you get over to Kevin? You're standing without your braces!"

"Oh my Lord!" shrieked Priscilla as she looked at her legs in unbelief, ""I can walk! I can walk without my braces! Oh Praise God! I can walk without my braces!"

She burst into tears and Angie ran over to her and the baby and they embraced in thanksgiving. Little Kevin, Angie and Priscilla wept together.

"Oh thank God, I can walk," Priscilla repeated in praise, "Thank you Lord so much! Oh Angie! This is the sign I've been waiting for! I asked God if He intended for me to have Philip again. I didn't want to do anything without His blessing. I asked Him for a sign to reveal His intention. Angie, I never felt that I was a complete woman for Philip, but God has removed my affliction! I know that He intends for us to be together now! Oh Goodness! It's eight o'clock! He'll be here in an hour! I must get ready! Don't tell anyone about this! I want this to be a surprise for him!"

Philip arrived at a few minutes past nine, and the children were anxiously waiting. They had prepared a celebration for him and he was surprised to see that even his old friend Simeon was there to greet him. He was touched by their enthusiasm, for they welcomed him back as a long awaited hero. As he climbed from the car, he was mobbed by several of the boys and Eddie Leone carried Joy to meet him. She was excited and she squeezed his neck in happiness when Eddie handed her to Philip. Though they didn't speak, Eddie and Philip extended their hands to bridge the barrier between them. Angie brought out his son and he stood in the midst of the shouting mob of children with Joy in one arm and Kevin in the other arm. Angie smiled and walked to Eddie's side. He looked for Priscilla, but didn't see her.

"The children want you to have ice cream and cake," shouted Angie above the noise.

"Where is Priscilla," asked Philip as he scanned the crowd for her.

"Oh! That's right," replied Angie as she pretended to recall, "She went up the hill to her mother's house. She asked me to tell you to come up there to see her."

"Did she say what she wanted?" asked Philip bewildered.

"She said something about giving your ring back," Angie replied.

He handed Joy back to Eddie and Angie took their son, Kevin and he walked up the hill to her mother's home. The mansion was a picture of perfection on the top of the hill. The walk seemed especially long today. He didn't blame her for taking her rings off and giving them back to him. After all, it was all over now. He knocked on the door and soon Elizabeth greeted him.

"Well Philip," she said in fondness, "it's good to see you again!"

"Hi, Mrs. Pomp," he said humbly, "it's good to see you again, too. Is Priscilla here?"

"No she isn't Philip," she replied with a smile, "she walked down to the flower garden. If you'll hurry, I'm sure that you'll find her there."

He turned and started down the hill to the garden. 'The garden of all places' he thought. It had all started here with his grandfather, and this was where it would end. His heart was heavy but he was still anxious to see Priscilla one last time. The words of a song he wrote for Priscilla once when he was pining for her came to his mind and the melody played in his heart. It was a song, which he and Priscilla sang and she also arranged for their act, before her health prohibited the rigorous travel their show demanded. He would sing.

'I don't know how we fell in love, but it was easy,
It settled on us like a dove, it was so easy.
But then I realized at last that I was hurting you,
I don't know how, I broke each vow, but it was easy.

I thought our love could never be, but it was easy,
And then I held you close to me, it was so easy,

Though I'm a shameful fool, I pray that you will stay with me.
I need you so, but if you go, it won't be easy.'

Philip would sing the bridge as well.

'I should apologize, but I can't speak,
Just you can dry these eyes that always weep.
Can't you see I'm paying for mistakes I've made,
Don't you know I'm sorry now, I don't know how to make it up to
you.'

Priscilla would sing the last verse, bursting out in a crescendo at the end.

'Sweetheart I'd walk through hell with you, it would be easy,
Our love and God would see us through, it would be easy.
I wait with open arms, a heart so warm, a love that's true,
I love you still, I always will, and it's so easy.
I love you still, I always will, and it's so easy.'

His heart was pounding in anxiety. He would have to give up his
Priscilla. What was the sense of dragging it out? He began to run down the
hill. He trotted past the lilac bushes and stopped in the middle of the garden. He looked for Priscilla. She was nowhere to be found.

"Priscilla," he called.

"Philip, I'm here," answered Priscilla as she stepped from behind the
lilac bushes.

He turned to see her walking toward him with outstretched arms and
tears streaming down her cheeks. He saw that her braces were gone and she
walked with the same grace, which she possessed before the crippling accident. For an instant, he stood motionless as she walked toward him crying
joyfully. Then, released from the shock, he ran to her and took her in his
arms and wept with her.

"Priscilla! Oh my precious Priscilla," he wept in joy, "you can walk without the braces! Oh thank the Most High God! You can walk without the
braces!"

"Oh Philip, He's been so wonderful to us," she sobbed as he kissed her
tenderly.

"You don't know how my soul wept because I thought I had lost you
forever," he said with a trembling voice.

"God was our only hope darling," she sobbed thankfully, "He just wouldn't let go of us. Now we can continue His work together."

"I thought that you wanted to give my ring back," he said as he wiped his eyes, "that's what Angie told me."

"I do want to give your ring back," she said as she smiled through her tears, "this is the ring you took off your finger when you left for that six month tour with Angie. I'm placing it back on your finger and this time it will stay. Now that the Lord has released me from my affliction, I fully intend that you will never have a reason to look at another woman again. I'm going to be a complete woman for you, just like I always wanted to be."

She pulled his head down to her lips and kissed him tenderly as tears of happiness moistened their lips.

In the background the sound of a singing troupe was merrily advancing toward them. Philip and Priscilla little noticed until they were almost upon them. Simeon was carrying Joy and holding to Eddie's arm. Angie marched beside Eddie carrying Kevin and Harold and Elizabeth were also singing in the group. The nursing staff and the children danced along and even the handicapped children were placed in wheel chairs to join in the celebration. They circled around Philip and Priscilla as the excited children laughed and danced.

"What's the occasion," shouted Philip to them, as he pulled Priscilla closer to himself and smiled at her.

"Haven't you heard," she shouted above the clamor, "every day's a holiday at Little Angels Nursing Home!"

"Hey Philip!" shouted Joy with glee, "let's sing 'Every Day's a Holiday!'"
And they did.

'Every day with you is a holiday, honey it's true.
Anything we do it's a holiday, darling with you.
I know that when I'm holding you it's a holiday,
All my dreams come true; It's a holiday,
Every hour is such a shower of blessing with you.
Believe me.
Troubles we go through it's a holiday if I'm with you.
Dreams that don't come true it's a holiday, living with you.
I know that we will always stay; it's a holiday,
So much in love this way, it's a holiday,
I know you'll always say it's a holiday too.

Dear I love you, need you too,
Morning, evening, night time too.
Darling how I would love to make you mine.
Love you know I want you all of the time.

Just picture you and me,
In love and strolling under the stars.
How happy we would be,
T'would be the grandest feeling by far.
Magnificent and sweet,
This love that fills each cell of my heart.
Divine and so complete,
And darling this is only the start.

Just picture you and me,
In love and strolling under the stars.
How happy we would be,
T'would be the grandest feeling by far.
Magnificent and sweet,
This love that fills each cell of my heart.
Divine and so complete,
And darling this is only the start.

Dear I love you, need you too,
Morning, evening, night time too.
Darling how I would love to make you mine.
Love you know I want you all of the time.

Every day with you is a holiday, honey it's true.
Anything we do it's a holiday, darling with you.
I know that when I'm holding you it's a holiday,
All my dreams come true; It's a holiday,
Every hour is such a shower of blessing with you.
Believe me.
Troubles we go through it's a holiday if I'm with you.
Dreams that don't come true it's a holiday, living with you.
I know that we will always stay; it's a holiday,
So much in love this way, it's a holiday,
I know you'll always say it's a holiday too.

I know that we will always stay; it's a holiday,
So much in love this way, it's a holiday,
I know you'll always say it's a holiday too.

*And you shall be called, the repairer of the breach, the restorer
of paths to dwell in.*

The New Beginning

0-595-33435-0